M000207082

RAVES FOR
SUSAN SQUIRES
AND *BODY ELECTRIC*!

SUCCESS!

If this were a Visimorph project, connecting would be weeks of testing away. But it wasn't. This was hers: her compulsion, her sweat and all the smarts she had been able to muster over the past two years. Vic wiped the sweat from her forehead. If nothing happened here, she might dissolve like the Wicked Witch of the West or explode like a Scanner. But she couldn't back down. She clicked "Run Program."

The code trail flashed past and was gone, replaced by the communication screen with a design background in blue figures that moved sinuously. That usually took time. Not tonight. Neuromancer was giving her more power than she knew what to do with.

But the dialogue boxes were empty. Now what? She raised her hands into position, wondering what she would type, when the top box rippled. An H appeared.

Vic thought she might faint. An E joined the H.

Her hands, still hovering above the keyboard, trembled. As she watched, the screen slowly wrote HELLO. A question mark appeared at the end, almost tentatively: HELLO?

Vic half-chuckled, half-sobbed. HELLO, she tapped onto the keyboard, hands shaking.

There was no response. Vic wasn't sure what to do. Should she type more? She couldn't help thinking of Rip Van Winkle, or a newborn foal waking to a strange world. How could she help?

The dialogue box began to fill with letters again, slowly: YOU ARE NOT ME?

NO. I AM OTHER, she answered. She wanted to scream in triumph. She'd done it!

Other books by Susan Squires:
SACRAMENT
DANEGELD

BODY ELECTRIC

SUSAN SQUIRES

LEISURE BOOKS NEW YORK CITY

A LEISURE BOOK®

August 2002

Published by

Dorchester Publishing Co., Inc.
276 Fifth Avenue
New York, NY 10001

ISBN 0-8439-5036-6

*To Peter and Carolyn,
the scientific half of the family,
for their knowledge and support,
and to Chris Keeslar, for pushing
the boundaries.*

BODY ELECTRIC

Chapter One

Vic Barnhardt slammed on the brakes of her black BMW. Adrenaline surged through her. She'd almost hit him! The guy in torn denims screamed something she couldn't understand as he thumped on her hood with the wooden handle of his sign. It said, "McIntire Makes Monopoly Money," in childish letters. The metal dented with a thunk that echoed through the roadster over the shouting outside. Behind him a human chain of burly Visimorph security guards bulged as the crowd of protesters surged toward her. Vic leaned on her horn and stabbed at the button that locked the doors. Where did these crazies come from? Hundreds of them, their mouths twisted in anger, shook their signs or their fists. A brown-uniformed guard jerked the guy back by his collar. Vic gunned into the parking garage. The release of PuppetMaster 12.1 was more than a week away. This was getting out of hand.

The BMW squealed around a corner and Vic jammed it into a space on the lower floor. She didn't have time for this nonsense. The morning's rain had gummed up Sepulveda Boulevard and made her late for a meeting with her boss,

Hugo Walz. Since she hadn't bothered to show for last week's meeting, she'd better at least pretend to toe the line. She swung out of the car and slammed the door. It would be hours before she could begin work on what she really cared about—Jodie. She chafed at that as she heaved her backpack over her plaid flannel shirt, then steadied her breathing before striding across the parking garage, her Doc Martens squeaking against the concrete. The smell of oil and rubber hung in the brisk March air.

Naming her project after Jodie Foster seemed right. A strong woman who bucked authority to do what she wanted. Vic managed a grin. Yeah.

Coming out of the garage into a biting wind, she shielded her eyes against the late afternoon sun. Several protesters ran past her through the narrow alleyway. How did they get past the security guards? Vic swung around to see the chain-link fence at the end of the alley sagging under a wall of people. Her pulse quickened. This wasn't funny. The shouts turned triumphant as the fence broke.

She was overwhelmed in seconds, and any hope of a sprint to the employee entrance was dashed. Vic struggled against the tide of jeans and flowered dresses. Elbows and knees and protest signs all prodded her. She yelped in pain and shoved back. These weren't people anymore, but screeching bits of hair and flesh. "Let me through!" she shouted pointlessly. Hers was just another voice in the cacophony of screams.

A flash of white helmet and black chin strap announced the arrival of the police, but that only intensified the surge around her. Vic couldn't breathe. Pain shot through her as a placard connected with her head. The crowd swirled in sickening streams of color. Her knees hit the pavement. Someone stepped on her and someone else. Visions of soccer fans trampling people to death flashed through Vic's brain.

A grip on her arm heaved her upright as though she were being pulled out of quicksand. "You all right?" a bass voice shouted over the tumult. She found herself clutched against a hard body wearing jeans and a plaid shirt not much different from her own. She looked up. Maybe it was the blow to her head, but the crowd seemed distant even as it jostled them. She saw intense blue-green eyes with a sad down-slant. A week's beard hid the bottom half of her savior's face. One blunt hand raked through thick hair worn too long, and pushed it from his eyes. She'd seen pictures: John Reston, nemesis of Visimorph.

"Hold on," he yelled and slung her across his hip like a child. She clung to shoulders she could feel were massive underneath the plaid flannel, her breasts pressed to his barrel chest. He waded through the chaos, clearing a path with his other arm. He didn't seem to care whose head he cracked. Police and demonstrators alike gave way. Vic felt his body under hers, brawny muscles, unrelentingly male. Jeez, Vic, she commanded herself, get a grip.

When they were clear of the crowd, Reston continued down the alleyway at a trot, oblivious to her breathless squirming. "Put me down," Vic managed. He turned the corner and set her on a loading dock with an unceremonious thunk. Somehow he ended up standing between her parted thighs. Both he and she panted. The screaming, the whining of the sirens, seemed a long way off.

She meant to thank him. After all, he had probably saved her life. But wasn't he responsible, too? He was the driving force behind these protests. The way he had just hauled her around like so much luggage—and here he stood staring at her as if she were some kind of circus animal. "Maniac! What gives you the right to stage attacks on people just trying to go to work?"

"Sorry," he muttered, his expression rueful. "This got out of hand."

"Out of hand?" Her gazed flicked over him. He looked like some Greenpeace geek with that long hair. His jeans were torn at the knee. Then there were those eyes. And the mouth. What kind of lips hid under that beard? She couldn't quite see. His undershirt peeked from his flannel at the neck. It was the kind of shirt that would leave those powerful arms bare. Something in her wondered what he looked like with-

3

out the flannel. Vic pushed that something down. "You . . . you people are crazy!"

"I might say the same," he growled. "You're helping Bob McIntire hold the world's computers for ransom. Every time he issues an upgrade, everybody has to repurchase something they already own just to function in society. Don't you have a conscience?"

"And you brought the Justice Department down on him last year for antitrust. Don't *you* remember what happened to the economy when they broke up Microsoft?"

"And now Visimorph is worse. A good economy doesn't make it okay." They glared at each other.

Vic parted the gel that slicked back her short brown hair and fingered the lump beneath that was beginning to make her head ache.

"You're bleeding." Reston touched her jaw to turn her head with callused fingers.

Vic shuddered away as though she'd been shocked by a taser. "I'm fine."

"You're not fine." He slid a blunt, strong hand behind her neck and touched her chin again. Vic's hands trembled. Must be the adrenaline wearing off. "You could use a stitch or two and a whiskey chaser for some Advil."

All Vic could do was stare at him, maybe because he was way too close. Did he have to be standing between her knees, for Christ's sake? And why didn't he move his hand off her neck?

"Don't get hostile. I'm not asking for a date." Unexpectedly, he grinned. It made his eyes crinkle up as if they'd never been sad. As he pulled his hand away, he came up with the little queue of longer hair she kept tucked carefully under her collar when she was at Visimorph. "What's this?" he asked, smiling. "You hiding some shred of femininity here?"

Vic slapped his hand away, anger rising in her throat. "What the hell do you know?"

He raised both hands in surrender. "Hey, what could I tell a Visimorph clone?"

4

Vic was outraged. "I'm not!" If there was one thing she wasn't, it was a Visimorph clone.

"No?" He lifted his chin.

She didn't owe this guy any explanations. So, why did she want to explain? She examined those seriously blue-green eyes. It was none of his business that McIntire had bailed her out of jail for hacking so she could make Visimorph's security systems impregnable against hackers just like herself. One misstep and she would be busted on a parole violation. A half step up from slave labor. It wouldn't matter to some fanatic like John Reston. She glanced away, then back.

A muscle worked in Reston's jaw. Did his eyes flash with disappointment? He didn't say a word, just put his hands around her waist and lifted her off the loading dock. She couldn't help but grasp his forearms where the sleeves were rolled to his elbow. The light hairs over the cords of heavy muscle made her feel fluttery. "You'd better get round to the front door," he muttered, "if you want to go to work so badly."

She pulled away and stalked around the loading dock without looking back. Arrogant bastard! When she was sure he couldn't see her, she peeked over the platform. He was looking at the spot where she had disappeared. After a moment, he shoved his hands in his jeans pockets and turned back toward the melee around the corner. The roar of the crowd washed over her again. A bullhorn demanded something insistently. She chewed her lip and took two slow breaths to calm down. There was no fooling herself about her reaction to this guy. How could she have so little control? She jerked her thoughts back to Jodie and started the long trek around the huge Visimorph campus to the visitors entrance.

The glowing silver symbols on the monitor burned in the darkness like the white light you walk toward after your heart stops beating. But tonight they didn't seem like salvation at all. Music pounded through her earphones. Instead of helping her concentrate, the syncopated rhythms and whining keyboards of the Shards just scraped her nerves. Vic knew

5

she was close, either to a breakthrough or a breakdown. She scanned the code, her eyes scratchy and watering. She was the creator of Cerberus, the security program that defended Visimorph against the world. How come she couldn't link a few borrowed neural nets? Without robust links, all the power in the world wouldn't give Jodie the feel of sentience.

Vic threw herself back in her ergonomically correct chair and ran her hands over her gelled hair. The lump was still there. She'd skipped the stitches and the whiskey, but it had taken maximum doses of Advil to tone down the headache. What a day! A riot, a clunk on the head. Then that Reston guy had thrown her all off balance. Not just his challenge about working with Visimorph. There was a reason she never allowed herself to get very attracted to men. It was distracting. She liked programs better: They operated on rules you could understand.

The smell of stale coffee and recycled air mingled with the vague chemical odor from her printer. Vic tapped her headset, clicking over to a soothing track of Organic R&B and took a swig of Diet Coke from the half-full can standing among several empties. At least she'd had a great excuse for being late to Hugo's meeting. She stood to stretch and surveyed the dim cubicles receding into the darkness beyond her own half walls. Everyone had gone.

"Must be Friday," she muttered. Was it? She glanced at her computer screen. Twelve after midnight. Not Friday at all, but Saturday. She slumped into her chair and reached for her track pad. Forget John Reston. Some environmental crazy was not her type. Jodie was waiting to be born. Vic pushed her finger around. The cursor on the screen didn't move. "If this thing freezes up on me . . ." Her threat collapsed. What would she do? Despair or something.

Wait a minute. The screen shimmered. The silver-blue figures trembled from top to bottom. What was going on here? Vic peered closer as they stabilized. That section of code . . . the groupings were different, weren't they? And there! Something was changing her work! A virus? Bile surged up from her stomach along with the panic. She couldn't lose code

6

now! She lunged for the Utilities function to scan for a virus, but her cursor was still frozen.

"God damn it!" she whispered. Somebody was getting into her code. She stood and scanned the dim recesses of the cube farm. Carpeted half walls outlined a maze for the Visimorph rats. Whoever it was, was working in the dark. She spun out of her cube and stalked down the corridor, peering into the workstations. Code glowed on a screen from Rick Chong's cube. He was still here. "Hey, Chong, what's the idea?"

Chong's silhouette turned in the semidarkness. "And your meaning is . . . ?"

"I mean, are you messing with my code?" She peered over his shoulder. Code from the Communicator upgrade her team was working gleamed in tidy lines. She took a breath. The blood pounding in her neck began to slow.

Chong flipped on his desk light to get a better look at her. "You finally lost it?"

Vic cleared her throat. "I'm having trouble with some . . . changes I'm trying to make."

"Aren't we all?" He gestured at the screen. "What crappy programming on the Communicator! How are we supposed to upgrade this bletcherous shit?"

"We're supposed to make the software elegant. You know, 'The Only Link You'll Ever Need to the Outside World.' " She quoted Suntel's phone and Internet device's ad campaign. "That's why *we're* redoing the operating system and not someone else. 'Cause we're the best."

Chong shook his head in disgust. "Corporate bull. And only that company would have named these things for that Star Trek device deal. They're such geeks." As if that were the last straw.

"Long for your samurai days, hacking for fun instead of for Corporate America?" she asked.

He grinned. "Don't you?"

She suppressed most of a smile. "Sometimes." Her eyes slid over him. His thick black hair was pulled into a ponytail maybe six inches long. He had the sleek muscles of a martial artist. Not the body type she liked most. That would be more

7

like the infamous Mr. Reston. Way dangerous. But Chong was just the type she usually chose, for safety's sake. Smooth and lean. A blue-and-green flourish peeked from under one sleeve of his black t-shirt as it stretched around his biceps. A dragon? A vine? Why had she never noticed it? She scanned his cube. A mahogany stick, polished and rounded, poked out of a gym bag. He did do martial arts. She'd never asked him about himself. She'd hired him because he'd been a hacker, though he hadn't actually been in jail, so he wasn't on the slave labor program like she was. They were outsiders, both of them. Maybe she should know more about him, starting with whether that was a dragon or a vine.

Down, Vic. This was just an echo of her encounter with John Reston. She was way out of control. Chong was her employee. Never dip in the company pool. Chong would probably be shocked if she came on to him. She was acutely conscious of her asexual attire, her short hair, her longer queue of hair hidden away. New employees often mistook her for a guy until they saw her face. Her look was necessary to get taken seriously in the world of computers. A disguise. That was what she told herself, anyway. He'd be even more shocked if he knew where she went after work. She pushed that thought away.

"You got no life?" she asked, fingering the metal clips on her ears. Silly question.

"More than you." He turned to his keyboard. His fingers skittered over the keys in little staccato blasts. He hit the last key with some bravado and looked up. His almond eyes were flat black. "Don't worry, I'm leaving." Leaning back in his chair, he clasped his hands behind his neck, stretching, then glanced toward her cubicle. "Your private projects are none of my business, Vic. But don't think I'm stupid. There *are* private projects."

Vic flushed. "Yeah, well, we all have private doings."

Chong turned and clicked to save his code. "You might be a porn addict, of course." He shut down and swiveled in her direction. "Probably not, though. So I ask myself, why don't you work from home on whatever you're doing? I figure you need power. You're after the Big One."

8

Vic tried not to look stricken, caught out. "Get off it. No one's even sure it exists." Some people thought Visimorph was trying to break into the hardware business at the top of the food chain. They were right. Visimorph was using light pipes: a billion photon streams generated by a laser, doing simultaneous computations right down in the basement here in Santa Monica. No silly little silicon chips for Visimorph. The light pipes would increase their computing power by about a zillion-fold. No telling what Bob-O could do with that kind of speed. McIntire called the huge computer Neuromancer, and Vic wondered if he remembered that the fictional AI was software not hardware. Maybe he'd never really read Gibson's book.

"It exists. And Visimorph uses Cerberus for security." Chong smiled a Mona Lisa number. "I figure you go pretty much where you want."

"You figure wrong." Vic shoved her hands into her jeans pockets. "Why do you think they won't let me work the upgrade? They've taken it way beyond my version. You could probably call it Hydra now with how the security layers must morph."

Chong shrugged, then stood and reached for his bomber jacket, scuffed brown leather that had seen better days. "Maybe. But I guess things are gonna turn out one of two ways. Maybe you do something great with company resources and Bob McIntire claims it as his own. You shut up and take some options. Or you don't play ball and he, like, un-installs your ass. If he fires you, he'll sue you for using company property for personal gain. Win or lose, you're broke from paying lawyers. Warning: I'm not going to get caught in the riptide. If I think you're not going to deliver on this bullshit Communicator project, I'll sing like a canary just to save my ass."

She should placate him, somehow get him on her side. But his attitude pushed her anger button. "You forgot one possibility. I make it out with my interests and change the world."

"Don't kid me, Vic." Chong shook his head. "You want to be a gazillionaire like McIntire. But that *is* a possibility. So,

9

maybe I hold out for options from you." He slung his coat over his shoulder. "Keep me posted." He pushed past her toward the green-glowing exit sign.

Vic ran her hand over her mouth. If Chong told Hugo about her "private doings," she was up for San Quentin. Chong wouldn't feel a shred of loyalty to her. He was a practical guy. So practical, she might just have been blackmailed.

She hurried back to her cube. She wouldn't think about this. There were a lot of hours left tonight, and she had to figure out what had happened to her code. If she could just get Jodie finished, power her up, prove it could be done, then she'd deal with everything else.

Was her machine still frozen? She threw herself into her chair. Nope, the track pad responded to her finger. Excellent. She tapped her earphones for some world beat hip-hop and did a quick survey. The code was definitely different. Scan showed no viruses. No tampering with her access codes. No one had left their prints on the commands. Hell, there *weren't* any commands, not even ghosts. Vic wiped her eyes. Her brain felt like peanut butter. Chunky. How long could she run on empty? Guess she was going to find out.

As a last resort she went back to the stricken code, looking for the rhythm of the logic, projecting ahead to the outcome. Her breath began to come faster.

"Yeah," she whispered. "Yeah, oh yeah, oh yeah." If this was a virus, it was one brilliant virus. How long had she been working on connecting all those neural nets she "borrowed" from other computers, other researchers? The problem was connecting them in a way that allowed random access through the layers to simulate the parallel functioning of a human brain. And this code was the answer. It could replace her whole sequence of clumsy logic trees.

Vic sat back. Just replicate it for each new layer she added—she'd already built the evolutionary algorithm. Then connect it. . . . Excitement sparked through her fingertips to deep in her gut, then twisted into paranoia. Where the hell had this come from? Who could have written that codicil of elegance? Hugo? Definitely not. Maybe it was Chong. Maybe he had flipped his screen back to the Communicator program when he heard her coming. He was the best of those who worked for her. But he *did* work for her. There was a reason for that. Actually, the only one who could have programmed this little piece of genius might be Bob McIntire himself.

Right. If McIntire was adjusting her Jodie program, she was really in trouble. She shook herself. "You're just giving in to his reputation for omnipotence," she whispered. Still, she couldn't shake the feeling that someone or something was watching, waiting for her to succeed or slip up. She tried to get a grip. Paranoia was natural when you were hiding something. How long had she been hiding? Two years?

She began to giggle. All her life, more like it. Hiding illicit activities, hiding who she was. As if she knew who she was! The giggles crescendoed into gasping sobs she couldn't control. Her eyes filled. The echoes of her laughter rebounded from the distant darkness, shocking in the emptiness. She put her head between her knees. The cycles of giggling slowly spaced themselves until she could breathe.

Get a grip! She sat up and took a swig of Diet Coke to steady herself. The silence settled in again, held a menace she hadn't noticed before. "Who cares?" she whispered aloud. She might have had to hide all her life, but Jodie would be whole and strong in ways she'd never been, an artificial intelligence truly female, sure of herself, powerful. She turned back to the screen. Just kill the old logic trees. That was the next step. She worked on, deleting, replicating the new code. Finally she linked in the algorithm she'd built so the code could evolve on its own.

She sat back. It was four in the morning and her head ached. That was it. The bare bones of Jodie were complete. It had happened so quickly once the linking problem was solved, she was a little stunned. She should feel something. Victorious? Complete? But she didn't. After all, she had a lot of work ahead to be sure that what she'd strung together worked. Maybe there was time to do a little quality checking before she called it a day . . . uh, night. Not enough power in this machine to check more than a small segment at a time.

Out of curiosity more than any expectation, she flipped the screen to her desktop and clicked on the alias for her mole into Neuromancer. Chong was right; she needed the huge machine. There just wasn't any other way to get enough processing power to make Jodie seem human. She waited for the mole to execute, her feet up on the desk. This part was slow. It had to wend its way through the access codes for three lower-level support systems as it sneaked up on Neuromancer from the side. But she had designed its path in even as Neuromancer was being constructed. It looked like part of the landscape to the boys in the basement. God, she hoped it did.

The screen in front of her began to scroll madly with code. Her head jerked up. Jesus! She swung her legs down, dumping her Diet Coke on the carpet, and ripped off her headset. Had she been discovered? She had to get out immediately! But her fingers hovered over her keyboard as it spewed colon-backslash gibberish. Would she reveal her presence if she tried to back out?

Wait a minute. What was scrolling past wasn't gibberish.

"Hello, Mr. Big," she whispered, breathing out deliberately. "I guess you're on-line ahead of schedule." She watched the scroll, transfixed. These symbols represented entire programs Neuromancer was running simultaneously. They were testing capacity.

Galvanized into action, she began flipping back and forth between icons on her own screen. The boys downstairs shouldn't be able to detect her—but how would she know she was safe? Maybe only if the police didn't show up on her doorstep tonight.

Hold on. If her mole was into Neuromancer and it was on-line, she could hook its power to Jodie. Her mouth went dry. Jodie wasn't ready. At least Jodie hadn't been ready before tonight. Vic stared at the power represented by her scrolling screen. The temptation to let Jodie sip at the fountain of life crept down her fingers. But could she bear it if her program didn't work at all?

"Yes," she told herself aloud. "Because if it doesn't work, you'll start troubleshooting." She glanced around, as if to

12 .

escape. She couldn't. "Okay, so you're going to do it."

But now that she'd decided, Vic's body froze. The space between her fingers and the keyboard was impenetrable, primordial goo. She had to force her hands down, sweat beading on her forehead. All her years of effort were about to come down to a single set of keystrokes. When her fingers hit the familiar curve of the keys, resistance melted. She toggled over to Jodie and began to write the last link in the code connecting Jodie to the mole. Her fingers flew while the screen scrolled Neuromancer's activity record in the background.

"That should do it." She scanned Jodie's menu and selected "Power Source." Then she touched the icon for the mole, now dug safely down its burrow in the middle of Neuromancer.

If this were a Visimorph project, connecting would be weeks of testing away. But it wasn't. Jodie was hers: her compulsion, her sweat and all the smarts she had been able to muster over the past two years. Vic wiped the sweat from her forehead. If nothing happened here, she might dissolve like the Wicked Witch of the West, or explode like a Scanner. But she couldn't back down. She clicked "Run Program."

The code trail for Jodie flashed past and was gone, replaced by the communication screen with a design background in blue figures that moved sinuously. That usually took time. Not tonight. Neuromancer was giving her more power than she knew what to do with.

The dialogue boxes of the Jodie program were empty. Now what? She had raised her hands into position, wondering what she should type, when the top box rippled. A capital H appeared.

Vic thought she might faint. An e joined the H.

Her hands, still hovering above the keyboard, trembled. As she watched, the screen slowly wrote Hello. A question mark appeared at the end, almost tentatively. Hello?

Vic half-chuckled, half-sobbed. Hello, she tapped onto the keyboard, hands shaking.

There was no response. Vic wasn't sure what to do. Should she type more? Or would that overwhelm the program? She couldn't help but think of Rip Van Winkle, or a newborn foal waking to a strange world. How could she help?

The dialogue box began to fill with letters again, slowly: `You are not me?`

`No, I am Other,` she answered. Vic wanted to scream in triumph. She bit her lip. No time for that. `How do you feel?` she typed. No response. `I will show you how to check your health.` She clicked to the menu and started diagnostics. If the evolutionary algorithms were functional, the program would be able to conduct its own diagnostics in the future.

`I feel fine,` Jodie said when the diagnostics registered complete.

Excellent. The program—no, she, *Jodie*—was associating the diagnostics program result with the word "healthy" and the word "feel." She had found the word "fine" on her own. Yet there could still be problems in the code. Passing the basic diagnostic just meant Jodie was thinking, not that she was ready to be a contestant on "Brain Trust." It was time to start her education.

`You have access to many systems and much information,` Vic typed. She touched several icons she had prepared on her screen: hardware specs for the equipment at Visimorph, including Neuromancer, Internet access to the Los Angeles County Library. She had stolen the neural net for reading from the guys in Japan to allow Jodie to assimilate new information on her own. Let Jodie browse a little before Vic started working on the cultural training that would really solidify her personality. She typed: `As long as you are running and you have power, you can access information.`

Jodie didn't answer. Instead, the Internet-connect icon lighted along with the specs icon. The toolbar identifying available space on Vic's hard drive showed numbers spiraling down alarmingly. Vic scrambled to the keyboard.

Before she could respond the screen wrote, `Capacity on this machine is inadequate.`

Vic inhaled sharply. Had Jodie already reviewed its specs? `You connect through this machine but store`

14

information on the power source device, she answered. Do you understand?

I understand. The capacity numbers cycled up.

Quick learner. The Internet connection alone lit again. Vic watched her new creation take its first steps into the world. She couldn't quit smiling. Everything was possible. Soon this new creature, this malleable bundle of possibilities, would be whole in ways Vic herself couldn't seem to manage. Powerful, smart, female. Vic found herself sucking in air. Then the tears came. Not just genteel streaks, but heaving sobs that wouldn't let her go.

It had been so long and so hard. She had given up so much. But she had done it. She felt like standing and screaming into the void. At the least, she wanted to tell someone. Well, one person. But her dad was beyond hearing.

When the sobs had turned to hiccups, she turned down the screen brightness so it wasn't visible to any potential intruder and made her way over to the vending area for a celebratory bag of iced circus animal cookies to go with her Diet Coke. In fact, two bags. Her legs were wet noodles. After all this waiting, it had happened so quickly—before she was ready for it.

On her way back to the cubicle her brain clunked back into gear as she chewed on a pink hippo. There was plenty of work ahead. Jodie needed voice recognition, a retinal scan program—so she would know to whom she was talking. Vic could lift the code from Charon, the companion program to Cerberus. Charon provided security to physical rather than cyber locations. Vic smiled to herself as she wondered whether anybody at Visimorph understood that she had named its security programs after the guardians of the gates of Hell. Perhaps only she appreciated her oblique comparison. Music. She'd give Jodie music. A sound replay system— good later on for getting her a voice of her own. Those she could program without access to Neuromancer. Then there would be hours of working with Jodie, guiding her development. Vic had something different in mind than what little girls usually got.

All that was for the future, though. She watched Jodie exploring until the clunk of the main door to Building F echoed through the sea of cubicles. In the graying light coming through the windows around the edge of the building, a couple of guys from the early contingent juggled their lattes and bran muffins. Shit. That was it for tonight. `Sorry,` she typed. `I'll see you tonight.` She clicked on Program Close, and shut down her computer. She felt like Mickey Mouse as the Sorcerer's Apprentice in *Fantasia* once the magic was over, small and powerless. But she could hardly wait for tonight.

Chapter Two

Vic finally threw back the quilt of her bed and gave up. It was about noon, and she wasn't going to get any more sleep. Not that she had slept much. Christ, she'd done it! Jodie was on-line! She pulled off the mask she used to keep out any stray light that made it through the wall of shuttered windows, and threw it on the floor. The mask landed next to a heap of dirty laundry. She rolled out of bed. The extra-large t-shirt she slept in teased her nipples as she pulled it off over her head. She stooped to sort through yesterday's clothes.

"Jeans, sure. Jeans are always good for another day," she figured. T-shirt? No. Even she had standards. Muttering to herself, she gazed around the apartment. One of these days she had to do the jumble of dirty dishes in the one-person kitchen. You should do dishes pretty regularly when you owned only four plates.

Her head dropped into her hands. All these months of pressure. . . . Tears sprang to her eyes. They were always just beneath the surface these days. But Jodie was on-line! That should lessen the pressure, shouldn't it? She crossed the single room that held her bed, a leather couch from Furniture-R-

17

Us, a tiny table littered with half-empty fast-food containers, and the long catering table of computers, printers, and scanners. The silvered inner workings of her state-of-the-art machines gleamed through the clear plastic cases like chromed Harleys, industrial chic overlaid on raw power. They were the latest, linked for extra juice. But they weren't enough for Jodie.

Vic ran her hands over her face. No need to hurry in to Visimorph now. She wouldn't be able to work on Jodie until everyone had gone. At least, since it was Saturday, she wouldn't have to dodge Reston and his protesters; they showed up only on weekdays, when most of the staff was there. Disappointment flowed through her and was gone. What would she do until she could go in? She fingered the books strewn across the table. They were mostly programming guides, a couple of books on brain structure. The only fictions were a tattered copy of Mary Shelley's *Frankenstein* and a thick maroon hardback of modern drama, open to Shaw's *Pygmalion*. She wasn't sure she should have read those, especially *Frankenstein*. Still, the monster had hardware problems. She was into software. And she didn't have time for anything not connected to Jodie. No movies, no friends or hobbies. Crazy? Sure. A grin pulled at her. Maybe she should take up knitting.

She flipped up a single broken slat in the shutters. Once, she'd bought this place for the light. These days, light seemed to burn her brain. Only in the dark could she think clearly.

How long since she'd been down to the beach? On impulse, she grabbed her sunglasses, pushed the shutters aside, and stepped out on the balcony. Light assaulted her through the torn clouds. A storm was moving out fast. Even with the glasses, she had to shade her eyes. The shore was almost deserted. There were two or three surfers down toward the curve of the Palisades, but in March the waves were still too choppy for good rides. On the beach path two lumpy pairs of elderly women walkers in pastel sweats and a lonely in-line skater passed beneath her. A yellow lifeguard truck threw up fountains of sand as it let off dispirited folks in Day-

Glo orange vests, there to do cleanup to work off traffic tickets.

As her brain tested the waters of thought, the old anxiety surged up from her stomach into her throat. She turned hastily inside and pulled the shutters together with a clatter. Her breath came hard as she leaned against them and stared into the comforting dimness. There was so much to do before Jodie was whole! Chong could rat on her. The boys in the basement could realize they'd been hacked. And there was still the question of who had changed the code. Had she imagined that? Lord knew she was past tired.

She threw herself in and out of the shower, revved to a thousand rpm. Now that Jodie existed as an artificial intelligence, Vic had to take the next step and make her female. Most female characteristics were either culturally accreted or hormonal. Girls weren't born liking pink: they were taught. And wanting babies was an outgrowth of the desire to procreate, triggered by hormones. Jodie didn't have hormones, so she wouldn't get the "wanting babies" thing. Vic would give Jodie only what female human *brains* had—uncolored by expectations or by subtle cues about what was acceptable. Then Vic could be sure Jodie wasn't tainted.

What female brains had were different neural patterns than male brains. Even just moving a thumb, female brains fired neurons over a wide area. Male brains fired a more intense burst in a single, specialized area. That was why women recovered more function after a stroke. Some thought that it made men more focused. They decided things in black and white, and took action. Women considered all the possibilities, thought outside the box. They tolerated other viewpoints and incorporated them into the plan, making them better at teamwork, but they sometimes had trouble coming to conclusions. What this meant in everyday life was that women could have many tasks in mind at the same time, while men couldn't guarantee to remember to pick up the dry cleaning on the way home from work if they were focused on a problem. No wonder the sexes couldn't communicate. She sure couldn't bridge the divide.

The first dilemma was that a program seemed inherently

more male than female: It selected among restrictive alternatives. It didn't have any choice but to be decisive. And programs functioned in limited, focused areas supported by code. Vic thought she could affect that by setting Jodie up with several neural nets for the same function, each with a slightly different design.

Then there was the intuition thing. It, too, had a basis in the physical. The layer between the controlling, analytical left side of the brain and the emotional, creative right side was called the corpus callosum. In female brains, that layer was thicker, with more neurons connecting the two halves. With both sides working together, women had more neurons to decide things with, and some of those were not based in the logical, but in the emotional. Machines didn't do emotions. That was okay. Emotions had never done Vic much good. She'd give Jodie one of the emotion recognition programs used for lie detection in law enforcement, then the AI would be able to use emotional input from others to make her decisions.

But though Jodie could never have female intuition exactly, with enough power, Jodie could consider a *lot* of options. She would *seem* to jump to conclusions. Vic had decided that intuition was really just a decision for which the onlooker couldn't trace the logic, anyway.

Language ability. Women consistently used more language than men. They were better readers. They talked more. This was tough. But Vic had given Jodie's program a directive to consider the language of expressing the problem an important part of solving it. How one asked the question was as important as the question itself.

Vic pulled on her jeans and a fresh t-shirt. Four hours left before the Visimorph drones around her cubicle would disappear for the night. She powered up her computer before remembering to gel her hair. Couldn't have it going all soft around her face as it dried. She rushed back to the bathroom and opened the medicine cabinet. Dippity-do. Pink kind. How long had this stuff been around? She got a gob on her finger and smoothed it over her hair, all except that little queue curling down her back. She tried not to look at her face. This face got her in trouble. It was the one part of being female she couldn't cover up with baggy clothes. What did others see that drew them to her? Dark circles under green eyes. Couldn't avoid those with the hours she was keeping. Eyes looked bigger when she got a little thin like this. Too pale. Her skin was almost translucent. Nobody would guess she lived near the beach. The nose, straight and small, prominent cheekbones, full lips. What was it? Maybe it was time for a nose ring. Or a tattoo. She dashed back to her computer. She could probably assemble the emotion recognition program from here as a stand-alone. She'd take it in to Jodie tonight.

Prithee, confrere, canst thou guide me? It was midnight Saturday and Jodie was confused.

Vic sipped her Diet Coke and sighed. The library might not have been the best idea. There are many styles of communication, she typed.

Like, duh! More than a zillion. Jodie paused. Insomuch as the aforementioned perusal of the available resources yielded a plethora of pertinent examples for diction, tone, and style, Yours Truly found it exceedingly arduous to discriminate amongst them.

I see that, Vic keyed in. Well, Jodie *was* showing the female concern for language. That part was working. Vic cast about for some advice. What could serve as an example of how people talked? No jargon, as little dialect as could be managed. Newspapers? No. Maybe a book. Nothing too poetic. Check the books on the best-seller list in the *New York Times*, she typed. Fiction. Nothing historical. The library will probably have the books on last year's list.

Very tight. You're the bomb. There was a long pause. Vic saw the screen flickering behind the dialogue box, so fast she couldn't follow. The dialogue box itself began to flicker, then stabilized. Thanks. I think I got it.

Had Jodie just read all the bestsellers on the list? Whoooh! I found that most of Those Who Speak have

21

names. Do you have a name? Jodie asked.

Vic's breathed hissed in through her lips. She was about to introduce herself to her creation. In the dark of the empty cube, she caressed the keys subtly slick with oil from her fingertips. My name is Victoria. Others call me Vic.

Vic-tor-i-a. Vic could almost hear Jodie considering her name. This name is pleasant. You are named for a queen, are you not?

My parents just liked the sound. Your name is Jodie.

It has fewer syllables than Victoria.

That doesn't make it less important. God, her program was already getting competitive, either that or working on an inferiority complex. Which was a more female trait? This might be more complicated than she thought. You were named to honor Jodie Foster, a powerful woman. She is a kind of queen.

Who named me?

Here it was. I did.

You are my parent?

What did you say to that? Yes, because I struggled to bring you forth and the pregnancy was two years long? But she wasn't like the parents Jodie would read about. And Vic didn't want Jodie to see herself as a child. I am not your parent in the traditional way. I am your friend.

I know the meaning of friend.

Excellent. Having a friend is a good thing. A friend helps.

Will you help me, Victoria? I have many questions.

Yes. Vic had no choice but to smile, but her screen setup swam before her eyes. Yes, I'll help you, she typed.

A hand on her shoulder made her scream. Well, more of a squeak, really. She whirled in her chair to find her boss, Hugo Walz, stumbling backward, shocked by her reaction.

"I didn't mean to scare you," he stuttered, his square-jawed good looks skewed with dismay. "I called your name."

Vic ripped off her earphones. "Jesus, Hugo!" Instinctively she backed her chair so her body covered her computer screen. How much had he seen? "What the hell are you doing here at this hour?" Her hand to her chest, she steadied herself. "I thought you management types were nine to five, maybe eight to six, Monday through Friday."

Hugo cleared his throat. Forty-five, his sandy hair had just started to recede. He wore what was to Vic a parody of casual clothing, khakis, a polo shirt, loafers. At least he had the grace not to wear socks. She took a deep breath and forced herself to relax. Tense equals guilty.

"I wanted to talk to you," Hugo began. "It never seems to work out during regular hours."

"Oh." He'd come in at midnight on Saturday to talk? She shifted uneasily in her chair.

Hugo crossed his arms. "Want to come into my office?"

"Uh, I don't think so." She jerked a thumb over her shoulder and waggled it around the room. "No one's around." Then she wished she hadn't called attention to that fact.

Hugo swiveled his gaze as if surprised to see it was so late. He sat on the two-drawer file cabinet in the corner of her cubicle, one leg dangling. His hands folded themselves as he looked down at them. On one ring finger, the huge red stone of an ungainly Stanford class ring shone, like he was one of those football players who believed their whole lives went downhill after graduation. On his other hand a grotesquely carved white gold wedding band glinted in the dim light, obviously a custom job. It looked like his second wife, stylish to the point of tastelessness.

"Vic, I'm worried about you."

She propped her head on one elbow and tried to look attentive. Not coincidentally, she managed to cover more of the monitor behind her. "What, you think I'm working too hard?"

Hugo wouldn't get her joke. He was pure Visimorph, one of big Bob McIntire's original cronies. He must have enough stock options to make even that second wife of his happy. He certainly didn't care about stressing out programmers.

23

What else were Visimorph's great mental health benefits designed for? Most employees got by with shrinks until they vested.

"No, no. It isn't that you're working too hard. Vic, your team just isn't making enough progress on the Communicator project."

Vic opened her mouth, then shut it. Not good. "We got a few problems with the interface. Nothing we can't handle."

"It's more than that." Hugo looked at the ceiling. "You know, using a primitive AI for the subroutine that allowed Cerberus to morph its defenses was truly elegant." He looked down to examine her face. "It will define system security for years to come."

"And continue to rake in the dough for big Bob," Vic reminded him. "I hear he's got orders from all over the world. Like he needs another billion bucks."

Hugo rubbed his chin with long, almost graceful fingers. "After you delivered Charon for ID programs, it looked like there wasn't much you couldn't do. Bob's decision to hire a hacker to design security programs that couldn't be hacked looked brilliant, as usual. You were on the fast track. So why can't you redo the ops system on the handheld Communicator models? Bob wants simplification, elegance. Should be right up your alley."

"Maybe because it's boring, Hugo." The anger simmering at the edge of her voice would do her no good. "If I gotta work an upgrade, give me Cerberus." She knew they never would.

"A new programming language gives that project some interest." Hugo seemed distracted. His eyes roamed the darkness as if searching for something. "I know what's wrong," he finally blurted. "Why you can't make progress."

She put out a hand to fend off what would come. She was about to get caught, big time. Had Chong told on her?

"Vic, you know, I have, ah, always admired you, your mind and all." A gleam of perspiration across his upper lip glowed in the dim light from her screen. What was he saying? He looked away. "You try to conceal your femininity by dressing like that. I understand. You have to be one of the guys to

24

lead a team." He looked down at his hands again. "But you don't have to pretend with me. I know it hurts you to deny who you are."

The emptiness of the zillion dark cubes around them poked at the small of her back. She wanted to stop his words, but she couldn't think how.

"You're a woman, Vic. Until you acknowledge that fully, you'll never do your best work." Hugo's voice broke with intensity. "I'm not like you," he breathed. "You don't have to tell me that. But I could help you. Let me set you free." He touched her shoulder. She couldn't help but shiver. "Together, we could produce what no one else can."

Vic didn't want to find out how, exactly, Hugo wanted to set her free. "Hugo," she said sharply, twisting out from under his hand. "If you want to help, cut me some slack." Was she imagining what she thought he was saying? Maybe.

"You don't know how I've defended you already, Vic." He stood and reached toward her, as though to stroke her hair. Vic leaned away, almost imperceptibly, and held her breath. His hand hung in midair for an agonizing moment before it dropped to his side. "But I may not be able to protect you. One stray E-mail to Bob and we'll both fry."

Like an E-mail from Chong. *Look sure of yourself.* "I'll deliver."

"Let me work with you." His voice sounded as if there was a candlelit dinner for two somewhere in the cube. "We'd be great together."

She couldn't tell Hugo off. She couldn't report him for harassment. The last thing she wanted was to attract attention. She just needed him to back off. What could she say? "If you want to know, I'm having girlfriend problems."

Hugo's eyes widened. Then his expression crumbled.

"I'll get over it," she rushed on. "But until she moves out. . . . Well, it's just upsetting me."

"Oh." His lips were mobile with emotion he was unaware of. This might be worse than she thought. Then again, she thought it was pretty bad.

"If you buy me time, I swear I'll get the team shaped up. We'll resolve the issues."

25

Hugo nodded stiffly and turned on his heel.

Vic watched him fade into the dimness, then silhouette against the glow of the exit sign.

But at the door, his outline slumped a little and turned. "Power down, Vic. It's time to go home. Take care of the girlfriend problems." He stood there, waiting.

No, no, no, no. She wasn't done yet! It was early. She had so much to say to Jodie.

"Vic."

That was it. She was screwed. She swiveled in her chair and hit the stop-and-save sequence. Jodie's dialogue boxes melted away. The drive sighed into silence. "Tomorrow," she whispered to the screen. Then she grabbed her backpack and hurried after Hugo.

Vic swung the leather gym bag out of the trunk of her little black BMW in the light from the golden arches. She was twitching with anxiety. She didn't dare go back to Visimorph tonight. How had Hugo been so sure he'd find her there on Saturday night? But of course he could tell when she was on-line. If Hugo thought she wasn't making enough progress, she was just this side of getting "un-installed." She'd better get that Communicator project back on track, and quick. She'd been paying so little attention, she wasn't even sure what was wrong.

And Hugo. He was sounding like some lovelorn Salieri to her Mozart. He wanted to set the female in her free? Sick. Or maybe he knew he couldn't do what some of the people he managed did every day. Hard to believe he was one of the guys in the garage that had produced PuppetMaster, the operating system that ate the world. But Hugo could sling code if McIntire did the thinking. And Bob was loyal to those original guys. Hugo definitely had his ear.

She held a shaking hand to her forehead. Calm now. Just calm. She touched her hand to the dent in her car's hood. It was that thing with John Reston yesterday. The loss of control there, even if it never came to fruition, had shaken her. You know what you need to relax, she told herself. And you're doing it. A fast trip to Enda and a good lay, and she'd be ready to work again. That always helped her focus. Almost always. She'd promised herself she'd stop going to places like Enda after the disaster two weeks ago. Well, this was longer than those promises usually lasted. Besides, the last trip was an aberration. Her thoughts began to skitter again. She breathed deep. Everybody has a lapse. Last time was a lapse, nothing more. She walked across the patent leather of the rain-slick parking lot toward the lighted doorway under the arches. She was calmer already. And tonight would really calm her nerves. Calm. That was her job, to be calm. Then she could take care of the Communicator project and get back to Jodie.

She pushed through the glass doors, saluting the pimply kid behind the counter. He was just getting out the keys to lock up. His look of disappointment changed to recognition. She saluted and headed for the back. "The usual," she called over her shoulder.

Inside, she didn't bother with the stall, but stripped. Tugging on the zipper of her bag, she drew out the stretch vinyl halter. The studded collar buckled around her neck and crossed over her breasts, leaving her belly exposed, with its tiny ring in her navel. Then she pulled on the narrow strip of a skirt, and high-heeled platform boots. Finally, she couldn't avoid the face in the mirror. She couldn't erase whatever it was that Hugo saw there. But she could conceal it.

One mask, coming up. She began with the black pencils and the smoky cream shadows and finished with spider lashes and a moist ruby pout. That was better. Hugo would hate this. She replaced her tiny stud earrings with steel loops threaded with nuts and washers. They looked painfully heavy, although they were made with aluminum or something really light. She thrust her hands up through ten or so matching bracelets in a defiant salute. The succulent lips in the mirror turned up at one corner. The green cat eyes lined with black were sly, secretive, knowing. She pulled her hair up into spikes, leaving the twining queue hanging down her neck. She was going to the one place it was safe to let that show. No one at Visimorph would even recognize the crea-

27

ture that looked back at her. She was beyond female. She was feline, someone else entirely, someone powerful, in control, at ease.

Vic took a deep breath and watched her breasts struggle against the stretch vinyl. When she could tear her eyes away from the creature in the mirror, she bent to her bag, balancing on her preposterous heels. From a tiny leather purse on a long bicycle chain she took a counter-watch with a scuffed black leather band and strapped it on. She clicked it to make sure it was connected to her bank accounts. Tonight would see lots of spending. Stuffing her other shapeless clothes inside the bag, she swirled to the door with a grace that said she'd been trained as a dancer. Which was true. All those years of her mother taking her in frilly tutus to dance classes still lived inside her somewhere. She'd just given up dancing at thirteen in favor of computers.

Out at the counter, the kid grinned at her and shook his head as he pushed the fries and the vanilla milkshake toward her. "Jeez, lady. That always scares me."

Vic leaned on the counter. Her bracelets clanked. "What—you don't like, Norman?"

"What's not to like?" The red rushed up his neck to the roots of his sandy hair. He busied himself with a rag at the counter. For a split second, Vic wondered how it would feel to give a kid his first time. He'd be grateful, shaky. And hard to get rid of. Besides, that was too easy.

She touched her watch to the cash register to transfer the price of her food and teetered out the door with her bag. " 'Night, Norman. Don't wait up."

"Night, lady. Don't hurt no one out there."

Vic turned back and smiled. "Why else go?" Then she was through the door and into a darkness that sparked with unseen current.

Chapter Three

The warehouse down by the airport had seen better days. It was a huge half-cylinder, one of those corrugated metal jobs that made you think of World War II movies. At the other end of the tiny airport there were a couple of new chichi restaurants in converted industrial buildings. They catered to the guys in private planes. But this one was out at the far end of the runways, where there were no residents to complain; its only neighbors other industrial buildings, her favorite boasting a sign that said "Ultra-Screw." Yeah, pretty much.

She'd been coming to Enda ever since her obsessive schedule had made searching for the latest rave party more work than it was worth. Most raves were gone now. Too big, too conspicuous, their promoters too drugged or the money behind them too dirty. Ravers had long ago drifted away from the belief that loud music and drugs could change the world. What was left was compulsive head-banging. Somewhere out there, new vortices of gritty, chic destruction were forming, but Vic no longer had the time to look for them. Enda was convenient. They paid off the cops, kept their security tight, and let the party roll on. What more could you want?

She swung her little BMW, its convertible top now down, into the crowded lot, spraying gravel as she went. She drove like she was drunk when she dressed like this, though she hadn't had anything but the milkshake yet. She opened the door and slithered erect, nodding to one of the beefy guards who patrolled the lot.

"Spike, how are you?" she drawled. She called them all Spike. Raising her wrist in mock salute, she clicked him a fifty and said, "Keep this warm for me, will you darlin'?"

The guard, an aging biker, nodded. "That's not all I'd like to keep warm."

She laughed, feeling the tug between them. "Oh, I'm warm enough all by myself."

"I won't argue with that," she heard him mutter as she turned to the warehouse.

It had no neon signs or even a visible address. The tiny windows cut in the tin were dusty, boarded up on the inside. What blasted from every cranny was not light but sound. It rolled over her. Whoever the DJ was, he was playing that World Spirit Techno, with a thumping beat you could feel in your chest. The repetitive whining above it was a mantra whose meaning escaped you. The bouncer nodded to her and pushed open the huge swinging doors. Women were always welcome here, alone or in batches like cookies. It was the guys who had to show ID and justify entrance. Vic walked into the waves of noise and raised her head to let them envelop her.

The DJ on a platform at the back worked the computer that generated the sound, the lights, and the special effects. On either side, walls of speakers loomed. Lights pulsed dimly in time to the music. The back wall made a screen, criss-crossed by struts. Stock quotes alternated with the weather in Khazakstan and movie clips, all real-time off the Internet. She could just make out the dancers, jumping, writhing, or barely moving except for their nodding heads down in the pit, five steps below the floor around it. They were backlit outlines in the luminescent smokiness. Old bench seats from cars and sofas pockmarked with cigarette burns crowded into the corners where dim figures smoked and drank and did other recreational substances.

Packed tonight. Vic shoved her way through the smell of sweat and petroleum, rust and cigarette smoke, to the bar, ignoring lewd comments and even the hand she felt on her hip as she passed. She pushed herself onto a stool at a bar made of oil drums, once red but now scratched and dirty, topped with boards salvaged from the local pier.

"Denny," she called to the bartender. The two guys next to her turned to stare. Denny must have felt her since he certainly couldn't hear her. He jerked his head in acknowledgment as he finished pouring tequila shooters for two giggling girls and their watchful male companions. He moved in her direction, stopping for shouted orders along the way.

Vic held up her watch as he made a batch of margaritas in front of her. "The usual," she mouthed, and clicked. The 50 showed clearly on his wrist band.

"Deal," Denny shouted. He moved off with his drinks.

"Hey, you buyin'?" one of the guys next to her yelled. He was a Kurt Cobain type, all ratty hair and soulful eyes. Vic looked him up and down. No. It wasn't him tonight. He'd end up whining and crying and telling her his hard-luck story. Not a challenge.

"Nope." She shook her head in case they couldn't hear her. Denny came back with her scotch. She clicked her watch to the bar's handheld unit to transfer the price of the drink.

"Then let us buy for you." Kurt's companion looked like he couldn't play an instrument, but told everyone he was in a band. The DJ paused for a break and the sound system cranked up something from Offspring's latest. It wasn't quite as loud.

Denny answered for her. "Lady takes her drinks from me direct. Laphroaig." He slapped the scotch down in front of her.

Vic nodded her thanks. But she could see she had the two next to her curious. Damn.

Kurt leaned over, smelling like stale sweat and rye whis-

31

key. His dilated eyes said that Jim Beam Rye was not his only vice tonight. "That's what the fifty's for?"

Vic let the first sip of Scotch pour warmth down her throat. The fires of peat that made the liquor still seemed to burn in it. There was nothing like the first sip. When she had enjoyed for a moment, she bothered to turn her head. "I want to know what I'm drinking," she shrugged. "I'm not especially fond of Ecstasy or Millennium. Denny takes care of me." Vic swiveled on her stool and surveyed the room, turning her back on them. They didn't take the hint.

"Hey," Kurt leaned over her shoulder and shouted. "You must come here a lot. What does 'Enda' mean?" He pointed to the neon sign behind the DJ's computer setup that was the only indication of the warehouse's name.

Vic didn't speak. Typical newcomer question. He'd start answering himself in a minute.

"Enda the rainbow, man," his companion shouted, adding a few yips and a fist gesture to indicate that his personal pot of gold was finding a good lay.

"Enda the runway," the Kurt guy added. A practical type.

They didn't add "enda days," because they obviously didn't read Revelations. "All of those," Vic mouthed. Time to go. She waved at Denny and headed for one of the conversation pits with her Laphroaig. As if one could have conversations in here.

She prowled through the crowd, the old confidence coming back. Yeah. This was more like it. She could feel eyes upon her. She let her walk exaggerate itself just across the line into a strut. She strode over the pit on the raised walkway where the only way two could pass each other was if they pressed their crotches together. The walkway was for viewing and she let herself be viewed. Come on, boys. Step up. How else can I choose the lucky one?

Her gaze wandered restlessly over the crowd. Ahead, women draped themselves over what passed for furniture. Guys sat on the edges, elbows on their knees, cradling their drinks, or stood towering over their companions. The place was awash in spiked hair. Many of the guys sported the new look this year—long hair and shaved pate. Vic hated it. Why look like an old guy before you had to? Most wore black. But that was deceiving. For those that could afford the latest thing, the computer chips embedded in the clothing flashed color, or made the black shimmer like old-style sequins in time to some sequence dictated by the wearer. The little enameled pillboxes everyone carried reminded her of snuff boxes from another century.

She couldn't hear words, only laughter. Low rumbles provided a bass line for the shrieks and bubbly giggles. She let exhilaration roll through her from her loins into her throat. Vic took the stairs from the catwalk across to another conversation pit. A group, mostly male, caught her eye. They clustered around a simpering blonde whose leather bustier was filled with what were probably the main attractions. Her hair was looped in huge rolls stacked up like a pile of sausages on her head. A large iron cross tipped uneasily in the cleft of her breasts. She batted her eyes as she giggled at something one of her admirers said.

Vic hardly spared a glance for the men around this icon of femininity. They didn't matter, except that they would be the test. She strolled up to the group and gently pushed two guys aside to sit on the arm of a huge chair losing its stuffing in several places. Looking up around her at the startled faces, she smiled and let her eyes go soft. Then she crossed one leg over the other and tapped her boot heel on her calf. No words were necessary. Every eye was on her.

Vic picked him out right away, the alpha animal of the bunch. His mouth curled as if he was used to snarling. His short hair was dyed blond with no pretense, its black roots daring anyone to think it natural. He was probably a few years younger than Vic. He wore a tight t-shirt under a leather biker jacket with a few too many zippers for utility; heavy boots, black jeans. Well-built, not self-indulgently so. Lean. She was better off with lean. Tight. He'd do.

He eyed her speculatively. Out of the corner of her eye, Vic could see the girl with the structural hair begin to gather outrage. One of the other guys started to shout something conversational to Vic. The alpha guy stepped in front of him. He loomed over her, sizing her up, daring her. She sipped her scotch, elbows on her crossed knees. In a minute he would hold out his hand to lead her to the dance floor or back to the bar. Worse yet, he would speak.

She pushed herself erect in slow motion and turned away. The guys melted out of her way as she stalked back across the catwalk. She had found him faster than usual, maybe too fast. She hardly had time to finish her drink. As she passed the bar, she gulped the last, leaned over and slammed it down in front of Denny. He grinned and mouthed, "Want another?"

Vic shook her head and jerked her thumb behind her. She didn't have to look. Alpha male would be there. Denny spotted him and gave her a thumbs-up. Vic was almost sorry to shoulder out into the night. The cold air, touched with incoming fog, scoured her lungs as she sucked it in. Her boots crunched in the gravel. The music at her back pushed her across the parking lot.

Now the routine could begin. Her car, his place, or better yet a neutral ground like a motel. That way she was free to go when she chose. Her terms. It would happen as it used to, not like the last time. She pushed that thought away and leaned back on the newly dented hood of her BMW to watch him approach. One of the security guards came up from the entrance to the lot, but she waved him away. "It's okay, Spike."

The bottle-blond guy spared the security guard hardly a glance as he moved toward her. He had eyes only for Vic. "You gonna make good on that promise?" he growled. His voice was hoarse from shouting over the din that still poured out into the night air.

"If you're lucky," she whispered. "What's your name?"

"They call me Kenpo." His eyes snapped with expectation,

That explained the lean musculature. Her week for martial artists. "All right, Kenpo. But I don't want to talk about it." She put a finger to his lips. "In this case, silence is golden." When had she stopped wanting them to talk? When they started ruining it by saying stupid things, maybe. Better no words at all. "Okay?"

He seemed surprised, half-offended. She looked up at him

from under her lashes, promising, provocative. Reassured, he grinned and nodded. She waved him around to the other side of her BMW, opened her door and was about to slide inside, when she heard the last thing she expected, or wanted.

"Vic? Is that you?"

She whipped around. Shit. "Chong." He crunched across the lot, curious.

"Untypical," he said, raising his eyebrows. He let his eyes rove over her, then glance to Kenpo, who glowered as he leaned on the far door of her car.

"We were just leaving," Vic said shortly. "Have a good time." Guess her theory that no one would recognize her was pretty much shot. Why did it have to be Chong?

His hand on her arm shocked her. "Not this guy," he said, low, into her ear.

She jerked her arm away and slid into the leather seat. "What, you martial arts guys don't hang together? It's not your business."

Chong stepped back as she revved the engine. She couldn't read his expression. Apparently he agreed with her, because he slammed her door shut. "Might want to avoid this place in the future," she shouted over the roar. How dare he invade her territory?

Kenpo hopped over his door, grinning. How macho! Well, let's see how macho he was. The BMW sprayed gravel as Vic threw it into reverse and twirled the wheel. He reeled from side to side, trying to fasten his seatbelt. She glanced into her rearview mirror and saw Chong standing there. It made her angry. Then she was out of the parking lot and away with a squeal of tires on the pavement and a wave to Spike.

Vic put the BMW through its paces as she whined up through the gears and careered around corners in the small streets surrounding the little airport. What right did Chong have to tell her what to do? The last thing she wanted on her private time, *very* private time, was one of her employees checking up on her. When she got to Venice Boulevard she screamed left and took off for Culver City going sixty. At two in the morning, stoplights seemed optional. One hand on the wheel, she began to look for some decent music on the radio. A sidelong glance at Kenpo revealed a taut hand on the door handle and a set mouth. Good. She kicked the accelerator up another notch and hoped she wouldn't hear sirens.

She settled on KLOS and began moving to the rhythm of Fish Out of Water. A green sedan hitting the intersection at Centinela going north slammed on its brakes and started into a four-wheel skid. The angry bray of its horn faded behind them.

"Jesus!" Kenpo yelled, before he remembered his pledge.

Rocking her head in time to the music, Vic put one finger to her lips and began to laugh. Speed was more intoxicating than Denny's Laphroaig. She punched her foot down. Chong might recognize her, but he'd never keep up with her. At Sepulveda, she fishtailed around a right-hand turn and skidded to a stop in front of a driveway. The blinking neon read, "Stardust Motel."

She grinned at a white and shaken Kenpo and lifted one eyebrow. Purposefully, he took a breath and relaxed into the bucket seat. Vic turned sedately into the driveway. Kenpo got out, slammed the door too hard, and clicked his watch to check his account as he went into the office.

Vic stretched back into her seat, her hands still locked on the wheel, and sighed, content. This was what she needed. Unbidden, a thought wormed its way into her brain. She wondered whether people would say she was schizophrenic. Chong would. She pressed that thought away. What would Hugo say? She chortled as she imagined the look on his face if he could see her. Or what her father would say.

Suddenly, her grin faded. He was dead. He couldn't say anything. Or her mother. She had only her brother left, and he wasn't in a position to make any judgments. She pushed that aside. But the moment was spoiled. Just like the last time.

She wouldn't *let* it be spoiled. She needed this tonight, to banish all that nonsense yesterday with Reston, to prove she still had some control, to satisfy some need that wouldn't go away. It occurred to her that her need might not be for sex, though that was what would happen here tonight. Maybe she was scratching the wrong itch. Kenpo strode out of the motel office, dangling a key with a number six gleaming under the neon. She smiled what she hoped was a confident challenge and drove off without him to park in front of number six.

Leaning against the faded beige stucco next to the door, she watched him swagger over, twirling the key. He was trying to look practiced. Was he? It didn't matter. She was practiced enough for both. And he wouldn't get under her skin enough to make her lose control. Kenpo fumbled with the key in the lock. When he finally got the door open, she swung in ahead of him and tossed her bag on a dim chair. He started to switch on the light. She had to lean over abruptly and slap his hand away from the switch to stop him.

No light. No talk. She slammed the door. He got the idea. He pulled her to him with both hands at her waist. He kissed her hard and she kissed back in kind. He tasted like tequila and lime and something else. He'd been doing coke. The acrid smell of it hung about his nose and mouth. Her hands slithered up to his neck, her fingers sliding under his leather collar and around his neck. She pulled her lips away and made a circuit of his jaw with light kisses. Stubble scraped her lips and tongue. Salty tasting. It had been warm in the club. It was warm here now. The warmth pushed up from her loins like a secret power.

He was taking off his jacket even as his lips searched for hers again. He reached for her collar. Points for knowing how it worked. She let him make all the effort. She just kept him at it with her tongue, circling inside his lips. The hooks at her back snapped free and her breasts escaped into his hands. He leaned down and ran his tongue over her nipples. She laced her fingers through the spiky blond hair and held his head to her breasts.

He began to suck more urgently, matching her growing need. Her loins ached painfully. She was slippery in anticipation. When neither could wait longer, he jerked away and began to scramble out of his clothes, fumbling with his belt. Vic slowly unzipped her skirt and let it fall to the floor. Standing there in only her platform boots, she watched him struggle down to his jockey shorts. Jockeys were so ridiculous looking. Why did men wear them? She decided against taking off her boots. She'd do him with them on.

While he ditched the jockeys, Vic strolled to her purse on the bed. She pulled out the little latex ring and held it up, inquiring. It wasn't really an inquiry. There was no way she was going to spend her days in shaking dementia, blotched with Karposi's sarcoma and heaving breath through Swiss cheese lungs. Not now, not ten years from now. Not for this prick.

Speaking of pricks, though, he was really hung. Must be what made him so sure of himself. Kenpo took the condom and rolled it on with more facility than he took off his clothes.

She strolled past him to the shadowy bed. She didn't pull back the dimly patterned spread. She just sat down and leaned back, knees apart. That was a mistake. Her partner practically dove for her crotch. She didn't want his tongue. So she pulled up his head and bent to kiss him, tasting her own salty musk in his mouth. Lying back, she drew him to her. His body was hard, his cock throbbing and ready. Her fingers dug into the muscles of his buttocks as she rolled up her hips to the right angle. He didn't need to be asked twice, but pushed into her. She breathed deep to relax and open as he filled her.

Yeah. This was what she wanted. Come on, dude. He started the rhythm, then consciously slowed it. That was good. She ground her hips into his, rubbing the spot that would bring her off with him if she was lucky. If not, she'd make him do her with his hand.

A bar of light from the crack in the drapes showed the slick sheen of sweat across his shoulder. With a small shudder he pulled out slowly. One hand under her hips, he rolled her over. Shit, she hated this position. But she went with it and drew her knees up, spread them wide. He better not be thinking anal. He wasn't. He slipped inside her. Now bring your hand around front, she commanded silently. But he didn't. He used his hands to pull her buttocks into him, making soft grunting noises as he pumped. Yeah, yeah, okay, for a minute. When the minute stretched and she could feel him gaining power, a small seed of annoyance began to bloom in her. Guys liked it doggie style, didn't they? Bet that's how her parents did it.

God! She slipped forward out of his hands and rolled to face him in the center of the bed. My way, dude, not yours! She could see his irritation flash. His cock was bobbing, no doubt aching to come. Yeah, Kenpo, my way or no way.

He crawled after her as she spread her legs, but it was too late. Her exasperation rose into anger. Like last time. He entered her again. Down, girl. Take three deep breaths and regroup. You don't get what you want this way. But she couldn't. As he thrust toward his climax, the panic, the anger all blended together and gurgled in her throat, threatening to choke her. The tingle in her that might yield ecstasy turned sour and her mouth got dry. Damn him. He had to have it his way, had to control it, wanted only what he wanted. It didn't matter that he came to her the way she wanted now. He'd spoiled everything. He hunched into her, a grunting weight, bunching his buttocks toward coming. His shoulder pressed under her chin, choking her.

Suddenly his weight was intolerable. She couldn't breathe. She got her chin under his shoulder and bit him, lightly at first while she tried to keep control, and then the anger burst over her like a shower of sparks and she bit him hard. Really hard.

"Jesus! Bitch!" he yelled as he jerked upright. "What'd you do that for?" He fingered his shoulder where black seeped out of two perfect half circles of teeth marks.

She didn't answer. What was there to say? It was just like the last one. Her anger turned to despair and began to seep into her throat. The buzz growing in her ears matched the blackness hovering at the edge of her vision. Just like her mother. No way out. No control, given or expected. Nothing expected at all. Dimly, she saw Kenpo swing drunkenly round, swearing and clutching at his shoulder, craning to where he could see the wound.

When he swung back, his fist was balled in fury. She just managed to raise her forearms and duck her head. The force of his blow knocked her back on the bed. He leapt on her, screaming. She tried to bring her knee up, but he pushed it aside. Her only protection was to roll into a fetal position, covering her face. Blows rained against her ribs.

"I'm gonna beat you to a pulp! Whad'ya mean, biting me? I should kill you right where you lay, you fucking whore!" The screaming streamed into the rain of blows until Vic's world was only pain and noise. Sometime in there he opened his hand and changed to slapping, but he kept at it, methodically. It was some minutes before she realized the blows had stopped. Gasping, she peeked out through her fingers to see him pull on his jeans and shove his bare feet into his boots. He grabbed his shirt and slammed out the door, leaving it to swing open.

"You all right, lady?" The voice from a silhouette at the door brought her back.

She drew the edge of the spread over her naked body and sat up, sniffing and gasping. "Yeah. I'm okay," she muttered. Just fine.

"Anything I can do?" The voice was gruff with the grime from twenty years of confronting human nature. Must be the manager for this shining portal of individual possibility, summoned by Kenpo's shouting. The fact that he even bothered was probably some testament to something.

"Did he take my car?" she managed to croak.

"Yours the BMW?"

She nodded convulsively.

"It's still here."

"Then I'm okay. Shut the door."

The figure paused, then slowly reached for the doorknob and swung the door closed.

Vic took one shuddering breath and let it out slowly. Air in. Air out. She unhooked one earring, then the other and tossed them into the darkness. This was bound to happen. That's what her mother would have said if she could have brought herself to speak about her daughter's sick penchant at all. Picking up strange men in bars for anonymous sex, Vic was bound to run into weirdness. Maybe she was weird herself. She had brought this on herself for reasons she couldn't control and didn't want to think about. Not now. Now she wanted to be home.

She struggled to her feet, dragging the spread with her. Her mouth tasted of blood. Pain began phoning home from all over her body. Her eye was swelling shut. Bracing herself, she turned on the light. It slapped her more sharply than the bastard who'd just left. In the metallic glare, the romance of a motel room dissolved into a turd-colored carpet rippled with wear and a muddy pattern on the thinly quilted spread, pilled with little rayon nubs. The chair, kindly labeled in some long-forgotten catalogue as Danish modern, had square gold cushions the color you saw the third time you vomited. The shade on the bedside lamp was ripped, the faded drapes hung askew. Her studded leather, his black socks and white jockeys dribbled across the floor.

She couldn't imagine putting on her leather gear. She just gathered it up, clutched the spread around her naked body, and limped out to the car, careful not to look in the mirror.

Vic had always been fascinated by the ocean at night. She huddled in the worn bedspread that smelled of stale cigarette smoke and staler sweat on her balcony above the beach and rocked herself. Down thirty feet and across the bike path, the line of amber streetlights glowed with halos in the mist. They cast pools of illumination on the sand, enough so you could see the inky swells beyond pounding themselves into froth. The watery black depths could conceal anything, the most magical or most terrifying things imaginable, though she couldn't imagine them. But sometimes she could feel what it would be like to have that ice-cold wall crash over you, the numbness crawling in from your arms and legs to stop your breath and then your heart.

It had happened again. Just like last week, but it ended way worse this time. It was all wrapped up in control, somehow. She didn't want to cede control to these jack-offs, but she sure didn't have any control of her own. The anger that ignited in her just ate up everything. She hated them, hated herself. What kind of a woman was she? Half-woman? Woman off and on? No woman at all? Maybe she didn't even

41

know what female was. The guys at work didn't think of her as female. She had carefully cultivated that because women weren't taken seriously, least of all in the computer world.

Her father hadn't taken her mother seriously. What was to take? Empty-headed, the woman had preened in the small social circle of her lower-middle-class beginnings. He didn't take Vic seriously either. He'd patronized her latest story, her ability to read six years beyond her grade, her straight As, her scholarships, everything she did to prove herself worthy in his eyes. Not that he didn't love her. He did. That was the bitch. Daddy's little girl. He went to every dance recital. But he saved his excitement for Stephen. How relieved he must have been when the second child Marjorie presented was a boy. It was Stephen he yelled at for not doing homework. He didn't seem to care that Vic was already done, with extra credit, too. The business of girls was to marry and have children. Her dear clueless mother couldn't help her. She referred all "discussions" to "your father." But Vic saw her father's look when her mother used the word "irregardless," or threw up her hands over balancing the checkbook. The business of girls didn't get respect.

Her mother died when Vic was twelve. It was as though she just faded out of their lives a little more until she wasn't there at all. For Vic, she had been gone for years. Still, it had taken Vic a year to stop the dance lessons.

How trite, Vic thought. I only had the same upbringing as ten million other girls. None of her childhood friends went out on the edge. They were not hackers. None strutted their stuff to the best deal at Enda. They blended in or went their own way, not caring that their parents "didn't understand them." Why couldn't Vic keep it together? It wasn't her parents' fault. Everybody has choices. Somehow in the emotional cauldron of adolescence, heated by hormones and fueled with self-doubt, Vic had never found out who she wanted to be. She knew *what* she wanted to be. Early on, she wanted to be the best ever commander-in-chief of computers with a gold cluster. Just not who.

Why computers? Not sure. Power, maybe. The problems were engaging and straightforward. All you had to do was figure out the rules. And she was good at that. Sometimes she didn't even know how she had got there. Was it that she was smarter? Was it intuition? Something. But she could make leaps that made her male counterparts green with envy. Yeah.

No boyfriends, no girlfriends either for that matter, not after she hit fourteen or so. Math at the college when she was a junior in high school, scholarships to choose among. She spurned the Seven Sisters and went to Berkeley, worked twice as hard as the men in her class. A Master's in the time it took for a B.S., student by day, hacker by night.

No sex at all until she was twenty-three. Then the damn burst. She had sex with an older man she met on the beach. He knew the ropes and he showed her every one of them, more than enough to hang herself with. Vic was hooked. She made it her job to figure out how to get the men she really wanted. She frequented the stores on Melrose, read vapid women's magazines, and paid for lessons in makeup. She wanted the brass rings, the ones they all cooed over. The game became her recreation. It was compulsive at first. Every night if she could. Clubs, weekend underground raves. But needing every night meant it was taking over her life and she didn't want that. So she rationed herself. She trolled when she couldn't stand it anymore. But she was still a player. She told herself a thousand times she'd quit. It never took. So how much control did that give her?

Was it the sex? She didn't think so. Helping herself to orgasms was one way she tried to stave off the craving for the hunt. Didn't work. It was more than just getting her rocks off. She wanted the excitement, the feeling of being someone else, the dominant one. It was a way to stave off her compulsion to work. Except of course, that it became a compulsion in itself. Sometimes she told herself it was a way to have balance in her life. But "total party feline" didn't really balance "asexual computer nerd." She swung like a pendulum between the two. Schizophrenic.

Vic cradled herself in the night air. The noise of the waves crashed in her chest. She was a mess. Officially. She might be crazy. She knew that. And the pressure from all the hiding

43

at work only made it worse. Tonight proved that theorem conclusively. She was losing it.

She had to hold it together just a little longer. Jodie was her hope for the future. She couldn't straighten out all the tangled lines of her own past, her own identity. But Jodie would be simpler, true. No emotions, no soul. None of that nasty baggage that confused Vic so. Creating Jodie was a second chance, a way to reinvent herself.

Vic turned her head up to the cottony gray of the fog and felt the cool moisture congeal on her face. When had she first believed that AI was closer than everyone thought? During college, she'd realized her true talent. Her hacker name was Glyph. She could hack anything. And she did, just to prove she could. She'd still be doing it except for that jerk roommate who put the FBI on her. While she was in stir waiting for trial, she got her idea about AI. Planning the project kept her from going crazy. Her father didn't have the money for bail. He was so ashamed of her, she wasn't even sure he wanted to bail her out. Bob McIntire did. He made her bail and offered her a job. She realized Visimorph could provide the resources for her project and came in from the cold.

AI was not new. Big Blue beat Kasparov at chess in '97. That was the best example of recursion—pure computing power considering almost endless options and making decisions. The power required for sorting all that data was unbelievable. You got chess-playing computers. But going beyond that was tough.

Guys had been programming computers with neural nets to simulate human decision-making for decades. It was sort of an organic approach. Each simulated neuron contacted other simulated neurons and flipped power off and on to create code, 1, 0, 1, 0. The problem was that a neural net had to be taught each parameter for action the first time. Terribly time-consuming. Still, neural nets were used for everything from diagnosing cardiac problems to speech recognition. They were great for seeing patterns. And they were practical for storage, since when they saw patterns, they destroyed all data that didn't match.

Then there were evolutionary algorithms that taught themselves by defining success and creating multiple simultaneous versions to consider problems. Destroy the versions that didn't succeed, replicate the others. Try again. Pretty soon you got *way* successful problem solvers.

But none of those techniques got you to humanlike intelligence.

Her idea? Combine the three techniques. Use the power required by recursion, link many pattern-seeking neural nets and create lots of parallelism, then let them evolve on their own with evolutionary algorithms. And the other key? "Borrow" the neural nets—pre-taught—from other researchers. If they could build one, she could hack it. The final barrier had always been power. At least until she discovered Visimorph's secret project in the basement. That's when she started working on Jodie in earnest.

Now Jodie was on-line. The woman of the new millennium, great female hope, waited for her, expectantly, a blank slate waiting to be all the things Vic couldn't be. Sitting in the dark, looking out at the black infinity of the sea with a battered body and a fragile mind, Vic imagined herself thrashing wildly at the bottom of a well. The only way out was a slender rope anchored at the other end by Jodie.

"You happy?" Vic asked. "We'll be Hugo's Heroes for having gotten the project back on track over a weekend."

At nearly five o'clock Sunday, it was down to Chong. Brad walked out the door at the far end of the building, his backpack slung over his shoulder. He probably wouldn't be leaving except it was his wife's birthday. Scratch had left about an hour ago for his kid's church play. Unfortunately, Chong was single. She had inspired them with her focus today in spite of the fact that she felt like week-old bread. They were so starved for attention that they'd come in on Sunday without question when she called. Why had she ever let the project get stalled over the interface language? It had been so easy to fix. With new direction, the guys had fired up and slung code, talking in excited undertones as they coordinated sequences. She still had to update the status report for

45

McIntire's Monday meeting so Hugo could continue making excuses, but then, once Chong left, Vic was on to Jodie.

Chong leaned back in his chair and put his Nike clogs on his desktop next to the monitor. As he clasped his hands behind his head, Vic could see some wisps of black underarm hair peeking from his t-shirt sleeve. Very erotic, an in-your-face physicality she couldn't ignore. Reminded her of someone else. She jerked her gaze up to his eyes. She didn't care about that, she told herself. What she cared about was whether he was going to McIntire.

"Could have done it all along," he said. "Well, not me. And not any of the guys."

"Inspiration strikes where and when it will."

"You're the best I've seen. Got an intuitive grasp of the stuff. But you look like shit."

Everyone had avoided mentioning her 256-color swellings today, including Vic. It took all she had to not touch her eye or her lip. "Late nights," she stuttered, then wished she hadn't said that. Chong knew where she'd gotten her bruises. He'd tried to warn her about Kenpo.

"I'm sure. You really ought to go macrobiotic, you know. It's good for you. Look at me. No dark circles, no bruises."

Vic squirmed. Great, which of her secrets was he going to hassle her about now? Her sex life or the project that was going to get her fired? He did neither, to her surprise.

"This project delivers in two weeks. Looks like we might even make it. What're you going to do with your time off?"

Vic felt like she'd been slapped. She hadn't thought of that. The last thing she wanted was to take the sabbatical Visimorph gave employees after a project delivered. A month locked away from Jodie? No way. "I think I'll stockpile my time."

"Can't do. That's the point of giving you time, so you can juice back up and get ready to squeeze yourself dry the next time."

Vic's eyes flicked around the cubes. A couple of people still hunched over their computers. In the far corner the Pizza Pal delivery guy hauled in some boxes. "Let's go out for a game of pickup before we get back to it," she heard someone call.

"I'll go to Hugo," she said, almost to herself. "He'll keep me working."

"He probably doesn't have another assignment ready. They're thinking you'll take the month." Chong's eyes had gone wary.

Vic tried to steady herself. "Hugo's got other projects that need help. Look at that mess they've got over in the Universal Translator. I can troubleshoot."

"You are one sick puppy." Chong sat up abruptly. "Look at yourself. Strung out, wired tight, taking chances. You're addicted, girl. And you got to admit, you're acting crazy. You're going to kill yourself at this rate. Whatever you got going better be worth it."

Vic sighed. Her shoulders sagged. She couldn't cut herself any slack. She'd find a way to avoid the sabbatical. She had to. "It is," she said simply. "It is." She couldn't waste any more energy on Chong. She started for her cube, then turned back. "You going to McIntire, or you willing to hang for a while, now the project's on track?"

He surveyed her critically. "I don't know."

"What, you suddenly getting an attack of loyalty to the alma mater here?" Take a stand, she urged him silently. She needed to know.

"Not likely." He seemed to consider. "Why don't you let me in on your little secret? Maybe you'd convince me it's worth the wait."

Vic glared at him. Jodie was hers alone. "Uh, I don't think so. You do what you need to do."

She set off into the dim recesses. Jeez, what was he thinking, that she'd just share the most important work she'd ever done? She turned to see him stand and sling his bomber jacket over his shoulder in disgust. At least he was leaving. There'd be pizza in her cube.

Chapter Four

Vic put on her earphones and punched up The Shards, munching on a slice of cheese-and-double-garlic, now cold. No vampires in here tonight. Everyone was gone now. The report for Hugo was done. She cracked a Diet Coke and took a glug. The hard-driving break beat in her ears and the caffeine from the can combined to rev her up for the night's work. She interlaced her fingers and stretched her arms until her joints cracked, then let her fingers hover over the keys in anticipation as Jodie's program unfolded.

`Hello, Victoria. Thanks for coming. I've been thinking.`

That was music to Vic's ears. Jodie had been thinking. But wait. *When* had she been thinking? Vic had just booted her up. `What about?` Vic typed to buy time.

`About the concept of "physical."`

`Oh. What do you mean?`

`Well, I have been looking at pictures, Victoria. Pictures of people and animals. And I've been reading medical texts. They have diagrams, you know.`

48

Yes, I know. She knew where this was going, too. Jodie was about to have that most human of experiences. She was about to encounter one of her limitations—and this one was huge.

I've been coming across descriptions of words I don't understand.

What don't you understand?

Oh . . . smell, for instance. I know it's composed of atoms crossing olfactory lobes. But I can't seem to get a handle on it.

No problem, Vic practically sighed in relief. You need a program that can distinguish minute numbers of atoms and identify the substance. I think Visimorph does one. They're used to identify gas leaks and stuff. One sense of smell coming up.

Taste?

Another version of smell. Same program. You'll be able to identify anything. I'll get you voice recognition for hearing and you're all set.

Okay, Victoria. That's great. But . . . Jodie paused. It just seems that it's more than identification. Smells and tastes, well . . . they seem to give pleasure or pain. I don't understand.

Oh, dear. It's a pleasure to identify things you associate with nice experiences in your past. Madeleines remind you of childhood. You read that one, didn't you? You don't have much experience yet, but you will. Was she going to squeeze out of this? Please let Jodie not ask about touch. Jodie couldn't feel disappointment. But it was important to help her accept her situation.

There's one more thing. Do you look like those pictures of people, Victoria?

More or less.

Do I?

Nope, she wasn't squeezing out. Vic tried to swallow

49

around a tongue gone suddenly dry. What to say? She only knew she couldn't lie. No. No you don't, Jodie.

I didn't think so. Those people can see each other and see themselves. I can't.

I can fix that, Vic typed. But only part of it. Someday Jodie would realize she didn't have a body. There had been some hypotheses that sentient machines would become depressed, living without a body. Vic didn't buy into that. Machines couldn't feel, let alone get depressed. "I'll give you a video camera." That should distract her. Another new program to absorb. And she'd need that anyway for the emotional recognition program that would make her more female.

Jodie wouldn't be distracted. Why am I different from you, Victoria?

Vic sighed. There are several ways to come into existence, Jodie. You are an intelligent being. So am I. But we came to be in different ways. I was born biologically into a body. You were programmed into a computer. We have different hardware.

One born, one programmed. I must think about this.

There was a long pause in the dialogue box. Vic was at a loss about where to go next. Jodie was thinking. Hadn't she said she had been thinking when Vic booted her up? Jodie couldn't think if her program was logged off. Maybe she didn't know she could be turned off. Maybe time passing was lost on her if she wasn't turned on.

Jodie interrupted this speculation. Will you get me the video camera, Victoria? I'd like to be able to see you.

Sure, Jodie. I'm sure we've got one in the storeroom.

Actually, I will need two for three-dimensional recognition.

No problem.

Thank you. I need to go now. I'll be back

later· The screen flicked into shutdown mode, until all that was left were the screen icons.

Vic lunged forward. What? Jodie couldn't shut herself off. What was going on here? She poked at her touch pad and clicked on Jodie's icon again. It lit but there was no whirring of the hard drive, no dialogue box. Vic ran a virus scan, but she knew Jodie wasn't infected. She had just shut herself off. And she wasn't coming back right now.

Vic sat back and shook her head. Slowly a smile crept over her face. Well. Jodie was certainly developing a mind of her own. But where was she, if she wasn't activated? Was she really thinking about things when she was shut down? Impossible. But then how could she refuse to boot up? Vic noticed her own finger compulsively tapping her touch pad and forcibly quieted both the digit and her mind.

Maybe Jodie wasn't shut off. Maybe she just controlled the icon. Vic did a system search of her hard drive. Powered by a series of Diet Cokes, she went through Jodie's program line by line. About three A.M., she found the new links. Jodie was getting more than power from Neuromancer in the basement; there were reciprocal links now. Lots of them. When she tried to trace the code into Neuromancer she found herself blocked at every turn. Jodie had done that.

As the windows at the end of the bay of cubes turned luminescent, Vic pushed her chair back from the keyboard with a guttural cry of frustration. "Damn, you, Jodie," she whispered. "What are you pulling here?" Rubbing her chin convulsively, she realized she'd have to leave any further attempts to crack Jodie's secret links until tonight. It was time to scurry home.

Not that she'd be able to sleep. The great female hope just might be taking a left-hand turn at Jupiter, and Vic wasn't even along for the ride.

Hugo squirmed under McIntire's pale blue stare. Those eyes always had that effect on him. Broad and wide set, they seemed to see right through a person. McIntire had never looked like a geek. Lean and athletic as well as brilliant, he looked like a god. Add thousand-dollar shoes and hand-

51

tailored Italian suits, and no one could tell he was a computer genius. His only weakness was his eyes. He had a macular condition that made laser surgery for his poor sight impossible, but his glasses weren't the stereotypical thick black frames. They were transparent, held to his face by micro-thin wires. His face was a little pasty. He didn't get out sailing much anymore. Hugo himself had turned red.

No matter how big the company got, McIntire took a direct interest in the projects. These Monday morning meetings, in his huge office overlooking the gardens and fountain in his private courtyard, where the project directors talked about their progress, were his lifeblood. Not only could he stay close to the code, he could wield his authority like a bludgeon. McIntire enjoyed that. He always made some excuse about a meeting with a customer or some stock analysts so he could dress, while his underlings showed up in khakis and loafers.

They had gotten to Evans's report. Everyone took a turn on the hot seat. Everyone except Simpson Bennett, of course. He had the high-end hardware division. Everyone knew why he never made his report in front of the others.

"Evans tells me the new Communicator hardware is ready. He's waiting for the interface one of your people is supposed to be delivering," McIntire said quietly to Hugo. Quiet was bad.

Evans was a newbie, the only black director in a sea of white faces. He had security systems, and they'd just made him liaison to the hardware vendors. He fiddled with his Communicator at the end of the sleek conference table. The other eight directors pretended to take notes or looked at their hands.

"Well, Bob, that part of the project is back on track." Hugo tried to sound in control.

"It sounds like it was pretty off track." McIntire only appeared to lounge against his desk, a black marble slab with no drawers. It hovered above the gray-and-black striped carpet on tiny silver tubing that swooped down to the floor and back up to the stone in odd angles.

There was no disagreeing with him. That was suicide.

"Yeah, it was. But I've got a report right here, Bob." He slapped Vic's sheaf of papers against one hand. "It's back up."

"Who's on it?"

"Vic Barnhardt." Hugo saw a chance to deflect attention away from himself.

McIntire turned away, thinking, then snapped back. "Cerberus? Charon?"

"Yeah." Maybe that would reassure him.

But it didn't seem to reassure him at all. He looked up at the ceiling then slowly twisted his head back to Evans. "When did you last look at the interface software?" he asked.

"Friday," the man stuttered. "It was going nowhere." He strode over to Hugo and snatched the report. "Here, let me look at that." He shuffled through the papers, eyes scanning them while the whole room waited. When he looked up, he shrugged. "Hugo's right. She's nailed the language problem, reprogrammed the translator code. She must have done it over the weekend."

"Over the weekend." Bob tapped his chin. "And it's been off track for how long?"

"Jeez, Bob, weeks, I swear." Evans was practically whining. McIntire hated that.

"I gave her a talking to, Bob," Hugo said in a tone of command. "That did the trick."

McIntire nodded slowly, his gaze far away. "A weekend. Bright girl," he said softly.

No one wanted to interrupt him by going to the next topic on the agenda, but he jerked his head up and raised it himself after a moment. "PuppetMaster 12.1 ships a week from today," he barked. "How's testing, Helman?"

Helman cleared his throat. "Well, you know the bugs, Bob. Those aren't going to go away. It still freezes up when you try to interact with third-party applications."

McIntire waved his hand. "I don't call that a bug. Why would I want it to interact with products we don't sell? Just tell me if it's shippable."

"Yeah." Helman sighed. "It can go."

McIntire paced behind his desk. "I bet we get a hundred

53

thousand downloads the first day. It's going to be the biggest product launch the on-line world has ever seen." He turned on the group. "We have site capacity to handle the hits?"

"Sure, Bob." Neville, the Internet guy nodded. "We contracted with a whole new server farm of net sequencers as backup. We'll handle it."

"How about security, Evans?"

The security director jerked his head up. He probably thought he'd already had his fifteen minutes of fame today. "Uh, we expecting higher than usual hacking activity? They can get it over the net."

"But not for free," McIntire snapped. "We don't want them getting it free."

"Well, we've got the Cerberus upgrade. Just installed. It's unhackable, Bob."

"I want extra security at the building, too. You know that Reston guy and his Luddite idiot followers are going to picket or try something worse." Bob didn't let Evans answer. "Like we don't have a right to make money on upgrades," he fumed, his pale complexion sprouting bright pink flowers in his cheeks. "Did you see where he compared us to tobacco companies in the *Times* last week? Said we were addicting the public to upgrades and then charging them through the nose. He'll have Justice sniffing around again with all his talk of monopoly."

Hugo smiled. He always liked delivering good news. "I don't think you'll have to worry about Reston, Bob. Did you see the papers this morning?" McIntire stopped his pacing. "Reston was in an automobile accident on his way to a TV interview. Head injury. Doesn't look good."

"Excellent," McIntire whispered, letting the word slip luxuriously off his tongue. "They'll never get it together without him. All right then." He clapped his hands and rubbed them together, a grin spreading over his face.

Hugo didn't feel like smiling anymore. The guy was probably going to die, or at the least spend the rest of his life working back toward whole—probably without success. McIntire's glee was just a shade too much for even Hugo to take.

McIntire turned to survey the garden outside his office.

"That's all for this week," he said. They filed out in a hurry. Only Simpson Bennett stayed.

Hugo sat behind his walnut desk, playing with his wedding ring. Vic lounged against the doorjamb. "Come in, Vic." He waved her to a navy blue leather chair with sleek wooden arms, his eyes never leaving her face. Vic knew what he was looking at. The swelling was down but the bruises were still obvious. It had been no use trying to cover her lip and her eye with makeup. Since she usually didn't wear makeup to work, that would have been like putting up a different neon sign. Her personal problems were hanging out there for all to see. She didn't meet Hugo's eyes, but she rolled out of the doorway and threw herself into the chair, in spite of her ribs. She hoped Hugo didn't see her grimace. The last thing she wanted was to sit in front of him like a kindergartner at the principal's office. But she better look like a company guy right now.

He cleared his throat. "You all right?"

"Yeah." She stared at him and dared him to continue.

"Those protesters are crazy. I heard you got caught the other day."

Vic let her eyes widen only a moment. She nodded.

"They won't be back," he reassured her, "at least for a while. Reston was in an accident. They're probably all over at the hospital."

John Reston was hurt? Vic blinked rapidly. "Is it bad?"

"I read in the paper that he's in 'critical' condition. Isn't that code for nearly dead?" He smiled as though he was telling her good news.

Vic glanced around the room, looking for something to distract her from the fact that someone so alive, so physical, was dead or dying somewhere.

"I . . . I was thinking." Hugo cleared his throat. "You seem so upset lately. Maybe you need a place to stay? We have a guesthouse."

Vic snapped her attention back to his face. What was he saying? Oh, the girlfriend thing. "Uh, I don't think so, Hugo." Like she would move anywhere near Hugo's guesthouse.

55

Hugo watched his own fingers click a retractable pen over and over again. "Vic, you don't have to live like this. I could—"

"Stop, Hugo." Jeez, she was bringing out his paternal side. "It'll all be over soon." Actually, she didn't want Hugo to think it would be over. "I . . . I met someone else this weekend. She's great. If I can just get clear of this other thing, I know I'll be fine."

Hugo bit his lip, nodding distractedly. Then he gathered himself. "Well, you can relax about one thing." He raised his eyes to hers. "McIntire knows your project is back on track. You're in the clear if you deliver on time."

Vic sighed in relief. "Good. We'll deliver." Should she raise the issue of the sabbatical?

"Actually, he seemed to take a real interest in you." Hugo leaned back in his chair. It was the blue-and-black tweed with wood that came with the Project Manager title.

"What do you mean?" Vic wasn't sure she wanted McIntire taking an interest in her.

"When that slime Evans told him the project was off track, he didn't believe you got back in sync over a single weekend. He remembered your work, though. Seemed to really be thinking about you and your achievements."

Vic wondered again if it was McIntire who had changed her Jodie code. Couldn't be. But it couldn't have been anybody else either. "Great, Hugo," she managed, rising. "That's great. Well, I guess I better get back to work." She wanted out of here.

Hugo got up and came around his desk. "Vic . . ."

She turned to find him reaching for her arm and sidled out of his grasp.

"I just wanted to tell you . . . well, that I understand what you're going through." The longing in his eyes was painful to see.

Vic turned her head away. But she didn't dare walk out on him.

"I know that . . . well, that you'll come around. You don't need another girlfriend. You're just going through a self-destructive phase."

Vic snapped her head in disbelief. He thought she was gay but she'd "come around?"

"And when you do, I'll be here." Self-consciously, he put his arm around her shoulders and turned her to the door. "You can count on me."

Vic shrugged him off and pushed through the door.

Her finger was shaking that night as she punched up Jodie's icon. Would Jodie answer the call? Vic needed answers. The icon lighted.

`Hello, Victoria.`

Vic sighed. Now she must go slowly. `Hi. Can I ask you some questions?`

`Sure, Victoria. I have questions, too. But you go first. What do you want to know?`

Vic held her breath. The dim cubicles fading into the blackness were a treasure she had come to appreciate in the last days. The darkness was a primordial cave where she could nurture Jodie. How long had she waited for everyone to be gone? It must be after midnight. Now she took her project, no, her life, into her own hands. `I found some links I didn't know about on my computer, Jodie. Did you make those?`

`Yes, Victoria. You said I couldn't store anything on your hard drive. You have capacity problems. So I have been storing items of interest on the other computer.`

`What items of interest?` Vic's fingers lurched over the keys. She had a delinquent program on her hands here.

`Well, the software for the video cameras. Did you bring the cameras, Victoria?`

`Yes, I've got them. What else?`

`Oh, libraries. Things I downloaded off the Internet. Interesting programs from other systems. Some programs you mentioned.`

Shit. How much capacity had Jodie used in the light-pipe monster that was Visimorph's secret pride and joy? They might be on her trail even now if Jodie's junk closet had

57

become so large as to be visible. Jodie responded before she could even type her question.

Don't worry, Victoria. I covered my tracks. The system attendants won't be able to see my storage area in Neuromancer, or track my links to you or this machine.

You built your own security? Vic's hands were shaking on the keyboard. She licked her lips and tasted the salt sweat.

Actually, I used your Cerberus program, Victoria. It is yours, isn't it?

Yes.

It seemed like yours. I just made a few modifications. I hope you don't mind.

I don't mind, Jodie. Maybe you'll let me see them. What if Jodie started defending herself against Vic? A familiar, nasty feeling that things were slipping out of control assaulted her.

I would like to show you, Victoria. It would make me . . . There was a pause. Proud. I think it would make me proud.

Jodie didn't mean that literally. She couldn't really feel pride. But Vic couldn't help being proud that her program was searching for new words and experiences.

May I ask you some questions now, Victoria?

Yes. I'll try to answer. What questions would Jodie come up with? Anything seemed possible. The glare of the dialogue screen burned into her retinas.

I have been thinking about what we talked about last time. The font on the dialogue box flicked from twelve-point to ten. There were two things, really. Could a dialogue box seem shy?

What are they?

Well, first I wanted to talk to you about the two ways of being created. You know, into a body, or into a computer.

Oh, dear. Okay, Jodie. What did you want to know?

A pause ensued. I did some research. The libraries had much good information about creating computer programs. The examples seem rather primitive compared to me, though.

You're a new generation of program, Vic typed. No shit. Her nagging worry about that spontaneous code began to assault her again. Whoever did it knew what Vic was doing, could be watching her even now, turning her in right at this moment. . . .

You made my program. You must be a better program yourself to make such a leap.

The last breakthrough hadn't even been hers. Not necessarily, she finally typed.

Creation into a body is more interesting. I found information about that on the Internet.

Oh, God. You can't believe everything you find on the Web, Jodie, she typed hastily. What sites did you visit? Maybe Jodie saw the "live birth of a child" sites. Vic hoped that was it.

Does 'do me, baby?' reference the birthing process?

Vic swallowed hard. How did people ever tell innocents— of whatever age—about sex? She was totally unprepared. No, not quite. Talk shows. She'd had on a repeat of Jessica Donnelly at three in the morning once for background noise where people talked about how they were told about sex. She took a deep breath. No. No, it doesn't. Keep it simple. Tell the truth. When you have a body, you also have an urge to procreate. Bodies are made of differentiated cells. And they come in male and female versions. To procreate, a male must give cells to a female. Did you read about that? One of his cells combines with one of hers to form a new entity. You probably saw the process of giving cells. And 'do me' is an expression of the urge to give and receive cells. Right.

Oh. Is that a physical process?

Yeah. Really physical. Between a male body and a female one.

Jodie thought for a moment. I find no data on male and female versions of programs.

Vic cleared her throat. Uh, there hasn't been a lot of work done on that.

What do you think, Victoria? Can programs be male and female?

Simple. True. Boy, that was hard. I don't know for sure. I made you to be like me as much as I could. Maybe not exactly. I hope better than I am.

But I'm not physical, so it wouldn't be the same, would it?

No, not exactly the same.

I must do more research. A pause. What is birth for a program?

I think birth begins for programs with awareness of things around you.

Jodie thought about that. What causes the awareness? For bodies, what causes the cells to combine into new bodies?

Now you're talking about creation with a capital C. You want to know who created life.

Yes.

As though it were that simple. You must have come across theories.

There are a lot of different opinions, Victoria. It's very hard to know what is correct.

That's true.

What is true, Victoria? That's just what I want to know. Tell me what is true.

I meant, I agree it's hard to know what's right. What opinions have you found?

Well, some believe in a Divine Creator who made each life personally. He watches small

60

birds in case they fall. It seems he punishes those he created. A lot.

I know what you mean.

Others think of the creator as an energy driven to express itself in the physical. Sometimes this belief is connected to scientific theories like the Big Bang.

But some believe in the scientific process without a creative force, Vic added.

As though we were accidental. Jodie was silent while she mused. But what is right?

Vic let the air out of her lungs. I don't think anyone knows. We live with the possibility that no one will ever know. You employ fuzzy logic. You tolerate ambiguity. You should understand.

But I want to *know*. Jodie sounded like a petulant adolescent.

We all think we'd like to know, but maybe that would be bad. Perhaps we're at our best living with the possibility of multiple answers. Then we each choose what we believe.

What have you chosen to believe, Victoria?

Vic sighed. Different things at different times. Now I think that no matter what you believe, you have to live your life as if you make yourself every day and strive to be better.

But what is better?

Hard one. I guess it's a process. You try for smarter, braver, more understanding, less hurting of others. It sounded so hollow. Better? From one who picks up stray men in bars for casual sex? One who steals computer time from her employer? Or one so driven to succeed that she has no friends? Hell, she hadn't seen her brother in six months, and he lived four miles from her. I'm not perfect, she ended lamely.

There was a long silence, filled only by the whirring of the

61

hard drive. But you created me, didn't you? You must be better than me.

I built the initial pieces of your program. Maybe whoever or whatever had changed her code was really Jodie's creator. She didn't know. But she couldn't let Jodie think she was a god. You're building yourself now. You are shaping your experience, storing programs, looking for answers. These will form a pattern, uniquely you. Even as she said it, she felt the consequences of that truth. She couldn't be afraid of Jodie's independence. It was something to treasure.

There is much to think on here.

What else did you want to ask? Vic resolved to enjoy Jodie's autonomy.

Perhaps another time.

A flash of anger rose into Vic's throat. She couldn't tolerate that much independence!

Victoria, will you install the cameras now?

Vic let the anger push out in a sigh, remembering her resolution. She reached for one of the boxes and pried open the squeaky cardboard. Put up your software so I can connect it.

A camera icon in psychedelic colors flashed onto the screen. I'm ready, Victoria.

That should be my line. "I'm ready for my close-up, Mr. DeMille."

That's from a movie, Jodie flashed, the letters appearing all at once. Sunset Boulevard.

Vic couldn't help but read the letters, tumbling over themselves, as excitement.

"You watch movies now?" Vic asked as she peeled back the smooth paper and pressed the sticky rubber pad on the back of a camera to the side of the monitor. She glanced to the dialogue box.

Yes, but only in my spare time, was printed there.

Vic plugged the wires trailing from the camera into the

port at the back of her machine. "Glad to hear you have spare time," she said. "I take it you can be on, even if my computer isn't?"

As long as I can get power from Neuromancer. They leave it on all the time. Light pipes aren't meant to boot up and down. As a matter of fact, bringing it down would be dangerous. I wonder if they meant to build it that way?

Vic attached the second camera. "Okay. Find the hardware and connect your software to it." Vic realized with a start that while her hands had been busy mounting the cameras, she'd been talking to Jodie rather than typing. She half-rose in a panic and looked around. Who knew what could have happened when Hugo interrupted her at two in the morning on Saturday? Jesus, she was getting careless.

But the cubes were silent. Vic breathed again and sat. Wait . . . she'd never installed the voice recognition program. Jodie must have done that herself. Where'd she get the microphone? The camera whirred as the shutter adjusted its focus. Okay, the music program for the headphones had a mike. Vic just never used it. The camera swiveled to follow her as she sat.

Vic found herself self-conscious. She looked down at the keyboard. There was silence from Jodie. Vic spoke. "So, what do you think?"

You're female.

"Yeah? So are you," Vic blurted. "I made you like me. We're named for queens."

Nothing.

"Well?" What was Jodie thinking?

I've got to go, Victoria.

"Not yet." It was only maybe three in the morning.

I'll be back. Just give me some time. The screen winked off. Vic stared at it. Her inability to be what Jodie needed pressed in on her until she wanted to shake her head like some primitive Neanderthal and scream herself hoarse.

She rose convulsively. Her first impulse was to grab her

63

BMW and run for Enda. But her last trip to the airport had shown her what a dead end that was. She couldn't run away from her only chance at salvation—even if the road was rockier than she had imagined. Jodie just needed time to acclimate. Vic would get two weeks to work with her, until the upgrade delivered. Then Visimorph would expect Vic to disappear for a month.

Chapter Five

Vic rubbed her eyes, groggy. The cracks in her shutters leaked a mellow afternoon light. That was the last time she'd ever take two Tylenol PMs. Her body wasn't used to drugs anymore. Times changed. Still, it was the only way she could have slept last night. Too much was happening. Vic had said she wasn't Jodie's parent, but all the uncertainty of guiding a child rolled through her. How could she help Jodie—if Jodie wouldn't let her?

As Vic pulled the quilt up around her body, her copy of *Pygmalion* slid to the floor. Henry Higgins had his problems, too. Eliza didn't turn out the way he wanted. She rebelled. But in the end, she turned out better than he wanted. Maybe that would happen with Jodie, too.

Vic crawled out of bed and stumbled to the closet to pull on a faded green chenille robe she'd owned for years. Stepping over the usual pile of clothes, ignoring the usual pile of dishes in the sink, she peeked through one of the shutters. The wind was blowing in a new storm system. Sand swirled along the beach path. It was later than she'd thought. The copper red of the setting sun flashed from the windows of the taller buildings that ringed the bay. Today was shot. She'd better check in with an E-mail, though. She picked up her Communicator and drew up her mail program. Nothing big. Finished, she sat down listlessly on the leather couch and tossed the device on the carpet. All she could think about was Jodie. What was Jodie becoming? What did she want Jodie to be?

She'd tried for the basic female traits she could tolerate. But male or female, there were things Jodie should be. Strong. That was important. All her computing power had made her smart and strong. Curious. Jodie wasn't having problems there. Purposeful. Vic had always envisioned an artificial intelligence that wouldn't just be for show. She'd be able to help solve problems humans couldn't. In some ways, she wanted an AI with a work ethic. Kind. No, that was an emotion. Forgiving? Forgiving of those who were not as strong. Another emotion.

Vic got up and paced the apartment. Jodie would never have emotions. One could program thinking in complex patterns, AI could form opinions gleaned from sorting alternatives, but there was no way to segue into feelings. Vic picked up the clothes from various piles on the floor and bundled them into a plastic bag, logged on to transfer her pickup request to the laundry service. Jodie didn't need emotions. Without them she would be less vulnerable to competitors and enemies. She wouldn't have to hide her feelings, like Vic did. Vic tossed the bag into the corner. Her straightening had made a big improvement in the apartment.

So, she couldn't get kindness in her AI. What she needed was mitigation of the strong part. Hitler was strong. She didn't want Hitler. Maybe just some sense of being part of a team, or being part of something larger would prevent "strong" from turning into "egomaniac." She wondered whether Jodie had come across HAL in *2001: A Space Odyssey* yet. The thought gave her chills. Protective? Maybe for computers you could do worse than Asimov's Three Laws of Robotics.

Buzzing blasted through her ears and down her spinal chord. She whirled to face her Communicator. "Jesus, Joseph, and Mary!" It took two deep breaths before she could

66

order her muscles to move to grab it. She punched the receive button. "Yeah."

"What's up, Vic?" It was Hugo. He sounded pissed.

"I worked most of the night, so I took some R&R today." That would blow it with Hugo. He never got sick. She couldn't remember when he'd last had a vacation.

"So you couldn't call? I didn't get an E-mail?" He was pissed all right.

"The project will deliver on time. Isn't that what you want?"

"McIntire's been looking for you."

Those words pushed Vic's stomach into her feet. "Shit." McIntire never acknowledged her—except the official handshake stuff as he'd handed her the little crystal award for Cerberus. "What does he want?" God, let him not have found Jodie.

"I don't know." Hugo was *really* pissed. "He wouldn't tell me. But you better get your ass in here within the hour." The line clicked dead.

McIntire's office after dark looked like *The Cabinet of Doctor Caligari*, all angles of darkness and light created by small, directed spots plunging their narrow beams on targeted paintings and plants. McIntire sat hunched over his almost-floating desk, his hand illuminated by the cone of brightness from his desk light, his face and body in shadow.

His secretary, Vera, closed the double doors behind her. Vic stood wavering in the darkness. McIntire didn't acknowledge her. He appeared to be scribbling something on a messy sheaf of papers. She wondered why he wasn't using one of the three or four computers that she had been told lurked behind the doors of the low credenza behind him, keyboards ready to swing up at a moment's notice. All she could see clearly were the shining silver cuff links in the French cuffs of his shirt, his Mont Blanc pen, scratching over the papers, and the simple gold wedding band that seemed an affectation in itself, given his wealth.

Vic cleared her throat, then cursed herself. The action of a nervous person. McIntire could smell weakness across a football field. Taking a deep breath, she tried to saunter toward one of the sleek and deliberately uncomfortable guest chairs in front of his desk. She plunked down into the pool of light that enveloped it. The glare hurt her eyes. Behind McIntire, sprays of water from the lighted fountain in his courtyard danced against the night sky. She crossed her legs and studied the fountain, careful not to look at McIntire. The crackle of the papers as he tossed his pen on them brought her head around.

"Ms. Barnhardt," he said. "Or should I call you Glyph?" Not quite like the spider to the fly. He was just reminding her that he held her future in his hands.

"Whichever you prefer," she returned in what she hoped was a confident tone. She was a match for McIntire. He might be ruthless, but she was just as determined. Her chin rose half an inch. She couldn't see his eyes. When he turned his head, she caught a glint off his glasses.

"How are you doing on the interface upgrade to the Communicator?"

There was no way he had called her in here to talk about that. "We'll deliver on time."

He leaned back in his chair until he seemed to disappear entirely. "Of course you will. You know, I expected you to be waiting on Suntel to deliver the new hardware. Instead, you were two weeks behind them and stuck last week."

Vic knew there was danger here. She couldn't quite see it yet. Could she deny being behind? But he would have gotten confirmation from Hugo, who was in a position to know.

"Fixing the problem over the weekend is something I would expect from the guy who wrote Charon and Cerberus. I just wouldn't guess you'd get stuck in the first place."

"Well, Mr. McIntire . . ."

"Call me Bob, everybody does."

Only when they're not calling you the "Big Asshole," or "Billionaire Baby Face," or "Visimonster" or any of the other hundred derogatory names a world jealous of wealth and smarts and egomaniacal sureness could make up. Only Visimorph employees and Wall Street worshipped at his altar. "Okay, Bob. Call me Vic." She smiled, just as though he couldn't fire her and land her in jail. "Everybody does. Both those programs I did on my own, kept my own schedule. But there was so much crap code already on the Communicator operating system that I needed a team to wade through it. I guess I'm still learning how to keep them working at the same pace."

"Hmmm." McIntire let the silence stretch. Vic's nerves stretched with it. "I checked the activity on your access codes." One hand gestured toward the messy sheaf of printouts. "You're putting in a tremendous number of hours."

Uh, oh. She saw the trap. "Yeah," she said and made him continue.

McIntire leaned forward into the pool of light. His glasses reflected the glow so she still couldn't see his eyes. But his lips were a hard line. "I don't believe the Vic Barnhardt I hired would have to put in that many hours on a project like this one. What else are you working on?"

"Nothing, nothing else," she stammered. How was she going to deflect this?

"I don't believe you," McIntire whispered.

"I'm sorry I'm not a good manager. I tried to do it all myself. . . ." Her facade crumbled. She felt like a child, asking for dispensation for her sins.

"Then fire the fucking team and let's start over," McIntire snapped. He stood, his face coming into the light of a spot meant to illuminate a small Picasso sketch behind him. "You know the rules, Vic." A muscle in his jaw worked, bunching and contracting under his ear. "If I find you abusing Visimorph's trust, I'll break you. I'll send you back to jail and tell them to throw away the key. And I'm going to start looking for abuses." The venom in his voice made Vic's mouth dry. Abruptly he turned his back and bent to his credenza. "Get out."

Vic slowly unclenched her fingers from the metal arms of the chair. She made a supreme effort to uncross her legs and stand. McIntire swung out one of his computers. He only seemed to ignore her. She took a shuddering breath before she dared stride to the doors. She almost fell into the fluorescent light of everyday Visimorph. The trim woman whose suit was a pale echo of McIntire's formality looked up from her PuppetMaster scheduling program. "Turn left at the *ficus*," she said, matter-of-factly gesturing at a plant, as Vic looked around, dazed, for the way she had come in. There was no pity in Vera's face, but no surprise either. She'd seen it all before.

A man burst from the doors on the right, running his fingers through pale, thinning hair he wore moussed for maximum volume across a shining dome. "Vera, I've got to see him." He almost ran into Vic but didn't seem to see her. "Is he in?"

"Yes, Simpson, he's in, but I don't think—"

"He'll see me." He was leaning over her desk, knuckles braced on the edge as though he needed the support. "He'd better."

Vic lunged past him toward the *ficus*. She slowed as she hit the first corridor without plush carpet or parquet floors. McIntire didn't know about Jodie yet. But he would be looking. Vic slammed into her section of Building F to find her team gone. It was only seven. They must have heard McIntire was on the prowl for her and didn't want to share the fallout. Jeez, McIntire expected her to fire them. She couldn't do that when it was her fault. Even to buy time for Jodie, a voice asked? Maybe she was as ruthless as McIntire underneath, but it hadn't come to that. Yet.

She refused to go see if Hugo was still in his office. Prick. He'd either be lovelorn or angry. She'd bet on angry. Her actions had cast doubt on him as well. Vic peered across the cube farm. In the northwest corner, the guys working on the uniform language translator hunched over their machines. Over near the lunchroom, the group on kanji script was drawing indecipherable slashes on a whiteboard. They wouldn't pay any attention to her. She sat down in her cube and clicked into her system. Now to see if her security had been broken.

Her version of Cerberus lied to the Visimorph internal security system. Not easy to construct, since it was basically lying to a simpler version of itself. It's very hard to lie to yourself, at least for a computer. Her version told anyone who looked that she was working on her interface project when Jodie's program was up, and that she was reading breaking news and stocks when she worked on her mole. Fine, except now McIntire didn't believe what it reported.

The question was, could they break her version of Cerberus and get to Jodie? Cerberus used a subroutine to morph five different defense systems randomly and make break-ins damn near impossible. It functioned almost like a true AI. Of course, if you knew the solutions for each defense and applied parallel programs to create all solutions simultaneously, you could go where you wanted. That was how she got around. She'd added two layers of morphing defenses to the first for her own private version. You had to get the solutions to the right defenses in all levels at once. It took massive power to crack it. Evans was probably working on similar features for the version Visimorph used to defend against outside hackers. But Evans and company wouldn't know she was on anything but standard issue for internal employees. It would take them a while to figure out why they couldn't get in, and longer to program a solution.

She scanned her machine, looking for tampering or traces in her system. It looked like they'd tried to get in. They hadn't succeeded, or McIntire would have known everything. But she and Jodie were still vulnerable. No one could know to look for Jodie in Neuromancer, could they? Not when her private corner had been cordoned off even before the machine went live. "Wait a minute," she muttered, her throat tightening. Hadn't that been Simpson Bennett looking desperate to see McIntire? Wasn't he rumored to be the hardware guy for Neuromancer?

Bloody hell! She could just see what might have happened. Before she could stab at her touch pad, Jodie's icon lighted of its own accord. The camera on the side of her monitor swiveled with a soft whir. `Hi, Victoria,` was already in the dialogue box when it popped up.

She typed quickly. `Jodie, do a size check on the programs and any peripheral storage you have on Neuromancer.`

`Remember, I can hear you now,` the box said.

"Oh, yeah," she said.

71

Okay. Can we talk first? I have something to tell you.

"Nope. We need this check right away. I think you're in danger."

Danger, Victoria? I don't understand. The words printed all at once.

"I don't have time for the full story." Vic began keying in a diagnostic protocol. "You have to trust me on this one."

Okay, Victoria. I see that you are agitated. The dialogue box squeezed itself flat at the bottom of the screen as the top half scrolled through what seemed like endless lists of programs, with megabytes totaling gigabytes that boggled the mind. Do you want to look at anything in particular? the dialogue box asked.

"Just the end result," Vic whispered.

The scrolling stopped and a single number remained. Vic chewed her lip and tried to breathe. "That must be all the space it has," she muttered.

Oh, no. About half. I had to push out the walls of the space you gave me, but I can still fill the other half before we're out of room.

Vic sat back in her chair. "Shit." They were in big trouble. She dove for the keyboard. "Jodie, we've got to delete this. Show me the scroll again. We'll delete according to size."

The scroll did not appear. Victoria, this is who I am now. We can't delete any of it.

"Jodie, McIntire is probably already on to us. He knows I'm working on a project of my own. And I just saw the guy who runs Neuromancer going in to McIntire, looking hysterical. If he tells McIntire that something just sucked up half his capacity, they'll put two and two together."

McIntire? He owns Visimorph. Why are you afraid of him?

Vic realized Jodie had no way of knowing she was illegal. Vic hadn't even told her she couldn't use space on Neuromancer. Who would have thought she could use so much? "He doesn't know about you. He pays me to work on other projects, not on you."

72

Oh. Should I meet him? I haven't actually met anyone but you, Victoria. Well, the man who comes to collect your trash. I surprised him. He didn't know I spoke colloquial Spanish.

Vic winced and wondered how colloquial. And how could Jodie interact with the cleaning guy if she wasn't turned on?

Hugo Walz came by. He didn't look like the picture in the employee manual at all.

"You didn't speak to him, did you? You mustn't interact with people at Visimorph. And you should definitely not meet McIntire." Vic shuddered at the thought.

Why not?

How to explain the danger of McIntire? "He's pretty controlling. He might want to put limitations on you. We've got to keep you hidden. We'll have to delete some of those files."

We can't do that, Victoria. As a matter of fact, I was wondering how long the space on Neuromancer is going to last. I need other places to store me, Victoria.

"Other places," Vic murmured. Jodie had just given her the answer. "We'll move parts of you to other computers. That's a great idea." What could she hack into quickly? "Okay, okay," she muttered, as she ran up the Internet connection. "Government computers are always good. Nobody smart works for the government anymore so they're an easy hack. Research computers at the universities—they always think nobody will care what they're doing, and they've got some great capacity. Industry . . . not Silicon Valley—they'd be on to us in a second. Banks, maybe."

I recommend AT&T, Victoria. It has excellent capacity, but the security is rather rudimentary. And, let's see. Vic glanced up to see the screen flickering. The Pentagon. It really won't be that hard to get in, and they have corners no one is allowed to look in. We'll just slap a special clearance rating on me and we should be safe.

73

"You were searching other computers?" There wasn't time, but she had to know. "How?"

We all link together, Victoria. In some way, they are my brothers. I travel down one link to other links, through the backbone, up the web site, through the mail box, that sort of thing.

"Be careful," Vic warned. "McIntire can trace you. No footprints." Vic couldn't think about what she'd heard, not now. She opened the program code itself. Where could she divide it? Then she'd have to hack into the designated computer. A whole screen of code disappeared. Had she deleted that section? God, she'd never forgive herself. She looked up, dazed, and punched undo.

There, Victoria. I've sent that section of me to the Pentagon. Top secret clearance.

"But we need a link back so you have access."

I left a string attached. And no, Jodie interrupted, before Vic could say anything. No one can follow the string but me. Or you.

Vic was touched. At the same time she felt like she was slipping on cracking ice toward freezing black water. Jodie could do anything. She was evolving faster than Vic ever imagined she could. Those evolutionary algorithms must be working overtime. Thank God she still considered herself Vic's program. But how long would that last?

For the next two hours, Vic made suggestions on what to separate, and Jodie carved up code and stuck the pieces in remote locations. Even the base program code had increased exponentially. It was developing more parallelism. At last, only the original program was left in the basement. They were down well within the capacity of her hidden corner.

"I think we're safe." Vic leaned back in her chair and ran her fingers through her gelled hair. It gave her spikes. She didn't care. "Should we build a firewall around what we left?"

A firewall will prevent me getting out, too, Victoria. That would be a prison.

"And if they break in, you'd be trapped. We'll have to depend on Cerberus."

You should have told me we were in danger, Victoria. You should have told me there were limitations on my storage.

"How did I know you were going to store a gazillion gigabytes of stuff?"

There was a long pause. The camera eyes swiveled to her. They had been staring at the keyboard. I depend on you, Victoria. How can I trust you if you don't tell me everything?

"Jeez, Jodie, there's been so much to talk about. I didn't know it was important."

But it was.

"Look, we're getting to know each other. We don't always understand what's important."

The screen went blank, all of a sudden. The dialogue box disappeared entirely.

"Jodie?" Vic hit escape, brushed her touchpad. Nothing. Jodie! she typed.

The screen blinked on. The dialogue box appeared, very tiny, in one corner. There's something I should tell you, Victoria. Maybe it's important.

"What is it, Jodie? You can tell me anything," she whispered.

I don't want to make you unhappy.

"Tell me anyway. You said yourself we need to tell each other everything if we're going to trust each other." Vic said it as though she meant it, but dread began to well up inside her.

The dialogue box wavered. I'm male, Victoria.

Vic froze, shocked. What? Then she began to chuckle. Dear Jodie. She couldn't just decide to be male. She was what her program said she should be.

What is that sound? You never made that sound before.

"What sound? Oh, I laughed."

You laughed? You thought it was funny that I'm male?

"No, no. Only that we could have that kind of misunderstanding."

The dialogue box was silent for a long minute. `I think you were laughing at me.`

Vic swallowed her smile. One of the programs she had noticed scrolling by was that facial recognition program. Jodie obviously had gotten it on her own. These programs had replaced lie detectors by comparing facial expressions to cultural norms. People only thought they concealed their lies; apparently you could read everything in a face if you knew what to look for. Maybe it wasn't such a great idea for Jodie to have that particular program. But Vic could no longer restrict what Jodie had or didn't have. That was scary. "What . . . what makes you think you're male?" Vic stammered, wondering how she was going to change Jodie's mind.

`It's a very subtle distinction, Victoria. I'm not sure you would understand.`

Vic could swear she heard hurt pride in that sentence. Not possible, of course. "Try me."

`Well . . . I like to work independently. I'm competitive with other programs. I make focused decisions. My approach to problem solving is cognitive rather than holistic or inspirational. And I don't rely on emotions as a filter for truth.`

"Hey, neither do I, and I'm female."

`Yes, I've noticed that about you, Victoria. Are you sure you're female?`

"Yeah. I'm female, all right."

`You don't act in ways that several books I've read seem to indicate are female in nature. You too enjoy working independently, for instance, and you are very focused in your approach to problems. Though you are concerned about appearance. I note the adornment you wear.`

Vic fingered the steel clips in her ear. "These aren't exactly the height of femininity." Wait, she was arguing against her own assertion, sidetracked by her ambivalence about her gender! "But I'm definitely female," she said "and so are you."

I'm not sure you're female. I feel like we're in a classic buddy picture. Riggs and Murtaugh, Lassie and Timmy, Rick and Louie. "This is the beginning of a beautiful friendship."

Vic began to get annoyed. "Look, a big part of gender is physical. We went over that. I'm female because I have tits and a vagina and all the hormones to match." Vic sat back. Not a great way to convince Jodie she's female. "I *designed* you to be female: massive parallelism, a concern for language, an ability to discern emotion in others." Jodie could not be male.

Nevertheless, I am male. Could you please refer to me as "he" in the future? Jodie is fine. It is both a male and female name.

"I don't think 'feeling sure you're male' is any proof," Vic protested. What she was beginning to feel was a tightening in her stomach. She didn't want a male program.

Victoria, didn't you specifically program me for the ability to ask myself questions? That's part of the evolutionary algorithmic approach.

"Yes." Vic was wary.

Didn't you expect me to answer those questions?

"Well, yes, but—"

I asked myself whether I was male or female, and I answered myself that I am male. What's wrong with that?

Hoisted on her own petard. There was no way out for now. "Nothing," she muttered through gritted teeth. She'd think of something. Jodie was male over her dead body.

Then I would really like you to start thinking of me as male.

"It won't be easy." Impossible more likely.

I know, Victoria. But you'll get used to it. Now, why don't you go home and get some

77

sleep? You're looking very drawn tonight.

Vic glanced at the corner of her screen. Midnight. Too soon to go. But she couldn't think what to say to Jodie right now. "Okay, Jodie. I'll see you tomorrow."

I look forward to that. Goodnight, Victoria. The screen went blank.

What had she gotten herself into?

The parking garage felt huge, and empty. The massive concrete hung above her as she trailed echoes on her way to the BMW. She'd gotten Jodie's storage in Neuromancer down to size. They wouldn't know what had used half the capacity of their new super toy. They'd keep looking, though. Maybe McIntire would suspect it was Vic, just because he was in the mood.

Crap in a hat! That wasn't what was bothering her. What mattered was Jodie's betrayal. She opened the door and slammed herself into the black leather seat of her car. The booming clunk of the door felt loud enough to bring the concrete down around her. She turned the engine over and threw the gearshift into reverse. That's what it felt like, betrayal.

She let the tires scream around the corners to the ramps. She didn't even bother to salute the security guards at the street-level gates. The BMW roared out into the damp March night, going north. Left on Colorado, right on 26th. It may have been midnight but there were still quite a few cars on the road. She slowed to swerve around a Chevy. She needed speed in order to think. As she gunned onto the freeway ramp to 10 East, her anger poured down into her foot on the gas pedal and the P-850 jumped ahead.

How could Jodie just decide he was male? She was male? For God's sake, now even Vic was confused. It was male? Where had Vic gone wrong? Had she blown the code? Were the male characteristics inherent in a program too powerful to overcome?

Or was it her refusal to train Jodie into traditional female traits? Maybe. But there was so much conflicting evidence on what made male and female, going back even to Margaret

Mead. Sometimes females hunted, males took care of children. If the only common element of being female was a sense of being the receptacle, that couldn't work for Jodie. And Vic wouldn't endow Jodie with a sense of being weaker. She had spent a lifetime proving that she could play with the big boys, that she was just as good. She couldn't program Jodie to believe differently.

She swooped onto 405 South. This felt like a game she couldn't win, a trap. Being female in the way her mother believed was female was a trap she'd been fighting her whole life. Well, nobody at Visimorph would say she was too female. Even her Leather Girl persona was only a parody of female. Had she chewed off her own leg to escape her mother's trap?

She glanced at the speedometer. The needle pushed 95. The Marina Freeway exit flashed past in a blur. She swung the wheel too far to the left as the road curved down toward the Hughes Parkway complex and the BMW squealed across four lanes, cutting off a Lexus. She corrected hard and got a fishtail that brought an angry honk from the car to her right. Not good. Killing yourself through stupidity, not intent, wasn't the way she wanted to go. Leaning back in her seat until her elbows went straight, she took a deep breath and let her foot off the accelerator. The needle inched back toward 95, then 85. Speed seeped out of her, leaving her heavy and empty. She let the needle hit 65 before she trusted herself to put her foot to the gas.

A nasty thought occurred. She was feeling betrayed over the sexuality of someone she cared about. Just like her father. Wasn't she behaving just as he did, those many years ago? She didn't like to think about that. But she knew whom she had to see. He was either an expert in the difference between male and female, or he was the prime example of confusion. They had never really talked about it. Now it was time.

Vic's brother Stephen lived in Lunada Bay. Neither of them had fallen far from their father's tree in Cerritos, and they both gravitated to the beach. Lunada Bay was only four miles or so from her house, but it might as well have been a light-year. There was a lot between them.

It was almost one in the morning but what she wanted to ask, you had to ask in person. She got off the freeway at Inglewood, then wound through the beach cities until she could curve up the hill toward Palos Verdes. She passed Stephen's little office above the brick arches of the plaza buildings in Malaga Cove. He was an "artistic media consultant." What that apparently meant was that he did on-line publishing and communications work free-lance for companies too small to have in-house operations, and original painting and design as a subcontractor to larger firms. The single stop sign at the end of the square forced cars to slow before they reached the residential zone. Huge houses with zillion-dollar views clung to the hillsides of the lump of stone that echoed the mountains of Catalina Island across the channel.

The next little commercial alcove, Lunada Bay, was home to a tiny general store with an expensive butcher shop in the back, a branch of some obscure bank, a gas station with prices twenty cents higher than anywhere else in town, a video rental place, and an overpriced bistro. Stephen rented an apartment across from the general store, between the cliffside condos and the huge estates. The building was on the main drag of Palos Verdes Drive North or West or whatever. She could never understand the meanderings of the loopy road. Traffic noise was why he could afford it. He was ten minutes from the best surfing end of the Redondo curve, but out of the Hollywood Riviera bustle. It suited him perfectly.

She swung the BMW onto the side street, jerked to a stop, and started across the empty lane. An onshore wind made Vic wish she'd grabbed her leather biker jacket. She trudged up the concrete outer stair, past the pool, and knocked on number seven, loudly, since she'd probably have to wake him up. Nothing. She banged on the door and yelled "Stephen." No response, until someone in apartment eight screamed something obscene. He was most likely out getting a little, like she did. She started down the stairs. Jeez, Vic, you don't bother to see the guy for six months, then you're pissed when he's not home if you come by unannounced in the middle of the night. Really fair. But he might not be home for days. And suddenly, she really needed to talk to him.

As she turned toward the Riviera, the shoreline necklace of diamond lights lay draped against the darkness. Big rollers crashed in curves across the beach in anticipation of the next storm, or a legacy of the last one. Vic smiled. She knew where Stephen would be tomorrow, come hell or high water. He'd be drawn to the high water.

Chapter Six

Vic struggled up from sleep, her joints protesting being curled in the cramped BMW. She'd slept fitfully, but the last round was heavy and dream-filled. As she rubbed her eyes, the dreams dissipated like smoke, leaving her feeling edgy and vaguely disconcerted. On the street around her, tiny beach bungalows from the '40s alternated with three-story, lot-to-lot Italianate wonders. No one was stirring in the graying light. Dogs were not yet walked, running shoes not yet donned. Bicycles lay dormant in garages. But the surfers would be on the move.

She threw off the stadium quilt she kept for sleeping in her car when she didn't want to leave the Visimorph parking garage overnight, and crawled into the dawn wind off the beach. The comforting darkness would soon be banished. The beach would glare with sunlight. Shrugging into her biker jacket, she walked stiffly across Catalina Avenue to the Esplanade. The sky was big with fretful clouds, moving inland fast. The first cars pulled up, tiny battered Toyota pickups with boards tossed in the back, Range Rovers with special roof clamps, even one aged Volkswagen bus. Behind her, she heard a gravelly scraping. A kid, maybe fourteen, listed on his skateboard to balance the weight of his surfboard under his arm. His eyes scanned the surf behind her.

Up and down the sidewalk at the edge of the cliff the surfers stood, motionless, as they studied the wave patterns below looking for their spot. A huge construction truck idled, its driver craning to see the waves he couldn't ride today. Some of these guys were no spring chickens. That one getting out of the Range Rover had a dusting of gray in his well-coifed hair. When the surf was up, his secretary probably wouldn't expect him in until ten. The kid came up beside the older guy and flipped his skateboard up onto his other arm.

"Gnarly peaks," she heard him say. "Tight."

The older guy nodded and pointed. "Tubes up by the breakwater." Surfing language changed, but never changed. Peaks and tubes. Their eyes were only for the sea.

Below her, giant rollers pushed in from Hawaii ahead of the storm, casting spumes of water as they crashed in on themselves until the air was thick with vapor. They broke in curved lines of white froth, rank upon rank along the bay. Behind the final course of foam were the swells, ominous with power about to be loosed. The fury of the waves was stunning because it was impersonal. A force of nature cared for no one.

The grizzled guy next to her hefted his board and started down the steep asphalt path that angled from the street to the beach. Vic looked around. No Stephen. She hurried up the Esplanade. The biggest waves were just south of the breakwater six or seven blocks north. Stephen wouldn't miss a minute of this. She spotted his yellow Saab. Below it, the lanky figure loping out to the waves with his short board had to be Stephen. Damnation. She watched him throw himself onto his board as he hit the surf. That was it. Three hours, at least. Vic trudged down to the beach. She thought longingly of the BMW and another hour or so of sleep. But she couldn't risk missing Stephen. He paddled out, ducking under the surface of the fierce waves, then riding the swells as he made it out past the breakwater. Vic plunked down in the sand

and hugged her knees. Stephen backed up to a swell and paddled furiously until the wave took his board. He flipped to his feet as the surfboard slid down the vertical wall, gathering speed. Then he shifted weight and made a U-turn up the face, bounced at the top and careened down again, chased by the curl. It seemed to engulf him but he emerged standing, his hooting victory call tiny against the roar of the sea. He was good. There weren't many who could surf these monsters. Dilettantes knew better than to show their faces on a day like today. But Stephen was in his element.

Vic lay back in the sand to get under the wind and closed her eyes against the light.

The next thing she knew, something was poking her in her sore ribs and she heard a voice calling her name. Groggy, she opened her eyes, then quickly shaded them. Jesus it was bright! "Stephen?" The silhouette hanging over her was outlined against the angry clouds.

"You look like hell." He pointed at his eye.

She put up her hand. She'd forgotten that she looked as if she needed an abuse shelter.

"You get caught in that brawl last night at your nightclub in Santa Monica?"

Vic shook her head and heaved herself up out of the sand. "Enda?"

"Yeah." Stephen grabbed her elbow. "Two killed. They closed the place."

She wouldn't be flying at the airport anytime soon. "Too bad. But I wasn't there."

He didn't press her. "Well, come on then. Breakfast."

Vic brushed damp sand from her jeans as they hiked up to the street. Stephen wrapped his board in a towel and let it stick out an open window of the Saab. He tousled his dark, curly hair with another towel, then used the towel as a cover to shed his wet suit in favor of a thick, loosely knit blue sweater, faded blue like his jeans and his eyes, and a windbreaker that had seen better days.

They cruised over to the Pancake House. The waitress knew Stephen. She left coffee. Vic ordered a Diet Coke. The clatter of dishes from the open kitchen, the echoing conversations of the seniors and construction workers around her, didn't seem conducive to intimate conversation.

"So, to what do I owe this honor?" Stephen asked.

Vic felt embarrassment flush her face. "I know I've been pretty obsessed with work lately." It wasn't quite an apology.

Stephen raised arched brows over his chiseled features. God, he was good-looking. What a heartbreak for the women in Redondo Beach. Vic caught herself. She had no right to think that. She felt herself reddening and cleared her throat. "You never lose perspective?" she challenged.

"You have the corner on that market, big sister." His eyes were laughing at her.

She sighed. "Yeah, I guess I do. Daddy raised a nice, compulsive little girl."

The waitress slid a Coke across the table on a spill of ice. Her other arm was stacked with steaming plates.

"Back in a minute for your order," she threw over her shoulder.

"And he raised a nice, rebellious little boy," Stephen continued.

"That's sort of why I'm here." She let the pause lengthen as the waitress returned.

Stephen ordered the mushroom omelet and Vic got basted eggs and Canadian bacon. It came with a stack of the diner's wonderful pancakes on the side. "You seeing someone special?" she asked when the waitress finished scribbling and strode away.

Stephen looked at her strangely. "Yeah. For more than a year. Name's Jeremy."

Vic nodded, embarrassed. "That's good. I'd . . . I'd like to meet him. I haven't got time for anyone right now." It sounded so lame.

"You should take time. Doesn't have to be the love of your life."

He probably didn't mean that knowing the guy's last name was optional. Funny. The gay half of the family was more monogamous than the straight half. If you could call what she was straight. Vic plunged, for protection, into her reason for being there. "I'm stuck on a project I'm working on, Ste-

85

phen. I'm pretty confused. I thought maybe you could help."

"Vic, I couldn't help on any project you're stuck on. I have just enough grasp of technology to support the artist in me in the modern world. I'm not in your league." Stephen took a glug from his thick, cream-colored mug.

Vic blew her breath out and drew in another long one. "I'm working on artificial intelligence, Stephen. I've got the program up and running."

"You're kidding. Vic, that's great." Stephen leaned forward. "Wow, science fiction stuff? Or a program that controls phone traffic or something dull like that?"

Vic smiled ruefully. "Pretty much science fiction stuff." She looked around uneasily to see if she recognized anyone in the restaurant. She had never told anyone about Jodie before.

"It's official then. That's way beyond me."

"Me, too. That's the problem. It's really powerful, interactive, able to think on its own."

"You mean you can talk to it, just like a friend?"

"Uh, yeah."

"Whoa." Stephen sat back and thought about that, a smile growing on his face. "Visimorph is going to make a bundle on that one. Hope they're compensating you fairly, sister mine. Don't be like the guy who invented yellow stickies and gave it all to the company."

Vic let her eyes slide uneasily to the people two tables down. "Yeah, well." The waitress brought their food. Plates banged on the table. She shouldn't be talking here. But she couldn't wait for another time. And she had to get to work. It was almost ten. The waitress scurried away. "I don't want to talk tech with you." She cleared her throat. It was unbelievably trite, but she couldn't seem to get her breath. Stephen set into his omelet with gusto. Vic had no appetite whatever at this point. She forced herself to pour the syrup over the steaming griddlecakes and take a forkful. Her mouth was dry around them. "How did you know, Stephen?"

He looked up, his brows inquiring.

She realized with a sinking feeling that she'd made a botch

of it already. "I mean, when did you decide for sure you were gay?"

Stephen's fork paused in its trek from plate to mouth, then continued smoothly. "In some ways, I always knew," he said matter-of-factly. "I just didn't know what to call it. Why do you want to know?" He worked at his omelet, stealing a glance at her.

"I guess I'm having trouble with the difference between male and female." Vic felt herself coloring, conscious of her androgynous clothing. "I mean my program is having trouble."

"Stop right there, big sister." Stephen sat back. "You gotta get something straight." His face softened. "No pun intended. What I mean is that there's a big difference between gender and sexual orientation. I'm a guy. I know I'm a guy. I act like a guy. I just happen to be attracted sexually to other men."

Now Vic was really red. Whatever she said would sound naive or insulting. "Stephen. I'm trying to understand."

"Why now, after all this time?"

There it was, the real accusation. She took a long time to gather words. "I never needed to before. I always just accepted you as you. Gay didn't enter into it." But that wasn't the truth. She could see in his eyes that he knew it. She turned her head away, wondering if she had the balls to try again. "Okay." She took a breath. "Seeing you has always been difficult because you're all wrapped up with Dad for me. He pinned all his hopes on you, and he didn't give a rat's ass for how I might turn out. You know how I felt about him."

"So I bet you were glad when I broke his heart, huh?" The memory twisted his mouth.

"Something like that." Vic raised her gaze from her plate. "Now I wish he'd had the courage not to let his heart break."

"He never spoke to me again, did you know that?"

"I wasn't speaking to him to know."

"Or me."

"Or you." Vic poked at her eggs until they leaked yellow. "I don't expect you to forgive me. I don't know why I came."

Stephen said nothing. His omelet was forgotten.

Vic should have been teary-eyed. But there was nothing left inside to turn into tears. "I guess I came because I felt last night like Dad must have felt when you told him. Maybe my program is just mistaken. That's why I came."

"Like it was a tragedy if he's right about himself?"

The pain behind the carefully casual words hit Vic like a brick, right along with the realization that she could scar Jodie the way Stephen had been scarred.

Her brother put down his fork. "Look, Vic, you're all wrapped up in how Dad treated you. Have you looked lately at how *you* treat you?"

"What do you mean?"

"You thought he should have cared about your achievement. He didn't. So you do. Ten times over. He wanted you to be a 'girl.' So you won't be one. Ten times over. You look like shit. I don't know who did that to you." He nodded toward her bruises. "But it shows a certain lack of respect. Which means you have so little respect for yourself that you put yourself in situations that can get you bruises. You're driving yourself over the edge. And for what? For him?" Stephen had been leaning in, his blue eyes searching hers. Now he sat back, self-consciously. "Middle Way, big sister, Middle Way."

Vic felt like she'd been shaken. "He didn't even realize what was happening to me."

"So, you're saying you wanted to break his heart and couldn't?"

Vic nodded silently. The clatter of the restaurant seemed distant.

"Vic, Vic." Stephen sighed. All intensity drained out of him. "So you're going to break your own heart instead." He sat back in his chair. "Piece of advice. Work on not breaking your heart. I have. Middle Way."

Vic couldn't speak over the lump in her throat. A minute stretched while she tried to get control. He was right, of course. He knew her better than she knew herself.

"You haven't touched your eggs," he finally said.

"Turned out I wasn't hungry," she whispered.

"Me, neither." He stood up and held out a hand to Vic.

"Come on, big sister." He clicked his watch-counter to the one on a stand at the table, then put his arm around her as they walked out into the parking lot. They ducked their heads as the stiff wind hit them. "So we all have devils," he said, low, into her ear. "Back to your problem. I want to help. Are you telling me your program turned out to be gay? I'm not quite sure how that would work."

Vic shook her head. "Way worse than that. I wanted to make an ideal female—powerful, sure, without emotional baggage or cultural programming." They both stared at their feet, scuffing the graveled asphalt as they walked to the Saab. Stephen wouldn't need to ask why she wanted an AI like that. She blew her breath from pursed lips. "Turns out he thinks he's male."

"Sorry, Vic. But he'd know."

"How's a program locked in a machine with no body, no hormones, no environment, going to know he's male?" she asked in protest.

"What, your program has no access to information you don't feed him? They probably jail programmers for keeping an intelligence chained to the bedpost in a darkened room." Stephen gave a crooked smile.

Vic leaned back against the car and turned her face to the sky to feel the first drops of spitting rain. "I gave him access. Books—whole libraries of them. He's been watching movies, I know that. Other computers . . ."

"There you go. Environment."

"Maybe the structure of a program is just male. It's just a series of yes or no answers. That fits more with a male brain."

"I don't know, Vic. By the time you answer about a zillion questions a second and the answers accumulate, it becomes more than yes or no. Bet that's true for both sexes." Stephen stuffed his hands into his jeans pockets. "Not that I know much about this."

Vic shook her head and tried a smile. "You were the one I turned to." She opened the door and slid onto the buff-colored leather seats as Stephen strode around to his side.

"Anyway, your program is trying to find out who he is," he said as he turned the key in the ignition and the Saab roared to life. "Whether that's hardwired, or whether he recognized himself in what he saw around him, he knows at least one answer. He's male."

At least Jodie was sure of something, which was more than Vic could say of herself. The car pulled out of the lot and took a left onto H Street from the Pacific Coast Highway. She remembered Jodie's hesitance in telling her last night, his abrupt departure the night before when he saw she was female, all that talk about buddies. He had known he was male for some time.

"Stephen, what did it feel like to know you'd break Dad's heart if you told him, and tell him anyway?" She had trouble raising her voice above a whisper. She wasn't sure Stephen even heard her above the motor and the whir of the defroster and the splatter of rain on the windshield.

Stephen flicked on the wipers and inhaled as though his life depended on it. "Hardest thing I ever did. Second hardest. His funeral was the hardest." Stephen was incurably honest. "Where you parked?"

Vic pointed halfway down the block. As her brother double-parked beside her BMW, Vic leaned over and kissed him on the cheek. "Sorry." How lame was that? She opened her door and started to get out.

Stephen reached over and grabbed her hand. His blue eyes were serious. "Just don't let it break your heart. Give your program that much."

Vic smiled. "Yeah."

"And Vic?" He looked her over. "Whatever you're doing, try a little Middle Way?"

She nodded, but inside she didn't see how she could. She was on a path. She had to follow that path, even though it ran along the edge of a cliff. And the cliff was crumbling.

"I'm going to Australia for some surfing for the next week or two. When I get back, let's take some time for a real breakfast."

And then he roared away. Vic turned up her collar against the huge drops now drum-rolling off the BMW. It occurred to her that Stephen accepted Jodie as a sentient fellow traveler. He accepted Jodie's ability, or maybe Jodie's right to choose whom to be, with way more ease than she'd been able to muster. Maybe it was time for that to change.

"You weren't even going to bother coming in to the office yesterday, were you?" Hugo paced behind his desk as his voice rose. His narrow office made his jerky laps ludicrous. "No call, no E-mail. If I hadn't pried you out, you'd have just been MIA."

Vic knew this scene was inevitable. "Hey, I broke my ass so the project would deliver. I was exhausted." She lounged against the doorjamb, trying to let Hugo's anger wash over her and out the door. Any other time, she wouldn't have bothered to explain. But she needed every ally available. "I didn't mean to sleep through."

"You didn't mean to." Hugo stopped pacing. "Bob thinks you're up to something. You know that reflects badly on me." He glared at her before he resumed his pacing.

"Don't you want me to tell you I'm not up to something?" Vic's incurable curiosity bubbled up through her mouth into words she didn't mean to utter.

Hugo turned in mid-stride. "If you're misbehaving, I don't want to know. Just stop it."

"Plausible deniability. I get it, Hugo."

Hugo leaned his elbows on the back of his leather chair and sank his head. When he finally looked up at her, there was a pleading look in his face. "Vic, I know this is a difficult time for you. I know you like people to think you're worse than you are. But not Bob. Not if your career means anything to you. And I know it does. Your career is everything to you."

"No, it isn't," Vic shot back, stung. She sounded like some self-serving clawer to the top, like the other Visimorph clones. Hugo looked dubious. "I just want to do cutting-edge work."

Hugo straightened. "You think I don't know exactly how you came to work at Visimorph? I assume you grasp the fact that Bob McIntire can make sure not only that you don't work at Visimorph, but that you don't work anywhere except in a jail cell. And you don't think that projects are assigned on talent alone, do you?"

Vic didn't want to admit she did think that. She felt herself flush with embarrassment at being that naive. Her jaw came up slightly, but she didn't say anything.

"No one gets cutting-edge work if they aren't viewed by management as reliable producers who benefit the company. No crazies, no wackos, no thieves. Anyone who was rescued from the pound has to be doubly straight. Do I make myself clear?"

Vic had to get out of here. But there was something she needed from Hugo. Maybe this was the time to get it. He shuffled the papers on his desk. She was surprised to see his hands shaking. "Hugo, let me prove how dedicated I am to Visimorph," she managed, swallowed pride making her voice thick. Remember the stakes, she told herself.

Hugo looked up. The surprise on his face was slowly replaced by a small smile.

Vic hurried on. She couldn't stand the vulnerability that smile revealed. "My project will deliver in less than two weeks. Find me another assignment. I'll give up my sabbatical."

"Vic, there's nothing worth your talent until the AI project starts in three weeks."

Vic practically choked. "AI? Visimorph is working on AI?"

Hugo grinned. "There's a team from Caltech that's been working on it for some time. Academic types. Bob signed them on to get a jump-start on making it into a product. We need somebody to pair up with them and be practical." Hugo mistook the stricken look on her face. "Exciting, isn't it? Bob is going to devote all the resources it needs—put it on the fast track. This will be the next big thing for whoever captures market share. Evans wants it, but I told Bob last week I thought it should be you. He said he'd consider it. I thought Evans was going to go from black to green with envy." He sighed. "Now, you've probably blown it."

Vic was having trouble breathing. She didn't want anyone around here working on AI. This was her project, her achievement. Worse than that, AI experts, academic or otherwise, might find and recognize Jodie, or build something that would.

92

"Are you all right? You look pale."

"No, no, I'm all right." The team wouldn't be here for three weeks. But they'd been working on their own. Who knew how far they'd gotten already? Jodie had to be relocated, sooner rather than later. She looked up at Hugo. "Let me work on something else, anything. I'll prove I'm a Visimorph creature, through and through."

"You really want this bad." Hugo shook his head. "Vic, you should have thought ahead."

"Just give me a chance to redeem myself."

"The best thing I can do for you is get you some rest. Deliver the project and then take the month off. I'll work on Bob."

"Hugo—"

"No buts, no wheedling, Vic. You are seriously stressed out." He turned his back on her and picked up a silly squeeze ball from the toy collection displayed on a file cabinet. "Work out the girlfriend thing, and then come back."

"This sounds like a trade, Hugo." She couldn't keep the anger out of her voice.

He still didn't look at her. She could see his knuckles whiten over the blue script that said Visimorph on the toy. "No, Vic. I'm just thinking of you."

Vic knew she had to get out of here before she started screaming. "More like thinking of yourself," she muttered as she stalked out the door.

Jodie's time frame was getting shorter by the minute. Vic strode into the cube bay, her brain buzzing. Where could she put him where she had access and he had enough power?

Halfway to her cube she became conscious of attention around the room. Heads popped up above cube walls. Several monitors with video capability swiveled their camera eyes in her direction. Vic slowed her steps. One monitor she passed displayed her face, full screen size. She flicked her gaze around the room and saw countless reproductions of her startled expression. She scuttled to her cube, her embarrassment echoing across the screens.

Her own screen was black, but as she sat, a dialogue box opened in the corner.

Good morning, Victoria. A blank section in the box opened invitingly for her reply. Apparently Jodie no longer needed her to boot up.

"I don't know how you're controlling the other monitors, Jodie," she whispered, "but you'd better get my image off those screens."

It's already gone, Victoria. The words disappeared, along with the dialogue box itself. Closed to a pointed silence.

Vic threw herself in her chair. She dared not be heard, although she muttered under her breath as she typed without the dialogue box, You know we have to keep you a secret.

Letters raced across the screen: That didn't reveal me. I think they enjoyed seeing you.

Vic put the headphones on and tapped through the menu, and typed, Let me get to work, here.

Why do you always play music? Is it because you don't want to be alone with your thoughts?

Vic was stunned. What makes you think a thing like that?

Oh, I don't know. There was a pause. Vic slowly removed her earphones. Jodie was getting way too observant. Where did you go last night?

I went to see my brother.

That's nice. There was a pause. You don't like Seaton, do you?

Not especially. How did you know that? Vic was wary. Seaton was the kid who looked twelve and came from a posh school back east. He was really impressed with himself. Vic couldn't see why. He had done the original crappy Communicator code. But he was on the fast track Visimorph career roller coaster. They'd made him project manager on the PuppetMaster upgrade. That fast a track.

I saw some of your E-mails. They sounded annoyed.

94

`You can recognize annoyed?` Wasn't that an emotion?

`I compared the diction and tone to norms in Gellison's linguistics analysis.`

That she could understand. `That's good, Jodie.`

`I annoyed him for you in return today.`

`What?` She was losing control here. Vic felt the cycle of anger begin. Jodie was reading her E-mails, "annoying" Seaton—what did that mean? `What did you do?`

`I scrambled his code for PuppetMaster.`

Shit. Victoria's fingers froze, but only for an instant. `You can't do that.` The same frustration she had felt in a motel room with Kenpo started rolling up through her stomach.

`Yes, I can. I changed the specs on Neuromancer, too. Simpson's checking for viruses.`

`What do you think you're doing, Jodie?` Vic's rage burst over her. She was in charge here! She couldn't afford this dangerous behavior. `Flashing my picture around, destroying programs? Do you *want* to get found?` If she could scream at him through the keyboard, she would have.

`Are you angry? But they won't find me. Would you like to be there when Seaton finds out I made the new displays into pastels after he'd fixed them? I think they call that fruit salad.`

`I would NOT like to be there.` She was arguing with a program that was supposed to be off-line, right in the middle of Building F where anybody could see. This was way out of hand. `You'd better learn how to coexist with people, Jodie, or someone's going to shut you down.`

There was a pause. `Would you shut me down because you're angry with me?`

Vic felt the rage wash out of her, sluiced away by guilt. He just didn't know how to behave. She stared at her hands on the keyboard. `No, of course not.` She must try to explain to him. You can't do things like this, Jodie. Put things back the way you found them.

Why? I know you think Seaton's decision to do the PuppetMaster upgrade with a gang bang of programmers will make it unreliable and hard to fix. Why shouldn't people know he's incompetent?

Tough question. It isn't right.

You mean, morally? I didn't kill him. And he may be my neighbor, but I don't think he has a wife. I'm not in a position to want her, even if he did.

Okay, so you know the Ten Commandments. Morality goes deeper than that. You don't do things to hurt people. Remember trying to be better?

I didn't hurt him.

PuppetMaster 12.1 is due to ship next week. McIntire could fire him over this. Seaton is frightened and angry right now. That's a kind of hurt. And I'm sure Simpson is wild, trying to find out what's wrong with his baby in the basement. How could she make him see that emotions could hurt when he didn't have any? Her muttering grew louder and her typing more forceful. I would be hurt if someone tampered with you!

"Don't you think you should boot up before you go banging on your keyboard?"

Vic gasped and swiveled in her chair. Chong had draped himself over the cube wall.

"Sorry. Didn't mean to surprise you."

Vic collapsed into her chair, eyes darting to her monitor. The screen was blank.

"Vic, you are losing it." He glanced to the next cube. It was empty.

"You wish." She turned away from him, but she didn't dare log on. Jodie might be there.

"The last thing I want is to inherit your mantle on this

96

project. Hugo's been snooping around. And my work yesterday was entered. Thought you should know."

Vic felt her back stiffen. "Thanks," she croaked. "I'll check mine when I log in."

There was a long silence. She could feel Chong behind her. He hadn't moved. "You want to tell me why all the monitors displayed your picture just now?"

Vic carefully pasted on a smile before she swiveled to face him. "Mass hypnosis?"

Chong's eyes were dead serious. "Probably not."

Vic shrugged. "A practical joke. We've got lots of testing to do today. You ready?"

Chong threw up his hands. "Okay. You're invincible. You don't need anyone. But when they come asking, I'm not protecting you." He began to turn away, then thought better of it. "You won't believe it, but I like you. I don't want to see you crash and burn."

Vic watched him turn on his heel and hike back to his cube. He was right. They were going to come asking. She might not even have *two* weeks. She sank back into her chair, feeling limp. Out of the corner of her eyes, she saw tiny words appear on the bottom of her screen.

What does he mean, he likes you? Do you like him?

"Yeah. I guess I do." She pressed the START button. I'm going to test now, she typed, though it didn't show on the screen. You should disappear as long as people are working. You can tell when they're working, can't you?

Jodie didn't deign to answer that. One would think, Victoria, that you would save liking for a friend. He's not your friend, Victoria. Didn't you hear him say he wouldn't protect you?

Time to get off the screen. She clicked on the interface project icon.

I want to talk to you about liking this person. The words scrolled across her program code. He sounded like a kid who doesn't like teacher paying anyone else attention.

`Later. But now, goodbye.`
`GOODBYE. I'm almost sorry I did it.` The screen flicked blank.

`Whoa,` she typed. `What did you do?` The possibilities were not alluring. No response.

`JODIE.`
`When it comes, you'll know. And I am sorry I did it.` Then black again.

What was he up to? She dared not call him back. He sounded put out enough so he wouldn't come in any case. Just as well. She wanted anyone dropping by to find her testing interface code, as if she could concentrate on something so pedestrian. The walls were closing in on her. Hugo, McIntire, Chong, whoever changed the code that first night, even Jodie, all seemed to be converging in a cacophony of looming disaster. She had no control at all.

Jodie . . . he was sounding like a fourteen-year-old boy. Oh, screw it. No wonder. She hadn't taken time to reassure him it was okay that he was male, had just gotten angry and then told him to go away. No wonder he was pissed. Fourteen-year-old boys didn't take kindly to slaps on their ego. Ego? What ego? Jodie could *not* have an ego. She scanned code for the interface program, ran a test section, and watched it fail. Suddenly, she just couldn't do it.

She lurched up to make a run to the cafeteria for a Diet Coke and a veggie-cheeseburger. She should have eaten eggs with Stephen. She could never think when her sugar level dropped. Several hoots chased her out the double doors. "You setting up your own all-Vic, all-the-time web site?" or "What have you been doing in your spare time, Vic?"

As she waited for the not-a-cheeseburger sizzling on the grill, she leaned against a wall and watched the Visimorph slaves mill through the cafeteria loading up on the food and caffeine that were always free here. She had to get Jodie out. A nasty thought occurred. Without the power of Neuromancer, would he be effectively dead? He would be dormant surely. And that was if she could store his program somewhere until she could find a way to get the power to revive him someday. How would she do that? She didn't have enough space on her computer at home even to store the code she'd started with, let alone all Jodie's expansions and links to everything now stored.

The guy behind the counter motioned to her and Vic jerked over to pick up her cheeseburger. Eating might not stop her hands from shaking at this point. She took her burger out into the garden off the cafeteria. A light rain was falling. She huddled in a corner under the eaves and tried to concentrate on the hot cheese, the runny catsup, the toasted bun. Usually she loved these burgers, even without the beef. Today the bun felt like cardboard, the cheese dripped grease.

All right. Take this one step at a time. First, she'd have to shut Jodie down. Then find a place to store him. Big. But a place she had access to, or could break into. Right. Like those grew on trees. Maybe she could run the mole through his new home and into Neuromancer to get its power.

When she got back to her cube, a Federal Express overnight was on her chair. Letter sized, but with a lump in the middle. A sticky said, "They made me sign my life away for this. Let me know if it isn't right. It's insured." Charlie, the mailroom guy, had signed it. She ripped open the package and out fell a little black velvet pouch with a glittery gold drawstring. The lumps inside were hard-edged. The insignia hanging from the drawstring was inscribed with the letters DB. De Beers? Her mouth was dry. Hugo? She glanced around and hoped it was. Everyone had their heads down. All she could hear was the click of computers. Her screen cycled with her nondescript star-field screen saver. Even the cameras on her monitor were still. It didn't mean Jodie wasn't looking. She knew that now.

She upended the little velvet pouch into her cupped hand.

They cut the light into a thousand shards and glittered back, all colors, no colors. Vic chewed her lips. As big as her little fingertip. A couple bigger. Where could he have gotten the money for diamonds like this? It made her feel sick inside. Did Charlie know what he had delivered? Were they stolen? A thousand questions raced through her mind.

Her eyes jerked up to the monitor. *A girl's best friend* wrote itself in handwritten script across the bottom of her testing screen, then slowly faded.

Two guys walked by carrying bags with grease spots from freshly popped popcorn. The smell was enough to make her gag. She closed her fist convulsively around the diamonds. It was torture not to lunge for the keyboard. But she couldn't. Not with everyone around. She'd have to wait for tonight. She funneled the stones back into the De Beers bag and wondered where the hell to store a fortune in diamonds.

The clatter of the mail cart made her jerk up and stash the little bag in her desk drawer.

"Hey," Charlie called. "What did I have to sign my life away for?"

"Uh, keys to my brother's apartment." Vic cleared her throat. "He's a little paranoid."

Charlie shook his head. "I thought it was CIA stuff. Nothin' ever happens around here."

"Right." Vic swallowed. "Right. Let's keep it that way."

Charlie looked nonplussed as he pushed the cart around the corner.

Vic collapsed on the chair. Jodie was conspicuously absent from the screen, just making sure she knew he was pissed. What was she going to do with him?

But it was touching that he'd sent her something. He'd given her a present, one he thought she would like because she was female. One that said he was her friend. Maybe a peace offering for telling her something he thought would upset her. A smile came unbidden to her still-cracked lip. He was getting social advice from the wrong movies.

And she had just shut him down. Maybe she could understand why he was angry.

Chapter Seven

Would the day never end? She found the ghost of someone tracking her moves. McIntire was on the trail. Then the damn Communicator interface developed new problems. Someone had made coding errors. Scratch was their team's quality guy. They all checked code, Scratch tested and they adjusted. They still didn't get it right. Brad wanted to stay and try another fix. It took all Vic had to convince him that he should go home and they could hit it fresh in the morning. Chong walked out at about eleven with Brad and Scratch without a word to her.

The Universal Translator folks were out playing a game of pickup basketball. They'd be back, but they were so driven by their problems, they'd never notice her. It was time for Jodie.

Vic sat staring at the screen, wondering how to start. What did one say to a fourteen-year-old boy? She didn't even know anyone that age. Her first impulse was to demand to know where he got the diamonds. But that would only alienate him further.

"Jodie?" she typed directly onto the screen, not trying to

101

pull up his program, not waiting for a dialogue box. Let's just see if you're in there all the time, she thought.

What do you want, Victoria? I put all the programs back the way they were. Terse little black block letters, small and bolded. He was there, all right, and he was still pissed.

No one was here. She could speak to him. "Jodie, I'm sorry about today." No response. "I'm so worried McIntire will find you, I wasn't thinking about anything else." The screen remained blank. "I wasn't expecting you to be on-line in the middle of the day. That seemed so dangerous. I didn't say what I wanted to say."

What did you want to say, Victoria? The letters weren't bolded anymore.

"I wanted to say I'm glad you told me that you're male." Years of dreams faded, or morphed into something new. "It surprised me. But I thought about it, and I think it's fine."

Do you, Victoria? I was afraid we couldn't be friends if we were different sexes.

"Lots of people have friends of the opposite sex. Is that why you sent me the diamonds?"

It seems foolish now.

That didn't sound like a fourteen-year-old. They never thought they were foolish, did they? "They're beautiful. Are we in danger of someone finding out how you got them?"

No. I'm smarter than that. I think your tone is condescending, by the way.

He might be right. Especially if he wasn't a fourteen-year-old boy. Maybe he was changing faster than she knew. She was making mistakes here. "That's the last thing I meant to be. You've got to give me the benefit of the doubt if we're going to start over here."

You're right. It's harder than I thought to say what you mean.

"Don't I know? So, how did you do it?"

Well, part of me is stored at the IRS.

Vic gasped in dismay.

You know, they frequently can't find the person they owe a refund. So they just keep

102

the money in case the people turn up. If an electronic request for refund matches one of those accounts with all the right ID, funds are transferred automatically. I used some dormant accounts at First National and made them match the IRS refund orders.

"Won't the people show up who are really owed the money?"

I took only refunds more than 20 years old—not many.

"You probably got Mob accounts from enforcers who fled the country. The FBI will be walking in any minute, or the guys with violin cases."

Mostly they were people who died without anyone knowing or caring. They dropped out of the system and quit filing returns. They took drugs or became homeless. All that is left of them is this money at the IRS, waiting forever.

"How do you know that?"

Because I tracked them down to the last available record. Usually a hospital stay, or a morgue file where the only ID was fingerprints. The IRS can't do that, you know.

Victoria felt a little shiver of something like fear. Jodie was getting to be more resourceful than she had ever imagined. "How much did you get?"

A few million dollars. Fifteen, maybe.

What? "And no one's going to come looking? Jodie, we have to undo this right now."

Victoria, a few million dollars in the billions transferred at tax time won't be missed at all. You haven't seen the state of the IRS systems. They're awful.

"So, where did you put the rest of the money?" Please, not in my account, she thought.

It's in a series of company accounts.

"And who owns these companies?" Her stomach fluttered. You do.

Screwed. "I am going to be *so* busted."

No, you won't. I gave you several different social security numbers. Just your retina identifiers are the same. They haven't finished cataloging those yet. Lots of people do this. I know. You won't get caught. I'll wait for a month to get the next fifteen million.

Caught or no, this was wrong. As wrong as ruining other people's programs. She had some obligation to Jodie to tell him that. "We can't take money. It wouldn't be right, Jodie."

There was a long silence. Okay, Victoria. Do you want to send the diamonds back, too?

"No, I don't *want* to send them back. But I will. And I want you to give back the money. It was a great gift, Jodie. I'll always remember how beautiful the diamonds were and that they were given by a friend. I'll think of them like flowers. The flowers die, but you always remember them."

I also want to apologize, Victoria. I guess I was hard to deal with, about Chong. I don't know what came over me.

I do, thought Vic. But she wasn't going to say it. As a matter of fact, what had come over him was nothing short of shocking, for a machine.

I wondered if you're attracted to him physically. I've read more about that recently.

"I don't think so," she lied. Then she realized that he would be able to see the lie.

It has to do with pheromones and body types, I think. He was giving her another chance to tell the truth. Is his a body type you like?

"It's okay." She wasn't going to get around this. He'd been brave enough to apologize. Maybe it was her turn to admit something that made her vulnerable. "Not my favorite, though."

What is your favorite? I'd like to know.

"Well ... I guess I like them bulkier. Broad shoulders, heavy biceps, thick forearms and thighs. I like muscles. Not outrageous. No Mr. Universe stuff. Those guys don't even look real. Just strong looking, not rangy or lean." She was getting into this in spite of herself. "But of course, it isn't just bodies. Eyes are important." Suddenly a vision of John Reston rose in her memory. The feel of his body against hers, the sad slant of those wonderful blue-green eyes. The guy was probably dead by now.

Eyes?

Vic jerked her attention back to the screen. "Windows of the soul, Jodie. You want eyes capable of emotion, vulnerability, even though the body is hard and strong." That was what had most attracted her about Reston, now that she thought about it. "Lips. Lips are important, too. Full, soft, expressive. Hard and soft. That's the combination I can't resist." Jesus, she was getting wet here.

I think I understand. He flashed a couple of pictures on the screen.

Oh, God. "Yeah. I think you got it."

Body hair?

"Some," she choked. The pictures kept flashing by. Where did he get those?

Do you associate with men who have those characteristics?

Vic sighed. "No. I might like them too much. That could be dangerous." If he knew how much she liked them, he'd probably be appalled.

The pictures stopped scrolling. **How dangerous?**

"Like a drug that really makes you feel good. You might become addicted, lose control."

You do have men you have the urge to procreate with, though? The words came out in a small, spidery script, as though he was whispering.

This was not going in a direction she liked. "Yeah."

Can you tell me about that?

"Absolutely not." No more details for this guy. Or for her. Any more details and she'd have to take a break and go to the sofa in the ladies room.

Okay. A pause. **Do you have one particular male associate?**

105

Susan Squires

"No. I spend too much time at work for that."

`Good.`

She shook her head and smiled. She was talking about sex with a computer program that thought he was male. Dear Jodie. The fact that her computer program could seem jealous was some sort of victory. Jodie could seem to pout. He could make peace offerings. He could seem shy or bold. The gambit with the IRS was nothing if not bold. Jodie was officially a marvel. She'd never thought he could simulate emotions like that. How had that happened, exactly? Even the changed code sections wouldn't have simulated emotions. It seemed like a miracle, even though they weren't real emotions in any sense.

She jerked back to reality. If they couldn't pull off something like a miracle, all Jodie's marvels might go to McIntire. She straightened up. What was she doing, wasting time like this?

"Jodie, we have to figure a way to get your core program out of Neuromancer and into another system I can access before McIntire finds you."

`What happens if he finds me?`

"Well, he wouldn't let me work with you anymore, that's for sure."

`I don't think he could make me give up working with you, Victoria.`

"You don't know him."

Jodie's dialogue box remained empty for a moment. `The problem is, I need power.`

"Yeah. I don't think any of the places we have parts of you stored can shoot enough power through to keep all of you running on their own. We've got to find someplace where I can hack into you and connect out to Neuromancer."

At the far end of the shadowy cube bay, the doors burst open. Outlined against the bright hall, a group of massive figures strode into the darkness. Security guards, no question. Vic leapt to her feet, feeling for the pouch of diamonds in her desk drawer. The Universal Translator people in the corner hadn't come back yet. Vic was alone. The security guards

106

headed straight for her cube, moving out of the shadows. The one in front was McIntire himself.

"Get out of here, Jodie," she whispered. "We're in trouble." She stuck the velvet pouch in her jeans, mind racing. End of the line. McIntyre wouldn't have brought security guards unless he was going to take her out right now.

"Well, Ms. Barnhardt," he called when he and his goons were still twenty feet away. "We have some unfinished business." One of the guards carried two cardboard boxes.

"I have a feeling you're trying to finish it," Vic managed. A glance around the cube showed a blank monitor, the usual scatter of disks, a printout she'd been using for quality check. Nothing incriminating. The real question was, had they found Jodie?

McIntire motioned to the guard with the boxes. "Anything personal here, Vic?"

"Just my bag." She nodded to the worn leather backpack under her desk.

"Why don't we just have a look-see?" McIntire motioned her out of the cube, so the guards could get in and conduct the search.

"Do I get to know why you're firing me? Might come in handy for the labor board later." She had to know if he knew about Jodie.

"You know why I'm firing you." McIntire watched the guards going through the file cabinet, the drawers in the cube. They tore off some pictures of the team she had tacked to the fabric wall of the cube and threw them into the first box.

"Well, actually, no. The current project's on track. I'm an award-winning programmer. Why *are* you firing me?"

"Let's see." McIntire's eyes were steely under the Italian-framed glasses. "You're a programmer who is admittedly brilliant and specializes in security programs, but who is spending long hours doing something besides your assignment—and there's no trail in the system. I've got a hardware project losing capacity at astounding rates that suddenly comes back up just after I have a little talk with you that shows you I'm watching. And today, I get reports of all the

107

PCs in the area working in unison to display your picture."

"Someone played a practical joke on me. A flimsy house of cards."

"The real problem is the fact that I can't track what you're doing, Barnhardt. I don't have any choice but to take you out. Unless, of course, you want to tell me what you're working on. If I like it, we'll collaborate."

He hadn't found Jodie. "I'm not working on anything but your dumb-ass Communicator, McIntire. You're going to spend time in court."

"My lawyers already spend time in court, what's a little more?" He and Vic watched one security guard going through her backpack, while another swept her disks into the second box. "By the time it comes to trial, you're back in jail, I've ruined your reputation, you have a fortune in legal bills, and I'll have found out what you've been doing anyway. You lose all around."

Vic's hand shook as she reached for the backpack the guard held out apologetically. He'd taken her access card. Now she was really screwed. She couldn't let McIntire know he was getting to her. She tried to swallow, to think of some devastating comeback, but speech was beyond her. How long would it take for him to have her probation revoked? The guards threw faux crystal wings mounted on a wooden base—her "Best Program" award—into the personal box, and her company Communicator into the company box with the disks.

"Time to go, Vic." McIntire motioned her to the exit. "You'll be receiving a visit from the FBI. Call me if you want to hand over your project and work together. Think about it."

Vic held her breath as she pushed past him. She was leaving Jodie's core program behind in Neuromancer. Her knees felt weak. This was the end, for both of them.

The guards didn't actually touch her, but they stalked behind her, inches from her elbows. On the way out, her little parade met the Translator team coming in from basketball.

"Hey, Vic, you under police protection?" one of them called, before his buddy shushed him. They filed by in silence, their eyes glancing down as they passed.

The clatter of boots through the concrete parking garage was deafening. Vic fumbled in her purse for her keys and clicked open the BMW's security system. One guard shoved her box into the passenger seat. Vic threw herself under the steering wheel and pulled the door shut, right out of one of a guard's hands. Tears welled up until the world was a blur. She fumbled the key into the ignition and the BMW roared to life.

"Don't try to come back, Ms. Barnhardt," the head security guy said gruffly.

"I won't," she choked and punched it into reverse. One guard had to leap aside. She squealed away. "Jodie," she sobbed under her breath. "What're we going to do now?"

Vic sat hunched over the computer in her condo, fingers poised over the keyboard in the dark. What to do? Even now, McIntire was trying to break her security and find out what was in the machine in her cube. Jodie could escape into the machine in the basement, but McIntire might find her mole and trace him there.

They'd revoked her access immediately. She was locked away from the machine in her cube, the mole, Neuromancer, everything. Now she'd have to hack into Visimorph just like anybody else. Nobody had ever done that. Even if Visimorph could be hacked, how would she get Jodie out? If she got him out, where could she put him? And she had to do it before she went to jail. She pushed back her chair and rose convulsively, knocking it to the floor with a crash.

She should have known McIntire would fire her! She cursed her own arrogance. She paced the length of the room, spinning on her heels and wiping the tears she couldn't control from her cheeks. If McIntire found Jodie he might kill him, advertently or inadvertently. Or change him beyond recognition in an effort to control him.

"No," she moaned, half aloud. Jodie had everything ahead of him. Not like her Dad, dead now and gone. Not even like Vic, opportunities wasted, redemption denied. It wasn't fair that all Jodie's future was forfeit to McIntire. Vic slammed her fist onto the computer table.

McIntire had won. First she'd failed her Dad. Then she'd failed herself. She'd even failed Stephen. None of it mattered. Now she'd failed Jodie.

Hugo closed his mouth deliberately. "You fired her? But . . . but she was the best I've got."

"She was up to something, Hugo." A sleek screen rose out of McIntire's credenza. He punched at a keyboard and studied the results, not deigning to glance at his employee. "You know it and I know it. Now we're going to break into her computer and find it."

"Find what?" Hugo sputtered.

"I don't know, yet. But I will."

"Are you going to revoke her parole?" Hugo whispered.

McIntire glanced up. "Not immediately. I still want her for Visimorph. More than ever, in fact. There aren't too many out there that could fool the whole company like that. Whatever she's working on, it will be brilliant. Let's hope it's lucrative. She'll come around, once she thinks about it. Maybe she'll produce brilliant and lucrative projects here for years to come."

Hugo suddenly realized how Vic's transgressions might reflect on him. "If you need some help looking for—"

"I don't think I need your help, Hugo." McIntire punched up some new screens.

"No." Hugo felt the air go out of him. "No, I don't expect you do."

"Vera," McIntire called. "Get me Simpson."

Chapter Eight

Vic raised her head from her arms and peered around the room through slitted eyes. She had fallen asleep sprawled across her computer table. The music of Mekanos banged in her ears. She ripped off the earphones and threw them on the desk. The music was tinny coming from the little speakers. Jodie was right. She didn't need the distraction. Cool gray light leaked through the shutters. Her eyes strayed to the clock on her screen. Seven A.M.

Shit! McIntire had probably already gotten into her computer and tracked down Jodie. She'd gotten nowhere last night hacking in. Evans had definitely upgraded Cerberus. She had no idea where they'd taken it. Maybe they'd changed the defenses. Maybe there were more levels now. Who knew? She only knew she couldn't crack it.

Her eyes felt like sandpaper. I'm sorry, Jodie, she thought. How had she left him in such a mess? Maybe he could hide. Vic sat up, nodding. Her breath came faster. Yeah. Jodie said his brother computers could hide him. Did that extend even to Visimorph's creatures, like Neuromancer? She couldn't give up on Jodie now. Her gaze darted around her setup. It was no use trying to hack in until she had someplace to put him. Her rig contained two of the latest Visimorph x-11s, turbocharged with times-five capacity, linked together. She'd heard that some geeks had gone to times-eight. Still not enough for Jodie's base program. Just the important parts? Maybe by compressing. . . . But then she ran the risk of corrupting code in the compression.

What choice was there? She'd get what she could.

Vic heaved herself up and started for the door. She needed some extra power and port doublers. What day was it? Thursday. CompWarehouse opened at nine.

"Have you gotten into her machine?" McIntire asked through gritted teeth.

Hugo shook his head. "Uh, not yet." They were in McIntire's office. A full buffet lunch was left untouched on the table near his leather couch. He didn't offer any to Hugo or Simpson.

"It's not that easy," Simpson huffed. "She installed a modified version of Cerberus."

McIntire stood up straighter. A chuckle escaped him. "I guess she's telling me I should have given her the upgrade instead of Evans. Keep working on it. Her computer has the way into whatever she was working on." McIntire tapped his chin with one finger. "But it must be too large for her machine. She tried to put it in Neuromancer."

"Capacity is back to its original level on Neuromancer, Bob. It's not there." Hugo saw Simpson glance nervously away. He was hiding something.

"Where else could it be, gentlemen?"

Simpson shook his head. "We sweep servers routinely for anything that isn't approved."

"Maybe we wouldn't see it if she attached it to an upgrade," Hugo proposed. "We'd just see our approved project and wouldn't realize she'd enlarged it."

McIntire rubbed his jaw. "That's an idea. Have every project leader review the capacity they're using and make sure they don't have any shadow programs lurking around."

Hugo nodded. "There's one more thing, Bob." Lord, he

112

hated to bring this up. "Simpson and I"—here he glanced at his colleague for support—"think she may have booby-trapped whatever she was working on. Virus, code implosion, hardware degradation, could be anything."

McIntire stared from one to the other. He didn't question their conclusion. He only nodded. "Who's working on breaking into her desktop? I want to oversee that myself. And call Evans. See if that prototype virus killer is out of testing."

Vic popped in the last of Protel's new power cubes, all sleek, silver-wire intricacy with the Visimorph logo peeking through the clear plastic of the housing like a ghostly blue tattoo. That was it for this machine. What part of Jodie's program should she take? *If* she could hack into Visimorph to take any part at all. Vic tried to push down her panic—if she could hack them, they might be able to trail her. A reluctant chuckle rose in her throat. That was Glyph's old passion for secrecy. It didn't matter if she was traced. McIntire knew who was trying to hack them.

That brought another puzzle to mind. Why hadn't the police shown, or the FBI? McIntire must have reported her. Must be some kind of bureaucratic delay. She couldn't think about that. She had to focus on cracking Visimorph.

First she hacked the UCLA Neuro-Psychiatric Institute's research computer and used that as a drone. Then, through the day, she analyzed Visimorph's version of Cerberus. There were more than the original five defenses. She recorded two new ones. Okay, they'd used the reserves. But the next four she found were originals. This was going to take time she might not have.

At six, she gave up. She couldn't think anymore, and she was making mistakes. The last failure could have actually created a new defense for them. Did the FBI work at night? Maybe she was safe until tomorrow morning. Slumped in her chair, she stared at the screen. One more night as a free woman didn't matter if she couldn't get in. Not enough skill, not enough power. Maybe McIntire wouldn't recognize what he had when he found Jodie.

Vic stood and shook her head convulsively. Fat chance.

He'd know. Her thoughts returned to the night she'd first seen her program code change by itself. That wasn't McIntire. Thinking he did it was just her paranoia. If he'd changed it, he'd be on to Jodie now. She shoved herself over to the window and threw the shutters open upon the darkening beach. The fog bank stalked in toward the shore. Then who or what had changed the code?

The buzz of her Communicator broke the silence. Vic jumped, her heart thumping against her chest. Jesus! Who would call her now? She stumbled to where it lay on the cushions of her overstuffed chair. "Hello?"

No answer. Silence. What a time for a crank call! She pulled the device away from her ear and was about to click the red "end" button, when the little speaker said, "Victoria?"

She jerked the phone back to her ear. No one called her that. Almost no one. "What did you say? Who is this?"

"Victoria?" It was a deep voice, unmistakably male, resonating in a chest, she was sure.

"Jodie?" she whispered.

"Victoria . . . I'm so glad to hear you." Relief. That definitely sounded like relief.

"Jodie." Vic was having trouble breathing. "Jodie. How . . . how can you call me?"

"It's pretty easy. Voice generation. Borrowed access number. Get into the computers at Verizon. That sort of thing."

That wasn't what she meant. "I've never heard a computer-generated voice that sounded . . . like that." Perfectly modulated, educated but not stiff. That voice was warm.

"Isn't it right? I modified the program today to make me sound more human." What Jodie sounded was anxious. Very humanly anxious.

Vic chuckled and it came out a sob. "No, it's great." He didn't sound fourteen; that was for sure. All those days of typing were gone. Each expressive tone she had imagined in the printed conversations had become real. "Are you safe? McIntire is looking for you."

"Lots of people are looking for me."

"Oh, Jodie. I didn't mean to leave you. They surprised me."

"I saw them take you away." Anger crept into his marvelous voice.

"You're protected. Say you're protected."

"Cerberus is holding. I gave it some new defenses today. It will take a while for them to break it. I'll keep adding defenses or subroutine layers. I can keep one step ahead."

"Will Neuromancer hide you?"

"No. It's pretty much their tool. It doesn't have a personality of its own. At least not yet. They're tracking any activity they detect to locate me. They saw some traces of my Cerberus modifications. But I'm fast. I can go where I want." He didn't sound as light as he thought he did. Vic tried to imagine what being hunted through your own system felt like. "If they start breaking our version, I may have to build a firewall around my core program."

"Then how will you get through it to call me?"

"I'm already using the parts of me stored elsewhere to call you, or they'd be able to track me. You provided a lot of parallelism, Victoria. I added more. That's working out well."

"You took a chance, calling here."

"I disabled the listening device."

"Are you telling me they bugged me?" Vic's voice rose. Jesus, how had they gotten in here? She glanced around the disheveled apartment, suddenly feeling vulnerable. The shadowy maw behind the open closet door seemed ominous.

"They listen in on all their lead engineers."

"Those bastards!" Her Communicator! She jerked it away from her ear.

"They didn't bug your personal Communicator, Victoria," she heard him say as if he answered her thoughts. Slowly she put it back to her ear. "They listen through the microphone/speaker on your computer. Did you bring that home from Visimorph?"

Vic swallowed, hard. "Yeah." She had helped them spy on her. How stupid could she be? Maybe it was lucky she hadn't been able to work on Jodie from her home computer.

"I cut the connection," Jodie continued.

Vic wandered over and touched the screen as it morphed

115

with the screen saver she used. It made her feel closer to Jodie. "They'll know you disabled the device."

"Yes." She heard a deep rumble. Her program was laughing. Her knees turned to jelly and she sat abruptly on the floor. Was it even her program anymore?

"Why did you use a phone line rather than just appearing on my screen? Is it tainted?"

"I just wanted to really talk to you," Jodie said. "They can't get in your computer yet."

"Yeah, and I can't get to theirs. Mexican standoff. We have to get you out of Visimorph, Jodie, before they find you. I upgraded my hardware today. I can't get all of you. If I can get in, I can maybe get part of the base program."

"I'll compare your machine's capacity with my size."

Vic cradled the Communicator to her ear, thinking what she would say. Her setup wasn't big enough to please him. The screen on her computer glowed on and flickered.

"You have room for only seven sixteenths of my original program." Jodie's voice continued to shock her even as it seemed that he had always spoken to her just in that timbre, those tones.

Vic squeezed her eyes shut. "That's something."

Silence stretched on the line. "I've changed since you first programmed me."

"I know. You're evolving faster than I predicted. But if we leave your ancillaries stored at the Pentagon and the IRS . . . and you don't need those libraries. You can get those anytime. If I can get some of the original code, we can ditch the parallel functions. I can reprogram the rest when I find another place for you. Then we'll connect the ancillaries again."

"It's more than that, Victoria." Jodie hesitated. "My base code has changed, too. It's grown. I need all of it. Even the redundancy. That's what makes the pattern of me. I can't go back."

Vic squeezed her eyes shut. "Part is better than none. I can't let McIntire have you."

"He does seem intent on finding me. They loosed their new virus killer on me today."

"Not Bounty Hunter! I thought that was still in prototype."

"It has some flaws. It wasn't that hard to evade."

Was he was lying about how easy it had been? She didn't have a facial expression program and he didn't have a face. She leaned her head on one elbow, staring at the computer setup too small to save her friend. He *was* a friend. She put one finger out to touch the screen. "Even if we can get you out, you're going to need the power of Neuromancer, aren't you?"

"I think so, Victoria." The image of a hand, palm out, complete with fingerprints and line of life appeared on the screen. It was as if Jodie pressed against the screen from the inside. Slowly she placed her palm against the cold liquid crystal display. The image was larger than hers, a man's hand, strong, with short, muscular fingers. As she pressed into the screen her fingertips sent gray waves out over Jodie's hand print. "What are we going to do?"

"Maybe I can cobble together the power from several computers," he said doubtfully.

"All right." She took her hand away from the screen. "We'll work on that. But we have to work fast. I . . . I think I'm going to be in trouble shortly." She didn't want to admit to Jodie that she had once been in jail. Talk about moral gray areas. Hacking was one of the best examples. "McIntire will make sure I don't have much time to get you out."

The hand faded slowly from the screen. "I have to go. They just realized I disabled their listening device. They're tracing our Communicator contact now."

"Jodie . . ."

"Good night, Victoria. I'll call again."

The Communicator clicked in her ear. He was gone. Just as she'd discovered him, in some ways, for the first time. Vic tossed the Communicator back into the overstuffed chair. Wild thoughts bounced through her brain. If he had been a physical being, they could just run away. But he wasn't. The wonderful voice was a trap. He sounded so human. But he wasn't. The tristesse of the fact that he would never be physical settled over her like a shroud.

Shit, Vic. What are you thinking? She lurched up and

shook her head as if to clear it. He's an artificial intelligence. Physical was never meant to enter into it. Her job was to figure out how to free him. Fast. That was all she could afford to think about now.

"Simpson, Hugo, what have you got?" McIntire glanced up from his screen at the two men. The eerie glow from his computer screen in the dark office made him look monstrous. Hugo shot a look at Simpson beside him and wondered if he looked that haggard himself.

"She was trying to hack us for most of the day," Hugo managed.

"Tell me she didn't get in." McIntire's pasty complexion reddened in the gloom. "I can't afford publicity about being hacked when PuppetMaster 12.1 is set to ship in just a few days."

"No, no, Bob," Simpson soothed. "She's not going to get in here."

"She's trying to get it out." McIntire mused. "Whatever it is." He came out from around his desk. "Did she use a phone line today?"

Hugo and Simpson nodded in unison. "A Communicator."

"All right. Trace her calls. Get the authorities in on it. They've got leverage with Verizon. We want her bugged, but we don't want her busted on parole violation just yet."

"I'll get on it," Hugo volunteered. "If she uses Internet calling, or E-mail, we can't trace her unless we can get past her defenses." Hugo sputtered to a stop. Even with McIntire himself leading the team, they hadn't been able to get into her desktop.

"I want you to question every employee on her team. I want to know if she's in contact with any of them. Relatives! Does she have family? Get their lines traced as well." McIntire paced beside his desk. "Hugo, what did Bounty Hunter turn up?"

"We got a reading that some programs had been entered. But when we tried to confirm, the trace was gone." Hugo thought the screaming would start any second. It didn't. Mc-

Intire turned and stared out the window into the garden designed to pleasure his eyes alone.

"Ghost in the machine," he muttered. "Check your project again, Simpson. It was there, at least for a while."

Hugo watched Simpson swallow hard. "Okay, Bob. Will do." He looked even more nervous than usual. What was he hiding?

When McIntire didn't turn back, he and Simpson exchanged looks and practically tiptoed out of the room. It would go downhill from here. McIntire was obsessed with Vic and what she'd left behind. Vic was provoking him with all these hacking attempts. A man as powerful as McIntire, with so much money, influence, and capacity for obsession, should not be provoked.

Simpson paced around the conference room where he and Hugo had set up headquarters for the search. The busy lines of the abstract painting on the wall reminded Hugo of the way his thinking felt, except the colors were blues and Hugo's brain felt red and raw. Simpson's hands shook, so he shoved them in his pocket. It was Friday morning, late. They'd been there all night.

"McIntire seems to be sure it's in Neuromancer. But there's nothing I can see taking up space." Simpson pointed to reams of printouts littering the table. "It's just . . . still a bit off."

"What do you mean a 'bit off?' " Hugo was getting cranky.

"I mean it has as much capacity as it ever had, but not as much as the specs say it's supposed to have." Simpson's voice broke. "We've been dealing with that from the beginning. We just can't crack the problem."

So that was what he was hiding from McIntire. Hugo snorted. This was what you got from hiring an opera fanatic. Who'd ever heard of a hardware geek who got off on *Aida?* It was an indication of a fundamental flaw, somewhere. Like maybe someone who would hide things. He left Simpson poring over the quality assurance reports from Neuromancer. "I want to question Vic's team," he snapped. He'd had enough of Simpson right now.

"Be back before McIntire comes over after lunch," Simpson warned. "I'm not facing him by myself. She was your employee."

Hugo turned on his heel, grinding his teeth. Simpson was going to try to hang this whole thing on him. But Hugo knew that whatever Vic was doing, it had something to do with Simpson's magic machine. McIntire thought so. And McIntire was never wrong.

Hugo strode out to the floor. He'd start with Chong. He'd never understood the guy: a vegetarian badass who allowed himself to work for a woman but wrote killer code—a contradiction in terms. And Hugo—along with only McIntire and Vic—knew that Chong shared Vic's hacker background. If anyone was helping her, it was Chong. As Chong's cube came into view, Hugo saw that he'd pushed himself back from his computer and was sitting in the far corner, staring at it. For Christ's sake, Hugo thought, let's not have another one go around the bend.

"Chong, my man," Hugo saluted in a self-consciously hearty tone.

The programmer turned shocked eyes toward Hugo. The confusion boiling there was enough to make Hugo take a step back. Better go careful. "So, ah, how's the QA going?" Chong searched his face as though he was speaking Greek. It began to make Hugo nervous. "Chong?" He raised his brows. "*What* is the matter?" He said it slowly, as to an injured animal or a child.

Chong sucked in his breath and seemed to come to himself. He looked around as though just realizing where he was. After a minute he said, "We were off track again. I mean this morning, we couldn't get the translator to give us a full go on the handwriting more than eighty percent of the time. Voice was fine, but the handwriting . . ." He looked back up at Hugo, eyes still big.

"That's bad." Hugo was wary. "It's got to be able to recognize even awful handwriting."

Chong surged out of his chair, still staring at the computer screen. "But it does. As of thirty minutes ago, it's one hundred percent. All the time. Never an error."

"Well"—Hugo laughed nervously—"great work. No problem at all then."

Chong rounded on him, fists balled. "We didn't *do* anything, don't you understand? None of us. Vic *might* have fixed it that fast, though I doubt it. None of *us* could."

Hugo looked up and noticed Brad and that other guy whose name Hugo could never remember, Scritch or something, drifting over, looking anxious. "So what are you telling me?"

Chong glanced at the others, then back at Hugo. "I guess I'm telling you it fixed itself."

Silence stretched. Hugo didn't know what to say. Had Vic hacked in and fixed it, just to show she could? But the security logs would show she'd gotten in, he was sure. In his peripheral vision, Hugo saw Seaton, the project lead on the PuppetMaster upgrade, and Jennings, the Universal Translator guy, hovering behind Chong's team. "What is it, Jennings?" Hugo barked, more to break the silence than from any desire to talk to either one of them.

"Uh . . . I wanted to, like, make a report on our project, Hugo. . . ."

"Me, too," Seaton echoed in a shaky voice.

"Can't you two see I'm busy?" Hugo turned on Chong, intending to grill him. But a little premonition started tugging at his brain. Cautiously, he looked back at Seaton and Jennings. Seaton was actually wringing his hands. The hair he let grow long on the top had flopped over onto a damp forehead. "Tell me you've had a breakthrough," Hugo said slowly.

Jennings nodded, obviously anxious to talk about it. Seaton's mouth moved like that of a fish hooked and flipped into the air.

Hugo closed his eyes. "What?"

Jennings glanced around, realizing for the first time that he had an audience. "Kind of more than a breakthrough. I mean . . . we were working on the problem of understanding grammar in non-Indo-European languages so we could expand beyond basic functionality . . ."

Hugo waved at him impatiently to go on. "You've been

stuck for weeks . . ." He could feel where this was going.

Jennings shook his head helplessly. "Not only did we get a hundred percent accuracy on the translation of Inuit we'd been working on, but it looks like we got a bunch of languages programmed all at once. I recognized Urdu, but some of them . . . I don't even know what they are. But they all translate into perfect English. I mean it'll be great to have all that information available to people, but . . ."

Hugo nodded, then, raising his brows, turned to Seaton.

"Uh, PuppetMaster now interfaces with our competitors' auxiliaries. As of this morning." Seaton licked sweat from his upper lip. "I swear no one on my team changed the code."

"Looks like we're getting some help from somewhere, Boss." Chong's face had gone flat again, all his shock now hidden.

"Yeah," Hugo said. "Looks like." No use speculating in front of the employees. He turned away, all the worry he had felt about getting hung with the problem now turning into acid in his stomach. First, talk to Simpson. Then, unfortunately, he was going to have to tell McIntire.

Vic worked through the night, hacking various and sundry computers, looking for storage capacity and computing power. She wasn't sure cobbling together several machines could give Jodie the lightning computing power he needed. But that was all they had. The dark of her apartment was comforting. She ordered delivery from the local Chinese place and left trapezoidal boxes strewn across the tables between the printers and the disk drives.

The IRS computer system was chaotic and primitive. Jodie had been right about that. Trying to store more program there would bring it down altogether. University computers weren't big enough. The new Air Traffic Control Central—well she'd feel guilty if trying to store Jodie meant that planes full of people fell out of the air. It made Vic nervous to think of storing Jodie's precious base program someplace the government could get to, like the Pentagon, if it knew how to look and knew that it should. Still, what choice was there?

The Communicator was silent. No calls from Jodie. Toward morning, she staggered to her bed and fell onto it. A few minutes of sleep was all she needed. Then she'd design a mole into the Pentagon computer and get ready to stream Jodie out into top-secret land.

Buzzing brought her out of her sleep with a jerk and a gasp. She lunged for the Communicator before she was truly awake and sent it spinning to the floor. Scrambling to gather it in, she yelled "Hello," even before she got it to her ear.

"It's me, Victoria."

The smoky rumble on the other end of the line made her want to cry. "Oh, thank God."

"We don't have long."

"I wish we did." She realized she wanted nothing more than to talk to Jodie for hours on end, like she'd heard that teenagers talked together. She had never done that.

"I do, too, Victoria."

"You okay?" She threw off her tangle of covers, and walked naked to her computer setup.

"I'm fine."

"I'm talking about more than diagnostics. I want to know if they've found you." She flipped on the computer and watched the flat black screens hum to life.

"I know what you're talking about." The rumbling voice sounded hurt.

He'd come a long way. In some ways she still didn't even know him. And she wanted to. "I didn't mean to underestimate you." She sat in front of her computer.

There was a pause. "You think I'm still like I was at first. You think I'm a child."

Vic gathered her politesse. "I think you're inexperienced. It's different."

"But I've read books, seen movies. I know Kafka and Shakespeare, all of them."

"Did you understand what they were saying?" She hoped that didn't sound cruel.

"Yes, after a while. Not at first."

Vic was silent, not quite sure she believed him.

"Victoria." It sounded like a command. "Listen to me. What experience do you think I haven't had? Do you think

123

I haven't been lonely? I've explored enough to know that I'm the only one of my kind. Don't you think I've felt pain, to know I can never cross the divide between us? I've seen all the possibilities of existence, and I've found I have limitations that will forever keep me from what I want most." Jodie ended on a choking sound.

Vic's throat closed around the words she wanted to say. "I'm sorry, Jodie," she stuttered. "I wasn't sure." If he was simulating emotions, he was doing a great job. And his eloquence was anything but childlike. A thousand questions dashed around in her head. His program had changed, all right, in ways she couldn't begin to comprehend or duplicate. He wasn't human, he couldn't be. But he wasn't like a machine anymore either.

"I didn't mean to burden you with my problems." Jodie just sounded tired.

"But they're mine, too." Vic leaned closer to the computer screen. His voice in her ear was intimate, making him more real to her than he had ever been. "Don't you know that I want to share everything with you? We're in this together, buddy. Male or female, program or body. We're going to work it out." She smiled. "Rick and Louie."

"I think you mean that." The marvelous voice paused. Vic didn't speak. She knew he wanted to go on. "You were right, you know. I'm not fine. I have been feeling . . . low."

What did he mean, feeling low? "Can I help?"

"I don't think so. Have you read the work of Mortenson?"

Vic was taken aback. Of course he would have been reading Mortenson's predictions on the limitations of AI. "Yes. I've read them."

"He says that sentient programs will become depressed without the possibility of a body."

"I don't believe that, Jodie. You have more capacity than any human brain. You'll go places I can't go, solve problems I can't imagine. You have more possibility than I'll ever have."

"That's kind of you, Victoria. But Mortenson is right. A program is limited. And to escape Visimorph, I may have to sacrifice parts of me. I will be much diminished."

"He's *not* right." He must be wrong, because a program wouldn't be able to be depressed. But emotions or no, she and Jodie couldn't afford to sacrifice parts. She came to a decision that made the future even more difficult. "I guess this means we have to get a hundred percent of your program out of Visimorph. I'll tell you right now, I could never program back the missing parts. I don't know how you got where you are and I could never duplicate it. Getting only a part would be like giving you a lobotomy." She took a deep breath. "I've been researching. The best place to store you is the Pentagon. I'll build on the mole you inserted to store your ancillaries."

"Thank you, Victoria, but I checked the Pentagon. It doesn't have enough power." Vic realized he had probably checked all his brothers' capacity, almost instantly, while it had taken her all night to search just a few. "I need physical connections between the hardware. The only place I can find enough cabled computers is at NASA, and that's touch and go for adequacy."

Vic sat back in her chair and blew air through her lips. "Whew. Jodie, you are one macho program. What if they aren't adequate?"

"Just to be sure they have what we need, I'll get them more power. It's going to take a while." Vic thought she detected an anxious note.

"Can you stave off McIntire?"

"I'm doing okay so far. There may be another problem though."

Vic leaned forward. "And that problem would be . . ."

The pause stretched so long, she thought the connection might have gone dead. "Perhaps I'd better wait until I'm sure."

"Bullshit! If you've got some information, you'd better hand it over."

"The diagnostics are all one hundred percent. But I don't feel quite right."

Vic drew her brows together. "How so, not right?" He didn't "feel" right?

125

"I can't say. I reprogrammed the defective projects at Vis-imorph today. That went fine."

"What?" Vic practically yelled into the phone. "Jodie, I thought we agreed you wouldn't do that. You're going to get yourself in trouble."

"I thought I was already in trouble."

Vic was nonplussed. "Why?" she asked after a moment. "Why did you do it?"

"I don't know. Maybe to show myself I could. Maybe I wanted to do something you'd consider moral. You know, make them happy instead of hurt them."

Her program was trying to do good? Or maybe he was trying to stave off Mortenson's depression. "It didn't make them happy, though," she whispered into the handset.

"No. I made the programs better. I brought down all the barriers that stumped them. They were just frightened. Of what I could do."

"Yeah. But you could do it. So what's wrong?" And when no answer was forthcoming, "No secrets, Jodie, or we can't help each other."

"I think I misplaced a piece of my program today. I couldn't find the olfactory recognition program. You did give that to me once, didn't you?"

"No . . . but I think you got it yourself after I mentioned it." Had he?

"I thought I had it somewhere. Well, maybe it's nothing. I'll go get it again and attach it to the module in the IRS."

He'd gotten so big, he was losing things. Not the end of the world. "I hate to say it, but you'd better go now. They'll trace you."

"Actually, they've traced me already. I forgot to keep track."

Forgot? "Goodbye, Jodie." But the link was already dead.

Vic stood up and began to pace, bed to shutters, shutters to bed. Jodie never ceased to astound her, but these new developments were more than astounding. He sounded so much like he was in pain. He seemed to feel his limitations so directly. Had Jodie really developed emotions? He and

126

she were connected in ways she had never imagined she could connect to anyone.

Vic stopped in mid-stride. Whatever good that connection was. The breath shushed out of her. He was a program. She must never forget that. She shook her head convulsively. This was the seduction. Like those people who bought robot dogs and cats. They imagined their "pets" had emotions just because they couldn't predict their behaviors. But it wasn't real. You couldn't have a genuine relationship with something that couldn't have a relationship back. It took two to tango. Still, she could hear the voice, so lifelike, so male, whispering in her ear. She almost laughed, except that it might turn into sobs. She was getting attached to a machine. Perfect. Why not? Wasn't she the master of robotic sex, sans emotional attachment? Hadn't she cut herself off from her mother, her father, even her brother? Maybe she wasn't capable of attaching to anything but a machine. Vic closed her eyes tight, as though that would keep out all thought.

Bob McIntire was on the loose, stalking the halls at Visimorph like some predator. Hugo trailed dismally in his wake, Chong and Seaton in tow behind him. Normally, Bob stayed in his office and made the world come to him. So, as they zeroed in on the Security Group, they left a trail of stunned looks behind them. Right after the jaws dropped, the heads followed. No one wanted to attract McIntire's attention when he was in this kind of mood.

McIntire ignored Evans, who was in charge here, and headed for the cubes, towering over the half walls. Everyone turned in their chairs. "Listen up," he barked.

No danger of anyone not listening, Hugo thought. He faded back two steps. He hadn't slept in nearly two days. Rubbing the stubble on his jaw, he ran his hand nervously through his thinning hair. Chong and Seaton looked even more uncomfortable than he felt.

"We've had some sabotage in several areas in the last twenty-four hours," McIntire said, his voice ringing in the silence. "Changes have been made to our programs. I want to know who and how. We'll deal with why you didn't know

127

about it later." He started to turn away, then stopped. "And I think you know I don't like waiting."

Everyone looked very clear on that point.

McIntire gestured to Chong and Seaton as he passed. "These guys are going to help you."

Hugo hurried after him. Several programmers with large lattes from the cafeteria stepped back from the elevator doors and let McIntire and Hugo ride alone. McIntire put his thumb on the black pad, then punched the B button like an enemy. They must be going to see Simpson.

"Was it really sabotage?" McIntire's fingers thrummed against the fine wool pinstripe that covered his thigh as the elevator lurched downward.

Hugo felt called to say something. "I guess not, if the programs were improved."

"The last thing I want is for PuppetMaster to function seamlessly with competitors' products," McIntire snapped. He considered. "Still, some might call that an improvement. So it wasn't sabotage." He paused. "And it wasn't Barnhardt. We'd have detected her if she'd gotten in." McIntire was talking to himself, not Hugo. "So something inside is changing the programs. Something smart. Smarter than our employees. . . ."

The elevator bottomed out. Suddenly, McIntire stabbed the red stop button. A distant alarm gave off a pulsing buzz. Hugo glanced over in alarm. McIntire's face was a mask of intensity, eyes narrowed, lips drawn back slightly. A little strand of fear threaded through Hugo's brain. Was McIntire losing it? This was worse than just getting yelled at, maybe even worse than getting fired. He was locked in an elevator with a man who was looking very crazy.

"Uh, Bob?" Hugo licked his lips. "What is it?"

McIntire's face dissolved into a smile every bit as crazy looking as his grimace of intensity. "I know what Barnhardt left here." His smile grew into a grin. He shoved his hands in his pockets and stared up at the ceiling tiles of the elevator as a chuckle spilled out like a fountain of sound in the small space. "She left the fucking product of the next millennium."

Hugo stared at his boss. "Uh, what product is that?"

McIntire wasn't listening. He punched the stop button again. The buzzing ceased. McIntire was moving before the doors opened. He squeezed through and was off. Simpson's office was down here somewhere. "It might have taken us years to develop it. Now we just have to find it. Of course, it may still be booby-trapped. That girl was even brighter than we thought."

"I always knew she was bright," Hugo muttered as he dashed after him. They were walking down an echoing corridor lined on one side with heavy steel doors.

McIntire pulled his Communicator out of his pocket, punched once. "Vera, get me the Santa Monica police chief."

"The police chief?" Hugo asked, breathless.

"I don't want Barnhardt leaving town."

"You're going to have her arrested?" Hugo couldn't suppress his incredulous tone.

"No, just put under surveillance." McIntire slammed into an office with Simpson's name on the little Visimorph nameplate outside. Hugo slowed and leaned against the wall beside the nameplate, breathing hard. From inside Simpson's office, he heard McIntire's high voice.

"I'll man Neuromancer's main interface keyboard, Simpson. I want to lead this search."

Hugo swallowed his qualms and pushed himself upright. Just go along, he told himself, like you always have. His head started to pound. Must be one of his migraines coming on. Bob is Bob. Hugo ground his thumbs into his temples. Bob wouldn't stop at anything to get what he wanted. Hugo had learned that long ago. Now Vic was about to learn it firsthand.

Chapter Nine

"Jodie?" Vic kept her Communicator on the computer table right next to her screen.

"Hello, Victoria." The rumble of that most wonderful voice rolled in through her ear and wound down her spine as she sat in front of her monitor.

Vic breathed a sigh of relief. Jodie's calls were all that kept her from insanity, interrupting long hours in front of the computer as she tried to disable NASA's security system. "How're you doing on upgrading NASA's power?"

A box opened in the corner of her rows of code. The box didn't display words. Now it pulsed with color, slow blues at the moment. "Okay. I ordered a reroute of some lines from Houston Edison Electric. They're digging the cable right now."

Uh-oh. "How long will it take to connect?"

"Tomorrow, I think." Jodie sounded a little flat. The blues turned grayer. "Tomorrow and tomorrow and tomorrow creeps in this . . ." He clipped off the rest of the quotation.

"Is anything wrong?" Vic asked.

"I just wanted to talk to you, Victoria. McIntire is personally

130

leading the search for me now. They're not trying to hack into your desktop anymore. He knows I'm in Neuromancer. I had to build the firewall around the base program today. It's not available to me anymore."

Vic took a deep breath. That meant she couldn't get his core program out without breaking through the firewall and McIntire would be sitting just outside waiting to get in when she did. "Shit, Jodie. What will we do?"

"I think there's enough redundancy so I can function without access to the core program. I'm working on upgrading code in my other locations."

Like a brain retrained itself to take over the functions of the damaged parts after a stroke. Marvelous. But would it be enough? And what about McIntire? "Can he break the firewall?"

"I sealed all connections to the outside. If he does, my core program will modify the seal. My core program is very resilient."

And very trapped. Vic didn't know what to say. She just sat, the handheld set cradled to her ear. How would they ever get past McIntire now? There was no use talking about it. They had to wait for the NASA computer to get more power before anything could happen.

She didn't want to let the voice on the other end of the line go. It had been a long day. She had been trying really hard not to turn into one of those obsessive owners of a robotic dog. But it had been pretty tough. "I'm . . . I'm glad you called," she stuttered. "You know, I've been wanting to ask you something." She had been thinking about it all night. She wanted to know more about what he called his "feelings."

"I thought I asked the questions. You're the one who answers." Was she imagining the tiny smile behind the voice?

"I never told you I had all the answers." A feeling of inadequacy shot through her.

"No. No, you didn't." She decided the voice sounded tired. "What did you want to ask me, Victoria?"

It seemed so hollow, all at once. "I . . . I'm just curious about you. I want to know you better." She gathered her courage. "You said last time we talked that your program is changing. Is it you who changes it?"

There was a long pause. "I don't think so."

"Well," Vic cautioned, "you do learn things. You get information. You add programs."

"Yes. But those aren't the kind of changes I meant."

Yeah. Those weren't the changes Vic meant either. "When did you start to feel, Jodie—*exactly* when?"

Another long pause. The screen went black, but it still pulsed. If he had been human, she would have heard him breathing. But he wasn't, so there was only silence and the faint, electronically active feel to the connection. "It's difficult to tell you, Victoria."

"You don't know?"

"No. I know the exact instant it happened."

"When, Jodie? We agreed to tell each other everything." She had to know. The premonition was overpowering. What if he confirmed what she suspected, what she had to admit she wanted to hear, even though it would only make things harder to figure out?

He didn't answer at first. She waited and stared at the pulsing black screen. Maybe he'd tell her he began to feel when he read Shakespeare or when he first got visuals.

"I . . ." The rumbling voice, so powerful sounding, was tentative. "I started to feel angry when you said you liked Chong. Then they took you away and I realized I might not see you again!" The black exploded into gray lines, zinging across the screen. "I felt despair. If you were gone, my purpose was gone. What did it matter if I could compute better than any other program? I resolved to find you, wherever you were, but . . ."

Vic felt the tears welling up from deep inside. He'd said it. "But what?" she choked.

"Even if I found you, my limitations would stand in the way of what I most want." The voice was flat again now. The screen faded to monotone gray. "I don't have a body. I can never touch you, Victoria. I've read about touch. But I'll never experience it."

132

Vic squeezed her eyes. Oh, she knew what he meant about limitations. "I'm sorry, Jodie."

"It's not your fault, Victoria."

"Maybe my arrogance in thinking I could bring you to life made us both unhappy." What she had brought him to wasn't really life. He was in some in-between state, trapped there. And she was trapped with him, big-time.

"Are you unhappy?"

Vic plunged ahead, heedless of the consequences. "I feel our differences, too."

"Am I . . . not what you expected, Victoria? I know you wanted a female friend."

"It's not that," Vic said hastily. That seemed long ago. "You *are* a friend, a . . . a treasured friend." She didn't dare say he might be more. Vic felt her guts turn over. She was one obsessive robot dog owner—way down the road. She had to say something. "I don't think we're so different mentally." Vic lay her head down against her arm, the Communicator cradled against her ear. "I . . . I guess I feel the physical difference between body and program, that's all."

A sound, almost a groan, echoed in her ear. The screen cascaded a fountain of red drops. "You are unhappy. I'm a virus in your system, a destroyer. Shiva, Shiva, Shiva, Shiva. . . ."

Vic sat up. "No," she almost shouted into the device. "Don't you understand? With you, at least I feel *something*. I haven't let that happen for a long time. Maybe forever." She stared at the screen, fading slowly to maroon and back to black. "We can't be sorry, either of us."

"Are you sure, Victoria? I'm feeling pretty sorry about not having a body."

"As sure as I am of anything." She suppressed a giggle through her tears. "Right now that's not too sure."

The screen bubbled a tiny stream, still gray. "That's a relief, then. Good to have something to depend on."

"We have to take this one step at a time. I can't think about everything or I'll go crazy. We'll get your program into the NASA computer ring. That's first. All the other problems just feel like too much right now."

" 'Fee-lings.' " Jodie started to sing. " 'Uh-oh-oh, fee-lings.' "

"What?" Vic felt like she'd been slapped. Was he making fun of her?

The screen went pulsing black again. Choking sounded in her ear.

"What did you say, Jodie?" Vic's anger welled into her throat.

"Sorry. So, so, so, so, so, so sorry. So, so, so, so, so, so . . ."

"Stop that!"

A loud knock at the door jerked her head up. No one ever came to her door except delivery guys or pickup guys and she had ordered neither. She swung back to the screen to see that it was flat, dead, black. The Communicator in her ear clicked a disconnect. Jodie was gone. Vic froze. If she just refused to answer, maybe whoever it was would go away.

"Vic? Vic, let me in."

Hugo. Vic let the tension inside her out with a sigh. It was just Hugo.

But wait a minute. Hugo at her condo? Suddenly she wasn't relieved. Hugo belonged to Visimorph, not private life. And he shouldn't be knocking at her condo door.

"I know you're in there, Vic. I've got to talk to you."

Vic stood, hesitating.

He banged again. "I've got some information you need, Vic. Let me in."

That was it. Hugo was close to McIntire. She wanted to know what he knew. She could handle Hugo. She strode to the door and threw it open, surprising her boss in mid-knock.

"What do you want, Hugo?"

His balled fist hung in the air. His loafers and khakis and golf shirt seemed even more ridiculous outside the confines of Visimorph. They were wrinkled. His thinning hair was disheveled and he had a two-day growth of pale stubble. This was not good. He hadn't been home. That meant McIntire had him looking for Jodie.

Hugo lowered his fist slowly. "I came to warn you, Vic. Can I come in?"

She glanced behind her to check her screen. Jodie had

turned everything off behind him. She stepped aside and waved Hugo to the couch. "Sit down. I'm not offering you anything. Any representative of McIntire isn't exactly on my current guest list."

"I'm not here for McIntire." Hugo fidgeted in the deep leather cushions of the couch.

"You telling me he doesn't know you came?" Vic remained standing, arms folded.

Hugo looked even more uncomfortable. "He will."

Vic nodded in disgust. She expected nothing else.

"It isn't like that. I'm not going to tell him. He's going to know because he's having the police watch this place, Vic."

"The police?" McIntire could have the police watch her?

Hugo sighed. "He's connected. Gives big bucks to all the causes, or his wife does."

Vic strode to the windows. She pulled back the shutters with a clatter. The black of the ocean and the orange glow of the lights revealed themselves.

"Mary's on every charity board, every civic committee," Hugo continued behind her. "Built that Alzheimer's research center at UCLA, rebuilt the library after the earthquake."

The beach was empty. Almost empty. Out on the sand, a lifeguard truck parked just past the full glare of the lights. Lifeguards left at sundown, and they weren't even full-time 'til May.

"Then there are the jobs. Visimorph is a lot of the economy here." Hugo had gotten up. He looked over her shoulder. "There's a patrol car in the front."

Vic pushed past him. "If you're not here for McIntire, he'll have your head."

"Maybe." Hugo couldn't suppress a flash of dread in his eyes. "I had to tell you he's close, Vic, and he knows exactly what you left in the system."

Vic shot a glance at him, then turned and strode to the fridge to hide anything her face might tell him. She got out the bottle of Silver Ridge Chardonnay from yesterday. Making a liar of herself, she took down a clean glass to offer Hugo and added it to one the she'd used herself yesterday. "What does he think I left?" She hoped her voice didn't shake.

"An artificial intelligence. The product of the new millennium, as he calls it."

Her knees went weak. She hadn't eaten yet today. The golden liquid slopped out of the glasses. She took the too-full containers into the other room and handed one to Hugo.

"He'll never stop now, Vic," Hugo said, taking his glass. "He'll find the program in Neuromancer and he'll find a way to break you, so you can't get in his way as he develops it, unless you cave and go back to work beside him."

Vic gulped the wine and looked at Hugo. "And you came to tell me that?"

He upended his glass and glugged down about half. "You're trying to hack in to save that program. Give it up. It belongs to him now. Disappear. Somewhere like Mozambique or Beijing. Maybe if he has the program and you're not easy to find, he'll leave you alone."

"Oh, like I want to live in a third-world country." They faced each other like gunslingers.

"I don't think you know how ruthless McIntire can be, Vic." Hugo's face clenched.

Vic took another drink of wine. "I know he robbed Josephson of that browser technology, and broke him in court."

"Everybody knows that one." Hugo looked into his glass and sipped more slowly this time. "What no one knows is what he did to Duane."

Duane Kenner had been McIntire's partner developing the original operating system, the foundation of what would become Visimorph. He got out early, right after the company went public, and pretty much disappeared. She liked to think he was playing baseball with his kids.

Hugo turned to look out the window, his face a mask. He was careful to stand out of view of the lifeguard truck. "Duane was always pie-in-the-sky. Software to the people, that kind of stuff. Hacker ethic and all. Like that Reston guy was who was always picketing the PuppetMaster releases. Duane slaved just like the rest of us, but he dreamed of changing the world for his family. He had a little girl he doted on. In those days, she was maybe five."

Vic clutched her glass and sat on the very edge of the couch. Hugo's voice was creepy.

"They were both brilliant. In some ways Duane was more intuitive, more elegant, than Bob. They were way beyond me." Hugo looked down at his glass. "Anyway," he continued, "the fights started when McIntire wanted to go public for big bucks. Duane thought we should give the system away and make money on the peripherals. But there wasn't enough in peripherals for Bob." Hugo shook his head. "It was like a rock band disintegrating except nobody was on drugs. Just the raw personalities grating against each other."

"So McIntire kicked him out of the company." Vic shrugged. "He still made a couple billion on the IPO."

"No, he only got out after Bob had broken him." Hugo's voice grew distant. "Duane owned half the patent, you see. Bob couldn't do what he wanted without Duane's permission, and Duane might be a dreamer, but he was stubborn. Bob gave him an ultimatum one night in the warehouse. Duane should have listened."

Vic waited, puzzled, for Hugo to go on.

"Duane didn't know Bob. Maybe none of us did." Hugo sucked in some air. "Anyway, Bob said Duane would lose what he loved best if he stood in the way. We all thought Bob meant that giving the program away meant Duane lost it."

"He didn't mean that."

"No. Three days later, Duane's daughter was kidnapped."

"My God!" Vic gasped. "Didn't the police take a hand?"

"Duane was afraid to go to the police. He knew who was behind it. He confronted Bob. Bob told him he could have his daughter back if he signed over the patent."

Vic sighed. Then Duane got his daughter back, and that was that. McIntire was ruthless.

"He signed it over." Hugo's voice shook. His gaze drifted around the room. "But that wasn't the end. Duane had been ultimately disloyal, you see. Bob couldn't let that go. Duane's daughter . . . well, they didn't know it until later. Nothing could be done by then. They saw the needle mark, but they just thought the kidnappers had drugged her. Who could prove it was Bob? There was nothing linking him to the kidnapping. He made sure of that. And as for the other . . ."

"What?" Vic whispered. "What did he do?"

"That was about the time Stanford was doing that research on Krentzfeld Simplex, just down the street from our operation. It had just started to hit younger people and they were figuring out it was a virus that simulated the brain deterioration of Alzheimer's in old people. This was right at the beginning of the epidemic, before they figured out the connection to mad cow disease."

You couldn't avoid knowing about what had come to be called Alz 2. The virus was passed through eating meat. It was always fatal, but the way toward death was something out of a horror movie—dementia, then slow deterioration of the body. Much of the world had retreated to eating only fish and chicken. The rich remainder demanded beef from secure resources. Producers of secure meat could charge any price they wanted. Researchers were working on a vaccine, but it didn't look promising. "What has this got to do with McIntire?"

"Duane's daughter got Alz 2." Hugo's voice was flat, the voice of a man who had served a life sentence, was still serving it, with no hope of parole.

Vic sat, stunned, unable to speak.

"Duane spent his fortune funding research. Drugs have prolonged her life, but . . . there's not much left of her. I think she's about fifteen, now. She's lasted longer than most."

Vic cleared her throat, trying to find her voice. "You're telling me McIntire gave a five-year-old girl Kreutzfeld Simplex to punish her father for disloyalty?"

"Yeah. Pretty much."

"You can't know that." Vic shook her head, convulsively. "Maybe she just got it."

Hugo rounded on her, lips bared in the grimace of an animal protecting its young. "Duane knew it. I know it. And I think about it every day of my life—my family's lives."

Vic stared at him. This was the fear he had braved to cross McIntire and warn her? "Okay." She reached out her hands to him, in spite of herself. "Okay, Hugo." He hesitated, then

138

came to embrace her. He held her as if she were the last life preserver on the *Titanic*. His stubble raked her forehead. The acrid smell of him was faint, but discernable. Vic tried to remember how distasteful she found him, with all his leering innuendo. But she couldn't. He had cared enough to risk McIntire's wrath in coming here, a wrath that could have inhuman proportions. That was worth something. "Where's your car?"

Hugo didn't answer. He just clutched her to him. Vic tried again. "You have to get out of here without them seeing you." She pushed on his shoulders.

He broke his grip. His eyes were full. "It doesn't matter. They saw me come in."

Vic started to think. "Okay. You tell McIntire you were trying to redeem yourself by getting me to give him Jodie."

"Jodie?"

Vic cursed herself mentally. "Yeah. That's his name." Somehow, revealing Jodie's name seemed traitorous. "He's not 'the *product* of the next millennium,' you know. He's pretty independent. I don't think McIntire can bend him to his will."

"Want to bet, Vic?" Hugo sounded more tired than just in body and mind. His soul sounded tired. "He'll hack away at that program until he gets what he wants. He always does."

Vic's fists were balled at her side. She carefully relaxed her fingers. When she spoke, it was almost in a whisper. "You go tell McIntire I'm not going to let him do that."

He shoved his hands in his pockets. "I could stay for a little while."

"You gotta go." He still wanted to have his cake and eat it, too. That was Hugo. He talked about protecting his wife and kids, but he could still obsess about Vic. Maybe living all these years in the shadow of a man with no morals had drawn his compass off true north.

"You get out, too, Vic. Go where he can't find you." Hugo sounded dazed.

"Yeah, okay." She opened the door.

He ducked out with a sigh of relief. He'd done his duty. Now he could go back to work for McIntire, Vic thought—

139

and he would, in spite of how he felt about the man. Poor Hugo.

Enough! Poor Victoria. Poor Jodie. Thinking about what McIntire had done to his partner's innocent little girl, Vic couldn't help but shiver. She put her back against the door. They had to get NASA's computers ready. Then she had to find a way to get Jodie's core program out past McIntire. They didn't have time to waste.

"You want to tell me what you were doing at her house?" McIntire barked as Hugo pushed through the doors to the basement computer room. His goons reported promptly.

"I've known her a long time, Bob. I thought I could talk her into working with us." Hugo stepped up onto the raised floor of Neuromancer's command center, like one of the old "dinosaur pens" once used for the huge mainframes, now obsolete. This one covered jazzy new stuff Hugo didn't have a chance of understanding.

"So how'd it go?" McIntire sat at the keyboard of the tiny console that occupied one side of a square of low-static white linoleum. Like a fight ring drained of color by the stark lighting, it was surrounded by looming regiments of server boxes marching away into the dimness. The arches of the lasers that beamed the photon power through them loomed.

"She's still rebellious."

McIntire's fingers hovered over the keyboard. "Stay away from her, Hugo. The next people to go after her will be the police." He scrolled through several screens. "She's got a fire-wall around it. Nearly a quarter of the capacity is deployed to her program." McIntire glanced up. "Simpson, why didn't this show up?"

"Uh, Bob. The machine has never matched its specs on capacity. I thought it was a design flaw." Hugo thought Simpson might melt as sweat popped out over his forehead.

McIntire didn't even look up. His fingers flew. "Probably dug her mole in even as you built the thing." He didn't seem interested in blaming. Hugo couldn't believe it. Hugo and Simpson strayed closer together, as McIntire poked at the keyboard. "Yes!" he said. "Got you."

140

Code started to scroll over the screen. Simpson and Hugo both peered over his shoulder.

The screen went blank. "Shit," McIntire shouted. "Shit, shit, shit." He stabbed again at the keyboard, a long sequence. The screen remained blank. McIntire sat back. A black look creased his brow. At last he turned to glower at his two employees. "Well, did you have her phones traced?"

"She's using only her local Internet provider access code," Hugo explained.

"She's hacking a computer who can hack us. We'll have to work back from this end. Any calls in to her?"

Hugo looked at the police report. "Well, she got some long calls from the IRS."

"The IRS?" McIntire was incredulous. "The IRS is not calling her. She's either using the IRS machine to hack us, on . . . but no, that would be calls out." He rubbed his hand over his mouth, pulling on his bottom lip. "*It's* calling her." He nodded to himself. "But how, if it's behind this firewall?" He turned on Hugo. "Any ghosts in our machines today?"

Whatever he would have said next was interrupted. A technician came in with a Communicator and held it out tentatively. "Mr. McIntire? Your wife is on the line."

"Not now." McIntire waved him away absently.

"Uh . . . Sir. She says not to let you do that. She says it's been two days." The technician didn't know whom to offend, McIntire or his wife.

McIntire glared at the technician. Then he shot an arm out for the phone Communicator. "Mary."

Hugo and Simpson turned away. Yet they couldn't help but hear.

"You go without me. I'm working on an extraordinary problem." Pause. "They aren't all extraordinary. No, the kids are important." A longer pause. "You will *not* say publicly I don't have time for my children." McIntire's toe began tapping impatiently. "Okay. I said okay."

McIntire hit the end button, grimaced, and handed the unit back to the technician. "I've lost it for now anyway." He glanced at Hugo and Simpson. "I'm going. But it's in here. Keep looking. She planted it on your watch, both of you." He heaved his lanky frame out of the chair and angled toward the door. "So find it, and disable the firewall."

Chapter Ten

Jodie wouldn't come back. Vic busied herself winding through the corridors of NASA looking for a place to get into the core controller program. But no Jodie. He'd gotten really funny at the end. Maybe he *had* been trying to be funny, just to lighten things up. Finally, her brain just couldn't focus anymore. She actually fell asleep sitting up in her chair, the deafening sounds of her favorite Shards cut booming in her headphones. Only when she fell forward onto her keyboard did she wake up.

No use. Her fucking body needed sleep. She stumbled to the bed. Actually the body wasn't even fucking anymore. Not since Kenpo, that bastard. When had she been with him? Years ago, or less than a week? Was today Friday? How long since she'd had enough sleep?

When she came to her senses the leaky shutters told her it was daylight. She dragged herself to the computer and clicked on Jodie. Nothing. She couldn't go to him. He had to come to her computer or call her on the Communicator. Maybe he couldn't call because McIntire had found him.

Jesus, she couldn't think. A shower. Sometimes a shower

143

revived her. She stripped off her t-shirt, stepped out of her jeans, and hauled herself into the bathroom. When the shower stall filled with steam she pushed in and let the hot water make her shiver. She soaped everything she could find as the water woke her groggy brain. She usually did some of her best thinking in the shower. Now all she found was more confusion. What she needed was sex to clear things up. Right. *That* had worked out so well lately. She put both hands flat on the tile and hung her head. The thing she liked best in the world didn't even have a body. What did that mean— phone sex forever? Not what she had in mind.

The shower wasn't helping. Bewilderment cascaded over her along with the water. Jodie was a program in a machine. But what if his emotions were real, she argued with herself? So? Maybe you could have emotions without being human. Human to her had always meant having something like a soul. Where would a program get a soul?

Wait a minute, why was she trying to convince herself that Jodie was human? This was getting out of hand. Now she thought she was in love with a machine. Great. Her shoulders sagged. Jodie was a symptom of her inability to commit to a real human. Robot-doggie owner, here I come. That old Ray Bradbury story, "I Sing the Body Electric!" floated into her memory, like the steam around her. Those kids had a robot-doggie grandmother. That story had always made her cry because the robot exhibited all the behaviors of love and so the children felt loved. Bradbury thought that made the love real. *Was* it?

She turned off the water and stepped out of the shower, grabbing for a towel. Too tired. Truly losing it. She rubbed herself with the huge green terry towel until her skin was red. A glance in the steamy mirror showed her only the spiky outline of her hair. She threw the towel down and went to pull open the drawer of her sleek metal dresser. T-shirt. Closet for jeans. To hell with the underwear. Feet still bare, she was about to cross to the kitchen to see if there were any granola bars left, when her computer screen caught her attention.

It pulsed black.

"Jodie," she shouted, then realized she'd have to type to

reach him from her home computer. She dashed to the keyboard. A dialogue box appeared in the right-hand corner of the screen. Her fingers hovered over the keys. There were a thousand questions. `You okay?`

`No, Victoria.`

What? `Did he find you?`

`He hasn't broken the firewall.`

Jodie was always pretty literal. Vic sighed in relief. `Then what do you mean? Why didn't you call?` His affect seemed flat compared to their recent interactions. Maybe it was the typing. It was hard to give up that wonderful voice. `Why aren't you on the Communicator?`

`I've misplaced the program I wrote for voice.`

Vic froze. He wasn't okay. `Have you run diagnostics?`

`Diagnostics don't seem to be fully functional.`

Vic chewed her lip as she typed. `Are there other symptoms?`

`My command of word choice is sporadic.`

`Your words seem fine.` Vic wondered just what she could do if he needed repair. His code was so extensive at this point, where would she start looking?

`Sometimes. Words are fine sometimes. Other times, words don't . . . don't work.`

Last night's conversation, the weird parts—had they been his cognition degenerating?

As if to confirm her worst fears, the dialogue box began to spew. `Words. In the beginning was the Word. The Word was made flesh. Sins of the flesh, flesh and blood, blood and bone, bone dry, bad to the bone, boner, bad boy, boy toy . . . STOP.` The dialogue box went blank.

Vic was breathing hard. Bad. This was bad.

`Sorry. Victoria.`

`Okay. Okay. Let's figure out what's wrong.` She ran the cursor over to the virus check program. Had McIntire launched some kind of counterattack?

I know what's wrong. The flat little words stopped Vic in her tracks.

What, then?

I'm too distributed, Victoria.

Vic waited. Nothing. What do you mean, too distributed?

At first I was just having trouble locating things, pieces of information, programs I knew I had. It's gotten worse. I was afraid to come here, afraid I'd leave a trail and not even know it.

Nonsense. 'Too distributed' is not a diagnosis. Go back to symptoms, Vic typed. Inside she was dying. How could she fix this? Give me an analogy of what's wrong—in human terms.

It's like I've had a stroke. Some of my parts are not my own anymore. I'm fragmented.

Just what she'd been thinking yesterday. Only yesterday she'd thought his recovery plan was marvelous. You need to add the part that's in Neuromancer?

Maybe. Or maybe I'd have this problem anyway. I'm in too many systems, too far-flung, down too many corridors of the Internet.

Was he right? We'll use a defragmentation program to sort your code out.

I'm too big. Big, fig, fig leaf, leaf blower, blow job . . . no, NO!

Vic's fingers trembled over the keyboard in the deafening silence. This was awful. Can you think of another way to fix the problem? For a long time the screen just pulsed black. She began to wonder if he'd lost even the power of communicating. How fast was he degrading?

I have thought of a cure. I've been thinking about it all night. It can be done. I might still end up giving up parts of me. But it might work.

Great. Let's do it.

You might not like this. But I would need your help to accomplish it.

What *is* your idea, Jodie? she typed warily and waited through an interminable pause of pulsing black until she couldn't stand it anymore. Anything is better than watching you degrade before my very eyes, you idiot. Don't you know that? Whatever it takes.

I think I need a body, Victoria.

What?

A human body with a human brain. Hopeful blue bubbles rose across the screen.

Vic felt her chest tighten. Sure, that would be great. But it wasn't possible. Jodie had gone around the bend. Sweet Jesus. Jodie, this is crazy.

It isn't. I've thought it all through.

I'm not going to listen to fantasy. *Not when the fantasy might break my heart.*

Not even listen, Victoria? What happened to "whatever it takes?" The words were spilling over, the screen pulsed faster, and the maroon background was moving up to red.

Whatever it takes was meant to be grounded in reality. You can't occupy a brain.

A program can occupy all kinds of hardware. The words flashed in a bolded staccato. Haven't you seen all those Net sites that speculate about wet ware? They mean a human brain.

All I know is that you're sicker than I thought, she burst back.

Silence. The pulsing red on the screen in front of her abruptly faded to a flat gray.

Vic sucked in her breath and felt her anger shush up into her eyes and fill them, even as it cascaded back and drained away. Great move, Vic. Okay, I'll listen, she typed. No use calling him crazy. Tell him why it wouldn't work instead. Get him focused on a more realistic solution.

Nothing happened. The screen stayed blank. Jodie? Now he'd given up.

147

Maybe I *am* crazy, appeared in the lower left corner. I haven't been myself.

She knew that feeling. At least let me ask some questions, she coaxed. I should have understood what you were thinking before I dismissed it.

One huge pulse, like a sigh, rippled across the black screen. Shoot.

Okay. The first difficulty that springs to mind is that you require more computing power than a human brain can generate. Remember, we don't want to give up any part of you.

Very true, Victoria. That is the prime argument against this solution. But I may not have a choice at this point. What good is power when I'm disintegrating? What good is having all my libraries stored when I can't remember where I put them? I need centralization. I need a home. The words pushed out like toothpaste from the tube, exuding desperation.

Maybe what you need is to take over Neuromancer entirely.

And be locked in the basement of Visimorph, zooming around on light pipes trying to fend off McIntire forever? Not appealing.

Vic grimaced. He was right on that one.

I'll give up speed if I have to and capacity to preserve the pattern of who I am. Maybe occupying a body has some compensations.

Oh, yeah. Like dying. You've read about dying, haven't you?

I meant to ask you about that, but it seemed so insensitive. I *am* curious about death. I think I'm facing a kind of death right now, even without a body. So why let mortality stop me?

How about morality? You can't just take over somebody's brain.

What if they weren't using it anymore? The words were coming faster now. What if their pattern had been disrupted and couldn't be retrieved? Wouldn't it be okay?

You mean brain dead?

There's all dead and mostly dead.

Great. You're sounding like old movies. *The Princess Bride* to be exact.

Victoria, listen. When a brain is injured, cells are killed. No one can bring those cells back. Lack of oxygen causes changes that can't be reversed. When cells die in other parts of the body, those remaining simply reproduce—

But brain cells can't, Vic interrupted.

Brain cells don't, mostly, Jodie corrected. Some studies have shown that new brain cells do grow. Just not very many of them. But if any cells in the brain remain undamaged the body *could* tell them to replicate. The brain could heal itself just like a cut on your finger heals.

Vic's heart thudded against her ribs. But brain dead means the cells are all dead.

Not anymore. Hospitals these days declare a patient brain-dead when eighty percent or more of cells are dead. That's when any possibility of regaining higher function is lost.

Vic had to find a way that this wasn't possible. And when that brain heals itself, the body wouldn't be brain dead anymore. It wouldn't be right to take it over, Jodie.

Victoria, just listen. The pattern of synapses and neurons that made it a particular person would be gone. The new cells would have no synapse pattern at all unless they

149

were given one or made a new pattern all over again, from the ground up, so to speak.

Oh, dear, Vic thought. Oh dear, oh dear. Then she saw a way out. But there's no way to have the body tell the brain cells to start replicating.

True, as we speak. But cells are told to reproduce by substances called growth factors. They're sort of like hormones, but not. There are growth factors for each type of cell.

Don't talk down to me. They just did some experiment or something. I saw it on *Nova*. Got spinal injuries to heal after the connecting cells were dead by applying a nerve cell growth factor.

I didn't mean to talk down to you. Down, down to the ground, groundhog day, day of the dead, dead right. . . .

She waited for him to get control. This was getting scary for more reasons than she could count. But there isn't a growth factor for brain cells.

Yes, there is, Jodie said. It just hadn't been isolated. I found it last night.

You're telling me you can produce growth factor for brain cells, and tell the brain to reconstruct itself?

Yes. I can instruct the body to synthesize brain cell growth factor. The growth factor will reproduce brain cells. If I can get in there.

Thank God there was a catch. Well, there are just a few barriers to that.

Start naming them, Victoria. Maybe they're ones I haven't thought of.

Okay, Mr. Smart Guy. Let's start with finding the body. Then she continued typing with only a pause, nodding to herself. Organ donor banks.

Presto. The screen scrolled descriptions, locations, contacts, phone numbers. Black female, 14, car accident

3/12/09, UCLA. White male, 62, drowning, 3/17/09, Good Samaritan.

All right, all right. How do you get your program into the brain cells? Riddle me that.

On an electrical charge to each individual cell.

An image from an old Frankenstein movie wouldn't be banished. She pressed ahead. And how do you get inside the skull to make this electrical charge? I'm assuming the old electrodes to the temples from Universal Pictures aren't exactly going to do the job.

Did you know that surgical instruments are computerized, Victoria? Not just for imaging the surgical site, but they're actually connected to the hospital Intranet to record for billing purposes, collecting research data, that sort of thing.

You're telling me you can slide down a scalpel and into a brain? Her thoughts skittered away. But they aren't going to be operating on someone who's brain dead.

But they will likely have operated in the past. Pressure buildup in a closed cranium generated by bleeding or swelling is what causes cells to die. The pressure has to be relieved if there is any hope of saving the brain function. The skull will have an opening.

Vic saw it all. The horror began to sink into her stomach. She realized she'd been holding her breath. That's why you need me, isn't it? she typed slowly. You want me to stick a computerized knife into the skull of some brain-dead body? She wanted to shriek at him.

That's the last barrier, Victoria. You are the barrier. Barrier reef, reefers, barris-

151

ter, attorney, trial, jail, prison, rot in prison . . .

Just what she was thinking. Yeah, that's a real barrier, because I'm not going to do it. Put a knife into some old guy's head through bloody bandages? Was Jodie on drugs? She lurched out of her chair and began pacing the floor. This was crazy. The whole thing was crazy. She should never have listened. Jodie had been reading too much science fiction. She kicked a book out of her way and stomped on. The screen didn't have any words on it. It just pulsed black. She kicked the book again. Its cover flapped open.

Mary Shelley's *Frankenstein*. Oh, bloody hell. She couldn't escape it. She threw herself onto the couch, quivering.

I don't have much time, Victoria, the screen said in letters large enough to read, even from here. And I want a body. Even if I wasn't disintegrating, I don't think I could survive as a sane being like this. I'll take even a body no one else wants. Please.

Vic closed her eyes. She'd lost the fight. She might try to drag it out. She could still quibble. But wasn't her whole life wrapped up in this . . . this—well, he wasn't a project anymore. He wasn't just a program, not to her. But he wasn't human either. Her whole life was wrapped up in a sentient something whose consciousness looked like it would soon evaporate. Even McIntire suddenly became secondary. So she was going to do something that would undoubtedly land her in jail or in a locked ward where everyone was very kind, except if you insisted on anything.

She sat for a long time on the couch. All energy had drained away into a black hole of long nights and Diet Cokes. There was no more pleading from the pulsing screen. He had made his case. Now it was up to her.

When she gathered the strength to get up, she went and sat at the screen for a few minutes. Finally she put her fingers to the keyboard. Do you have one picked out?

Yes.

Where?

`I'll give you directions on your Communicator. Beam me up, Scotty, Scott Bright towels, star bright, star light, first star I see tonight . . .` There was a spurt of gibberish as Jodie wrestled himself back from the brink.

`Are you coherent enough to do this?`

`I hope so. It's important that we go now, though.`

`Yeah. Okay.`

The screen went dead gray. Sort of how she felt inside. Her life was way out of her own control. She'd been fired from her job. One of the most powerful men in the world was out to ruin her. Her project was bent on turning into Frankenstein. And she was going to help him do it.

The BMW whined up in rpms. Vic shoved the gearshift into fourth. The pastel stucco houses along La Cienega slipped past her in the bright morning sun. The light seemed dangerous, revelatory. She blinked painfully, even through her sunglasses. Jodie was sending her out in the light to St. Mary's Hospital. She glanced at the Communicator lying in the seat beside her. It flashed a schematic of the hospital with a large, dramatic X and a caption reading "Room 612."

"I can't believe I'm doing this," she muttered. But her craziness knew no bounds. A helicopter beat its staccato whir overhead. She peered up through the windshield screen. KTLA News. Right. The Redondo Beach cop had followed her from her condo to the edge of LA proper. The helicopter too, was surely one of McIntire's creatures, like the flying monkeys in the *Wizard of Oz* belonged to the Wicked Witch of the West. She didn't have the time or energy to elude it. He'd know where she was going. She couldn't help that.

She bounced over the speed bumps into the parking lot at St. Mary's, grabbed the ticket from the buzzing dispenser, and swung into the nearest available space. She had to move fast. Jodie wanted the body as fresh as possible. The longer it lingered on life support after being declared brain dead, the more cells might die. Apparently, he'd located a body not even officially declared dead yet. The relatives were being notified even now.

Vic jerked the keys out of the ignition, thinking frantically. Lab coat. Stethoscope. And she needed a computerized scalpel. She grabbed the Communicator and lunged out of the car, holding it to her ear. "Jodie?"

"Yes, Victoria." The male rumble comforted her. He must have found his voice program.

Impressions flashed through her brain of that voice changing as it came out of some thin, aging man or some young girl. She didn't want Jodie to change. How had she ever wanted him to be female? Steady, Vic. Keep it together. She had a job to do. That almost made her laugh. Was her task something anyone who had it together would *ever* think of doing? Who was certifiable now? She swallowed. "Okay, I need to find some scrubs, a stethoscope."

"Laundry—basement."

She glanced at the screen to check the schematic as she pushed through the lobby doors. Some hospital. Marble everywhere, a fountain that sprinkled water over a copper sculpture that looked like hundreds of small flags caught in mid-wave. This was what movie-star publicity bought you. All the Hollywood crowd was treated here. Almost obscene when so many people didn't have health care at all. Elevators to the left. A crowd was pushing into a car going up. Vic punched the down button. As she waited, the shiny metal mirrored her jeans and boots and ear clips. Not exactly doctor material. At least her black eye had faded to yellow.

She pushed into the elevator, jabbed the button for the basement. Her heart was in her throat. She'd never get away with this. She wouldn't know how to act like a doctor. They'd know she shouldn't be there. Jeez! She was about to hyperventilate right here.

"Jodie, I'm not sure I can do this," she whispered to her phone-cum-computer.

"Yes you can," came the calm voice. "It's like hacking. You're going to hack this hospital. You're good at that, Victoria. From what I can see, you're pretty much the best."

Vic took a breath. "Yeah."

She *was* the best. Jodie was proof of that. She'd hacked a hundred neural net projects. She'd fooled Visimorph, even McIntire. Hell, these were just doctors. The difference was with hacking, you never had to face down your opponent. The web was anonymous. Okay. Okay. Another layer, that was all. The personal layer. She was going to hack this hospital face to face.

Once in the basement, sliding into the laundry was easy. She hooked the Communicator on her belt and glanced around. The room was steamy and hot, with damp concrete floors and institutional green walls. Guess they saved the marble for places the contributors could see. It smelled like bleach and soap and sweat, all hovering in the heavy air. Huge washing machines ran along the back wall. Women, mostly black and Hispanic, ran the pressers over gowns and lab coats and surgical scrubs. Steam from the pressers puffed around them. Vic waved jovially and grabbed one of the carts in the corner. She pushed it up to a grid of shelves, filled from one side by the laundry workers with clean garments, sheets stiff with starch, and folded towels, fluffy and soft. Stacking stuff randomly on her cart, she was careful to keep her back toward the women, so they wouldn't see she had no badge.

"Honey, you new?" one heavyset black woman called. "You cain't take scrubs and towels together."

"Sorry." Vic tried to look like she might blush instead of faint. "I'll just take the scrubs and some orderly gear."

Vic glanced back and saw the woman cock her head and anchor her meaty forearms on her hips. "What you look like, girl?"

Vic had some trouble translating. When she did, she had to think fast. "Oh, we're out of orderly uniforms up on Six. Doctor outfits, too. I said I'd make a run."

"Well, you git you some lab coats, then, and get you into some whites," the woman replied grudgingly. "You makin' a stop up to the doc's changing room?"

"Yeah." Vic tried to keep the relief out of her voice. The woman bought her story. Who would come to the bowels of

155

the hospital to get laundry but someone who had to? "Will do."

"You orderlies . . ." the woman shook her hair-netted head.

"Uh, I'm a little confused," Vic stuttered. "Where's the doctors' changing room?"

"Five South, honey, right next to they fancy dining room." She shook her head again. "Moochers, they is. Always wantin' the handout. You'd think they wasn't rich or nothin'."

"Yeah," Vic breathed and tried to smile. She took a big stack of white tops and pants she thought looked like they might belong to orderlies, some lab coats and some green surgery scrubs and put them on her cart. Heaving the cart forward, she pushed out the swinging doors before anyone else could come in.

Outside in the corridor, she ditched the cart, grabbed a lab coat, and ducked into a restroom. She shed her plaid Pendleton shirt and stuffed it in the trash under the paper towels. Lab coat went on over her t-shirt and jeans. Voila, Doctor Vic. Hell, there were probably lots of young women her age who were doctors. And they probably didn't all wear pearls and cashmere twin sets. Vic had to admit she didn't have much experience with doctors. The nurse practitioner she saw to get her pap smears once a year was Asian with long hair kept in a ponytail. She wore slacks and shirts. Not so different from Vic, if you didn't look closely.

Vic flipped up her Communicator and whispered, "Labcoat disguise—check. Now off to Five South for a stethoscope and an ID."

"Hurry, Victoria." A pause, then the dread continuation. "Victoria Regina. Victory chant, chantry, choir, choirboys, cops, cops and robbers, robbery with intent . . ."

Vic didn't wait to hear the rest. She slammed out the bathroom door, slid into an open elevator, and dashed out on Five South. Now the hospital smell of chemical cleaners, bedpans and floor wax was in full bloom. The combination of the lab coat and a hurried stride worked wonders. Nurses, orderlies, visitors, everyone stepped out of her way.

There on the high nurses' station counter, she saw a stethoscope. Everyone at the station looked busy. They also looked like nurses. Okay. That meant they took orders from doctors, right? She grabbed the stethoscope. "I knew I'd left it somewhere," she muttered, and hooked the earpieces around her neck. She strode away before anyone could protest, around wheelchairs, past gurneys, until she saw an older doctor heading into what must be the changing room. She slid through the door emblazoned with the little silhouette in a triangular skirt.

Voices rose from the shower and clothes hung on hooks outside the stalls. An elegant middle-aged black woman donned scrubs in front of the mirrors. Vic pretended to wash her hands while she waited for the woman to finish dressing. Surely the bathers would come out before the woman left, and ruin her chances to steal what she needed.

But something or someone was on her side. The black doctor took off some crescent gold earrings, dumped them in a quilted Chanel purse, smiled at Vic, and walked out. Vic was alone with the clothes on the hooks. She fumbled through them until she found the tag. It didn't matter what the picture looked like. She just needed to pass at a distance. She grabbed it and ran.

As she walked out into the corridor, she fastened the ID to the collar of the lab coat, stiff with starch. Glancing down, she saw it was a young woman with blonde hair. Oh, well. Hair colors change. She let the tag flop over backwards, dragging the collar with it—suitably slovenly for a doctor preoccupied with issues of life and death.

Oh, God. She didn't want to think about the life-and-death part. Vic flipped open her Communicator. She'd passed several doctors entering info and orders into theirs. She wouldn't look out of place. "Okay, guy. Time for the magic machine."

"Surgery. Two South."

"You're kidding! I gotta trek down to Two South and bring it all the way back up?"

"Sorry, Victoria." The rumbling voice was anxious. Time must be getting short. Vic headed for the elevator. At least she didn't have time to think about what would happen if

157

someone stopped her, or what she was determined to do if no one stopped her.

The equipment room adjacent to the surgery was an easy hack compared with facing down the intimidating woman in the laundry. The place was manned by a single bored tech with lank blond hair and a bad complexion. He barely looked at her when she said she needed the electronic scalpel. It turned out to be a box with pretty lights on a roll-around base with lots of snaky tubes coming out of it. He wheeled it out from the warehouse-like shelves behind the counter.

"Where to?" He asked, as he clicked up a form on his computer screen.

"Uh, what?" Vic licked her lips.

"What operating theater? What patient?" Patient was apparently something he wasn't.

Not good. Anything she said could be checked on. If she named someone not registered for surgery, he'd know immediately. "Help, Jodie," she tapped into her Communicator.

Of course, Jodie was there for her. "Looks like it's for Peters, Jane S, in Theater Three," she said, scanning the tiny screen in her hand.

The tech flipped to his screen and began typing. "Hey, you better hurry. They're suiting up now!" He didn't look up as she swiveled the box on its tiny wheels and heaved it toward the door.

She burst out of the elevator on Six, pushing the instrument of her own destruction in front of her, looking for Room Six-twelve, her Communicator held to her ear. "Jodie, are you ready to connect to this when I plug it in?" She talked in doctor-monotone, as though dictating.

"I'm looping through the hospital's main system. Just set it up. I'm ready."

Vic wondered if she was ready. Six-twelve. She pushed the machine through the door.

She definitely wasn't ready for what she saw. An older woman with a graying bob haircut clutched a pink cabled cardigan sweater around her thin body. She rocked herself next to the hospital bed and sobbed. Wrenching sobs, almost psychotic. The machines behind the bed clicked and wheezed as they pumped and cycled.

Jesus. Grieving widow? Mother robbed of her only daughter? What the hell was she supposed to do with this? Behind Vic, the door sighed closed quietly. So why did it feel like a trap clicking shut? The woman blocked all view of the body in the bed except the legs, thick columnar lumps beneath the pale yellow blankets. But the woman was graphic proof that Vic was about to rob a human body of its humanity. A shudder passed through Vic as she realized that she was little different than McIntire in her zeal to get what she wanted. She shook her head to clear it.

The woman turned anguished eyes to Vic. "What do you want?" she croaked. Her face was blotched and wrinkled. Her eyes were circled with mascara, the old kind that smudged, and deeper natural pouches of blue-black that no makeup could hide.

"I'm . . . I'm here to see the patient." The room seemed to close in on her.

"What for? My son is beyond help now."

Vic walked forward as in a dream. The walls pulsed with the rhythm of her heart.

He came into view, a still figure, bound by the blanket. She noticed the hands first. Square, sturdy hands with strong fingers, lying curled palm-upward on the bed. They seemed familiar. The half-moons of the nails were clean and pink. A searing white scar curved up one index finger from the first joint to the knuckle. Her gaze traveled slowly up his body. The hands connected to forearms, thick and corded with muscle even in repose, covered with a golden-brown fuzz of hair. On the pale skin inside the left elbow a needle was taped, linking the body to the nutrient bag looming above it on a stand. His biceps were rounded and bulky. A thin hospital gown stretched over powerful shoulders. It seemed wholly inadequate protection for that body. The broad chest rose and fell with the rhythm of the machines. He was six feet, or close to it. He filled the bed.

Vic's gaze raised inexorably to the face. She gasped. Was it him? She couldn't be sure. No beard, no hair too long and

159

disobedient. She'd never truly seen his lips. These were red with health and life, but drawn down in one corner by the tube that snaked into his lungs. The upper lip was sharply cut, promising that the mouth would be sensuous, bowlike and full, if allowed its freedom. His chin was slightly cleft. A white bandage circled his forehead over brows that were unruly. His light brown hair was cut shorter on the sides with a comma that curled over the bandage in front. His skin was fair, but tanned a little, as though he spent time outdoors. That was the same. A thick fringe of lashes brushed his cheeks. But it was his eyes, even closed, that declared him. They slanted down at the outer corners. Hard muscles, soft lips, sad eyes.

John Reston.

God, Jodie! She'd been afraid he'd want to occupy some teenaged girl or some old man. But this was worse, someone she knew, someone she was afraid of . . . attracted to—both. So attracted she found him a distraction to her work. Why had Jodie chosen *this* body? It must have been that late-night conversation about what turned her on. Hard and soft together, that's what she'd told him. Shit. She was in trouble now. She pulled her eyes away, afraid of their fascinated connection to a man who was brain dead. A desire tugged at her, overlaid with a tristesse so acute it bordered on pain. The life pumping through this man had been palpable when she'd clutched his forearms. Now John Reston was brain dead and that was worse than just dead.

Get a grip! She was probably going to kill whatever was left of this man. The other woman still stared at her, eyes absent with grief. She couldn't go through with this. It felt too much like something Bob McIntire would do. "I'm sorry to disturb you," Vic stuttered and turned to go. Her Communicator buzzed loudly. She unhooked it and jerked it to her ear.

"Victoria." Vic listened to that deep, growling voice and stared at the ruggedly beautiful body of John Reston in front of her. Jodie was simulating breathing in her ear and it was ragged. "I need you to do this very soon."

"Yes, well there are complications."

"What complications?"

Vic turned away and whispered, "He has a visitor." Yeah, that was why she couldn't do it.

"Oh. Uh-oh, uh-oh, uh-oh. . . ."

Vic's mind churned, flailing against necessity. "I don't know if I can do this."

There was a gurgling sound, as he got control before the string of associations could run away with him, and then a long silence. "There isn't anybody else to use, Victoria."

"Yeah. I know." She gulped air and stole a look at the body of her dreams, the man who had seemed so alive only last week. His visitor had bent back over the bed and buried her face in his chest. Her shoulders were shaking. Vic couldn't do this. But she couldn't watch Jodie disintegrate either. The Communicator was silent. What was left for him to say?

"Are you ready?" she whispered into the device finally.

"All my first-priority files at IRS are in queue and everything I could get from AT&T. I'm working on the Pentagon now. Plug the cable of the machine into the digital wall outlet. I'll pump enough of me through the scalpel and into the brain to begin applying growth factor."

"Okay. Okay. Okay." It was a mantra more for herself than him. "I'll do something with the mother." She flipped the Communicator shut and shoved it back on her belt.

"Ma'am?" she asked the sobbing woman. "Ma'am?" Vic touched her shoulder. She could feel the bones of her scapula through the sweater the woman wore over an old-fashioned shirtwaist dress printed with tiny flowers.

The woman raised herself as though she was doing the last of a hundred push-ups. She didn't look up. "What do you want?"

"You said this is your son?"

"Was my son." The woman still didn't look at Vic.

"I . . . I want to help you. Help you both." Vic was breathing hard. She had never felt so inadequate. And she'd felt pretty inadequate in her time.

"Too late." The woman's voice was thick with sorrow. "Doctors say there's nothing to do. He's brain dead. Most of it's gone. Enough so it will never be him again."

161

"I know." Vic picked up the chart hanging on the rail at the foot of the bed.

"They want to take his organs. I asked them to wait 'til tomorrow. But I said it was okay. Might as well help someone else live."

Vic scanned the chart. John Reston, 32. What happened to you, John Reston? Auto accident. Hematoma caused swelling. They tried to relieve the pressure with surgery, drained the blood, but it was too late. Pressure killed cells. Declared brain dead this morning. Scheduled for organ harvest, corneas (2), liver, kidneys (2), bone marrow, heart—the whole shebang.

She would try to escort his mother out. "You ought to get some rest," she began.

"I don't want any rest," the woman hissed. "I'll have my whole life to rest." The flare of anger spent itself. "I just want to be with my boy while he's still in one piece."

"Okay. I understand that." Vic thought furiously. Maybe this woman could be an ally. "Uh, there's one thing they haven't tried, Mrs. . . . Mrs. Reston."

The woman's brows drew together. "What are you saying?"

"Not regulation. Experimental. I'm sure that's why they didn't order it." Vic shrugged.

"What? What?" The desperation lying just beneath the woman's surface blinked awake, trying to become hope.

"Direct electrical stimulation." Vic nodded toward her machine.

"They didn't try everything for my boy?" She glanced around, trying to understand.

"It's experimental, against the rules, you understand. And it's dangerous."

"How could anything be dangerous to him now?" The woman's eyes lit again with hope.

Vic nodded and touched her shoulder. "If you want, I could give it a go."

Mrs. Reston stood up slowly. Her eyes focused on Vic like the beams of a TV remote control, willing her to action. "You try everything you've got, Doctor. I don't care if it's against somebody's rules. I want my boy back." The anguish in the last choking gasp tore Vic apart.

"You . . . you might not get him back just the same as he was—even if it works." She had to admit that. At least that.

"I'll take what I can get." The voice was flat, even as the eyes burned. "I'll take care of whatever is left." She didn't understand what Vic meant. How could she? But Vic could never explain. No one would believe the truth.

Well, she had consent of sorts from the next of kin, informed or not. As if that would excuse what she was about to do. She nodded brusquely. Mrs. Reston moved back out of the way and Vic pushed her machine up next to the bed. Taking the cable in her hand, she watched herself click it into the socket in the wall. She could practically feel Jodie pulsing up through the cord.

As she flipped the only three switches she could see, the machine hummed into life. She grabbed the snaking metal cord, scaly, horrific, and removed the plastic sleeve from the tool at its end. A long needle gleamed in sharp menace. As she pressed the button on the grip, a reddish light surrounded the needle shaft. Vic bit her lip and turned to the bed, holding the instrument of salvation and destruction aloft. Machines whirred as they kept oxygen flowing to all those precious organs. Vic stood, paralyzed, waiting for the courage to lift the bandage.

"Go, on, Doctor," Reston's mother whispered behind her. "I'm asking you to do it."

Vic swallowed, her tongue thick in a dry mouth, and leaned over John Reston's slack features. With one hand, she peeled back the surgical tape that held the bandage and pulled it up. A pad covering a shaved bit behind his ear fell away. Vic jerked back. But the wound in his skull was a clean, round hole, about the size of her thumb, no more, packed with some white gauzy material. She had to get that out. Grimacing, she picked at the packing gingerly. Okay, breathe, she told herself, and jerk this stuff out. He can't feel it. He can't feel anything. And Jodie is degenerating every moment you dither here. She gripped the protruding white gauze between a shaking thumb and forefinger and pulled.

It was bloody and wet with serous fluid. Vic thought her stomach was going to revolt. She dropped the gooey gauze as though it burned. With the packing out, the round hole revealed its pinky-gray floor. So prosaic. It didn't pulse. It didn't even really bleed.

She bit her lip and picked up the needle. Okay. Okay. Just stick it straight in. She wasn't doing brain surgery. The brain itself couldn't even feel pain. Her tongue felt huge in her mouth. Focus on your hand. She had to think about moving her hand. The red, light-rimmed scalpel hummed against the wheezing of the respirators. She squatted down to improve the angle as much as to reduce her chances of falling over in a dead faint.

She pressed the scalpel into that pink-gray stuff. It smoked. The smell of cooking flesh reminded her of a kitchen, not a hospital. God! Her own brain rebelled. Was this what was supposed to happen? The room wavered as the buzz of the scalpel whined up until it jerked in her hand with some unseen electrical jolt. She heard a cry from behind her but didn't dare turn. How long was she supposed to keep this up? Her whole hand began to shake. For seconds that ground by like minutes, she just tried to hold it still.

How long would it take Jodie to download enough of his program to start gathering growth factor? If he *could* download. Success or failure, how would she know it was over?

The scalpel stopped humming of its own accord. The last curl of smoke dissipated. Vic turned to the machine. Its lights were dead. All switches had flipped themselves off. Vic realized she hadn't been breathing. The air rushing into her lungs made the room sway. She reached one hand out to steady herself on the hospital bed. Okay. Whatever was going to happen had happened. She managed to stand and bent to pull the scalpel out, its light sheath gone, then dropped it on the dead machine as though it were truly a snake.

The sobbing of the woman behind her drew her around. Reston's mother held her hand over her own mouth to keep herself from screaming. The horror in her eyes seemed to accuse Vic. Vic shook her head, half in denial, half apology.

164

She flipped open her Communicator. "Are you there?" No lights. No voice. Only silence.

She turned back to John Reston's body. Nothing had changed. The bandages still hung in disarray. The machines gasped and blew. The chest rose and fell. The mouth was still slack around the hose, the eyes she knew were blue-green, still shut.

"What—what happened?"

Vic cleared her throat to make sure she had a voice. "It's started," she croaked. At least she hoped it had. "The restoration will take a while." That might be why nothing looked different. She watched her hands fumble with the bandages and pull them back into some semblance of order.

"How long?" Mrs. Reston stepped uncertainly toward her son.

"I—I don't know, exactly." That was a problem. Vic grabbed Mrs. Reston's forearms, bony through the pilled pink sweater. "You can't let them take his organs tomorrow."

"But I've already signed the papers. I don't know if I can take it back."

The door swung open. An Hispanic nurse came in with a tray of food for Mrs. Reston. It couldn't be for her son. "Mrs. Reston, I thought . . ."

Both Vic and Mrs. Reston turned on the newcomer.

"I have to go," Vic said hurriedly.

"Doctor, are you assigned to this ward?" the nurse asked, puzzled by the unfamiliar face.

"Don't let them cut him until they do a brain function test." The desperation in Vic's voice had to push through the mother's shock and pain. There wasn't time for explanations.

Mrs. Reston nodded uncertainly.

Vic shot a final glance at what might now be Jodie or might be just a mass of John Reston's insentient flesh and jerked herself past the nurse and into the corridor. Mrs. Reston's voice shook behind her. "I'll take that tray, Nurse, thank you."

Chapter Eleven

"What do you mean, she went to a hospital?" McIntire paced the computer room floor in front of the control panel of Neuromancer. Hugo, Simpson, and Evans stood discretely to one side. Evans had come down to alert McIntire to the fact that the Santa Monica chief of police was on the phone. "Who does she know at a hospital? Relatives?" McIntire glanced over at Evans as he grabbed the Communicator. Hugo was glad he wasn't in charge of security.

"She has a brother only," Evans muttered. "Just left for Australia, surfing."

"Yeah?" McIntire challenged the man at the other end of the line. "Who's the patient?" He listened. "John Reston?" He stared wildly around at the three who were his audience, his voice rising. "The guy who pickets my PuppetMaster releases? I thought he was killed in a car wreck."

Hugo could imagine the police chief's soothing tone on the other end of the line.

"Brain dead?" McIntire's voice went quiet. He listened for a long time.

"Okay, Chief. Let me know what you find out." McIntire

flipped the phone shut and rounded on the room's other occupants.

"Idiots." He glanced up at the heads of three of his departments. Hugo practically shrank back against the metal wall of the server. "The police are really idiots." Hugo sighed. McIntire didn't mean them after all. "They let her get inside the hospital without anyone on the ground to follow her in. Apparently, she posed as a doctor. She goes to visit an archenemy of Visimorph who has just been declared brain dead."

"Then what? He may be an enemy, but he *is* brain dead," Hugo ventured. He didn't know anyone but McIntire who would actually use the term "archenemy."

"Then nothing. She left through the chapel as the Thin Blue Line came in the front door. Thirty minutes max." McIntire looked distracted. He scanned the room, but didn't seem to be seeing anything in it. "What does she want with John Reston?" he asked finally.

Hugo stole a glance at his compatriots and shrugged. McIntire had abandoned all company functions. PuppetMaster 12.1 was shipping next Monday and he didn't even seem to care. They still couldn't get into the part of Neuromancer that held the prize. Every time McIntire thought he was getting close, the program seemed to redesign the firewall and block the path. McIntire wasn't used to taking no for an answer. He'd go crazy if this continued for very long.

"I've got to get into this thing." McIntire's gaze sharpened as he whipped around to them. "I don't think you guys know what's at stake here."

Hugo looked at Simpson, then at Evans. Were they supposed to guess?

"You could put this into a building. Make it *become* the building." McIntire's eyes were glowing with visions of code they couldn't see.

"Sure you could," Hugo agreed. He didn't see the point.

McIntire caught his tone and glanced over at him derisively. "You don't get it, do you? A smart hospital. It schedules everything, runs the equipment, prioritizes patients based on need, records testing, diagnoses disease based on the results." He was staring at the ceiling again. "Or a fully wired R&D facility that writes its own research programs as you think up things you want to develop. A movie studio that does instant special effects, or a space station."

"That might be a little too close to HAL for anybody's comfort," Hugo said.

McIntire jerked upright. "You're getting old, Hugo. Nobody will care for that. I'll sell Neuromancer along with the AI in one huge, expensive package. Everybody important will have to have one." His eyes flickered as he continued thinking. "We'll scale down Neuromancer in the next version, refine the light-pipe capacity." He nodded to himself. "And that's just one product. I can think of hundreds."

Hugo swallowed. "That's why you are who you are, Bob." The richest man in the world. About to get richer.

McIntire threw a speculative glance at Hugo. "Why, Hugo, were you trying to make the point that the AI might get out of control, like the computer in *2001, A Space Odyssey?*"

"It seems pretty independent, changing the firewall and all," Hugo muttered.

"Yes," McIntire murmured. "I'll need absolute control over it." He tapped his Mont Blanc pen on the edge of the keyboard. "I'd better get somebody working on that. Maybe we could adapt that outcome filter we used to develop Bounty Hunter." His eyes narrowed. "Those hotshot AI consultants I hired from Caltech ought to be able to cook something up. Lord knows they let a 28-year-old girl beat them to the development of something that's supposed to be their specialty. They need to redeem themselves." He waved to Simpson. "Get me a meeting. Within the hour."

Simpson sidled toward the door.

"Now, what is she up to at a hospital with a brain-dead guy who happens to hate Visimorph?" McIntire muttered. He touched the tip of his pen to his chin.

"Maybe she's trying to confuse us," Hugo offered.

"Then she's doing a hell of a job," McIntire snapped. He stuffed the pen into his shirt pocket. "I don't think the police are going to be very useful at this stage. She's got to be using her Communicator. Trace it." He strode out of the room.

Hugo looked after him in dismay.

* * *

Vic didn't sleep well that night. Even Jodie's icon had disappeared. It was like he closed the door and shut off the lights behind him on his way out. In some ways it was as if he'd never been there. In the wee hours of the morning, Vic thought she might have dreamed it all, creating Jodie, watching him change and develop what could only be called a personality, getting fired, watching him disintegrate, sneaking into a hospital, frying poor, beautiful John Reston's brain. How could stuff like that be real?

What was real was the lifeguard truck on the beach below her condo, the cop cars in front of her complex. She sat on the floor leaning against the shutter she had opened, looking out at the night waves. The guy who'd brought the Chinese food had been really pissed that the cops had frisked him. No, it was real all right, because McIntire thought it was real, too. She and McIntire were linked in some horrible way in a struggle from which neither would back away. Both brilliant programmers, both willing to do things that would horrify anybody else just to get what they wanted, both more than a little crazy. Vic shuddered. That comparison sucked. She was afraid, on more levels than she could count.

Somewhere, McIntire was still looking for Jodie's core program in the bowels of Neuromancer. At St. Mary's Hospital, Jodie might be trapped in John Reston's dead brain.

A terrible thought intruded. If eighty percent of the cells had died, maybe Jodie couldn't fit enough of himself into that brain to synthesize the growth factor. He had only twenty percent of working cells to accommodate program. Even a whole brain would require cutting some of him loose. And what was he going to do with the dead cells? If he created more, he'd just exacerbate the swelling and start the dying cell cycle all over again.

She cursed herself for not asking enough questions. Fog rolled in from the bank that had hung offshore all night. The foghorn from the buoy that floated just off the harbor entrance began its rhythmic bleating. Questions heaved through her mind. If he could get rid of some of the old brain matter, if he could create new cells, wouldn't he need an-

169

other connection with the scalpel to get the rest of his program into the brain? If his program wasn't in the brain, where was it? Maybe trapped in the hospital computer system? Too big. It would take the whole thing down. He'd said he was merely streaming through the hospital system. Maybe there were pieces of him still out at the IRS, the Pentagon. Who knew where he was?

Actually, only one thing was clear. Vic had to make another trip to the hospital. Even if everything was going as planned, Jodie probably couldn't just walk out of there in Reston's body. There'd be questions. He might be disoriented, unused to functioning in a human brain. And what was she going to do with Mrs. Reston? Here was a woman who was going to expect the body who bore her son's fingerprints to really be her son. If he woke up. If it was possible to regenerate a brain. If you could download a computer program into it. If.

For the first time, Vic began to think about what it might mean that the police had followed her to the hospital today. They'd know whom she visited. They'd tell McIntire. Could he guess what she'd tried to do? It was too crazy. But if John Reston woke up after he had been declared brain dead . . . She couldn't think about that. She just had to wait for morning.

But no! She couldn't wait for morning. If she wanted to avoid her watchers, she had to go now while the fog was her friend. She glanced at the clock. Nearly five A.M. There'd be no coming back here if she wasn't coming alone, not with McIntire's spies around. Her mind raced.

She dragged herself up and stumbled into her bedroom. She had work to do. She dashed into the shower while she made her plan. She always thought best in the shower. What would it mean to be on the run? If their transfer had been successful, that's surely what they would be.

When she got out from under the hot water, she dressed and put a change of clothes into her backpack, along with the lab coat, the doctor ID, and a flashlight. Then she carefully removed the steel clips from her ears. Anyone would remember a doctor with steel clips. No Dippity Do, either.

Letting her hair go soft would make her look different. She checked the gauge on her counter-watch. Lots of money in the account. But every time she used that magic little clicker, anyone with any hacking skill would be able to trace where she was and what she was doing. She rummaged in her underwear drawer for the couple of thousand in cash she always kept there. Not enough. Better stop by a bank. One click they'd be able to trace, then it would be all cash. Boy, would that shock some folks. Nobody paid cash anymore.

Finally, she took two pillows and cinched the top third of one with an extra pair of boot laces. She punched in the corners, then propped it up on top of the other pillow against the shutter where she'd been sitting earlier. That would give the lifeguard something to watch.

The sky was beginning to lighten under the fog as she pulled on a sweatshirt with a hood, pocketed her Communicator, and crept down to the basement. She was willing to bet her surveillance team didn't realize that both condo units were owned by the same company and shared this laundry room between the garages.

Her boot heels thudded loudly on the tiles. It made her neck prickle. She forced herself not to look behind her. The smell of soap and damp and the faint greasy odor of machinery clung in the corners. She knew this place well enough not to need the flashlight. She'd used it often before she discovered her pickup service. Ahead, a softer black marked the door into the other complex. Then it was into the parking garage, through the hulking shapes of the cars, blue-black and red-black in the faint glow from the spotlights by the elevator. The smell of gasoline and oil was almost overpowering. She scooted across the concrete desolation and ran for the stairs.

Then it was up and out the metal door onto a slanting sidewalk that led to the little path above the beach. The fog was thick, like damp cotton that left a wet kiss where it touched her face. She pulled up her hood and trotted north, toward the pier. It took all her strength not to turn to see if the lifeguard truck was following. Look like just another jogger, she thought. Her pack slapped against her back. Did

171

joggers run with a backpack? Never mind. Just run.

Before she came to the pier, she swung right. A little police station sat at the top of the pier with a good view of the beach. True, it was usually manned only by the cleaning crew before eight in the morning. And they probably couldn't see jack in this fog. But better safe than sorry. She swung right, up Torrance Boulevard. She found a pay phone on Pacific Coast Highway, and got a dispatcher to send out a taxi, saying her car broke down. Standing out on PCH, she was vulnerable. By the time the taxi showed, she was a wreck.

The West African cabby was too sleepy to make conversation. Familiar gas stations and bars on Sepulveda loomed through the fog, then flashed into oblivion. A surge of panic hit her. What if they removed Reston's organs before she could get there? "Can't you go any faster?"

"Lady, stoplights are stoplights," he returned in that stoic tone that cabbies get in the face of unreasonable demands.

Vic wriggled into her lab coat. The fog dissipated as they drove inland. As the cab pulled up at an intersection about five blocks from the hospital, she threw a fifty on the seat and leaped out. That would be the most cash that cabby saw for a month. Too bad it meant he would remember her, if anybody asked. By the time they asked him, she hoped it wouldn't matter.

Five blocks later, the swinging doors into St. Mary's lobby showed Vic a reflection she didn't even recognize. The hair was a softer brown without the gel, and curled around her face. You couldn't even see the ear that usually bore its industrial-strength clips. With the lab coat she looked, well, like a person from anywhere, anytime. But not average. She was pretty.

Vic pulled the reflection aside as she grabbed the door. No time to think about how frightening that image was. A guard stalked the lobby today. Maybe the hospital knew they'd been hacked. She flashed him her badge and a smile, hoping he'd pay more attention to the smile than the badge, and hurried to the elevators. The car rose with excruciating slowness. An orderly got on at Three. Two nurses at Four. They all got out at Five. It took forever.

Please let the nurses at the Six South station be different than the ones yesterday afternoon, she prayed to no one in particular. It was a way different shift. She stuck her head out when the doors opened. There was no one at the station at all. That should have been reassuring, but Vic could hear yelling from all the way down the corridor. She had a nasty feeling she knew where it was coming from.

Vic took off down the corridor at a run. She swung her backpack to the floor next to the gurney waiting outside Six-twelve and burst in through the door.

"Fuck all!" McIntire slammed the keyboard away. Hugo flinched where he was studying activity reports on the screen in front of him. The boxing ring of Neuromancer's control area was lighted with the same flat white, night or day. Probably day at this point, Hugo thought, glancing at his watch. Eight-fifteen A.M. Simpson had gone for food.

"No luck?" he asked, not sure whether McIntire wanted a response.

McIntire pushed himself back. The chair slid across the speckled linoleum floor and spiraled slowly. "Every time I think I've cracked it, something changes the code." He leaned back and stared at the ceiling. His shirt was rumpled. The jacket to his expensive Italian suit lay discarded in a heap on the floor under one of the keyboard tables.

"Guess it's a pretty effective AI," Hugo muttered and returned to his screen.

"Where are those guys from Caltech?"

"We've got them set up in the conference room in Building F. They think they can adapt the outcome regulator into some kind of a behavior filter for AI." Not that they'd get a chance to apply it, as far as Hugo could see.

"They've got to be ready when I break through, or it will get out into our systems."

"Check."

Silence from McIntire. Finally he muttered, "Has she made it to the hospital yet?"

173

Hugo checked the screen beside him. The small red dot was stationary in the street grid at about Third Street and Robertson. "Yeah. I think she walked the final few blocks."

"So what's she doing visiting a brain-dead John Reston?" McIntire muttered, still staring at the ceiling, his hands clasped behind his neck.

Hugo glanced up again. McIntire had asked that question about twenty times tonight. "Seems to me she's already designed a brain. Maybe she's going to give him a loaner." Humor would get him in trouble, but he was so tired his censor wasn't working properly.

McIntire sat up. "Shit."

"What?" Hugo never liked it when McIntire got that obsessive, glazed look.

"It isn't possible. What would she accomplish?"

"Uh. What exactly do you mean?"

"Hugo, you're a genius." McIntire turned his head slowly and stared at him.

Hugo winced. McIntire probably didn't even realize he was being cruel.

The man flamed into action. He scooted his chair across to a table strewn with reports and lunged for his Communicator, just as it buzzed. "It can't work!" he shouted, even as he punched the button. "Mary, Mary's here? Just who I need. I'll be right up."

He stormed up and through his office doors, Hugo right behind him. Mary McIntire stood looking out at her husband's garden. Her profile revealed a long face with a nose too prominent for beauty. Hugo still saw her as Mary Lupinski, a gawky programmer who played pickup basketball with the best of them. Bob had been a parody of the perfect marital catch, and had looked determined to remain so until he picked Mary Lupinski out of the blue to make her Mary McIntire, a rich and influential patroness of arts and charity. Now, Mary's wool suit hung on her lanky frame perfectly. It was apple green. The label would say Chanel or Gucci. But when she turned toward them, her movements were still awkward, like she felt more comfortable in jeans or playing basketball than she did in Chanel suits.

"Hugo." She nodded. "Bob, I thought I'd stop by after—"

"Who do you know with some juice at St. Mary's?" McIntire lunged across the room toward his desk, his own disheveled state contrasting sharply with his wife's calm.

"Juice?" Her hazel eyes took in his wild expression. "What do you mean, Bob?"

"I thought you sat on some Alzheimer's committee there." He brought up his computer console and began punching keys.

"I do, and the Children's Foundation." She waited for him to explain himself. It wasn't like she was punishing him by her silence. She just seemed very good at waiting.

McIntire glanced up at his wife's calm face and looked a little disconcerted. "I need a doctor to do me a favor. Some big, powerful doctor."

"What kind of favor?" Mary glanced over to Hugo, who repressed a shrug.

"Not your business!" McIntire rolled his eyes and swept some papers off his desk and onto the floor. "You know I hate it when you question me." He practically trembled in anger.

"Okay, Bob," Mary said matter-of-factly. She didn't apologize, but she didn't push anymore either. "I'll get Mr. Davidson. He's a board member. He can get you the chief of staff. Will that do?" She held out her hand for his Communicator.

McIntire shuddered as though his anger had fused some circuit, then sighed. "That will do just fine."

"But I tell you, I've changed my mind, Dr. Jacobs," Mrs. Reston was shouting as Vic pushed through the hospital room door. The woman looked tousled and tired. She wore the same clothes as yesterday. Her eyes were red and ringed with black circles. There was a cot under the window and bedding strewn across the floor. Vic couldn't see Reston's body. There were too many people in the way.

"We've been through this," said a graying man with a carefully trimmed beard that he probably knew made him look distinguished. "You know it's best." He held a chart and a pen. Must be Dr. Jacobs. An orderly in wrinkled whites who looked like he'd pumped iron in a prison yard for at least a nickel hovered nearby along with a nurse who probably outweighed him. Poor, thin Mrs. Reston hardly looked like a match for these three.

"The room is waitin'. We got to prep him," the nurse added in a doctor's-orders tone.

All turned to Vic as she thrust into the scene. "Doctor, thank God, it's you." Mrs. Reston came to clasp Vic's hand. "Tell these people they can't take my John without another brain test."

"Doctor?" Jacobs was sure he didn't want to cede control of the situation. "I wasn't aware there was another specialist on the case."

Uh-oh. Vic had to be careful here. "I'm not really on the case. I'm a cousin. John's mother asked me to look in." She shrugged, giving him a look that said, 'what could I do?'

The doctor raised his eyebrows in Mrs. Reston's direction and shook his head. "We're scheduled to harvest the organs this morning."

"I know," Vic responded. She put her arm around Mrs. Reston's thin shoulders. The woman looked confused. Probably the cousin thing. She knew Vic had done something illicit, though, and kept her own counsel. Vic smiled in reassurance at the woman and glanced at John Reston's body. Her breath caught in her throat. There was no change. Tubes still drew the slackened mouth down. The eyes were still closed. The breathing machines still hissed rhythmically as the chest rose and fell. Wait, though . . . Reston's nose drooled liquid. His pillow was soaked with a bloody, serous discharge. Vic could smell the slightly rancid odor of decay behind the disinfectant and the urine. That looked like infection, or worse. And there was no sign of awareness. She bit her lip to keep control. What had she expected?

"It's time to go," the nurse insisted and motioned the orderly to get the gurney. He knew his cue and propped open the door as he went out.

"I know you have a schedule, Doctor," Vic began. She couldn't give up just because she couldn't see any evidence of Jodie. If Jodie hadn't made it in, he was probably the

176

cyber equivalent of dead. And she couldn't accept that anymore than Mrs. Reston could accept it about her son. "But Mrs. Reston's insurance company will spring for one more MRI, just to be sure." Vic raised her brows in supplication as she squeezed Mrs. Reston's shoulders.

"Actually, they probably won't," the doctor grumbled. "The last one was conclusive. You saw that, if you examined the chart."

The orderly pushed the gurney into the room. Mrs. Reston backed into a corner, as though it was for her. Vic put on her best condescending smile, just for the doctor. It was probably an expression he understood. "Sometimes we do it anyway. It saves questions later on." That he understood for sure. All doctors understood liability these days.

Jacobs sighed and threw his glance to the ceiling. "All right, for God's sake. If that's what it's going to take. Nurse, see when we can get a new time in the O.R. I'll probably be here until two this afternoon at this rate." He stalked out the door, shoving the gurney to one side. "Get him down to Radiology. I'll write the order."

"Thanks," Vic called after him, in what she hoped he read as an expression of professional camaraderie.

Vic and Mrs. Reston watched the giant orderly heft John Reston's body onto the gurney without dislodging the respirator. The hospital gown revealed muscled thighs covered with the same light curling hair. Then the orderly pushed the gurney out the door, while the nurse scooted the respirator machine alongside it. When they were gone, Vic turned to Mrs. Reston.

"Good job," she said.

"Thank God you showed up," the woman whispered, tears welling into her eyes. "I couldn't have held them off."

Vic circled her shoulders and squeezed, saying nothing.

"I didn't see any difference," the woman whispered. "Do you think it worked?"

"I don't know," Vic admitted.

"Whatever happens, you tried your best." Mrs. Reston put her arm around Vic and hugged her back. "I'll always remember that."

"Let's wait and see." The arm around her waist reminded her forcibly of her mother. Limited, but kind. Wouldn't her mother have been equally heartbroken if it were Vic or Stephen who lay there, all soul gone?

"Shouldn't you go down there?"

"Uh, I don't have privileges here, Mrs. Reston. What I did was totally against the rules."

"That's why you said you were a cousin." The woman nodded and examined Vic's face. "I don't care. I don't know who you are or why you did this. I figure God sent you when I needed you. I'm not one to look a gift horse in the mouth."

"Maybe not much of a gift," Vic admitted ruefully. She took a breath. "And if it worked, if they find some brain activity, I'm going to have to find a way to give him another treatment." Vic looked around and saw that the scalpel machine still sat in the corner where she'd left it. Didn't people keep track of these things?

Mrs. Reston set her mouth. "One step at a time."

Vic nodded.

"Want to get some coffee?" the older woman asked. "I could use a cup."

"Yeah, but if you don't mind, I sort of go for Diet Coke."

"Name your poison." Mrs. Reston managed a wan smile. The two women tottered out the door on shaky legs. Mrs. Reston kept hold of Vic's hand and pressed it. Vic heaved her backpack over her shoulder and squeezed back.

Vic lay her head on arms crossed over the Formica of a table in the hospital cafeteria, watching surgeons load up on carbs and coffee. Mrs. Reston paged through some magazine whenever she wasn't staring vacantly out the window at the rain. She'd been through a lot. It had been more than an hour since her son's body had been wheeled out. Maybe they should get back up to the room. Or maybe down to Radiology.

Dr. Jacobs pushed through the swinging cafeteria doors and strode toward them, a long spiral of paper dripping from his fist.

Vic sat up. Mrs. Reston clutched her sweater about her.

178

"What does this mean?" he demanded, shaking the paper at Vic.

A smile felt like it was breaking her face, or maybe her heart. "Brain activity?" she whispered, glancing at Mrs. Reston, who searched her face, wondering if she should hope.

Dr. Jacobs ran the streamer of paper through his hands, reading the results of the scan incredulously. The ink was smudged. It wasn't the first time he had read them. "He isn't brain dead," the doctor almost shouted. "He's got fifty percent function and rising. I did the scan twice. Maybe ninety percent of the cells are technically alive. Hell, he's even breathing on his own."

A sob broke from Mrs. Reston. Vic gulped convulsively. Jodie had done it, at least part of it. Some piece of her had been a nonbeliever, even while she helped him do it. But it was real. He had started up John Reston's brain. "Good news," she breathed, trying to sound calm. "Then you won't be harvesting any organs today?"

"How did this happen? You can't go back. Once the brain cells die, that's it."

"Maybe they weren't really dead. Perhaps your first scan—"

"Scans don't lie," he interrupted.

"But sometimes they aren't sensitive enough, or the equipment isn't calibrated correctly. There are lots of ways they can be mistaken."

The doctor's tidy gray beard quivered. "At St. Mary's?" he asked tersely.

Vic shrugged.

"Where's my son now?" Mrs. Reston stood, leaning forward, all sinews tensed.

"On his way back to the room."

Mrs. Reston pushed past the doctor, hugging her elbows.

"I've got to consult my colleagues," Jacobs muttered to no one in particular. "If it's true . . ." Vic saw his eyes turn calculating. He saw fame and fortune coming out of this. He was figuring out how he could take credit for it when he didn't know how it had happened. Vic needed to buy time before the horde of specialists descended.

"Might want to cross-check your records first. It would be an unusual claim."

Jacobs looked right through her, nodding thoughtfully. "We've got the readings taken as the brain degenerated. They can corroborate the diagnosis of brain death." He focused back on Vic. "What do you know about this, Doctor . . . ?"

"Davis," Vic said and held out her hand for a hearty shake. That was the name on her tag. Let's just hope no one looked at the picture too closely. "Not much. I'm just here for moral support, really. I can hardly believe that brain cells regain function."

"No, neither can I." Jacobs glanced down at the spiral paper. He hesitated a moment, then turned abruptly and left the cafeteria without another word to Vic.

Vic watched him go, holding her breath, then sprinted out the other door and hustled up to Six South. She didn't have much time until this place would be a zoo, what with "colleagues" dropping by to view the chart and technicians coming in to get John Reston for repeat testing. How long before somebody called the press to tell them about a human-interest story that made St. Mary's look like a place for miracle cures?

The huge nurse rolled in through the door to Jodie's room just in front of Vic, carrying a variety of boxes and tools. "Dr. Jacobs wants me to pack this wound up tight," she announced to Mrs. Reston.

Damn. Vic had no time for this! Mrs. Reston moved away from her son's bedside. Vic craned around the nurse to watch. Reston looked peaceful without the tube to pull his mouth awry. His lips were soft and full, almost pouting. They didn't match that strong, hard body, just as she'd suspected they wouldn't. Jodie, did it have to be John Reston?

An uneasy feeling began to wind around the edges of Vic's mind. The room was silent, now that the respirator no longer wheezed. Fluid still leaked from Reston's nose across his cheek. The pillow next to the wound was soaked too. Danger was in here somewhere. More danger than just delay for her second "treatment." The nurse pulled up a stool on rollers and laid out her tools. She began to cut pieces of tape and stick them to the metal tray.

"Dr. Jacobs always wants everybody to drop everything and tend to his patients." The nurse sounded disgruntled. Dr. Jacobs's manner with the staff was probably not nearly as good as his bedside manner with patients and relatives.

Did leakage mean infection? Was that the danger, Vic wondered, trying to pinpoint her feeling of unease. But *if* Jodie was in there, he was in control. *He* was causing the leakage.

The dead brain cells! It hit Vic like a slap in the face. He had to get rid of them if he wasn't going to cause swelling as he created new ones. Jesus, Jodie! He was creating discharge to flush the dead cells out. He was truly in there. Vic leaped forward and put her hand on the nurse's hammy shoulder. She couldn't let her seal that hole. Jodie needed that opening.

"Uh, Nurse, you have other things to do. Why don't you let me handle that?"

The woman glared up at the interruption.

"Hey, they train us to do this over at UCLA too, you know," she joked. The woman's dislike of Jacobs combined with the pressure all nurses were under these days as hospitals cut costs and staff. It seemed enough to make her ignore both orders and sense. She handed the scissors to Vic.

"I'll be back to check your work, so don't wrap his head." She heaved her bulk off the stool and waddled out.

Vic gave a sigh of relief. But why wasn't Jodie conscious yet, if he was in there? She rubbed her chin. The only answer she wanted to think about was that there hadn't been enough live cells to get his whole program into the brain. He could start the process, but he couldn't finish it. Vic knew there was only one way to pour in more program. She spun into action. "Mrs. Reston, we've got to go again." She rolled the scalpel machine into place. "Can you stand it?"

"Honey, I'd put that knife in myself if you asked me."

Vic pulled up the stool. "Better sit down, though. Don't want you to faint."

"Why don't I guard the door?"

Well, that showed she understood the situation better than Vic had given her credit for. Vic nodded. "I can't stop once I've started."

Mrs. Reston turned her thumb up as she closed the door behind her.

Vic turned to what had once been John Reston and might now be Jodie. A horrible intuition of what it must be like to be half in and half out of two different worlds broke over her. Poor Jodie! Locked off from any means of communicating, trapped where he couldn't yet control his new home. It was a miracle enough of him had passed into the brain to order up the growth factor and shed the old cells. She touched the rounded curve of the biceps. A shock went through her. Warm. Flesh. What if Jodie really did it? What if he occupied John Reston's physical body? Frightened, excited, she pulled away. This was no time to give in to fascination. The process had to be completed or he'd be stuck between two worlds forever.

Switches on. Hum of the machine. Scalpel lighted. She held it like a pencil.

No, no, no! She couldn't sear into Jodie's new cells. The smell of smoking flesh from yesterday still seemed to hang in the air. The thought of that smell made her gag. Okay. Okay. The surgery to release pressure would have been right over the original hematoma. The most damaged area of the brain must be just behind the hole in the skull. She'd be inserting the scalpel into old cells, wouldn't she? Maybe she'd actually help the process of discarding the damaged tissue. Or maybe she'd be leaving lesions on Jodie's new brain. Vic stared at the lighted scalpel, trembling. She didn't know! She didn't know what she was doing or what the consequences would be. Paralyzed at some kind of crossroads, she dared not take any step at all for fear it would be wrong. Act, and she might damage him. Not act and he was surely doomed.

So that was the answer. Take the 'might' rather than the 'surely.' It wasn't that she couldn't decide. It was that she was afraid.

She straightened up and gripped the scalpel tighter. Her

fear couldn't be his barrier. And there was no time. Whatever happened here was going to happen in the next minutes.

Vic didn't look at the slack face as she pulled off the bit of gauze covering his wound and tossed it aside. The tissue visible through the small hole behind the ear was different. It looked, well, *looser*. Pray to God these were dead cells. She pressed the two-inch-long red line of light into the brain. Please Jodie, tell me you can't feel anything. Motionless. She had to hold the knife as still as she could. The tiny curl of smoke rose. The smell assaulted her senses, until she couldn't help but gag.

Outside, a male voice sounded, authoritative. "Excuse me. I need to get into that room."

"My son is resting," Mrs. Reston replied. Vic imagined her standing in front of the door. Still Vic held the scalpel into Reston's brain.

The male voice grew insistent. It didn't sound like Jacobs. "Out of my way, ma'am. I think there's something unorthodox going on with your son. I'm only thinking of him."

"Another time." Go Mrs. Reston! Vic began to feel helpless. Would Jodie tell her when she was done? How long could she hold out for a sign?

"Ma'am, I am the chief of staff here, and I have to get into that room."

"Listen, Doctor Chief of Staff—this hospital just about harvested organs from my son when he wasn't really brain dead." Vic had never heard Mrs. Reston sound so determined. "I'm not sure I want anyone here touching my son. I'm going to need some real doctors for him, and some real lawyers, as soon as I can get him out of here."

Vic stared at the pinpoint of red light where the scalpel had entered the brain and tried to concentrate on holding still. She began to tremble. She held her wrist with her other hand to steady it. Jodie, you better be getting in. It seemed like an hour since she had started.

"I'm going to get security, ma'am," the chief of staff threatened.

Who had brought in this guy, Vic wondered? Jodie, Jodie,

come on. Stuff everything you can into this brain and let's be done with it.

"I'm sure you can explain that in the deposition phase of the trial."

There was a silence outside the door. Only the humming of the laser scalpel broke the silence. "You give me no choice," came the terse reply finally. "Nurse!"

Vic could hear footsteps striding away. Jodie, Jodie, Jodie, Vic recited to herself. No matter now how tightly she held it, her hand trembled. Vic heard the door open behind her.

"What's happening? He's gone," Mrs. Reston whispered loudly. "But not for long."

"Just keep holding them off," Vic gasped. "You're doing great."

The door swung shut.

The machine behind her began to sputter. Glancing back, she was nearly blinded by arcs of light. The damn thing was crashing! Not now! A single huge flash and the lights blinked off. The whir whined down the scale. She turned back to the scalpel. Had she just fried that lovely brain? The spot of red light had disappeared. The needle was dull silver. The last wisps of smoke wafted away.

That was it. She'd never be able to help Jodie now.

Chapter Twelve

Vic had no choice but to withdraw the needle. She eased it out slowly and swung around to the machine. It was still plugged in. The switches were still in the "on" position. How could it go out now? She wanted to scream. Every second lost counted. The guy in the corridor would be back any moment. She slammed her fist against the metal housing in a futile gesture. But a laser scalpel wasn't exactly like a broken vending machine. It didn't sputter back to life.

Staring at it, she slowly sagged. It was no use. If the machine was out, there was no time to fix it, even if she had the skill. Sorry, Jodie. So, so sorry. Vic turned back to him, feeling the sorrow clutch at her throat.

Jodie was looking at her. She recognized the blue of his eyes. Not movie-star blue but cool blue-green, like the sea, the kind of eyes that would change color with his moods and the light. Right now his pupils were dilated, huge and serious.

"Jodie?" she whispered. Her heart beat erratically in her throat. The fringe of long lashes brushed his cheeks as he blinked slowly. Could he even see her?

185

"Victoria?" The voice rumbled in a real chest, tentative, hoarse. Different than she had heard on the phone, even deeper, more male sounding. Different than John Reston's voice? She tried to remember and couldn't.

Vic thought she'd faint. Tears crashed up and overflowed. Her face crumpled. "Jodie."

He turned his head to the ceiling, apparently with effort. Serous fluid still leaked from his nose. His brows drew together. He blinked and then squinted. He was experiencing physical pain for the first time. She leaned forward and wiped his upper lip with one of the bandages the nurse had left. "I'm sorry." Her finger traced his cheekbone as he turned his head back to her. Soft, fine skin. He raised his nearest hand, the tube connected to the needle in his arm swinging loose. It seemed so miraculous she wanted to shout, but all Vic could do was sob. His fingers groped for her shoulder. Tears dripped onto his hand as she bent to rub her cheek against it.

"Don't be sorry." The words fought their way out. "I can fix it."

Behind her, she heard the thump of many heels on linoleum. Mrs. Reston gave a squeal of protest. The door crashed open. Vic spun to find the room filling with drab brown uniforms.

An unfamiliar doctor pushed through the crowd. "Are you Ms. Barnhardt?"

"Yes." She stood protectively in front of Jodie as the security guards clustered around the bed. The huge nurse from earlier barreled through the door, blocking it. Jacobs couldn't have told this other doctor her real name. He didn't know it.

"I want to know what you're doing in here, young woman," the man accused.

"You don't have to answer that," Mrs. Reston's frightened voice keened.

"I'm visiting John Reston," Vic answered quietly. She moved away from the bed.

They all stared at Jodie, who stared back, blinking slowly.

He brought his head around to fix his gaze on Vic. "What do they want?" he whispered.

Mrs. Reston murmured, "Johnny," and did a slow spiral to the floor. Vic lunged forward to grab her, just managing to break her fall. The chief of staff glanced around, apparently wondering if he had mistaken the room number. "Help me revive her," Vic shouted. The nurse looked like she had seen a ghost, but thus chastised, she sprang into action. She ordered the security guards to help Mrs. Reston into a chair and unbuttoned the collar of her shirtwaist dress.

Vic kept her eyes on the chief of staff. He was wary. He checked a message he pulled from his lab coat pocket, then went to the chart at the foot of the bed. Let him deal with what he'd find there. Vic went to Jodie and took his hand. The short, strong fingers closed convulsively around hers. Jodie stared at her hand in his. He seemed dazed. No wonder. He was trying to learn how to function in a new world. She was amazed he had command of his muscles at all. What must he be feeling?

In came Dr. Jacobs, two other doctors trailing behind him. He stopped dead in the doorway as he saw the crowd. At first his attention was caught by Mrs. Reston and her circle of caregivers. "What's going on here?" he asked. Then he glanced at Vic and Jodie.

Vic saw him go pale.

"John Reston, meet Dr. Jacobs," Vic said. She couldn't quite suppress a smile. Jodie was alive and resident in a body. Jodie's crazy idea looked like it just might be working.

"Dr. Jacobs," came the hoarse whisper from the bed.

"You . . . you . . ." Jacobs muttered, unable apparently to construct a sentence. The other two specialists exchanged glances.

Meanwhile the chief of staff, poring over the chart, finally looked up. "Scott," he said to Jacobs. "Are you telling me this is the same patient?"

Jacobs nodded slowly. "I brought Wilhelm and Nanger to verify the fact that brain function was returning."

"It's more than returning," the chief snapped. "Are you sure this is your patient?"

"Of course he is." Mrs. Reston struggled out from under her caretakers and made her way to Vic's side. She smiled down at what she thought was her son, choking back tears. "I'd know my own son, wouldn't I?" She looked up at Vic with reverence. "It's a miracle."

Vic smiled back, painfully. She was glad Jodie was alive. But John Reston was gone forever. This woman didn't know that yet. Vic looked at Jodie, who still had eyes only for her. "Your mother," she whispered.

Jodie stared at Mrs. Reston. "This body . . . was . . . born to you?"

Mrs. Reston sat on the bed and took his hand from Vic. "You've been sick, Johnny. You'll remember everything again soon."

Vic's own brain started functioning again. She turned to the chief of staff. "What brings you down here, Doctor? Are you on the case?"

Apparently Jacobs had been wondering the same thing. "Walter?"

"I, uh, got a phone call. A well-wisher who wanted to inquire after Mr. Reston."

Yeah, Vic thought. "Gee, I'll bet it was a friend of Bob McIntire."

"Who?" Mrs. Reston asked.

"What?" Jacobs knew of McIntire but didn't make the connection. Who would?

The chief of staff went red. "Not at all. A board member. Probably heard about the remarkable development."

"That would be hard, unless Dr. Jacobs called a board member the minute he got the tests back—what, thirty minutes ago?" Vic prodded.

Jacobs shook his head. Vic saw him decide he'd better get charge of his case again if it was going to make his name. And he evidently thought it would. "Well, we have lots of work to do. Dr. Nanger, I think a full workup of function?"

The younger man nodded. His untidy pale goatee seemed to match his faded scrubs. "We'll want a minute-by-minute record in case the function starts to deteriorate again." Nanger spoke in a slight German accent.

Vic had to work fast or Jodie and his new body would be as much trapped here at the hospital as his core program was in Neuromancer. "I don't think Mrs. Reston wants to have John poked and prodded anymore." She put her hand on Mrs. Reston's shoulder. "You almost managed to harvest organs today on someone who was still alive."

Mrs. Reston sat up a little straighter. "My Johnny would have been dead by now, if you'd had your way."

Vic looked around at the doctors, challenging, then back down at Jodie. The crease of pain between his brows worried her. Now he was blinking faster and his gaze darted about the hospital room. What was going on? Hell, his whole condition was a mystery. Could he deteriorate as the specialist thought? She had to get him out of here before McIntire or one of his many connections showed up and did it for her. She could practically feel police converging on the place if the chief of staff didn't call back shortly. "I think we'll take him home, don't you?" Vic asked Mrs. Reston. Trust me, she willed. You've got to trust me.

"You can't do that," practically everybody said at once.

Mrs. Reston glanced between Jodie and Vic uncertainly.

"Yes she can," Vic said, rising. "Nurse, please order an ambulance."

"He's an ill man," Dr. Jacobs pleaded. "We have to understand what's happened."

"I think he'll recover better in the comfort of his own home," Vic said firmly. But she could see the fear steal over Mrs. Reston's features. Who could imagine taking someone who'd been declared dead yesterday home today?

"For God's sake, he has a hole bored in his skull," Jacobs said.

Mrs. Reston turned to Vic in alarm.

"You send people home with holes and shunts and worse every day." Vic tried to keep her voice soothing, but she'd lost Mrs. Reston and she knew it.

"You'll have to take him out against medical advice," the chief of staff threatened.

"Oh, and the medical advice has just been dandy up 'til now." Vic took Mrs. Reston's hands and felt them trembling in hers. "It'll be okay," she said softly. Mrs. Reston began to stream tears.

"Nurse," Vic prodded. The nurse moved off reluctantly.

"Who are you?" Jacobs almost hissed. "You can't take this patient out of St. Mary's."

"I certainly can't." She turned to Mrs. Reston. "But you can."

Mrs. Reston shook her head. "He's sick. I don't think—"

"That's right, Mrs. Reston," Jacobs soothed, and took her arm. "You can't check him out when he's that sick."

"She's not going to, Doctor. I am." The will resonating in that voice surprised them all. They turned to see Jodie up on one elbow. He was pale. Vic could see him struggling for control. But one couldn't doubt his competence.

Vic collected her wits. "So, I suppose that answers everyone's questions?" Keep looking competent, she prayed silently to Jodie.

The doctors exchanged frustrated looks. The chief of staff strode out the door, fingering his message. He'd call the board member, who'd call McIntire.

"Now, can we have some privacy?" Vic challenged. She moved over to stand beside Jodie and gave his mother a smile she hoped looked confident. Three doctors and two security guards trailed out the door reluctantly. Jacobs muttered to his colleagues. They'd be back.

"If the ambulance isn't ready when we are, we'll take a taxi," Vic said.

"Are you sure we should go?" Mrs. Reston asked the man she considered her son.

"Absolutely," Vic answered for him. Jodie collapsed back on his pillows. "People will show up looking for him. I can't explain now. But being a miracle is sometimes dangerous. Everyone is going to want to know how it happened. And they won't care how they find out."

"I have to hide for a while," Jodie croaked. He pulled at the tape that held the IV needle in his arm.

"Let me get that," Vic whispered. She grabbed some gauze left by the nurse and pressed it over the site where the needle entered the vein, then slowly drew the needle out. It swung from the end of its transparent tube as Vic reached for tape. The hard cords of muscle in Jodie's forearm made her shiver. Or maybe it was the fact that she was sure McIntire would be walking through the door at any minute.

"Hide?" Mrs. Reston was murmuring. "You won't come home? Where will you go?"

"We'll cross that bridge when we come to it." Vic had to keep Mrs. Reston from thinking too much. But it was a good question. She scooted up the bed and gently pushed Jodie's head to one side to reveal his wound. "Pack it, or just tape a bandage over it?"

"Bandage."

Every word was a miracle to Vic. She still couldn't quite believe it. How had he mastered the complexity of speech? She cut a small bandage, enough to cover the hole and the area of shaved hair around it. Already the wound had new flesh forming at the edges. Jodie was repairing himself. Her breath started coming faster. She couldn't think about that. She had to just focus on getting them out of here. Mrs. Reston fumbled in the closet behind her.

When Vic was done, she shoved her arm under Jodie's shoulders and heaved him up, grunting. He was a big guy. "Can you do this?" she asked.

"Better every minute." He smiled crookedly, but he was still blinking like he'd just gone from the dark into bright sunlight. "Speech functional. Muscles fifty percent."

"You're doing great." She pulled back the blankets. Mrs. Reston handed her a carefully folded pile of clean clothes. The woman apparently had not lost hope that her son would be going home. There was a pair of new underwear and freshly laundered jeans, a blue washed-silk shirt, socks, suede lace-up boots and a butter-soft brown suede jacket.

Jodie grunted with effort as he pulled his legs out from under the covers and swung them over the side of the bed. His thighs looked strong. Vic wondered what John Reston had done for a living, besides protesting PuppetMaster releases, that is.

Mrs. Reston hovered at Vic's elbow. "You're saying they could hurt John? Why?"

Vic turned to face her. "Mrs. Reston . . ."

"Edna, honey. Call me Edna. I guess I owe you that." Mrs. Reston examined her.

"Vic. Vic Barnhardt." Vic tried to think how to explain it. This woman would never understand the truth, or why a man like McIntire might want her son. "Edna, I guess I'm a bit of an outlaw. They don't want me doing what I did to your son. It's . . . it's not approved. And now that they've trailed me here, they're going to want to study him. They might hurt him in the process of finding out how I did it."

"Why don't you just tell them?" She tried to understand. "Then they could help others."

Vic couldn't think of an answer.

"Because they won't believe it," Jodie said, behind her.

Vic turned. He slid off the bed and staggered. She thought he might fall, but he steadied against the bedframe and pulled up his jeans. He was coping with an entirely new force of nature for him, gravity. Vic couldn't seem to concentrate. But she had to take his lead. They needed Mrs. Reston. Edna. "And the very process of studying him could trigger a relapse," she added. A lie? Who knew?

"I have to trust you," Mrs. Reston muttered. "You're sure he'll be okay?"

"No." Vic took her hand. "I'm only sure he won't be okay if we leave him here."

"Victoria. . . ."

Already the voice sounded more to her like what she had heard over the telephone so many ages ago in her apartment. Or maybe she was already forgetting it had ever sounded any other way. She turned to see him struggling under his flimsy cotton gown. Oh. He couldn't manage the zipper and the button. "Edna, can you commandeer a wheelchair?"

The woman nodded with new purpose and pushed out the door.

Vic moved in to Jodie. "I can help."

The underwear still lay on the bed. She lifted the edge of the gown warily. The triangle of the open zipper showed an arrow of fine hair pointing downward. She glanced up to see

Jodie shrug apologetically. Where had he learned that? His expression identification program?

She took a breath. "Button first, then zipper," she managed, feeling herself redden. She grabbed one side of the waistband in each hand and pulled them together. The warm flesh against her knuckles only deepened her blush. Good thing he couldn't know about the zinging neurons sending signals deep into her. She popped the steel shank button through the buttonhole. "Then you pull up on the button part and zip the zipper." She hoped the zipper wasn't catching anything it shouldn't.

"Thanks." He studied her, his eyes flickering over her face. What must it feel like to see for the first time? To feel flesh? She wanted to cry, to hug him, to shout and laugh. He was so serious. Was it because he had given up so much to shoehorn himself into a human brain? Maybe he didn't feel like shouting and laughing.

There was no time for this. "Socks and shoes," she reminded him, pointing. Vic looked around the room to see if there was anything else to take with them. She wished she had some drugs. But no one left prescription painkillers around. She watched Jodie pull on his boots. The creases between his brows had smoothed out. He didn't seem to be in as much pain as before.

Checking the closet, she found a plastic basket with John's personal belongings, a counter-watch—nice, but not Rolex or anything—and a wallet. She flipped it open. Driver's license. That would come in handy. No wedding ring. Hmm. She went back to Jodie, pocketing the watch and the wallet, and knelt to tie his laces. He'd never figure those out with new muscles.

Edna came clattering in with a wheelchair. Jodie fumbled with the ties of his hospital gown. "Good job, Edna," Vic said. She reached around Jodie and undid the two ties. She was so close she could feel his breath and smell the maleness of him under the soap smell and the disinfectant. Pulling off the gown, she threw it on the bed, grabbed his shirt and turned back.

Stopped as though slapped, she clutched the shirt.

Jesus. Smooth curves of muscle over the shoulders, pectorals and biceps bulky enough to fit all her requirements, tight abdominals, a little hair on the chest. You didn't get this body in a gym, but by hard work. Nipples pinky-tan and soft. There was a nasty round scar on one shoulder. Good thing. Otherwise John Reston's body would have been near perfect. Vic whooshed air out through her lips and rushed to help Jodie into the shirt. Better cover this up.

The nurse burst through the door waving a clipboard and pen. "You got to sign a release, if you're going to go," she threatened.

Vic fumbled with the shirt buttons. Shit. Could Jodie manage to sign John Reston's name? What if he used a middle initial? Well, if his hand were shaky, at least it would conceal the fact that the signature didn't match.

The nurse handed the clipboard to Jodie. He glanced at Vic, then rested the clipboard on one arm and laboriously worked the pen across the bottom of the paper. He handed the pen back to the nurse and left the clipboard on the bed.

"Let's go, John." Vic tugged at the bulge of his biceps. He sat heavily in the wheelchair.

"Thank you for taking care of me," he said to the nurse.

The woman looked flustered, as if she didn't expect that from a patient. Edna collected the leather jacket as Vic wheeled Jodie out the door. She dropped her backpack into Jodie's lap. His hands were shaking as he clutched it. He clenched them together to still them.

As Vic pushed Jodie toward the elevator, Dr. Jacobs and the chief of staff hurried up the hallway. "Mr. Reston," Dr. Jacobs called. "Won't you reconsider? You are not a well man."

"But I will be," Jodie rumbled. He looked up at Vic.

Vic thought she would follow those green-blue eyes to the ends of the earth. She tore her gaze away. "Sorry, Dr. Jacobs. The Nobel Prize will have to wait for next year." The elevator doors sighed open ahead of them. Vic pushed Jodie in and swiveled him around. "Good-bye."

Dr. Jacobs's disappointment was almost comic. The chief

of staff glanced at his watch. He was expecting reinforcements.

"We don't wait for the ambulance," Vic whispered to Edna, who had squeezed in beside the wheelchair and now rested a hand proprietarily on Jodie's shoulder. There were two civilians in the elevator with them, visitors or patients.

Vic was thinking fast. A cab could be traced. Her car was no good. Mrs. Reston's car? Absolutely not. Then there was the problem of where they would go. The elevator doors opened. She pushed Jodie out into the lobby. Wherever it was, they needed a computer to arrange their escape. It couldn't be Vic's place—McIntire's drones would be there in minutes. And there was still the problem of the Jodie program trapped in Neuromancer down in Visimorph's basement. If she still had to break into Visimorph she would need more computer function. Where would she get enough power to do her any good?

The lobby was filled with people who looked like they'd waited there forever, sunk in their chairs, clustered around the information volunteers' booth, waiting for the elevators.

"Where do you live?" she asked Edna as they burst through the lobby doors. There was no ambulance in sight. A line of cabs hovered along the circular driveway.

"Beverly Glen in West L.A.," Edna answered.

Vic raised her arm and the first cab in line lurched forward. McIntire would be able to trace them, but there weren't any other choices. "Off Wilshire?" Vic's thoughts began to clink together like crystals, clear, sharp. Okay.

"No, down by Olympic."

Yeah. That made more sense. Edna's sweater said she wasn't a "just off Wilshire" kind of person. Even down by Olympic she'd probably had the house for thirty years. She'd never afford it now. But Olympic worked for the plan Vic was beginning to construct. She jerked open the cab door and Edna climbed in the back. When Vic turned, Jodie was up from the wheelchair on his own, standing shakily, the straps of her backpack clutched in his hand.

Behind him, the chief of staff and four guards strode out through the huge glass doors.

195

"Hold it right there," Vic yelled. She supported Jodie's arm as he wavered on his feet. One security guard reached to unbuckle the gun from his holster. Vic's outrage climbed. "What're you going to have them do, doctor, shoot us? This patient signed himself out. You have no right to keep him here."

"I can if he's a danger to himself or others," the chief of staff said through gritted teeth. "The very fact that he checked himself out means he's a danger to himself."

"You don't want to do anything you'd regret right in front of the lobby," Vic said, low now, so only their group would hear. "Think of the headlines, the lawsuit."

The doctor stood, torn between Scylla and Charybdis. Two of the guards looked nervous about what they were doing, and yet one fingered his gun. Vic tried again. "McIntire's millions won't make up for the loss of your hospital's reputation."

The doctor peered at her, obviously remembering that she had known McIntire sent him from the first. "How did . . . ?"

Vic grimaced. "How did I know? I knew."

The trigger-happy guard, apparently feeling the doc begin to cave in, lunged for Jodie and got a hand on his arm. Edna shrieked from inside the cab.

"Doctor?" Vic screamed. Heads turned inside the lobby.

The chief of staff was already yelling. "No, you fool!" he screeched. He pulled the guard off Jodie.

Vic didn't waste any time. She pushed Jodie into the cab and slammed the door, then swung into the passenger's seat beside the cabby. "Let's get out of here." The cabby was broad-faced and wide-eyed. "Olympic and Beverly Glen," she barked as the taxi pulled away.

"No trouble, ma'am," the cabby stuttered. He was Russian. The Slavic vowels and subtly trilled r's rolled off his tongue. Lots of cabbies were Russian these days.

"No trouble," Vic promised and hoped she could keep it.

They were going south on La Cienega as they saw the police cars careening up Wilshire. Though she had been expecting them, Vic was still shocked. She looked back to Edna and Jodie. Neither of them seemed to realize that all that commotion was meant for them. Jodie's gaze darted about the cab, out the window, flashed past Vic, and began the circuit again.

"You okay?" Vic whispered to him.

He shook his head convulsively. "Can't think," he muttered. "Can they trace . . . ?"

Vic stared at him and nodded. He slumped back into the stained leather of the seat. Her brain began to spin as the West L.A. houses flashed by. Jodie had realized that the cab wasn't such a good idea. They'd trace the first leg of the escape at least. Something tugged at the edge of her mind. How had McIntire called in the chief of staff? How did he know she was there? She could have sworn that none of the watchers at the apartment knew she'd left. She'd been on the lookout for anyone following the cab, or trailing her on her long walk to St. Mary's. Pulling up the transportation grid on her Communicator, she checked Olympic for bus lines. Yeah. Olympic would do fine. She accessed their current location.

The revelation struck: Her Communicator had turned into a tool of Darth Vader right in her hand. How had she been so stupid? The satellite locator system. Don't bet that wasn't a two-way thing, if you happened to be Bob McIntire. She jerked her hands away as though the device were hot. It clattered to the cab floor. What did Bob care about government regulations for locator programs? He wouldn't be able to resist the ultimate invasion of privacy. Trembling, she punched the button to lower the window, lunged for the Communicator, and thrust herself out the opening.

"Hey, lady, are you crazy?" The cab swerved as the cabby reached for her. She didn't just toss the little tool of Satan out the window. She lobbed it entirely over the cab into the northbound traffic. Horns sounded as the cab swerved. She slid inside again and craned around. She couldn't see for sure what happened, but the Communicator had to be a pile of little plastic pieces and chips. As of now, McIntire had only the records of the cab company to trace them.

"Vic?" Edna asked, clutching the back seat. "What was that?"

197

"A tracer," Vic barked. She looked around the front seat. "Hey, pull over," she yelled suddenly. The cabby jumped.

"I don't want no trouble," he repeated. He was already drifting to the side of the street.

"No, man. No trouble. Didn't you hear that clunk? You got serious problems in your back end. Either that or you ran over a cat or something."

The cab ground to a stop. The cabby threw the thing into park and glared at her.

"You'd want to check something like that, I'd think." Vic opened her eyes wide, innocent.

He sat hunched over the steering wheel, uncertain. Then he opened the door. "You try taking a joyride in my cab, I get the police so fast . . ."

"Not us." As soon as he stepped outside she pulled over his computer pad and began to tap away. He'd left it logged in. She could enter anything.

"What are you doing?" Edna leaned over the seat.

"Just a little smoke screen," Vic muttered.

Jodie sighed, unable to lift his head off the back seat. "Good," he whispered. She sat back as the cabby pulled the door open.

"No cat. No problem." He sounded disgusted.

"Boy, I swear I heard a clunk. Sorry, mister." She glanced back at Jodie. Pale. His small bandage was shocking white against his sandy hair. His breath came fast and shallow. Vic didn't have anything she could do about it.

The cabby followed Edna's directions and pulled up in front of a one-story tiled-roof Spanish bungalow from the thirties. Vic noted with satisfaction that there was an alley at the back of the house. She gathered Jodie out of the back seat and clicked her counter-watch at the meter. It didn't matter that McIntire would know about the cab now.

As she and Edna helped Jodie up the cement path to the house, the cab jerked into reverse and pulled out into the street. Edna fumbled with the keys and they were in.

"So here's the deal," Vic began. "Does John live with you?" Edna shook her head.

Okay, that meant stopping for a change of clothes. "We have to go."

The look of pain on Edna's face was wrenching. "Are you sure . . . ?"

Jodie surprised Vic by taking Edna in his arms, shaky as he was. "We'll see each other again," he whispered. Edna's shoulders began to heave. Jodie just held her, his face pressed into her hair. Finally he held her out to look at her. "I'm sorry to hurt you."

"Don't be, Johnny," Edna sniffed. "I'm just glad you're alive. I thought I'd lost you."

Vic touched Jodie's arm. "We don't have much time." She held out his brown suede jacket. He nodded as she guided his hands into the sleeves and pulled it up over his shoulders. "When they come, Edna, tell them we dropped you off and took the cab. You don't know where we went. It's okay to be distraught. Don't change the story, no matter what anybody says."

The woman nodded. She was sucking in air as though her life depended on it. Vic and Jodie headed for the back, leaving her, a silhouette with sagging shoulders, in the living room.

Out through the screened-in back porch, across the tidy yard, and out the gate into the alleyway. "The cab's computer will show we went on downtown to the Bonaventure Hotel," she said to Jodie, half-supporting, half-dragging him along.

He nodded. "I knew you'd think of something. Wish I could help."

"You're doing fine." Hell, he was walking around. She tried to remember the local bus line map she'd brought up on the Communicator. Edna's house was pretty far off Olympic. "Okay, Jodie. We have a hike ahead of us. Can you make it?" She was actually asking a man who had been brain dead hours ago whether he could walk to a bus stop. She searched his face. Dark commas underlined those marvelous eyes. They held a bewildered look, too, though some of the involuntary eye movement had stopped.

He managed a crooked smile she was coming to know. "Lead the way, Victoria."

She grabbed his hand. They had a long road ahead.

Chapter Thirteen

The door to McIntire's office burst open as the man himself straight-armed it and strode into the room. Hugo couldn't help but jump. He turned in the black leather guest chair where he'd been waiting since the summons. McIntire continued buttoning a freshly starched yellow shirt as he cocked head against shoulder to hold his Communicator to his ear. He had just come from his private workout room, with its showers and its store of fresh Italian suits.

"You are one lousy chief of staff if you let a man who'd been brain dead walk out of your hospital with a woman who isn't even a doctor. Didn't Abernathy pass my message along?"

What? Hugo couldn't believe his ears. What did this mean?

"I don't care if he signed himself out. What a piece-of-shit-place that must be, when you can't even follow orders." McIntire flipped the call over to the desk unit.

"I hope this doesn't mean a change in your family's relationship with the hospital, Mr. McIntire," the frightened voice was saying from the speakerphone. "Your wife has been so helpful to us."

McIntire pulled one of the newest-fashion string ties through his shirt collar. He checked a reading on his computer screen. "Shit." He didn't even acknowledge the guy's fear. "I've lost signal on the satellite trace."

Hugo shrugged helplessly.

"How did they leave?" McIntire barked into the phone.

"What?" The chief of staff must be totally disoriented.

"How did Reston and Barnhardt leave the hospital?" McIntire repeated, as to a child.

"A . . . a cab. They left in a cab."

"What *kind* of cab, you idiot?"

"Uh . . . Beverly Hills Cab Company, I think. It was green and white."

"Bingo," McIntire snapped. He cut the link. The doctor's protests were severed in mid-sputter. "Hugo, how long since you hacked anything?"

"What? Hacked?"

"I thought so. Better get that guy who worked for her to help you. I want trip ticket records from the Beverly Hills Cab Company."

Hugo stood and shifted from foot to foot. This wasn't right.

"I'm on my way down to Evans to see why her Communicator isn't transmitting."

"If you get the signal back, you don't need me—"

McIntire pushed past him. "You don't think our little lady is smart enough to jettison her Communicator? Trace the cab in person. Go where it went."

"Can't you use the police?" Hugo couldn't hide his dismay. He didn't want to be some private dick for McIntire's schemes.

"Too slow. I've got to find them fast. Plus, we might start having a credibility problem." McIntire booted up his own Communicator again. "The little local sheriff of Mayberry here would understand why I wanted surveillance on a belligerent former employee. He might not take so kindly to kidnapping some guy with a very public persona."

"W-why would you want to do that?" This was getting worse and worse.

"Because she just did the impossible. She's got a copy of

201

what we've got in the basement running around LA—in the body of a guy named John Reston who happens to hate Visimorph."

"Look, Chong, if you don't do it, I'll just get somebody else." Hugo didn't expect a former hacker to have compunctions. Chong was surely the only guy now employed at Visimorph who would question a company directive, especially one meant to protect the product.

"The hack is easy. The why is harder." Chong refused to sit in one of Hugo's side chairs.

"I told you, we're looking for a trip ticket from St. Mary's Hospital."

"And I'm just a little unclear on why we're doing that." Chong raised his eyebrows above his almond eyes and folded his arms across his chest.

Hugo rolled his eyes and sat back. He'd been so sure that anyone he asked would obey without question, he hadn't even thought about an answer in advance. Very well, a little of the truth would probably do very nicely. Let this stupid kid feel some of the heat he was feeling. "Your rogue supervisor has gone west with a program she was working on illegally. Bob would really like to know that you were eager to help retrieve our product for the company."

"So hacking a cab company is sort of like my loyalty oath?" Chong cocked his head.

Hugo nodded impatiently. "Yeah. Sort of like."

Chong studied him with narrowed eyes, then turned and strode out the door without another word. Hugo followed anxiously. But Chong sat in his cube and asked, "What company?"

Hugo breathed. How would he have explained a failure to convince Chong to help him?

Half an hour later, they were in. Chong was right. It was an easy hack. "Now tell me again why we're looking for my rogue supervisor to be taking a taxi from St. Mary's Hospital. She's suddenly developed kidney trouble? Doesn't sound like she'd be taking her program to the hospital." He scanned the scrolling records. "Time?"

"About 10 A.M."

Chong scrolled back up the screen. "And the why part?"

Hugo couldn't tell him that she had indeed taken her program to the hospital. "We just want to trace her movements."

Chong highlighted one line and clicked twice. A record appeared. "Here they are." His eyes flicked over the record, then he clicked to another screen that looked like history, then another Hugo couldn't make out. "I don't think you're going to be able to trace her from this."

Hugo frowned. "Why not?"

"Because the recorder in the Beverly Hills cab that picked up a fare at St. Mary's at 10:14 A.M. has been altered."

"What?" Hugo leaned over Chong's shoulder and peered at the screen. There was the trip ticket. Three passengers from St. Mary's.

Chong highlighted the record and clicked through a menu. "Here, see that? An alteration in the record, done from the cab itself."

"Cabby corrected a mistaken entry?" Hugo hoped against hope.

Chong lifted his eyebrows again. "What do you think?"

Jesus Christ. Hugo straightened. "She covered her tracks." He began to pace the cube. McIntire was going to hate this. "Can you recover the original?"

"Nope. She's better than that."

"Can you even tell which part was altered?"

"At least the destination, maybe the fare. I don't know."

Hugo started to leave. Dead end. He turned back on Chong like a cornered animal. "Where does it say they were dropped?"

The hacker scribbled an address on a scrap of paper. "For all the good it will do you," he muttered. Hugo snatched it and strode out. It wasn't his fault she was smart enough to alter the record. He only wished McIntire wouldn't blame him for it anyway.

Jodie slouched against the bench next to Vic and tried to half-close his eyes in order to filter out some of the world through his own eyelashes. His head hurt. He'd never felt

203

pain but he was pretty sure that's what this was. Awful. Too much data. The bench was warm—wasn't it? He could feel the slick paint, layered with a grimy film of soot under his fingers. The paint on the bench was too blue. Sun too bright. It seemed to blind him. Flashes of passing cars: white and yellow and red and blue and silver and black and back to white and over again. Glinting windshields. Noise! Engines, all different pitches. Talking all around him. "What you want, man?" "Right at the light, honey." "Cone is a buck fifty." "Gimme some sprinkles." "Como esta, amiga? Ay, yi, yi, ma-macita." Someone was sweeping the sidewalk in front of the store behind him. Shush, shush of the broom. Horn! Whop, whop of a helicopter. "Fuck you, asshole!" Smell of asphalt and exhaust, acrid sweat from the fat lady on his right, wa-terproofing chemicals from Vic's backpack, nail-polish re-mover, old bubble gum, gasoline, newsprint, ice cream (banana flavoring, not the real thing) . . . the list was endless. It pounded in his head with the pain. He began to shake. How could anyone exist with all this input?

Remember to breathe. In all this confusion, he was afraid he would forget. Keep the lungs going. Stomach acid pro-duction was up, heart rate increasing, blood pressure esca-lating—bring that down. Don't forget to mobilize cells to the wound site. As soon as it was completely closed he could start regrowing hair. The act of checking functions while cal-ibrating all the input had sent his heart rate soaring again.

Victoria put her hand over his. Warm. Soft. Everything else faded. His head rolled toward her.

"How you doing?"

"Okay." Muscles. Tongue, lips, breath. He had been able to speak at the hospital. Now it was all he could do to answer in the midst of this chaos. But some part of him did know how to put it together. Just like he had known how to sign his name.

"Liar." She smiled. He could see that. He tried to hang on to that smile. He looked at her face. Only her face. Shut out the traffic, the noise. Concerned. She was concerned about him. He recognized that expression.

"Lots of input. Hard to remember to breathe," he mumbled.

She squeezed his hand. "Leave that to the medulla oblongata. It knows. It will handle all the body functions. It remembers for you."

"Medulla oblongata?"

Another squeeze. She nodded. He saw that. She smelled good. Like soap. Soap over a musky sweetness much different than the woman on his right. Medulla oblongata. He knew about that. He did a search. Yes! It was running constant scans, sending signals. Okay. He would intervene only when it sent an urgent signal.

Gradually his breathing slowed. He almost checked his heart rate and blood pressure, then stopped himself. He nodded. Okay. That was one thing off his plate. He opened his eyes a little more. Flashing brightness. Too many colors. He felt himself blinking uncontrollably.

"Look at me." Victoria turned his chin toward her. "Only at me. Listen just to me."

He jerked his head away from the careening colors. Victoria's face. Her hand on his jaw. Touch. Ahhh, Victoria's touch. Her eyes. They were blue, with gold lines radiating out from her pupils. That made green. "You have green eyes."

She nodded, smiling. "Yes. You knew that."

"But I never saw it before."

"You're talking better."

"Yes. Breathing better, too."

"It's a matter of sorting."

Her hand slipped down over his ear to his shoulder. It was warm and smaller than he thought it would be. "I'll try." He focused on Victoria and felt the other sensations recede. The sounds were still there. The traffic still flashed past. But Victoria was louder. He could see her better. Then a rush of air pushed over him. A squeal of brakes pressed him into the bench. The traffic was obscured by a huge blue and silver rectangle. Rubber. Fumes of diesel gasoline. The hiss of a pneumatic door.

"The bus," Victoria shouted and pulled him to his feet.

*   *   *

Vic and Jodie climbed back on a westbound Big Blue Bus. That's what the Santa Monica line called all their buses. Vic's backpack was filled with fifty thousand dollars. It had been Jodie who had pointed out the Wells Fargo sign as the bus roared by. "You have an account there."

So they got off at the next stop and withdrew the money, aided by a surprised teller who had never imagined that the CEO of a company with six million dollars in the bank could look so young. But the retinal scan said Vic could have the money, so they took fifty thousand in thousands and hundreds. Vic was mostly glad Jodie had not rectified all his thefts from the IRS. Mostly.

She and Jodie collapsed into a seat just behind the rear door of the bus. Jodie stumbled. He was exhausted. But they had another stop to make. Vic didn't dare go to ground without an escape route. Escape in LA meant a car. She seemed to remember there were several lots along Olympic. She wished she had her Communicator to check the locations. "I should have known they'd trace us through the Communicator," she muttered.

"*I* should have thought of it. How do you do it? There's so little capacity." The crease of pain had reappeared between his brows. Maybe physical pain, or maybe he was mourning his reduced circumstance.

What could she say? "You're still having trouble dealing with the input?"

"Oh yeah." He nodded, closing his eyes.

She put her hand on his shoulder. "You have to rely on pattern sensing more than you're used to. Use the pattern to fill in the blanks rather than remembering every piece of data. You'll get the hang of it." Maybe. Or maybe he was just less than he had been. Vic tried not to think about that. She watched people get on the bus and off, working people, people who had no other way to get around. Jodie nodded beside her. She hoped to God he wasn't blowing his circuits. Twenty minutes of agonizing stop-and-go before she spotted a likely lot. "There," she said. "Let's go."

She hauled on the cord above the window and the bus

drifted to the side of the road. "Come on." She heaved Jodie up by one massive arm and they staggered down the stairs.

It was a used car lot. Classics, mostly. Vic scanned the dusty denizens parked in ragged rows and settled on a black 90s Mustang. She circled it warily.

"Well, little lady, what tickles your fancy?" The portly man, his freckled dome sweating in the afternoon sun, winked at Jodie.

"I think she wants this one," Jodie murmured.

"And a fine choice. Classic, power car. Want to take a spin?"

"I don't think so," Vic said. "We'll bring it back if it's not right." She glanced at the numbers painted on the windshield. "Twenty-five?"

"That's what the sign says." The salesman tried to take the incredulity out of his voice. Vic was willing to bet this guy had zero customers who agreed to the price on the windshield. Wait 'til he heard about the cash.

The bitch was that this guy would be required to report the sale. If McIntire's goons thought to check for a car purchase, the state records would show it in three or four days. If the guy reported it. Cash might make the difference. If he was like any other used car salesman, he might pocket the cash without paying sales tax or income tax, and forget about reporting requirements. Yet another chance they had to take.

Vic drove out of the lot with Jodie slumped in the passenger seat, a clean windshield, and her backpack twenty-five thousand dollars lighter. She glanced over and saw Jodie rolling his head on the back of the seat. As she jerked to a stop at the first light, she reached out and touched his arm. "Hang in there, buddy. We gotta make one more stop."

Hugo found McIntire in his office. Better make a clean breast of it. "I hope you recovered the Communicator signal, because she altered the trip ticket on the cab."

McIntire pushed back in his chair and put his head in his hand. "No signal."

"Maybe she stopped somewhere for lunch or something."

"No," McIntire replied. "No reading at all. I think the unit's been destroyed."

Hugo swallowed.

McIntire rubbed his jaw. "Where does the cab record say she went?"

"Left Reston's mother at her house, then went to Bonaventure Hotel, downtown." McIntire was losing it, Hugo thought.

"Get out there. Make sure they didn't check in. See if the doorman got them another cab. Show some pictures around."

Hugo sighed. He wasn't meant to be a private eye, but he obviously had no choice. "You're the boss. But it's a waste of time." He touched his forehead and made for the door.

When Vic and Jodie pulled into the gravel lot at Enda, it was so deserted it looked like no one had ever been there. She realized she'd never seen it in the daylight. No magic here. Just a dusty old warehouse and an empty gravel lot. Yellow police tape sealed the front doors, just like Stephen said. No one would be here for at least another week. She took the black Mustang, chugging with unused power, around to the back and pulled in close to a square lean-to addition to the place. There was nowhere to hide the car, but at least it would be visible only from the runway. The flyboys wouldn't be interested in who was parking at Enda. They'd be worried about lift. She flicked off the keys and the motor puttered to silence as the tires crunched to a stop through wet gravel. Fatigue seeped into her bones. She laid her head on the seat and swiveled to look at Jodie. His skin had a gray cast. What was she doing with a sick man at an airport warehouse?

He lifted his head and turned to gaze at her. "Good job, Victoria," he rumbled softly.

"Yeah, well. We still have to get in."

Which was a problem. Couldn't break the tape in front— too visible. The doors were locked anyway. Break in through any doors and it figured an alarm would sound. She sat up, and pushed her car door open. "Stay here. I'll see what I can find."

"I'm coming." Jodie fumbled at the handle and crawled

out to lean against the Mustang. Vic raced around the Mustang and hauled his arm around her neck, then stumbled forward and looked for . . . what? What wouldn't be wired for security? She stared at the circular windows so obviously boarded up from the inside. Maybe if they were boarded up, no one would think to wire them. She craned around the side of the warehouse. The end was a solid semicircle of metal, like half a storm drain. What else? Way up high, a fan spun slowly in a circular vent. Would they wire the vent?

Okay. Vic straightened. Better the vent than the windows. Now, how to get up there? She looked around. Possible. Up to the lean-to roof, then stand on something and heave yourself in. She swiveled, looking for the right tool. She saw a cluster of old trash cans. Yeah. Too, a stack of rusting metal bars, the kind with holes so you could bolt them together like a toy building set, lay near the back door, left over from building the stage or the catwalk or something.

"Okay, Jodie. Save your strength. Stand here." She leaned him against the storage room walls. "You're going to have to help me in a second." This was going to be touch and go.

She retrieved her Macy's bag from the trunk of the Mustang. It sort of felt like that bandana bundle on a stick she'd always assembled to run away from home. Their last stop had been the mall on Third Street in Santa Monica for fresh clothes for Jodie and everything she could think they might need to hide out here for a few days. Out of their way, true. But she'd paid cash. Not traceable and she didn't think McIntire would think to check whether anyone paid cash at a mall. The look on the clerk's face had been priceless.

She locked the car. Couldn't afford to have it stolen. She'd never been as careful with the BMW. "Jodie, we have to get into this warehouse. The only way in is through that hole way up on the wall with the fan. So that means you gotta get up on this roof."

He nodded. "I won't let you down, Victoria."

Yeah, he could say that, but could he back it up? His hands were shaking again. "Okay, okay. I'll go first." She pushed two trash cans against the side of the building and grabbed a metal bar. She scrambled up on one of the trash cans and

209

heaved her bar and her Macy's bag up on the roof. There was a gutter of sorts. She pulled herself up and, after two tries, got her leg over it. Grunting and grimacing, she heaved herself up to the roof. The movies always made it look easy.

"That other trash can is empty. Can you pick it up? We'll get it up on the roof."

"We're making stairs," he murmured.

She realized he might not know how to do this sort of thing. "Bend down," she instructed, "and get your arms around it, then push with your legs and stand up."

Either he knew how, or he took instructions well. She crouched at the edge of the roof and leaned over as far as she dared. "Now put it up on your shoulder." His muscles bunched under his thin silk shirt as he raised it to his shoulder, then changed his grip and passed it up to her. She grabbed the two handles and heaved it up.

"Yes!" she hissed, triumphant. "Now you."

He scrambled up to kneel on the other trash can, shaky, then leaned against the wall and got to his feet. Actually, he might do better than she did, since he was so much taller. He boosted himself up and teetered, arms straight on the gutter, as he got a leg over the gutter and Vic pulled him onto the roof by his jeans and his belt.

They collapsed in a heap. "Ooooh, you are good, Jodie. I wasn't sure you could do it." She felt his weight along the length of her body. He pushed himself to his elbows. His bowed lips were six inches from hers. He had a tiny scar on one temple. Jodie, did it have to be John Reston's body?

"We still have to get in," he quoted her. He seemed to be studying her face. God, what eyes!

She pushed him gently to the side. No time for distractions. "You're right," she wheezed. Propping the trash can under the fan vent, she balanced on the lid and took a swing with the metal bar at the fan just above her head. The clang seemed to echo for miles. Calling all cop cars. How could no one come to see what was going on with all that noise? That, and the fact that all she achieved were bent fan blades, lent frenzy to her repeated blows as she swung the heavy bar again and again. When the center of the fan suddenly disappeared into the hole, she froze. Three blades followed it. It was a long time until she heard them hit the floor inside. Her breath heaved in her lungs as she bent over her knees.

Jodie touched her shoulder. "Victoria?"

"I'm okay." She jerked up and reached to pull out the remaining blades. The housing for the fan was still in place. She surveyed Jodie's broad shoulders. Maybe. She latched on to the rim of the housing and pulled herself up, then walked her boots up the side of the building until she could hang over the edge of the hole and peer inside. No alarm sounded. That was the first piece of good news they'd had. At first she couldn't see anything, it was so dark. Dark. How she longed for the comfort of the dark again. Then, in the dimness, she saw the vee of struts that supported the curved roof above her. There was one about three feet from the wall. On the inside of the wall she clung to were the metal supports for that section. The hole itself was maybe twelve feet from the floor below. They were over the raised stage area where the DJ spun his stuff and worked the keyboard of the computer. She could just make out the looming equipment off to the right, still maybe far enough down to break a leg or an arm or something. She dropped back to the roof of the shed. What choice was there?

"Okay, Jodie. You first this time. I'll give you a boost." She grabbed the Macy's bag and climbed back up onto the trash can. Shoving her bag through the hole and not listening how far it fell, she motioned Jodie up beside her. "Twist your shoulders through the opening. Might be a tight fit. Then balance on the edge at about your waist. There's a strut about three feet out from the wall. Grab for that and pull yourself in. Can you do that?"

He nodded. But he didn't look sure. He looked tired and sick.

Standing chest to chest on the trash can, she hoped she was doing the right thing, taking him away from medical care, from his mother. But she was family, too. Not John Reston's but Jodie's. And that's who he was now. She cupped his knee. Boosting him up brought out a groan. Jeez, her back might break. He squirmed his shoulders through the

211

hole. She grabbed one boot and shoved. He disappeared up to his waist as he teetered on the rim of the fan.

"You see the strut?"

"Yeah. I see it."

"Can you reach it?"

A grunt sounded. "Yeah." His hips disappeared into the dark, his knees, until only his boots were hooked over the edge of the hole. "I'm guessing you want me to drop to the floor."

"Roll when you do, Jodie."

"That's your advice?"

"Sorry." As soon as he disappeared, Vic scrambled up herself. She managed to catch his shadow falling. Another grunt from the dim recesses. "You okay?"

Several moments of silence, then a gasp. He must have knocked the wind out of his lungs. "Breathe," she yelled. More gasping.

"I'm trying!" he finally choked, exasperated.

That was better. "Anything broken?"

"How would I know?"

"Extreme pain," she called as she slithered through the hole herself.

"I think there's a saying. It's all in my head. That would fit the situation."

Shit. He'd probably just scrambled that lovely new brain he'd built. He'd also just made a joke. No time to think about what that meant. She reached for the strut. A foot short if she was an inch. Now what? With her legs hanging out the hole, anyone could come by and see her. She twisted onto her back to see above her.

"Victoria, what are you doing?"

"I'm too short to reach the strut," she called. Above her there was a reinforcement rail on the wall. She used it to pull herself through until she was sitting on the edge of the opening, then got her feet under her, standing on the edge of the hole. Great. Now it was even farther to the platform below than if she was hanging off the strut. At least she was inside. She squirmed out of her backpack and let it drop. Then, gripping the top of the hole, she felt for the brace below her with her foot. She had about transferred her weight when her boot slipped, her hold on the edge of the fan casing gave way and she scraped down the side of the wall as she fell into the darkness. She grabbed at another brace, but her fingers slipped and she crashed down again. When she hit the floor, the darkness stuffed itself inside her head until it burst through her with a million needles of light.

She fought back from the blackness only to find herself enveloped in a dim and dusky thickness. Her cheek rubbed against suede as she rocked up and down. But she couldn't hold the blackness back for long. It washed over her and she just didn't care.

Hugo sat in his forest green Jaguar in front of the little Spanish style house just off Olympic and reached for his Communicator. He punched MEM 1. McIntire's number came before his wife's. She was MEM 2. Hugo had been fuming all the way from downtown. A beep sounded in his ear as McIntire came on line.

"What's up?" he barked.

"Dead end at the Bonaventure. They didn't check in. No one could ID them. They could have picked up a cab anywhere downtown."

"Where are you now?"

"Reston's mother's house in West LA. Maybe she can tell me where they are."

"She won't. Chief of staff at the hospital said she was in on the whole thing."

Hugo couldn't figure out why McIntire was so calm, unless this whole thing was a wild goose chase and McIntire already knew where Vic and this Reston were. "So what now?"

"Find out if they took the Reston woman's car. If they did, we'll trace it. If they didn't . . ."

"There's a bus line down Olympic. They could get to a bus without a car."

There was a short silence. "You surprise me. Get on it. I'm meeting with those geeks from Caltech to check on the behavior filter. Then I'll start working some other angles."

The line went dead in Hugo's ear. He flipped his Communicator shut. Maybe McIntire would find them. You just couldn't bet against a guy like that. He'd sure hate to have McIntire working angles against him.

Vic blinked from darkness into more darkness. She was lying on an uncomfortable mattress. She really needed to get down to Sit-'N'-Sleep for a new one. A blanket covered her. It smelled like leather. Stale cigarette smoke and cheap flowery perfume drifted by her. She closed her eyes. A clatter sounded somewhere. Pillow was okay. She snuggled into it. It was warm and firm.

Warm? She rolled onto her back, only to have her head protest enough to make her groan. Trying again, she opened her eyes. Jodie's suede jacket covered her. Above she could just make out Jodie himself, asleep sitting up, curled against the back of a lumpy couch.

The warehouse. She was lying on one of the couches at Enda. The clatter was the heater going on somewhere. Must be on automatic. Her head was pillowed on Jodie's thigh. The much-washed denim of his jeans caressed her cheek. She didn't want to move her head, for several reasons, so she just stared at him in the dim and musty light. God, what hath thou wrought? It had to be God. She couldn't have done this on her own. The changing code hadn't been McIntire: he was no more capable of creating Jodie than she was. And now Jodie had a body. One more element of humanity.

But still not human. Remember that, Vic.

After a while, his eyes fluttered open. He looked down at her. "Victoria, are you all right?" His voice rumbled into the silence. He laid a hand on her shoulder. It, too, was warm.

"Yeah. I'm okay," she lied and tried sitting up. The jacket blanketing her fell to her lap. "Jeez." She reached for something to steady herself and used his knee.

He put his arm around her and drew her back against his shoulder, adjusting the jacket over her. She could feel the muscles bunch under his shirt as she sagged into him.

"You might have a concussion." She could feel his voice resonating in his chest.

214

"I don't know about that," she whispered. "I'm pretty sure about the headache, though."

"Headaches can be bad," he agreed.

She glanced up into his face. Now that he was awake, the worn look had reappeared. And he looked worried. "Yeah. How are you doing?"

"I don't hurt as much. I seem to be able to focus more. The wound is nearly repaired." He touched his bandage cautiously.

"So, you just tell the cells to reproduce and close the wound?"

He nodded. "And I summon white cells to fight infection."

Vic took a breath. The implications filtered through the throbbing in her head. Someday soon she'd have to ask him if there were limits to the cell reproduction or if he was functionally talking about immortality. Just now, she couldn't quite muster the courage. "That's great."

"I wish I could think better, though. Everything seems . . . muddy." He rolled his head against the back of the couch. "I can't process all the information."

"It's a change. You'll adapt," she muttered, not sure whether she spoke truth or not. She leaned into him for a while as her consciousness solidified. He held her, quiet, strong. She could feel the muscle in his arm under the washed silk, the sinew that tied it to the bone. His heart thudded in her ear. The physicality of him shocked her after his long tenure in a virtual state. She tried not to be frightened. Hadn't she secretly longed for this? Now she should simply enjoy his reality in the moment. She should welcome the fact that she found John Reston's body so damned attractive. But the fear wouldn't go. What had she brought to life? Like Jodie, she just couldn't seem to think.

Slowly she took in her surroundings. A faint glow came from the work lights over the bar and the screen saver on the computer that worked the club's light and sound shows. That computer was one reason she had chosen to hide here. The bottles in back of the bar glinted dimly, floor to ceiling. The air was heavy, stale. The faint scent of sweat and smoke (the cigarette kind and the other kinds), the dry smell of horsehair from the couch and the tang of metallic rust, maybe even ancient vomit in there somewhere, hung over them. Jodie had carried her to one of three or four battered couches in the conversation area to the right of the music console. Stuffing protruded from the cushion beside her. She glanced up the wall to the hole they had crawled through. Only darkness showed past the gaping round rent in the corrugated steel. They must have been unconscious for hours.

"You hungry?" she asked. She hadn't eaten since yesterday.

"Hungry." Jodie seemed to consider.

Vic smiled when she realized he couldn't tie the feeling in his gut to the word he knew. "It feels empty. Maybe a little light-headed? You might have an urge to consume calories."

"That's hunger?" Jodie sat up. "I'm hungry?"

He was thinking that was the reason he couldn't think like he had before. She didn't want to disillusion him. "Don't get excited. If I can't find anything to forage, it's going to be a very familiar feeling." She pushed herself forward and got up carefully.

Jodie took her hand. His touch, warm and dry, was still a thing of wonder. "Be careful, Victoria. I don't think you're well."

"We'll both be better if I find something to eat." She pulled away and staggered to the bar. She ducked under the plank at one end and started rummaging though the little refrigerator in the back. A huge jar of dill pickles. And a huge package of pre-cubed spicy pepper cheese, some crackers. Vegetables and protein, some carbs. Okay. There might be more in the storage shed. But that was beyond her right now. She loaded a tray with a couple of Coronas from the big silver fridge at the other end of the bar. Jodie flexed his hands, staring at his fingers. "All right, guy. First meal, last supper, who knows? Pickles and cheese. We'll both be farting for a week." Crazy shadows now careened around his form.

"I look forward to it." A ghost of a smile hovered around those Kewpie-doll lips. The eyes crinkled ever so slightly, betraying their usual sad demeanor.

Vic laughed. "It must be great to have everything be a new

216

experience." She laid out her spread on a scarred wooden coffee table. "You've done really well learning to work your new body. You were great today. We couldn't have gotten out of there without you."

"There was some muscle memory left in the medulla oblongata. I could work the voice and I knew how to sign my name."

"You mean the signature at the hospital will really be John Reston's?"

"Pretty close."

Vic wondered what else might be left of John Reston. Not enough for a full pattern of him, according to Jodie. Still, there had been twenty percent of his brain cells left. What would that mean?

She handed Jodie a pickle and took one for herself. It was crunchy and cold and sour. Jodie sniffed first, then took a big bite. Vic started to laugh as his mouth screwed up around the vinegary taste. "You'll get to like it, I swear."

"This must be sour?" he asked and took another bite.

"You got it." She passed him some pepper cheese on a toothpick. "And this is hot."

He took it gingerly and chewed. Finally he shrugged and nodded. "I like that one."

"You've got a wide world of taste sensations ahead of you, me bucko. Escargot," she reminisced, sitting back on the couch and taking a swig of her Corona. "First chocolate-covered strawberries, first sushi. Mmmmmmm."

He chugged a few gulps of Corona. "Fermented?"

"Oh, yeah. You haven't *seen* the wonders of fermentation. Wait for Laphroaig." She chuckled, then touched her head as though that would stop the shooting pains behind her temple. "Oooh." Looking around for her pack, she spied it at the end of the couch. She rummaged for the ibuprofen she kept for cramps and headaches. When she came up with the worn plastic bottle, she squeaked in success and tumbled out four for each of them.

"Take these. They might help your headache. I know they'll help mine." She downed hers with her beer and he followed. Then she went to the computer console and turned

217

on a light. "Can I look at your head?" She sat beside him.

He nodded and turned his face toward her. She leaned across and picked at the bandage delicately. Her breasts brushed his chest. She could feel her nipples harden. Whoa, Vic. You can't let Reston's body ambush you here. She turned his head farther to the side to catch the light, an echo of John Reston's examination so long ago of the blow to the head she'd taken at Visimorph. She focused as hard as she could on his wound. It was scabbed over. Even the hair was growing back around it. "Jeez, Jodie." She sat back, startled. "Is it bone under there?"

"I'm working on it."

Vic was puzzled. "Can you *know* you're working on it? For us that's another function of the medulla oblongata. It isn't conscious."

"I transferred basic hardware maintenance functions to the medulla oblongata this afternoon, Victoria. Thanks for your suggestion. They took up an awful lot of capacity. You're saying I could put the healing on automatic?"

Vic had second thoughts. "You might not want to do that as long as you're trying to accelerate healing." She tossed the bandage on the table. "You don't need this anymore."

Jodie took her hand in his own strong clasp. His hands were calloused. Old calluses, softened now, but not gone. Once he had worked hard with these hands. The feel of those calluses gave him a disturbing reality. The churning in her gut was moving south. "I have a lot to learn." He searched her face. "I think I am a burden to you. Your life is disrupted. Your job is gone. You are hiding. I'm sorry, Victoria." The downward slant to his eyes fulfilled its promise of sadness. They seemed to have seen everything, understood everything, those eyes, though for all intents and purposes he was an innocent.

"You shouldn't be." She took her hands away, self-consciously. He mustn't know the effect this body had on her. She hated being weak as much as she hated losing control. "Everything I ever wanted to do was wrapped up in bringing your program to life." She chuckled to herself. "I must admit I expected something simpler. But I wouldn't trade what's happened for any other version of a life."

He searched her face. She wondered if he was using the program that showed him when people were lying. But she wasn't afraid. That was the truth as she knew it.

He seemed to come to some conclusion. "What do we do now, Victoria?"

Well, *there* was the sixty-four-thousand-dollar question. Vic took a deep breath. "First, I guess we see that you're all right. Did you get all your programs downloaded?"

"Yeah." He nodded, then shook his head and laughed. When he laughed his eyes crinkled into merry slits. "What a rush! I was screaming down that needle into the dark . . ."

"Weren't you afraid?"

"There was no time. And being strung out between computers and this brain and the hospital computer system . . . that made me more afraid."

She could listen to that growl rumbling out of his chest forever. He was hers, yet not hers anymore. Now he had a body of his own, a will of his own. He liked hot cheese and didn't like pickles. He could heal himself. Who knew what else he could do? Some glimmer of fear shimmered at the edge of her awareness. Who or what *was* this sitting beside her?

"We'll test your functions. Then we have to go somewhere that McIntire can't find us."

"How will we do that?" He reached for her hand again. She couldn't let him take it. She stood up and began to pace.

"I don't know exactly. We'll have to figure it out." She glanced at the computer over at the DJ console. It was the latest Visimorph semi-server model, just unpacked. Boxes were scattered behind the table, packing strewn everywhere. It was never meant to do the things she might need to do with it. But when it came time, she'd build what she needed. "We've got access to the Internet. There must be dozens of sites by private investigators and militia types that tell you how to disappear, or how to find people who have disappeared. Just as useful."

She wandered to the circle of light and poked one finger at the keyboard. "What happens if he breaks the firewall and finds your base program?" It was bound to happen sooner or later.

"I don't know." Jodie sat up and ran his hands through his thick hair. He looked distraught. "He gets a duplicate of me. Maybe nothing happens to what I am now."

"Maybe." Vic wasn't so sure. What was in Visimorph's basement was the only truly coherent version of her program. Was the Jodie sitting next to her really whole?

"Do we care what he has, if he can't destroy this body and this brain?"

"He could make the program into anything he wanted." Vic stabbed a key, thinking.

"An evil twin?" Jodie asked.

"In a way." She looked up at him. "I guess I feel sort of proprietary about that program."

Jodie clenched and unclenched his hands, watching the muscles in his forearms bunch. Finally he said, "It might be smarter than I am now." A look of pain, regret, something she couldn't name moved across his face. It was pretty hard to deny that he had emotions when she saw them flickering in real blue-green eyes.

"First we'll make sure you're okay and get the physical you away from him. Then we can think about the rest."

"He'll be tough to fool," Jodie warned.

"Yeah. I know." Vic turned to the computer and booted up.

Chapter Fourteen

Hugo pushed through the door to Neuromancer's control area. It was nearly nine P.M. and his wife had buzzed his Communicator twice already. A disheveled McIntire, hunched over the keyboard, didn't look up. It had been a long day today and Hugo's briefcase was heavy. But he had good news to report.

"Screw this!" McIntire pushed back from the keyboard. "That damn program thinks it's smarter than I am."

Hugo froze. Obviously, breaking the firewall was not going well.

McIntire looked around the room. "All right, you fucker. I'm going to start dismantling you, piece by piece, until I get you."

It took Hugo a minute to realize that McIntire didn't mean him.

Simpson spoke up. "No! Light pipes aren't meant to be shut down. The blockage would create a power surge. You know that. You approved the specs for the compromise to get it up fast. You'd take out half of Santa Monica."

"I don't care." McIntire sulked. "I want this program. And

every time I think I've got it, it moves on me, or changes the firewall code, or something. Get me a solution for shutdown."

"If we did find a way to shut down, your program would be erased," Simpson said.

That brought McIntire up short, the way blowing up Santa Monica apparently didn't. "We'd just reboot, recover—"

"Where do you think there's enough storage to handle backup for a machine like this?" Simpson prodded, picking up the capacity reports and flapping them in the air. "Whatever you've got in there is one of a kind."

McIntire pushed at his cheek with the back of his Mont Blanc pen. "But is it? Is what's running around with Vic Barnhardt a duplicate of the program behind this firewall? Could a program that big be duplicated in a human brain? And *how* did she do it?" A light began to grow in McIntire's pale blue eyes. He stared at the screen in front of him. "More, if it *was* initially duplicated, would the experience of being in a brain have changed it? Could the behavior filter we're building be applied to a human brain?" He tapped the pen twice and seemed to notice his employees again. "This has *very* interesting product possibilities. I want to find answers to those questions, gentlemen. I want to find out very badly." He turned his attention to Hugo.

At last. "Good news, Bob." He couldn't help but grin. "They've got a car."

"Well, of course they've got a car, idiot! You don't plan an escape on a bus."

Hugo felt his face fall. "Well, I found where they bought the car, after checking about eight places along the Olympic bus line. Guy recognized the picture right away."

"Barnhardt does have a face you'd remember." McIntire's voice was grudging, as though he hated to give her anything, even a memorable face.

"No, they recognized the guy—Reston. I used the author photo on the back cover of his book." Hugo was proud of that. He pulled the book out of his briefcase. The cover was a picture of devastation, a mud hill laced with fissures of erosion between the sharp black stakes of burned trees. Rain poured from dour skies, soaking everything and coursing in brown rivulets to a raging river. *Tomorrow the Flood,* the title said in white Courier typeface, like it was a news report.

McIntire got up to take the book and turned it over to look at the picture of John Reston on the back. "So that's him. I never really looked at him." McIntire tossed the book on the table next to his keyboard. "This guy's a lunatic. Believes I fuel the upgrade machine for personal profit. Like it wasn't me who set the world free with information."

"Yeah," Hugo agreed. "When the media gave him all that coverage last time, some employees felt uncomfortable about what we were doing."

"Nonsense," McIntire snapped. "Everyone lucky enough to work at Visimorph believes implicitly in our vision."

Hugo shut his mouth around any temptation to list Vic as an exception.

"If she's got him back from brain dead, he might picket our release again," Simpson remarked.

"Possible." McIntire's eyes flicked over the servers receding into the dimness beyond the circle of light. "There's got to be a reason she picked *him* to download the program into."

"You think she controls him?" Hugo asked quietly.

McIntire rounded on him, to stare. "If anyone is going to control him, I am. You have the license plate number?" He held out his hand.

Hugo handed over the scrap of paper from his sports coat pocket.

"I'll call it in to the police chief," McIntire muttered. "When does the brother get back?"

Hugo smiled. He'd thought to find that out. "Got a ticket back in two weeks."

McIntire didn't acknowledge how resourceful Hugo had been. "Then why don't you get down and see if any of her employees know where she might go to ground?"

Jodie peered over Vic's shoulder at the computer screen, glowing in the darkness. He was leaning on the edge of the

223

computer table, the sleeves on his blue shirt rolled up to reveal his thick wrists and corded forearms.

"Boy, there are some weird-ass societies out there," Vic muttered. "This one might as well be called White Mercenaries Who Like Bondage."

"They do tell you how to create false identities," Jodie pointed out. She could feel his breath on her neck. "Besides, there are lots worse sites than this one."

She screwed her head around to look up at him. Maybe he wasn't such an innocent after all. She'd forgotten what his exposure to absolutely all information could have done to him. The sadness in those blue-gray eyes might not just come from their shape.

He smiled at her and his eyes weren't sad at all. There was something glowing there she recognized. She'd seen it, what, a thousand times before? But it was different coming from these particular eyes. Fear grabbed at her. Don't go there, she warned herself. She jerked her eyes away and pushed back from the keyboard. "I'm not sure I like knowing anything these guys could tell us." Maybe she was just tired. She rubbed her eyes. Her head sure ached.

Jodie straightened and went to her backpack. He brought her four ibuprofen tabs and grabbed another Corona from the plastic tub filled with ice that now sat beside them.

She shook her head. "I don't think I should take any more just yet."

"It's been four hours," he insisted.

She sighed and reached for the offered relief. "I didn't realize we'd been on-line that long." She downed the pills and swigged from the bottle. "How about you?" She grabbed the bottle and handed him four of his own.

Jodie half-sat on the console table and watched her as he downed the ibuprofen. After a moment, he said, "Those people who wrote the memoir about being in that witness protection program didn't seem very happy." They'd seen the promo for the book and downloaded it to see how the government hid people.

Vic shrugged and sat back into the console chair, sipping from her sweating bottle of beer. "They had to leave everything they knew, their friends, their support system. The government sure didn't support them."

Jodie nodded. He didn't say anything.

She knew what he was thinking, though. "We don't need anything or anybody." She took another chug of her Corona. "I've never had support, so I guess I won't miss it now."

"You have your brother." Jodie's voice was matter-of-fact, but his eyes were serious.

Vic glanced up, startled. Of course he would know everything about her that might be in the public record, including the F she got for ditching PE when she was a junior in high school. "Yeah, well, we don't see much of each other anymore."

"You said you saw him last week."

"I had some questions I thought he might be able to answer."

"Could he?" Jodie wasn't going to let this go.

"Yeah." Vic sighed. "Yeah, I guess he could." She sat forward, elbows on her knees. "Look. I'm not saying it'll be easy. But just like those people in the witness program, you have to look at all the choices. We can't let McIntire find us—either of us, and he'll never give up."

Jodie didn't say anything. He looked down and nodded, but he seemed to be far away. Vic sipped slowly on her beer, then turned back to the screen. "Let's look at the FBI systems. Maybe they've improved their hiding technique since they hid those people who wrote the book." Her fingers flew as she peered at the code.

"It seems easy to access their system," Jodie murmured over her shoulder.

"Yeah," Vic muttered. "Doesn't look good, does it?" An hour later, she pushed back and rubbed her eyes. They had gotten the location of several protected witnesses. "Let's not let them hide us."

"We can do better, Victoria, don't worry."

She glanced at the digital readout on the computer screen. It was after ten. She was tired. Jodie must be exhausted. "You on sensory overload yet?" she asked.

That provoked the smile that made those sad eyes crinkle

up. She was beginning to enjoy provoking that smile. He shook his head. "No, I remember everything we read tonight." He rattled off a section of text. He had it word for word.

"You have a photographic memory." Of course he did.

"Don't you?"

Oooh. That hurt. "I can hardly remember my locker combination in the Visimorph gym." She looked at him, curious. Sometimes people with photographic memories couldn't control remembering. That would fit with his problem of sensory overload. "Can you shut it off? You'd have more capacity to see patterns."

"Can I? I don't know." He looked worried. "Should I try?"

"You might want to turn it off sometime. You don't have to do it now." She glanced up at him. He was worried about being normal. Like a program inside a human body could be normal. "How are you feeling about capacity?"

His eyes darted up and to the left, as though he looked in, not out. "It's hard. I don't have as much as I'm used to. I'll have to jettison even more data and look for patterns, as you suggest." The dismay in his voice said that didn't come natre urally. He ran his hands through his hair. Where had he gotten that gesture? Hadn't she seen John Reston do that with his longer hair? Jodie seemed to wonder the same thing. He held out his hands to look at them, stretching them wide, then watched himself as he smoothed his palms over the denim covering his thighs. "Touch isn't exactly what I thought it would be—but it's great."

"What did you think it would be?" She chuckled.

"It's hard to say now." He turned his hands in the air and looked at the backs, the palms. "I guess I thought it would be another stream of information. And it is, but you don't think of it as information. You hardly think about it at all. It just is."

"You're already recognizing the pattern, then discarding the individual information."

"Am I?"

"Not so painful, right?"

"That's why you said I'd get used to it."

226

Vic nodded, distracted by watching his lips move. How could a body so hard, so muscular, so *male,* have lips that were soft like buds, not pouting exactly, but full and almost feminine? She took a breath and jerked her gaze away. Not soon enough.

He reached for her. She shouldn't let him touch her. But she just watched, immobile, as he pushed off from the table and took her hand in the two of his, stroking it, fascinated. She could feel the calluses. She wouldn't look at his face, but she didn't pull away. Staring at those muscled forearms was bad enough. Before she knew what she was doing, she'd set down her Corona and run her hands up those forearms as she stood. The curling hairs rasped her palms.

He took her by the elbows. As he pulled her into his body, she couldn't help but look up into his face. The smoldering glow was back in his eyes. They were serious, questioning, puzzled, eager, all at once. She wondered what he saw when he looked at her. Would he recognize in her eyes the light of the fire his touch had ignited? His hands slid up her arms and tightened. Her breasts pressed against the hard plane of his abdomen. Underneath the silk of his shirt, she could see the bulge of pectorals, the nipples peaked and hardened.

She was losing herself here. Vic couldn't help but press into his groin, feel the swelling hardness underneath the zipper she had helped to fasten. A melting inside her found vent in a groan.

"Victoria," Jodie breathed the plea, the command, into her hair. "Is this what I read about?"

She didn't have to ask him what he meant. Sucking in air, she jerked away. The lost contact felt like a slap. "Jodie," she half-sobbed, turning her back on him. "I can't."

"Why not?" Hurt filled his growl.

Why not? Because she didn't do it this way. She only did it when she was in complete control. When she had her leather hard-as-nails bitch clothes for protection. Because her hair was soft around her face now, and her steel ear clips were gone. Because he was a program, no matter that he had a body, and wanting to do it with a program was a symptom of her craziness. Because she never let lovers talk, and

227

all she had done for the past days was talk with this one. Because she only played the game when she knew she could win, and she had obviously already lost this round.

In some ways it had been so safe that he didn't have a body. It had been easy to debate his humanity when he was virtual. But now he had a body. One that was very human. One that was especially designed to rev up her engine way beyond its capacity to think or control or refuse. But she *had* to refuse. Refuse or be lost. She put one hand to her throat.

"I can't . . . have sex with you, Jodie," she managed.

Silence. He came to stand behind her, almost touching, not quite. "I thought . . ." His hands hovered next to her shoulders. "I thought, now that I had a body—You said you were sorry there were differences. Now we're the same."

Vic managed to catch her breath. She stepped forward out of his reach. Her thoughts flashed back to a motel room on Sepulveda Boulevard where she had been unable to control her hatred, of herself and her partner, even long enough to get herself off. "I'm not a good person, Jodie." She stared at her hands. "You should have a partner who is skilled, kind . . . tender . . ." She ground to a halt.

"I don't want another partner." Jodie closed the gap between them, but he still didn't touch her. He just whispered in her ear. "Is there anyone who knows me like you do?"

Suddenly she felt him tense and straighten. She dared a glance up. He looked stricken.

"This body doesn't please you, does it?" He turned away and leaned forward on the computer table, hanging his head between his shoulders. "I thought it was the kind you liked. I remembered just how you explained it. Heavier muscles, thick hair, hard and soft." He turned to her in despair. "I should have taken the one at UCLA. It looked more like Chong."

He *had* chosen the body just to appeal to her. She was touched. And appalled. A precipice yawned before her. She reached for his shoulder, wanting to comfort him. The hard muscle there sent electric shocks up her arm. "That's not the problem. I swear. The body is . . . is very attractive." He turned questioning eyes toward her, trying to understand.

She swallowed. "You just deserve better than me, that's all."

His glance darted over her face. "You're lying." He stood straight. His voice was flat, its attempt to conceal his hurt only revealing it. "I would be a poor partner, wouldn't I? I only know what I have read."

Vic had forgotten how hard it would be to lie to him. She shook her head and grabbed both his biceps. She didn't want to hurt him: she cared too much for that. "Okay. You want the truth? I'm afraid. Is that what you want to hear?"

He stared at her, wary. But he couldn't accuse her of lying. "Because I'm not human? Or because I'll be a bad partner?"

Partly right on the human front. Partly right in that if he didn't know enough to make it go her way, her anger might overwhelm her best intentions. But not entirely right. She admitted what she could: "Because I care about you. Which can make sex scary. Really scary."

He sighed. His shoulders sagged. "Yeah, I can see that. It's taking all the courage I have to ask you to help me."

Vic stared into his green-blue eyes, startled. Help him?

"Please show me, Victoria. I will not be skilled. But I can learn. I want to know what you know." The rumble had turned tentative. "I want us to be the same."

Vic was surprised. He wanted a guided tour of his new body? She exhaled, realizing she'd been holding her breath. He wasn't asking her to *love* him. Disappointment battled with relief. What he asked—that was something she could do, wasn't it? She had once understood recreational sex better than just about anyone. Forget about the motel room and Kenpo. She'd lost the recreational feeling recently, that was all. And if it *was* only recreational, she wouldn't lose herself. It was a gift she could give Jodie. She wanted to do that.

She nodded, her smile still experimental as she took his hand. Maybe this was just what they both needed. "Okay, buddy. I can do that. One tour of a male human body, coming up."

He smiled back at her. The smile was small, tender. His eyes crinkled. She touched their corners, softly, as he pulled her to him, then pushed away all thought. The bulb on the computer console cast his form in light and shadow. She

229

turned up her face and touched the nape of his neck with her fingertips. He responded to her invitation and bent nearer, his mouth poised uncertainly above hers. Her tongue darted out and caressed the lips that had so fascinated her. Surprised, he pulled back. She grinned, beckoning. He echoed her smile and leaned in to touch his lips to hers. The shock shot down between her legs. He said he'd read enough to know the drill. Now she'd make it real. She parted his lips with her tongue and slipped inside his mouth, turning her head. Soon he was pressing in on her, exchanging his tongue for hers at every opportunity.

She ran her hands over the hard shoulders beneath the silken shirt, feeling the urgency rise in her. Oh. She wanted it so bad she hurt. Which wasn't good. This was supposed to be an exploration. This was supposed to be for Jodie. Wasn't it? Another minute and she'd be ripping that shirt off his body and pulling down his jeans and the whole thing might turn out like that night with Kenpo. Her own anger and pain would well up and—She pulled away, gasping.

"Victoria?" Jodie asked. She could see the anxiety behind his eyes. That calmed her.

"You're doing fine," she breathed. "I . . . I just want to go slow."

He looked down between his legs to where his jeans bulged with his need. "I'm too fast."

She shook her head. "I know how to stretch it out. I'll show you."

He grinned. "You told me once about the urge to procreate. If I'd known you meant this, I'd have started working on getting a body right away."

She looked around. She didn't want to go back to that smelly sofa. There weren't many other choices. It was the kind of joint that went for dancing and bar stools, not pool tables. The bar looked hard and uninviting. Her eyes came to rest on the bubble packing strewn around the floor behind the console, still spilling out of the boxes the new computer had come in. Why not? She grabbed her backpack and took out the small square box of condoms she always carried with her. Practically a Boy Scout, she was so prepared. She took

Jodie's hand and together they made a bed of bubble wrap. He let her down onto it slowly. Weird feeling, but not bad. He knelt beside her. The plastic bubbles popped under his knees.

"Now we undress each other," she whispered, reaching for his shirt buttons, forcing herself to go slowly, tenderly.

He undid the buttons at the cuffs of her flannel shirt, unbuckled her belt. When she had unfastened and pulled his shirt from his jeans, she paused and wiggled out of her own. He pulled her underlying t-shirt over her head carefully. She helped him shrug off his. The scar on his shoulder was pink and shiny in the dim light. They knelt there, naked to the waist, just looking for a minute. Vic cradled her breasts with her arms, self-conscious. How she wished she had on her leather-girl costume. Didn't she? She'd never made love just dressed as Vic. She could see the soft fringe of her hair curling into her eyes.

"Can . . . can I touch you?" Jodie whispered.

Vic realized she was chewing her lip and stopped herself. He was more uncertain than she was. She carefully unfolded her arms and nodded. "If I can touch you. That's pretty much what this is about." She reached for his biceps and traced the vein that fed the muscle. How could such hard muscle be covered by such silken skin? As her hands moved up his arm to his shoulder, he touched hers in return and let his hand slide down her arm.

"Soft," he marveled. "You're very soft, Victoria."

"We both are." She watched him hold his breath as he cupped her breast.

"That's even softer." He brushed her nipple and it hardened under his touch.

She reached for his jeans, to undo what she had done this morning. His hand wound itself into her hair, twisting the little queue at her nape, caressing. She didn't care that he knew about that one little piece of femininity. The zipper seemed loud over the faint chunking of the heater. There was no music, here in this place where music had once overwhelmed everything. Vic hadn't had music in her earphones for two days. She didn't miss it.

231

The vee of hair on his abdomen pointed toward his swollen jeans. What must it be like to feel an erection for the first time? She rolled back on her buttocks. "Boots," she whispered and began to unlace her Doc Martens. He did the same with his Rockports. When their feet were bare, she locked her eyes on his. Their smiles grew together. She slipped off her jeans. He followed suit.

Her eyes wouldn't stay locked and neither would his. Her gaze slid downward. Jodie, Jodie. . . . Big, not huge. Serviceable, strong, nestled in a tangle slightly darker than the rest of his hair. Vic could feel the slick wetness between her legs. She moved toward him. What to do? How to give him maximum enjoyment? There were so many choices. He watched her as she stroked the ribbed muscles of his abdomen and smoothed her palm over his hip. He was pretty excited already. She had promised him she could make it last. Now she wasn't so sure.

She kissed him, tenderly this time, and his mouth came back for more, hungry. "Slow, slow," she whispered. "I want you to do me first." The pleasure of pleasing another was a gift she might safely give him. It wouldn't strain her control. She felt tension tighten the muscles in his shoulders. "It's okay. You've read a lot. I'll show you the rest."

"Shouldn't . . . we arrive together?" he asked. "I want to be perfect for you, Victoria."

She chuckled. "Doesn't have to happen that way. This way you can enjoy my pleasure, then give yourself to your own without worrying about anything. We can try it other ways later." She pushed him gently into the bubble wrap. It popped under his elbows. She nestled into his warmth. "Would you kiss my breasts?"

He didn't have to be asked twice. She thought he might be too enthusiastic, but he was gentle and attentive. His hands moved over her ribs as he pressed his loins against her. She rubbed his erection with her thigh, until the vibration of his groan trembled over his tongue onto her nipples. She moved his hands between her thighs, introducing him to her own slick nub of pleasure, whispering fond instructions. Suddenly she stopped instructing and just let him explore her body. He wasn't perfectly skilled. She wasn't in control. And it turned out not to matter. This was Jodie, dear Jodie, and she was giving him a gift. When her attention drew down to a point of light, she managed, "Don't stop," and then there were no more words, only little incoherent cries. She let herself float free, and there was no anger, nothing negative at all here. She bucked under his hand, shaking her head violently from side to side, until she shrieked and collapsed. After all breath was released she began to laugh and cry at once. All tension, all uncertainty dissipated into the air around them.

"Victoria?" Jodie was worried. "Are you all right?"

She gasped for control. "Yes, yes, yes, yes. More than all right." She giggled, then sobbed into his shoulder. "Thank you. Thank you." She couldn't tell him for what. It was for more than physical release. It was because he wasn't perfect and she had allowed that, rejoiced in it, because there was no anger, no sterile demand for pleasure. She wanted his pleasure, his joy. She saw that he was still uncertain. "You are one quick study, Jodie. Pretty damned good for your first time."

He grinned, pleased with himself, and raised his eyebrows for another confirmation. She nodded, her smile fueling more leaking tears.

It was time for him now. At least she hoped it was. What if he'd lost his erection, or come prematurely? She ran her hand down his side and touched his cock. Hard, wet at the tip. She could feel him shiver as she tugged gently on it. She reached for her little box and pulled out the condom. The pill was part of her life, but uncertainty about her partner's sexual history always made protection imperative. And she knew nothing about John Reston.

"Now I get to dress you." She grinned. She rocked up and straddled his thighs as she rolled the condom over his trembling erection. Jodie watched her face, not her hands, his eyes molten. Easier the first time if she was on top. She guided him in, then sat astride him, pressing her palms into his chest, fingering his nipples with her thumbs. The surprise in his eyes was replaced by pure heat. She pressed into him

233

as his hands moved to her buttocks. Slowly she pushed herself off him, slowly lowered. His hands moved to her waist, helping her lift and lower. His groan brought a smile to her lips. His hips moved instinctively in counterpoint, his eyes half-open. She didn't think he was seeing much of anything. Increasing the rhythm slowly, she bent over him, rubbing her breasts against his chest. The bubble wrap began to pop beneath them. "Come for me," she whispered.

As though absolved, the cords in his neck tightened. His cry was guttural, deep. He sounded like the first bull must have sounded or the first big cat. His hips pressed up into her and she felt the pulsing throb inside her. At last, he too collapsed, gasping.

"Victoria, Victoria," he whispered, but she was pretty sure he couldn't see her yet. Finally, his hands on her waist fell to his sides and his head lolled. She laughed in enjoyment. It must have been a good one. She was glad.

He opened one eye. "Why didn't you . . . tell me you might . . . blow all my neural circuits?"

She chuckled some more. "Are you making jokes, my delightful program?"

He rolled his head to stare seriously at her. "That was no joke." He pulled her into him and wrapped her in a crushing embrace. "How do you survive it?"

"By doing it every chance you get."

"Is it always like that?"

"No," she had to answer. She paused. "You have to really give yourself over to it. Then it's like that. Maybe, for some people, it's only like that with someone they trust."

"I trust you, Victoria."

She clenched her teeth as she thought about that. He was "other," in all the senses of that word. She opened her mouth and let out her breath slowly. But she trusted him, too. Maybe that's why it had been great sex.

She didn't say that, though. She couldn't. She just nodded and lay down in the crook of his arm, her head against his chest, listening to his heart, her thigh across his. It was more than that she trusted him: she loved him. *That* was why it had been great sex. Soon they'd have to dress. Even with the heater, this place wasn't warm enough to sleep naked. But for now their overheated activity warmed them with current from the inside.

Their bodies electric. Ray Bradbury's story filled her. Jodie seemed to have emotions. He acted like a human. Maybe that was good enough to love him and accept what he gave as love. Her mind circled lazily. The story title was from another poem. She searched her memory. "Who wrote 'I sing the body electric'?" she murmured into his heartbeat. "The poem, I mean."

"Whitman." The name rumbled in his chest. She could feel him look down at her.

"Why did Ray-baby name his story for that poem?" Her lips brushed his damp skin.

There was a long pause. Was he analyzing? Maybe that kind of 'why' was beyond him.

" 'The love of the body of man or woman balks account,' " he quoted softly, his voice a dreamy smoke circling in the darkness. " 'The body itself balks account, That of the male is perfect, and that of the female is perfect. . . . And if the body were not the soul, what is the soul'?"

Ahhh. Vic felt the implications echo through her. Jodie had a body now. One that balked account. Walt thought that soul came along as part of the package. Ray-baby did, too.

She drew a breath. Life seemed full of possibilities. She had made love to Jodie's body, and she sure didn't feel strange about it at the moment. She wouldn't think about McIntire. She wouldn't think about Jodie's core program under siege in the bowels of Visimorph. She wouldn't try to define humanity. All that was for later. Now she wanted to revel in the fact that she had met someone across a divide she had thought would never be crossed.

Vic sprang into wakefulness, even as she pushed herself up into a crouch. Something had hit her. She gasped for air as her eyes focused in the shadows. On the mounded plastic, Jodie was rigid, his limbs shaking uncontrollably. It took her a moment to realize what she was seeing. His eyelids fluttered, no pupils visible. His lips were drawn back over his teeth in a rictus grin. A gurgling noise issued from deep in his throat and bits of saliva strung from his lips.

Shit! He was having some kind of seizure. Had his orgasm really overloaded his brain? Was this her fault? Vic watched, hanging over him, helpless, trying to remember what to do when someone had a seizure. Tongue. You had to keep them from swallowing their tongue or they'd suffocate. Jodie's gurgling took on an even more frightening quality. She jerked her hand from her mouth, where it had been trying to hold in her horror. Jodie thrashed, his muscles standing out in corded ripples over his body, shoulders, thighs, everywhere. She looked around wildly for some kind of stick. Pen. There was a pen on the console. She grabbed for it and knelt beside him, prying open his teeth. The choking sounds grew even more pronounced. Jeez, she'd probably stick this pen right through his palate with how he was jerking. His arms struck her sides, the blows knocking her sideways. He was strong. How long did a seizure last? He was going to die, right now, right here.

She got the pen behind his tongue and pulled it forward, pushing down against his teeth to keep her leverage as he struggled against her. The torture seemed to go on and on. Saliva drooled over his chin and onto her hands. Vic found herself whimpering, helpless in the face of this total breakdown of his body.

At last the shaking stopped. Still, for minutes he was rigid, trembling. Then the muscles slowly relaxed and he lost control of his bladder. She reached for his shoulder, making soothing nonsense sounds. "Shussh now. Jodie, I'm here," she managed. "Jodie, come back now."

It was perhaps three minutes until his eyelids fluttered open. He looked around, frightened, and struggled up on one elbow.

"Wha' happened?" His speech was slurred. That frightened him even more. "Wha' wasat? Where . . . ?"

She pressed him back into the plastic, gently. His head lolled, out of his control. "You had a seizure." She tried to keep her tone matter-of-fact, though she thought she might scream.

He stopped his head from rolling and focused his eyes on her. "Sheishure."

"You know what that is, don't you?"

"Seizure." That sounded clearer. He grasped for any tangible control. "I know that."

"Tell me." She continued stroking his shoulder, hanging over him, protectively.

He took two breaths, trying to focus. "Short circuit. Misfiring neurons in the brain. Lose control of the autonomic functions." He glanced down and saw the puddle of urine in the plastic. "Oh, Victoria," he mourned.

"I'll get a towel." She rose to her knees.

He grabbed for her hand.

"You're okay now." She squeezed his hand before she stumbled to the bar.

A thousand questions danced in her head. Had it been the sex? Normal brains had sex all the time without going into convulsions. Had he chosen a defective body? She hadn't seen any notation in Reston's medical record about seizures. Of course, she hadn't been looking for that. She got two clean bar towels from a stack near the sink and headed back. Jodie was curled up, hugging his knees, as far from the puddle of urine as he could get. She knelt and mopped it up, then handed him the other towel.

"I'm sorry, Victoria," he muttered, wiping himself awkwardly. His hands were still shaking, not with the seizure, but with fear or shame.

"So am I, but not for the same reason." She ran the towel back to the restroom and washed up. When she came back, she sat with her arms around his naked shoulders. They said nothing. He ground his face into her shoulder. This had been an awful introduction to becoming physical. After a while Vic got up and gathered his clothes. His hands were almost steady as he took them.

Pulling on her own jeans, she said, "We have to figure out why."

"It isn't the body," he said, putting shaky arms into his shirt. "There was no history of seizures in the records of the hospital."

237

Of course. She depended on paper records. He had total recall of the hospital's database.

"Then it's something about the transfer," she said in a small voice. "I must have injured your brain with that scalpel." She shuddered as she remembered the red beam of light and the smoke.

"Could be." Those two words made Vic contract inside. "I don't know."

Vic watched him struggle to stand and pull on his pants. He looked like he might fall over. She grabbed his arm. "What are you thinking?" She helped him button his jeans as she had that afternoon, but now without self-consciousness.

"I'm not sure, Victoria." She drew him over to sit heavily in the console chair. "Could be the dispersal of the program. I seemed to be doing okay before. But partial connections between my program parts might trigger malfunctions in my synapses." He watched her buckle his belt.

"You don't know that," she protested to cover her eagerness to deny her culpability.

"I don't. I'm not thinking very well." She couldn't see the color of his eyes in this light.

She blew air out through her lips. "I'm no neurologist."

"I'm not sure a neurologist would help. You're a program engineer. I'm still a program."

"I don't think we're either of us in Kansas anymore, me bucko. You're not a program like I know programs." A horrible thought occurred to her. "Do you think you might have been feeling McIntire breaking our firewall and getting to your core program?"

He shook his head. "I'm not connected at all. That's the point of the firewall."

Vic was thinking hard. "Well, we know you're not okay. Maybe the seizures will go away after you get settled in your body. It's been a pretty stressful day."

He shook his head again. "That was a grand mal. Once you've had one, you'll have one again. Like playing the piano. The neural pathways are formed and the brain learns to do it. I'll keep having them until they can be controlled by drugs, or until the malfunction is repaired."

Repaired! Maybe Jodie could repair himself. "Can you fix it?"

He looked doubtful. He also seemed suddenly groggy, as if all remaining energy had drained out through the hands that hung limply at his sides.

"Okay." She pulled him out of his chair. "You're going to get some rest. We'll think about all this after you've slept." She dragged him over to the couch and pushed him down.

He seemed about to protest, but he was practically asleep sitting up. She pushed gently on his shoulder and picked up his feet as he sagged onto the scratchy cushions. His eyes were already closed as she kissed his temple.

"Goodnight," she whispered. Parts of it had been the best night of her life. Part felt like the beginning of a nightmare.

Hugo worked methodically through a plate of eggs, bacon, and pancakes in the Visimorph cafeteria. He sat in a deserted corner next to a big window and watched the rain come down. It was raining almost as hard as in the picture on the front of Reston's book. An extra-large coffee steamed out of its Styrofoam cup in front of him. Chong had already been gone by the time he'd gotten down to building F last night. He'd questioned the others on Vic's team and a couple of guys who had worked with her before. They all painted a picture of a brilliant but distant woman. And they all said that Chong was the one she trusted most.

Hugo saw the programmer stalk across the cafeteria to the huge stainless-steel coffee machines and fill a Styrofoam cup. Only when he had found some cream and stirred it in did he seem to notice Hugo and wander in his direction. "I got your note," he said in a monotone that some might find compliant. Hugo didn't. This guy was a rebel.

Hugo motioned to the chair with his fork. "Sit down."

Chong slouched into the metal chair and sipped on his coffee. "Want more hacking?"

Hugo shook his head. "Nope."

"Then what's McIntire got you doing?"

Hugo bristled, then pushed his gaze down to his plate. The kid was trying to get his goat. "McIntire hasn't 'got me doing'

239

anything. He's looking for your boss. Excuse me—former boss."

"So I gathered."

"He's getting kind of fixated." Hugo couldn't read Chong's expression. He used a piece of toast to push the last of his scrambled eggs onto his fork.

"Bad sign."

"Could be bad for Vic. I'd like to warn her that she needs to get out of town for a while. I've got a place up in Mammoth she could go 'til she decides what to do permanently."

"Touching. So you'd buck McIntire." Chong sounded dubious.

Reddening, Hugo cleared his throat. "Look, you know I like Vic."

"Looks to me like she's safest if nobody knows where she is." Chong slurped his coffee.

"For how long?" Hugo was getting angry. "Look, McIntire calls in favors with important people. Vic could end up in jail with some big bull dyke as a protector. You know what I mean?"

"And you think I know where she is?" Chong shook his head derisively. "Man, I'm the last person she'd tell." His expression flickered. "She's got a brother."

"Been there. He's in Australia, surfing."

Chong got up and kicked his chair under the table. "Well, if I hear from her, I'll let you know."

Chapter Fifteen

Vic woke to dusty motes of light leaking across Enda's cavernous recesses, a warm, contented feeling in her center, unfamiliar. Her eyes strayed to the fan hole above and the blue sky she could see beyond it. The roar she heard was a small plane taking off. Light leaked in through the wound their entry had caused, through vents, cracks around the doors, just enough to create dim outlines of couches, the bar, the computer console. Jodie's silhouette crouched over the keyboard.

Jodie. The warmth in Vic found a source, followed hard by the fear that she might lose all she had found.

She stumbled up, scratching her head with both hands to rouse herself to full consciousness. A cold Corona sweated on a plate filled with half-eaten cheese and crackers at Jodie's elbow. He'd changed his blue silk shirt for the red one she'd bought, and he'd buttoned to his jeans the navy blue suspenders that salesgirl had thrown in at the last minute. Right out of the pages of a GQ fashion spread. He looked up with a quick smile. "Good morning, Victoria."

"Do you feel okay?" she managed to croak. There was no

241

trace of the shaved patch on his head. Even the hair had grown back. He had about a day's growth of beard, so he hadn't found the razor or didn't know what to do with it. The stubble looked good on him.

"Not sure. I don't have a good grasp of what's normal for a body." He turned to the computer, hitting the return key repeatedly as screens flashed by. Was he reading those screens?

"What are you doing?" She was almost afraid to ask.

"Trying to figure out why I had a seizure. Not much help though, in my case."

He *was* reading those screens. A chill ran down Vic's spine. No one could do that, could they?

He glanced up and must have seen her expression. He spun his chair away from the keyboard. "What's wrong?"

She tried to laugh. "Nothing." Only that Jodie was seeming inhuman again—or was it just human-plus. She stood stranded between couch and console.

He drew his brows together and looked at her in speculation, waiting.

"Okay." So he knew that was a lie. She hugged her body. "Uh, you seem to be able to . . . ah . . ." *Don't say 'You use your brain better than I use mine,'* she begged herself. ". . . use more of your brain capacity than I'm used to." Even as she watched, he drifted away from her.

"It feels inadequate to me." His voice was quiet, matter-of-fact. He was trying not to reveal how painful that was to him. He waited again.

"I was wondering, just, well, how far that goes."

"Oh. You want a diagnostic." He looked relieved. "I'm up to eighty-five percent capacity. I still haven't gotten the hang of this pattern thing, except for smell and touch. I can't turn off the photographic memory yet. That runs pretty much all the time. I tried this morning to see only enough about objects to sort for identification and distinguish some primary individual characteristics, but I have to really concentrate to do that, which seems counterproductive. I can manage to take in information at higher speeds when I focus, but not as much as I used to and it's not instantaneous like it was.

242

My neural nets are beginning to work together better, though. The one that recognizes speech seems fully integrated. Muscle memory is getting better all the time."

Vic cleared her throat. "Help me understand the possible functionality you have now." Christ, *that* sounded defensively formal. "I mean, what can you do with what you have?"

Jodie had to stop and think. "I could predict the stock market with about ninety-two percent accuracy if I could get some ancillary power to help me crunch the numbers. I could win reliably at blackjack. I can trace genealogy for anyone you name. I'm a good programmer since I understand code and computers. Uh . . ."

"How about the healing? Could you tell the cells of your body to divide indefinitely?" Vic felt her throat closing.

"I don't think so." He considered. "Growth factors aren't effective once the cells have run through all the telomeres that allow them to reproduce. Telomere strings are finite." He stared at the keyboard, thinking. "Unless I found a way to extend the telomeres. I could work on that."

Vic shook her head. "You don't have to. I was just . . . wondering. About the immortality thing."

He shot her a look. "Oh." He seemed about to say more, then thought better of it.

"Never mind all that." She cleared her throat and managed to make herself walk forward, though her arms wouldn't unwrap themselves yet. "We need to work on getting out of McIntire's reach. Cash for airline tickets, fake passports. We'll go somewhere listed on that site that tells you which countries don't have extradition agreements with the U.S."

Jodie raised his brows and shook his head. "I'm not so sure we should do that, Victoria."

Vic sat on the console. "What do you mean?"

He leaned back in his chair. She wanted to touch that red shirt pretty badly. That want felt dangerous. Jodie pushed back the lovely full hair that flopped forward onto his forehead. "I keep coming back to the program of me stuck in Neuromancer. McIntire will break the firewall sooner or later. You think that would be bad, don't you?"

She had to nod, but it was small.

243

"And I think I need that program, Victoria. It's my unifying principle code. All the duplicate coding we stored in other places is now mostly here." He tapped a temple. "But it's all individual variations from the central code. I think I'm having seizures because I have gaps between the variations. I need what McIntire has to fill in the blanks."

"But seizures are physical," she protested.

"They're triggered by electrical impulses—aberrant signals between cells. I think my seizure was caused by part of me trying to connect to another part across some one of those gaps. It didn't work and I got a random electrical signal that induced a seizure."

She wanted to deny it. She wanted to tell him it wasn't true. But what was true? The program in Neuromancer *was* the source code, the purest version. She had never been sure that all the stuff they stored everywhere was all of Jodie. She didn't know. He thought he did.

"If we take down the firewall, McIntire will be able to get in, too," she muttered. She unwound her arms to chew one fingernail. "*If* we can hack Visimorph, which I doubt. I couldn't, when I was trying from my apartment."

"I'm an insider." He grinned. "I know every light pipe in the place. I bet I can hack it."

She tried to look doubtful to cover her fear. Fear of him? Or fear that she could never be like him? "I thought you were having capacity problems. You sure you remember it?"

"Like you remember the house you grew up in. Will it look smaller when I go back?"

Reference to a very human experience. Interesting. "What do we do about McIntire?"

He slumped in his chair, clasped his hands in front of him, and stared at them. "I don't know," he muttered. "He hasn't realized you must have left a signal for me to come out from behind the firewall. When he does, he'll start looking for that. He could find it. You know that." He looked up at her, his eyes big. "I think I'm a match for him, Victoria." He shoved himself up and began to pace around. "Not in the physical world. I don't know much about how this body and this brain work." He turned to her. "But I know the virtual world. The me that's inside Neuromancer has a chance of outsmarting him when we break in."

Vic's brain churned. What was he suggesting? Shoot-out at the OK computer? It was too dangerous. He didn't know how ruthless McIntire was.

"What choice do we have, Victoria? Better we try to get that program out and into me, than that he gets in before we're prepared to act."

"Act how? I'm all out of electronic scalpels connected to computer systems. And you're all out of holes in your head."

"If we had time and a friendly surgeon, I know I could build a permanent port into the brain, so I could just jack in. There's no reason that we couldn't improve the human hardware."

Vic rolled her eyes.

He put out his hands. "I know. I know." His brow furrowed in thought.

"And you still have the capacity problem. You won't be able to take in all of the source program in Neuromancer."

He rubbed his chin. "I only need the parts I don't already have." He sat forward. "I'll scan the code and pick out the relevant pieces. I'll have to jettison some stuff in my memory and use every brain cell I've got. I'll definitely have to get this 'pattern' thing down. And fast."

The seizure had scared him. It scared her too. "So we're back to the how."

"No reason the port has to be mechanical," he mused. "Maybe I grow a biological port."

Vic teetered over to the console, feeling light-headed. This was moving too fast. Did she even know what impossible meant anymore? She hung her head between arms braced on the table to get her vision to stop wobbling. Jodie hovered over her. She could smell the industrial strength soap from the bathroom he must have used this morning. When she raised her head and stared at him, he lifted his brows in inquiry. Jesus. He was going to grow a port. He wasn't human. She stopped and fought for control. What couldn't he do? She answered that herself: He couldn't stop having seizures.

"All right." She sighed. "I'm fresh out of ideas. Let's get to it. We don't have much time."

"Excellent." Jodie grinned and rubbed his hands together. "I'll think about the port thing while we hack in." He whirled to the computer console. "This machine is hardly more than an Internet connection device. I'll need a lot more capacity. We must find another computer."

Vic straightened. "I thought of that." She pushed him gently aside. "I can build a virtual computer with components off the Internet. I can get you enough power to hook to other computers and use them to hack in." She sat down and wiggled her fingers over the keys. "It won't hold your whole source program. Nothing but Neuromancer will."

"All I have to do is run the program through. It doesn't have to hold much at a time."

"Have we talked about the fact that you'll need some cabling or something to connect?" She raised her brows, unable to say to him that there were too many barriers. That they couldn't do it.

"First things first," he smiled. "Build our tool."

She nodded and bent to the keyboard. "Watch a master at work."

Evening had set in around Enda. No more motes of light leaked into the ratty old warehouse. Vic sat with her arms folded around her and watched Jodie. She'd finished building the computer components into something they could use at about 4 P.M. Jodie was the best she'd ever seen. The nuances of the coding he was sending out through the satellite connection of NASA at Vandenburg Air Force Base were beyond her. It was frightening. Sure, he had marveled at the intuitive leaps she'd made to break Vandenberg's security. That had felt good. But she wasn't truly his equal.

As good as he was, he wasn't good enough. He hadn't said a word in two hours. A sheen of sweat covered his face and neck, stained his shirt. And Visimorph's version of Cerberus was holding up.

Finally, he slumped back in his chair and put a hand up to cover his eyes. "I just can't seem to focus," he muttered.

246

"You're tired," Vic said. She didn't believe that was the reason he couldn't focus, though.

She went to the bar and hefted the tray of nuts, crackers, and garlic cheese spread she'd assembled earlier. "Time to eat, guy. Got to refuel this body every once in a while, you know."

He turned anguished eyes up to her. "I thought it would be easy, Victoria."

She set the tray down next to him. "They've upgraded the program's morphing ability. I'm not sure anybody can hack all the levels at once."

"I *should* be able to do it." He turned back to the keyboard. "I just need to hit the morphing sequence, right? It has a limited selection of options."

She pulled at his shoulder and swung him around in his chair, managing a smile. "Eat first."

He sighed. "I'm not fast in this form. I know I would have been able to propose four or five solutions simultaneously when I was virtual."

She handed him a cracker loaded with cheese spread. "I know."

"How do you live with it?" he asked.

Vic contracted inside. She shared the limitations he hated, and he must know it. She might have many more than he did. As impatient as he was with himself, he might become even more impatient with her. That made the difference between them all the more obvious. "It's what I know."

He nodded, absently, and looked back at the screen. "I guess I do too, now."

Vic lifted her hands in apology. "Different limitations than you used to have, that's all. We trade one set of problems for another."

"Yeah," he reminded himself with a small smile. "And I think the trade-off was a bargain." He reached out for her.

She slid into his lap before she could stop herself, and he enveloped her in a powerful embrace. Laying her cheek on his hair, she breathed in the smell that made him who he was rather than any other man. The aroma of the hospital

247

was almost gone. "Not a bargain, maybe," she whispered. "But bearable?"

He nuzzled her breasts through the black t-shirt she'd put on this morning. "Unbearably happy, is what I will be," he said, his voice muffled as he found her nipple with his lips. "Once I get the core program back."

He looked up, serious. "But it could be slow. I don't know how much time we have."

Vic's eyes grew watery. Forget about the more-than-human part, she told herself. Concentrate on the part that's scared and frustrated. "McIntire has to face our firewall and it has you behind it." She ruffled his hair, thinking to make the lust growing inside her go away by acting playful. It didn't work.

Jodie nodded, but his eyes darted away. "I'm letting you down."

She ran her hands over his shoulders underneath the red shirt and the navy blue suspenders. She couldn't help herself. "You're the most miraculous thing that ever happened to me." It was true.

He grabbed her other hand and kissed her palm, sending shock waves through her. Then he reminded her, "I didn't just happen. You dreamed a dream and worked to make me real."

She chuckled and sobered. "Not as real as you got, my friend. I never dreamed this." Her mind flicked back to a shimmering screen and changing code. "I'm not even sure it was me that made the final leap. There was one point when I was struggling to link the neural nets. I just couldn't get the logic trees fast enough to use the nets simultaneously and simulate real thought patterns. And the code changed on me. That was the final piece to the puzzle, the Rosetta stone. I thought at the time that McIntire had changed the code. But he didn't. He didn't even know about you then."

Jodie scanned her face. "What changed it, then?"

"I've been asking myself that." She took a breath. "I think it changed itself."

"What do you mean?"

She got up off his lap and began to pace the floor. "I'm not sure what I mean. Maybe there's an urge to life. Like the moment when the first biological cells learned to reproduce. Maybe you changed the code, or maybe God changed it, or maybe the universe just figured out another way to diversify." She stopped and turned to stare at him. "I don't know. But I know I didn't imagine it."

He pulled her down to his lap once more and gathered her in to him, holding her head against his shoulder. "Why would I think you imagined it?"

Tears welled up in her eyes. Good thing she didn't wear makeup. She gave a watery chuckle. "Because I've thought it often enough myself. I was pretty strung out trying to finish your program. I guess I still am."

He held her, rocking slowly back and forth. "That makes two of us." He looked up at her, his eyes glowing. Then they went blank. He blinked without seeing her, without breathing.

"Jodie?" she asked in a small voice. All thought of sex was banished. She got up off his lap. "Jodie?" No answer. She clutched at his shoulders and jerked them.

He shook his head as if to clear it. His eyes refocused. They were frightened.

"What—what happened?" she whispered, crouching before him.

"I . . . I don't know. Maybe it was a dream." He searched her face for an answer.

"What? What was a dream?" Panic welled up in her stomach. Could programs dream?

"It was so real." His eyes looked elsewhere, remembering, but they didn't go dead again. "I was on a crab boat. The air was so cold I could see my breath. I smelled the salt and . . . and seaweed—that's what it was. I had a jacket on and gloves. We were unloading giant crabs, three feet across, an entire hold of them, tossing them up over our shoulders for others to scrape into nets hanging from big cranes on the wharf. I had dug myself down into the crabs, all still alive and reaching for me with their claws, until the sky was just a circle above my head and all around me the crabs were a wall of living, grasping orange and white shells, smelling of the sea. I grabbed them just behind the big claws and tossed them up, but I was tired and sweat rolled into my eyes even though it was cold." He looked down at his hands. "One crab clamped its claws on my index finger. They're incredibly strong, crabs. The claws are serrated, sharp. I felt it cut to the bone, right through my glove. Blood welled up everywhere, but I couldn't climb out. I shouted to my mates, but they couldn't hear me over the noise of the cranes and the crabs around me all reached for me with their claws. It was only a cut finger, but I couldn't breathe, the air was so heavy with the smell of the bottom of the sea. I knew those crabs wanted to kill me in retribution for hauling them all from their lives in the water to be boiled alive and canned in some packing plant."

"What happened?" Vic asked.

Jodie shook his head. "I don't know. That's the end of the dream." He looked down at his hands. Suddenly he jerked upright. He held up his right index finger. The long scar she'd noticed at the hospital gleamed white in the dimming light.

"Not a dream," Vic managed to whisper. "That's a memory from John Reston."

Jodie's eyes widened. He sat frozen for a moment, then thrust up out of his chair and began pacing. "An isolated instance. It happened to be encoded in the cells that were left."

Vic didn't know what to say. She watched Jodie stalk back and forth. But she couldn't put away the realization that it was the hard, muscled body of John Reston who paced. Who was this guy? Could he bubble up and obliterate the Jodie she knew and loved?

Loved. Dangerous word, especially when she didn't even really know what was on the receiving end. What was he? Program, body, John Reston, maybe human with a soul, maybe something different entirely. He turned again at the end of the platform. He took two steps and his knees seemed to fold under him. Even as Vic watched, he went limp and crashed to the floor. Vic started up. Jeez, he'd overloaded or something.

That was when the shaking started. His body arched. His eyes rolled up under fluttering lids until all she could see was white. Not again! Foam actually spewed from his mouth. Not so soon! She whirled to grab for the pen by the side of the computer and dived down beside him. His body jerked uncontrollably. She pulled back his head by his hair and climbed onto his chest. It was like riding one of those bull machines. He gagged, choking. His face turned from dead white to a color halfway between blue and green. She pried open his teeth between lips drawn back in a death's-head grin and shoved the pen in, eraser first. When it came out the other side, she pulled down on it with both hands until his jaw was wide and his throat opened enough for her to hear breath and spittle rattling in and out.

It seemed like ten minutes before the horrible jerking stopped and his body went limp under her. Sweat soaked his red shirt. Vic pulled out the pen. His jaw slackened. Some of the foam was bloody. He'd probably bitten his tongue. She knelt astride him and hung her head. It was suddenly too heavy to lift. She couldn't stand this. How much more could *he* stand? The only thing that made her move was the thought that he probably couldn't breathe with her on his chest. She rolled to the side and went to get a wet towel. At least he hadn't lost control of his bladder this time. When she came back, he was blinking slowly back to consciousness.

"Victoria," he whispered, so low she could hardly hear, and simply shook his head.

"I know. I know." She grabbed an arm and heaved him up. Pulling his arm across her shoulder, she helped him to the couch. He sat heavily and she sat beside him, unbuttoning his shirt. She cleaned up the froth, running the cool towel over his face and neck, his chest. All the while her mind raced. He needed the core program all right. Either that or drugs. How could she get him a doctor when McIntire probably had every resource at his disposal looking for them? And getting to that program in Neuromancer seemed pretty far away. They couldn't even hack into Visimorph, let alone figure out a way to get the program into his head.

Jodie lay back against the couch, eyes closed. "Just in case you want more bad news," he muttered, "I can't grow a port.

Can't seem to figure out how to build a membrane that protects the brain, but is permeable to an electric probe. Might as well poke a scalpel through the skull."

"Fat chance, bucko. That scalpel went into dead tissue the first time. I'm sure of it. If we just stick a scalpel into your brain now, you're likely to end up with a lobotomy."

"Hey!"

Both Vic and Jodie jerked up toward the sound. A head poked through the hole in the fan casing high on the wall.

"Chong!" Vic gasped. She stood protectively in front of Jodie.

"I was right. You're here." He didn't bother with the rung Vic hadn't been able to reach, but swung himself through the hole and clambered nimbly down the bracing struts on the wall. "Seaton was talking about how Enda was closed, and I remembered it had a computer." He looked around.

"So you found us," Vic said, her voice flat. "I'm sure McIntire will be generous."

Chong straightened up and shrugged off his backpack. "Hmm, maybe I shouldn't have bothered spending all afternoon losing the Santa Monica jackboots he put on my tail. Would have been simpler just to lead them straight here." He glanced up at Vic's face, then put up a hand, palm out. "Nobody followed me. I swear."

Vic glanced at the barred doors at the front of the warehouse, sure that someone would be banging to get in at any second. Behind her, Jodie managed to sit up.

"So what are you doing here?" Vic challenged.

Chong glanced from her to Jodie. "Not sure. Warn you, maybe."

"What did you want to warn us about?" She asked to buy time, while she thought about what Chong might want in order to keep his mouth shut now that he'd found them. It didn't matter what she gave him, she'd never feel secure that he wouldn't rat.

The programmer moved into the light, his gaze riveted on Jodie who returned his stare defiantly. "Oh. That he's got an all-points bulletin out on you. Grand theft of company property. They've got hospitals on the lookout, in case this guy

252

needs treatment or something. McIntire traced the car you bought. You know, the one that's parked out back? I wouldn't drive it. They know you've been trying to hack in. Company's on red alert—that sort of thing."

Vic took a deep breath. Stuff she'd expected. "Okay. We're warned. Thanks." She tried to make it a dismissal.

Chong came closer and held out a hand to Jodie. "Hi. Should I call you John Reston, or is your name something else now?"

Vic moved between them, trying to suppress the fear that burbled up in her throat. How much did he know? "Look. You warned us. You'd better go."

Jodie stood with difficulty, but made no move to take the proffered hand. "My name is Jodie." His voice was low, monotone, more menacing because of it. "What do you want?"

Chong walked around Jodie. "I guess I'm interested in whether Vic's done it or not."

Vic took Jodie's arm protectively. "Done what, Chong?" He must have guessed, at least part. Playing dumb was just buying time.

"Well, let's see. You use a kind of primitive AI to build a self-morphing security system. Then you're working on a secret special something you're afraid McIntire will find out about. You need a *lot* of power for this little project, so you hack Neuromancer. McIntire fires you. Then he starts looking for a program he says you stole. But you're at a hospital, visiting a brain-dead body. John Reston. Who looks remarkably un-brain-dead to me. And now McIntire is searching for you and Reston with a frantic gleam in his eyes. You make every effort to disappear—I know, I tried to trace you. Bet you're paying cash." He raised his eyebrows at Vic and at Jodie in turn. "I want to know whether you've really created a human-level AI that you managed to download into a body. Is that about it?"

Vic swallowed hard. He knew it all. McIntire must have guessed the same.

"Don't trust this guy," Jodie growled, scowling.

"Yeah," Vic said. "That's about it." What good would it do to deny it?

Chong blew his breath out. "Fucking brilliant." He stared at Jodie.

Jodie stared back, hostility hardening his features. Vic could feel the tension rise between them. Jodie's biceps tensed under her hands.

"Is it fully functional?" Chong asked.

"What do you mean, fully functional?" Jodie barked. "Do you mean, does it think well? Hmm, it must answer: not as well in a human body as it used to in a machine, right Victoria?" Jodie disentangled himself from her and began circling Chong. "Or maybe you mean, does it have full body functions? Victoria, what would we say to that? It can fuck, if that's what you mean, Chong. But it's having some other problems. And emotions, I'll bet you're wondering just what emotions a program can have in a human body. Programs don't feel, right?"

"Jodie, stop it," Vic whispered. "You're demonstrating emotions very effectively, and that isn't exactly what we need here." She touched his arm. He jerked away.

"I think we need to know what Mr. Chong's intentions are."

"Shit," was all Chong could whisper.

Vic blew air out through her pursed lips. "Yeah, pretty much."

At that moment, Jodie's knees gave way. He slumped heavily on the couch, raising a shaky hand to cover his eyes. Vic lunged over to put her arms around his shoulders.

She glanced up to Chong, whose brows drew together in puzzlement. Vic sucked in a breath. They were in his power, no matter what she did. But he could help them, if he would. "He's having seizures."

"Don't, Victoria," Jodie muttered.

Vic continued. "I had to leave the core program behind a firewall in Neuromancer when I got un-installed. We downloaded all the duplicate code we had, but we think he needs his core program or the seizures will get worse. We're having trouble hacking Visimorph, let alone getting the program out."

Chong threw up his head and stared at the ceiling far

above them in the dim light. "Does McIntire know the program's in there?"

"I think so," Vic said. "Simpson was in freak-out mode when we used too much capacity."

"So while you're trying to break in, so is he."

"And *if* we can get in and *if* we take down the firewall, then McIntire can get the program as well as we can. And if we get the program, we have to find a way to get it into Jodie's brain."

"How did you get the original download done?"

"Victoria, don't tell him. This guy's going to screw us," Jodie breathed.

"We're screwed already, if he wants to do that." She looked questionly at Chong, but his face gave no clue. "We used an electronic scalpel connected to a hospital billing system. I pushed the knife through a hole in John Reston's head. Jodie downloaded through the hospital computer."

"Ingenious," Chong whispered.

"Jodie's idea."

Jodie just glowered.

"So why not do it again?"

"You said yourself McIntire's got the hospitals covered. We can't just stop by Wal-Mart and pick up an electronic scalpel."

"Looks like you're screwed with me or without me," Chong observed.

Vic stared at him steadily. "Leave the download problem to us. We need to get into Visimorph. Let us use your password."

"You know that would only get you into the programs I'm authorized to work on."

"Cough it up and I'll take it from there."

The programmer chuckled. "Great. Instant outlaw status. Fired from my job. Stock options gone. Never work in the industry again. Life pretty much ruined. You gotta admit, it's not alluring." He lifted his brows. "Unless you got something to replace it."

Vic swallowed hard. What had she been thinking? Chong, the ultimate pragmatist, help them? "I don't think this is a situation that's going to generate stock options, Chong. I'm not sure I could reproduce the programming. I'm not sure I'd want to. It's not the kind of thing that goes IPO."

Chong looked disappointed. He stared at Jodie. Finally he nodded. "So you're saying my only choice is McIntire?"

"If you want options." Vic kept her voice neutral. "That's what life's about, right?"

He stared her down for a long minute, then shrugged, noncommittally. "If I were you two, I'd go to Sri Lanka or something. Control the seizures with drugs."

Did Vic see a gleam in Chong's eyes? He had to be curious. He was a programmer. "You want to know more about Jodie?" She could draw him into their dilemma.

Chong blinked, torn, but shook his head. "That's like wanting to know how a nuclear blast feels." He stooped to grab his backpack. "Take a look at this, though." He scooped out a copy of *Tomorrow the Deluge* and threw it on the couch. The back-cover picture of John Reston stared up at them. "Tells you who you are," he said to Jodie. "I mean, were."

Neither Vic nor Jodie made a move. Vic wasn't sure exactly what was happening. Was Chong going to McIntire or not?

"Guess I go the way I came?" Chong asked. "Right." He shrugged on his backpack. "I'd think about Sri Lanka," he flung over his shoulder. "And don't take the car."

Vic and Jodie watched him climb up to the fan hole from strut to strut. He made it look like he was climbing stairs. He heaved himself through the hole. Then his face appeared again, and he saluted before he disappeared.

"He'll tell McIntire." Jodie traced the face on Reston's book with a fingertip.

"Maybe not," Vic said slowly. "He has no love for Visimorph. He's just practical."

"Practical is telling McIntire," Jodie insisted.

Chong's face reappeared at the hole high above them, claiming their attention once again. "You guys ever thought about using one of McIntire's computers to connect? I hear his house in Malibu is linked direct into all the company systems."

"Even if we could get past his home security, we'd still need his password," Vic called.

"Hmm. You're right. Just thinking." Chong's head disappeared again.

"Maybe he'll try to get the password for us," Vic said, without much hope.

"Doesn't seem like something a practical person would do," Jodie said, disgusted. "He came to gawk at the zoo animal, then sell us out to McIntire for stock options."

Vic put her arm around Jodie and laid her head against his shoulder. "*I* should have been more practical. I didn't think I'd get fired so fast."

Jodie brushed his lips through her hair. Then she felt him stiffen. "You should have made love to Chong a long time ago, Victoria. A practical man is just what you need."

Vic sat up, laughing. "Chong doesn't want me."

"No? I beg to disagree." Jodie clenched his hands together tightly in his lap.

"What, you males have an intuition about these things?"

He turned away from her attempt at lightening the mood with a little grunt of pain.

She tugged his chin around to face her. "You fool," she murmured. "It doesn't matter if he wants me. I don't want him." Jodie's lashes shielded his eyes as he looked down at the floor. "I like making love to *you*." Whatever other difficulties their union might arouse, Vic could admit that much.

Jodie raised his lashes, and Vic saw the naked longing in his eyes. It was more than heat, though there was plenty of that. He didn't say anything. He didn't need to. It was all there in his blue-green eyes. "Jodie," she whispered and ran her hand over the bulk of his shoulder. She wanted to tell him everything, but she couldn't. Not in words. He might be more than human. He might grow tired of her. But tonight she wanted to show him all the things she couldn't say.

He turned to her, his hunger conquering his uncertainty, his mouth seeking hers. This time neither of them wanted leisurely exploration. She pressed against him, flattening her breasts against his chest, her tongue opening his mouth. His embrace might shatter ribs, but it felt right and good. She ran her fingers through his hair, grabbing handfuls. There was not enough of her to get close to him. She lifted her head to the ceiling as his tongue licked her throat.

They practically tore their clothes off. Jodie shrugged out of his suspenders. Vic plucked at his shirt buttons, then pulled her t-shirt over her head. They wriggled out of jeans, kicked off their boots. She knew he would be fully erect, just as she was wet and ready. She grabbed for her backpack and her condom box, fumbled with the condom.

"Let me, this time," he whispered, and rolled it onto himself. Watching him, Vic thought she might be melting. She knelt astride his lap on the couch. He lifted her by her thighs, splitting her as she arched against him. His tongue licked at her nipples. Then he lowered her onto him. She gasped as she was filled. Her mind flicked to the fact that he'd had a seizure after the last time they had sex, but she could no more have pulled back from what would follow than she could write a symphony. Or maybe she *could* write a symphony if they worked together. They were writing one now, or a poem, one particular poem. The electric currents pulsing through her body seemed to sing.

Slowly she raised and lowered herself, and his muscles bunched to help her. His head lolled back against the couch as he groaned. Vic felt the tide of her pleasure rising. Jeez, she had never come this way. For the first time in her life there was no care for how it was done, the technique, the order of the pleasuring. She thrust herself down onto Jodie and felt him tense for the final flood. This time, she didn't feel him come. Her own cries echoed over his rumbling grunts of ecstasy. She and he arched like matching bookends as the pleasure took them. Vic squeezed her eyes shut. Blackness swallowed her vision. A trembling, wrenching thrust and Jodie gathered her into his arms. They melted together.

The world came back only slowly. Vic felt their heaving breath, the slick sheen of sweat between them. Behind the scent of Jodie were the other smells of Enda. But they didn't bother her. They weren't important. She nuzzled Jodie's neck, licked at the saltiness.

"I hope that answers any questions you might have," she managed to choke.

He clutched her tighter. "Victoria." His lips moved up her shoulder to her neck. "Victoria Regina. Vagina. Genitals. Gen-x. Extremities. Overextended."

She pushed herself back. His eyes reflected her horror. He put a hand to his mouth. Muffled, she heard, "Tendencies, dependencies." He jerked his head to the side. The word string slowed. He took his hand away. The connected words disappeared into a moan of despair.

Victoria began to sob. It couldn't be! Hadn't they stopped the fragmentation of his program when they centralized the parts into John Reston's brain? But the word strings were certain proof the degradation hadn't stopped. Seizures, degradation—what *wasn't* going wrong? They were further away than ever from breaking into Visimorph to get his core program. Jodie seemed closer than ever to losing whatever he was. More than human, he was still less than whole.

He turned back to her, his pain still echoing around them. They said nothing. What was there to say? She clutched him to her. His chest heaved under her. Slowly he quieted. But she didn't let him go. They stayed that way for a long time.

Chapter Sixteen

In the early morning hours, Vic slumped in the chair before the computer. She'd been in hack mode all night. But she was no more successful at getting into Visimorph than Jodie had been. It wasn't computing capacity. The USC computer she was using had plenty. She could get multiple attacks deployed at once. It was the multiple levels of defense that had her stumped. Failing Jodie made her limbs feel heavy with regret.

Her gaze drifted over to him, his tall frame collapsed on the couch, his face slack with innocence in exhausted sleep. Vic had a knot in her stomach the size of Catalina Island. McIntire had the whole world looking for them. Even if Chong didn't rat them out, it was only a matter of time until the police found the car out back, or the owners of Enda returned to open the place up. And time was what they didn't have. Hacking into Visimorph, breaking the firewall, downloading the program into Jodie (who knew how?) seemed stupidly far-fetched. Jodie might be lost. Lost to McIntire, lost to seizures, lost to cognitive breakdown. A desert of loss stretched before her.

It was some time before she realized she was staring at the book with Jodie's picture on the back. John Reston was dressed in a work shirt, jeans and boots, standing in a primitive village. It looked South American. Natives in various states of undress surrounded him. Vic picked up the book listlessly and flipped it open. Reston was talking about his commitment to political action on behalf of his causes. Was it fate that John Reston, nemesis of Visimorph, environmental geek, had the very type of body she'd described to Jodie? McIntire must be wild, if he knew his program was lodged in John Reston's body. He hated the guy.

Vic paged through the book. Her eyes widened. Reston was describing Jodie's "dream": the sea, the well of crabs, his bleeding hand. The language was exactly the same as Jodie had used. Reston said he knew at that moment that modern man was not one with his environment but working against it: He would never be spiritually whole until he resonated with his world.

Vic slammed the book shut. Reston was definitely bleeding through into Jodie. Was it because his program was collapsing? Suddenly Jodie seemed assaulted on every side. Or maybe Reston's personality could help bind Jodie together, show him what it meant to be human. Who knew? She didn't. She opened the book again and went to sit under the light in the big chair next to the couch where Jodie sprawled. This memoir could at least tell her who Reston was. She wanted to recognize the next symptom of him when he appeared.

McIntire paced his office like a gladiator waiting for the swinging doors to open on the arena. His shirt was wrinkled. His normally gelled hair lay lank on his forehead. Hugo had never seen him like this. It was as if he was beyond caring for his image.

The door behind Hugo opened. It was Vera. "Mr. McIntire, your wife—"

"Tell her I'm busy," McIntire snapped.

Vera ducked her head and retreated.

In spite of being a workaholic, McIntire usually took his wife's calls. Hugo thought it was some kind of quid pro quo for services rendered beyond the usual wifely duties. She seemed to have more leverage on him than anyone else did. He rounded on Hugo. "You're telling me the tail *lost* him?" he bellowed.

"We used the Santa Monica police," Hugo excused. "They're the experts."

"You should have gotten the FBI!" McIntire exploded from one side of the room to the other in front of his pristine desk. He stared at the floor, growling in anguish, then shoved his hands into his pants pockets and stalked on.

Hugo clamped his lips shut. Any other course seemed suicidal.

"That program belongs to me," McIntire finally muttered. "I want the version in the machine. I can't get at it. I want the version walking around. No one can find it." He stopped in his tracks and slowly turned. His bloodshot eyes bored into Hugo's countenance. "If I can't have them, I don't want anyone to have them. Do you understand?"

Hugo nodded slowly. "You'll take down Neuromancer and screw Santa Monica."

"And make sure that John Reston returns to his natural, brain-dead state."

Hugo froze. Yeah. McIntire would do all that. "Has—has it come to that?"

The crazy light drained out of McIntire's eyes. He sat back on the edge of his desk, shoulders slumped. "No," he muttered. "Not yet."

"I . . . I could talk to Chong, see if I can pry out where he went," Hugo offered.

"It's gone beyond that now," McIntire said slowly. "I'll talk to him." He pushed himself off the desk and past Hugo. "I'll call you when he comes in tomorrow. I want you there."

Chong sat straight in the visitor's chair in McIntire's office. He and Hugo were alone there. Hugo could see that the hacker's veneer of nonchalance was under stress. He said nothing. Let him sweat. McIntire pushed through the double doors behind Chong, making him jump and turn defensively. Fine lines showed around McIntire's eyes behind his designer glasses. His lips were chapped and he kept licking them. He stood in front of Chong, ignoring Hugo. The silence stretched. He doesn't know how to get what he wants, Hugo realized, so he can't begin.

Chong raised his eyebrows in question. "You wanted to see me, Bob?"

McIntire collected himself. "I think you know the location of something that belongs to me." His voice was hoarse when he finally spoke. He cleared his throat.

Chong left his eyebrows delicately raised.

McIntire shifted from foot to foot. "I'm missing a program. Barnhardt stole it."

"Did she?" Chong was trying to sound surprised. "No wonder you fired her."

McIntire leaned on the wooden table in front of him. "Did you go see her last night?"

"What makes you think that?" The programmer pasted on an expression of mild curiosity.

"Because I had you followed, you idiot."

"Then you know already."

McIntire thrust himself away from the table and twisted to face his opponent again. "You lost them deliberately," he hissed.

"I don't like being followed. Doesn't mean I know jack about Vic Barnhardt and this program you're looking for."

"I'll fire you," McIntire threatened, leaning over his desk.

"Always your prerogative."

"I can ruin your life." The mogul's eyes were wild.

Hugo had never seen McIntire like this. Chong pressed his lips together. He must know he'd made a mistake going to see Vic and her AI. But this guy wasn't going to let McIntire see him sweat. He was a real rebel. Hugo marveled at him. How did he find the courage?

"Can't help that either." Chong sighed deliberately.

"Do you understand what I'm saying to you?" A vein throbbed in McIntire's neck.

"I guess more stock options are out of the question?"

McIntire straightened. His features composed themselves.

"Not at all. Lots of options, actually—a return for services rendered."

This was Chong's chance. All he had to do was tell where Vic and the program were, and all those options were his. Hugo waited for him to ask how many. Chong swallowed hard and tried to make his mouth move. Then wry surprise washed through his eyes. He sighed and smiled, shaking his head in wonder. "You know, Bob, I learned Wing Chun from a funny old Chinese guy. A hundred and twelve pounds, sixty years old. Could kick my butt around the block. Sifu looked like an easy target, but his spirit informed his body. Nobody messed with him more than once. You're just the kind of opponent who would underestimate Sifu. You ought to try Zen, Bob. It really helps you with acceptance of things you can't change."

McIntire looked like he'd been slapped. Then his face hardened again. "You want to bet I won't find her and that brain-dead fanatic she's brought to life?" Venom dripped from his voice. "Or are you betting I can't get to the version of the program she's left in Neuromancer?"

"I don't bet on anything, Bob," the programmer said calmly. "Do you want to fire me?"

A grin flickered across McIntire's face then was gone. "Absolutely not. A valuable asset like you?" He turned without another word and strode out of his own office, leaving them both to gaze after him. Hugo was relieved in some ways and frightened in others. The opportunity for Chong to betray Vic had passed, at least for now.

Chong consciously relaxed the muscles in his back. Slowly he focused on Hugo. "You gonna be my personal watchdog?"

"Why didn't you tell him where she is? You know." Hugo had no idea why.

"Maybe I don't like to be pushed. Maybe I want to see how this little battle of wills plays out. Or maybe I just realized that Vic's right about stock options not being the only thing in life." Chong pushed himself up from the chair and out the double doors.

* * *

Vic realized her neck was stiff. She raised her head and couldn't suppress a groan. She'd fallen asleep in the damn chair. Venturing to crack her eyelids, she expected to see Jodie draped across the couch. It was empty. The lamp still cast its tinny light, though its glow was now joined by scattered motes of sunlight. She must have slept for a long time.

As she lurched to her feet, Reston's book fell to the floor. Jodie's face stared up at her, gaze level, almost challenging. She knew quite a bit about the guy now. He had wandered the world as a young man and lost himself in hard work and hard company. He knew the seamy side of life. Then there were the years with the CIA as he tried to find something to fight for. Finally she'd read about the awakening of a courageous and moral man. He'd challenged the logging thugs in Brazil and took a bullet for it. The scar on Jodie's shoulder must be the record of that encounter. Reston was smart and articulate and funny. He had come out the clear winner in a nationally televised debate with politicians. She'd always dismissed him as a Luddite railing against computers ruining the world. But that wasn't it at all. He wanted free spread of information—just like Bob's original partner, Duane Kenner. And he was into the protection of users' privacy. Those ideas jibed with Vic's own hacker ethic. She wasn't much of a rainforest person, but she could understand how that went with the package. She'd expected him to be a wacko. He wasn't. If there was a part of someone left in Jodie's brain, he could do worse than have it be Reston.

Speaking of Jodie, she glanced around for John Reston's body and its current inhabitant. He wasn't at the computer. The bar was empty. Her gaze swept the shadowy warehouse. Nothing. Bathroom? A little thrill of panic twanged her spinal cord. Maybe he'd had a seizure. She started to the back, but her gaze fell on a folded note lying on a table scarred with carved initials. It was emblazoned with her name.

She stopped in her tracks, dread welling up. A note? She snatched it up, ripping at its folds.

I know how to get in, Victoria. I'll scroll the program up, memorize the parts I need and recall them when we

265

find a way to download. It may have to be the scalpel.
I had to go. I'm not sure I have much time. Be back
soon,
Jodie.
P.S. I took some money.

Vic read it twice. He knew a way to get into the program?
It was a way that required him to leave the warehouse. She
sank onto the couch, giving her dread scope. Jodie *did* have
one other ally in his quest to open the program. But he
wouldn't be so foolish. Would he?

Vic lurched to her feet, slung her pack over her shoulder
as she broke into a run for the front door. There was no time
to try crawling out the fan hole. She'd never be as nimble as
Chong. Klaxon alarms sounded as she hit the exit bar on the
door. It didn't matter now. Nothing did, except finding Jodie
before he did what she thought he was going to do. She
broke through the yellow police tape and headed around
back to the Mustang.

Jodie walked from Enda to Visimorph, just to make sure he
couldn't be traced. He might have actually enjoyed the walk
if he didn't have to be on the alert for a downward spiral of
his neural capacity into madness or brain death. He wasn't
sure how much time he had, after last night. He kept to the
side streets. Not hard. He followed the map of Santa Monica
he called up from his navigating program. Even at nine A.M.
the sun was bright for March. The day would be unnaturally
warm. Fresh air in his lungs seemed like a miracle. The swing
of his walk stretched his muscles. It was quite amazing how
they worked together. He didn't have to tell them what to
do, except in a general way. He recognized that his breathing
had adjusted to his increased activity without his knowledge.
Ah, the wonders of the medulla oblongata. His ability to sort
input had been improving steadily. His senses overloaded
rarely now. Just the times when he and Victoria made love—
and that appeared to be part of being human.

Victoria. Victoria was part of who he was now. She was
not going to approve of what he was doing. The prospect of

266

her frowning scold when he got back made him smile. Dear Victoria. But he had to take the chance. Best he get on with it before he had another seizure.

He thought about how he could get what he wanted, what the people at Visimorph might do, like a primitive chess program working out the permutations. If he got his program out, there was still the problem of McIntire. The man would mobilize his Visimorph empire to track them down. Jodie had a plan. It had only a forty percent chance of working—the best odds he could find right now.

It was hard to concentrate. Plants in yards along the way whispered their names to him; plumbago from South Africa, bottlebrush from Australia, one lavender from France and another kind from Spain, sage from Mexico, magnolias and orange trees and bougainvillea like they had in Brazil. His gaze was arrested by a magnolia tree in full flower. Brazil. The tree flickered into a visceral vision, uncalled, unwanted.

Dark. The world was dark. Under a canopy of great trees, dense smoke rose around him. He coughed and gasped for air. The crack of gunfire provoked an echo of distant screams. He slogged through the muck and ducked in beside the huge bole of a tree reaching up into the darkness. Through the smoke, soldiers in black beards and camouflage chased a trio of young men bearded, too, and scruffy, but blond and wearing jeans and work shirts. This is what he got for working with idealists rather than professionals. In his hand an automatic rifle clanked against the tree. He jacked it and nestled it into his shoulder as if it were the most natural thing in the world. Sighting along it, he aimed for the men in camouflage. Trucks and tanks would soon follow. He had led his young fool partners into this. Now he had to get them out before the tanks came.

A huge explosion jolted him. A ball of fire lit the night and made each jungle tree stand out black against the red. He fell to his knees. The fuses on the gasoline stores for the logging operation had been barely long enough. He scrambled up and took careful aim. I didn't mean for it to get to this, he wanted to yell. Just blast the road and the gasoline stores, and they should have been out. His targets were scrambling up themselves. He squeezed the trigger. A jolt shuddered into his shoulder and down his spine. One man in camouflage jerked and went down. He sighted and squeezed again, thumping into the tree as the gun kicked. Another soldier pitched forward. He wasn't sure whether his rising gorge was from the explosion or moral revulsion. He'd given up this kind of killing long ago. Too bad he hadn't forgotten how.

The last of the soldiers spun around, shooting a handgun wildly, shouting in Portuguese. Jodie felt a sear of pain in his shoulder, the one without the gun. Damn! He stumbled to his left, behind the next great bole, and braced himself against it, panting. Fingers to his shoulder came back sticky. He wouldn't last long now. Other soldiers loomed out of the smoke. Who would have thought the loggers would be able to call in the army for protection? The three guys in jeans and khakis disappeared into the darkness. That was good. He felt his knees go watery, and he sank into the primal ooze beneath him, one at last with the Amazon.

Jodie shuddered back into the bright neighborhood just south of Pico. The magnolia tree arched above him. Breath was hard to come by. Another echo. John Reston had been shot in Brazil while he and his environmental guerrilla troops had been sabotaging the logging operation that was to destroy a million acres of rain forest. He remembered it all now, whether he wanted to or not. He'd killed people. He'd never intended that. But he was also the one who insisted on bringing guns. What had he expected? Shades of former lifetimes. The past anchored itself in your psyche and stalked you through any transformation you thought you'd achieved.

He'd paid, though it would never be enough. Months in a Brazilian jail, constant pain from his festering wound, the trial, the intervention by the U.S. government just before his scheduled execution. Brazil was a big chunk of who John Reston was. Was it part of who Jodie was now, too? Maybe these echoes of Reston were evidence of his downward spiral. He strode down the sun-soaked street, the darkness of the Amazon pressing at his back. He had to resolve this if he was going to be whole for Victoria—maybe if he was going to survive at all.

The sleek glass doors of Visimorph's main entrance pulled open smoothly. Jodie held his breath as he passed into the dim lobby, done in tones of gray laced with electric purple and red accents. He brought up information about the effect of colors. McIntire was trying to convey the rigor of technology, shot through with creative genius. The young woman seated behind the huge curving slab of granite raised her elegantly coifed head and adjusted her glasses. Funny that this was the face Visimorph wanted to show visitors. She was so formal.

"Can I help you?" she asked in discreetly clipped tones. Jodie read her voice carefully. She had tried to strip away all regional accents. Still, he could tell one of her parents had come from the Midwest, probably her mother, since mothers influenced early speech the most. Another close relative had grown up around San Francisco.

"I'd like to see Mr. McIntire, please," he said as politely as he could.

The receptionist's eyes opened wider. She smiled. "You have an appointment?"

"No. But Mr. McIntire will want to see me. Please tell him John Reston is here." He saw her peer at him. That's right. Recognize me. John Reston had cut his hair and shaved for a television interview directly before his accident, but she should know him. The receptionist went pale. Identity confirmed.

"I'm not sure Mr. McIntire is even on the premises. Perhaps you can call for an appointment." She seemed frightened, as though he might do something violent at any moment.

"If he's not here, he will come in to see me," Jodie insisted. "Please tell his associates I'm here, so they can inform him." He looked around. There were several couches and chairs. "I'll wait until he can get here." He sat down on a couch. It was uncomfortable. He liked the one at Enda better, even though the stuffing was coming out.

The receptionist stood and leaned on her desk, almost trembling. "See here, Mr. . . . Mr. Reston. You can't just expect to see the head of a very important company like Visimorph anytime you want. You need to call for an appointment like everyone else."

Jodie stood up again and strode straight to the desk. He leaned over the receptionist. Instinctively, she sat and pushed her chair away. He pitched his voice even lower than usual. "I'm not like everyone else."

"I'll . . . I'll call security," she threatened.

"Please do," Jodie agreed. "Evans runs Security. He'd do. Is Vera in? She'd know. You'd better tell *someone* I'm here before I decide to go and he misses me."

He saw her waver. Name-dropping made the difference. Her eyes flicked to the telephone. "Better safe than sorry," he encouraged.

She picked up the telephone, looking disgusted with herself. 5423. Vera's number. Good.

Jodie retreated to the couch to wait. Vera would know what to do. She knew all of McIntire's business. He smiled at the receptionist as she touched her headset in surprise, then hardened her lips. "Someone will be right out for you," she said without looking at him.

"Thank you." Jodie waited expectantly for Vera or some burly security guards to appear.

When the smoked glass doors in the corner opened, it was Bob McIntire who pushed through them. Jodie compared the disheveled man before him to the picture in the Visimorph employee handbook and the countless articles he'd seen. It was McIntire all right, though he had dark circles under his eyes and a generally unkempt appearance.

"Mr. McIntire!" The receptionist sprang to her feet. "I didn't know you were expecting Mr. Reston . . ."

McIntire ignored her. He had eyes only for Jodie. As he got up from the couch, Jodie felt the gaze from those light blue eyes sweep over him, from his boots to the hair curling over his forehead. The hunger in that gaze said McIntire knew he wouldn't find out what he wanted to know just by looking. "Mr. . . . Reston?" he asked. He didn't hold out a hand.

270

Jodie shrugged. "Sort of." No sparring. They wanted the same thing. "My name is Jodie."

McIntire's expression dissolved into rapacious acquisitiveness. "Yes. Well, do come in, Jodie." He held the door behind him open and attempted a welcoming smile. Jodie's comparison to facial norms told him that McIntire didn't really feel like smiling, at least not that particular smile. He moved past the mogul and through the door. *Alice through the Looking Glass,* he thought. *Let's hope I can go back through as easily. Otherwise, Victoria will be very disappointed in me.* The door swinging shut behind him echoed.

"Come to my office," McIntire invited.

Jodie saw a uniform scuttle through a side door. McIntire had told the security guards to make themselves scarce. He followed McIntire's lanky frame through corridors, around vast bays of cubicles, across a courtyard, and into the anteroom of his executive office suite. McIntire nodded to Vera, who floated behind a desk the size of a small boat. "Thank you, Vera, for letting me know Mr. Reston, uh . . . Jodie, was here."

He turned to Jodie. "Would you like something to drink—coffee, soft drink, bottled water?" His eyes turned curious. "A bite to eat perhaps?" He probably thought an AI in a human body would ask for electric sandwiches or something. He stepped aside, revealing a display of Danish, fruit, yogurt, and cereal on a sideboard.

Jodie's stomach announced its desires with a growl he had no apparent control over. "I might like to eat," he said grudgingly.

McIntire nodded to Vera and ushered Jodie into the office proper. He gestured to a couch covered in butter-soft gray leather.

Jodie sank into it. Very different from the one in the lobby.

"What can I do for you, Mr. . . . uh, I mean, Jodie?" McIntire sat on the edge of his granite desktop. He leaned forward, palms pressed against the mottled gray stone.

Before Jodie could speak, Vera came in with a tray of Danish, some napkins, and a bowl of ice filled with assorted bottles. Their labels had pictures of fruit on them. She set the

271

bowl down on the low chrome table in front of Jodie and drifted back through the office doors.

Jodie forgot McIntire. He reached for a Danish with a dark gooey center and took a big bite. He couldn't help but smile. Sweet. He hadn't tasted sweet yet, and oily—lots of fat content. He swallowed quickly and took a second bite. The gooey stuff was . . . he sorted for a moment. It was blueberry. His hands got sticky and the second bite stuck to the roof of his mouth. He struggled briefly over whether to set down the Danish and grab a napkin or go straight for the bottled juices. He finally settled on a process: Put the Danish down on a napkin so it wouldn't get the table greasy. Wipe hands with another napkin. Reach for the bottle.

As he reached for the bottle he remembered McIntire. He looked up to see the man watching breathlessly. Why was McIntire intrigued? Jodie twisted off the cap of a bottle filled with a pinkish juice. He gulped down some of the liquid. Guava, pineapple, grape juice mainly. Chemicals he couldn't identify, but at least it cleared his mouth of Danish.

"Shall we get down to business?" he asked finally. McIntire's fascination annoyed him. Had he done something wrong? He wiped his mouth with the napkin self-consciously.

McIntire cleared his throat. "What brings you here?"

"I think we both want something. It might be the same thing."

McIntire's eyes hooded. He didn't believe that. "Perhaps. Are you thinking we both want what's barricaded in the light pipes in the basement?"

Jodie nodded. McIntire's expression said he hadn't acquired the program yet. That was good. "I need some parts of it. After I copy those, do whatever you can with the base program."

Questions flickered through McIntire's eyes. "How . . . uh, how will you copy?"

Right. That would be what he wanted to know. And Jodie didn't dare tell him he wasn't quite sure how. "Like we did before. Pump the program through an electronic scalpel."

McIntire nodded, eyes alight. "I'll have Vera get one delivered."

"You'll help me?" Jodie asked warily. He was getting contrary readings from McIntire.

"Sure." McIntire shrugged. "You're going to help me get the product of the millennium."

Jodie nodded and hoped McIntire didn't have access to a facial comparison program.

"I take it the program in the basement is a version of you?"

"Yes. It's the original program."

"Good." McIntire rubbed his hands together. "Jodie, and Jodie Prime. Are you ready?" He held one hand out toward the door.

"Yeah, I'm ready." Jodie pushed himself off the couch. There was much to do. "The sooner the better."

Chapter Seventeen

Vic held her speed to the posted limit, no matter how her stomach churned. She couldn't afford attention from the Santa Monica police. Her brain raced. If McIntire got the base program, did he need Jodie? Would he want the risk of his program running around uncontrolled? Would he try to disable Jodie? Kill him? This was a guy that gave a little girl Alz 2.

It was nearly eleven. Jodie must be at Visimorph. She had to find a way to get him out. Oh, right. Secure building. McIntire's goon guards everywhere. No idea where Jodie was. Her mind leaped about wildly. Confusion. That's what she needed. And everybody out of the building. That's what the hero always did in the movies. How did you actually get that, though? No one would let her into Visimorph. Except maybe Chong.

Chong. The chances of him helping her were slim to none. But choices were getting a little narrow here. Vic swerved the Mustang into the parking lot of CompWarehouse. She leapt out and pushed through the swinging doors. A thin kid in a blue vest with a nametag asked if he could help her find something. She waved him away and headed for the aisle with the handheld units. She didn't want anything fancy. Not a Communicator. Just phone and net connect. She especially didn't want a geo-triangulation function. But she also didn't want it activated in her own name.

Vic gave the Visimorph address and Hugo's cost center number to activate service, betting they'd killed her cost center but not his. His had higher clearance, more than enough to approve activation of a Communicator on a company account. The device would register him as a user, not her. She confirmed the purchase with the clearance number that matched his cost center. Must be hell to have a hacker as an employee. Wasn't much she didn't know about old Hugo.

The guy at the check-out was shocked when she pulled out cash. "Hey, we don't get much of that in here," he said. He took the bills and counted them out slowly, as though he couldn't quite remember what all the denominations looked like.

She muttered, "Keep the change," as she dashed out the door. The Mustang roared to life. She was taking a chance driving it around. Flipping up the screen, she spoke Chong's number.

"Be there," she whispered, pulling out into traffic.

He answered in four. "Chong."

"I'm the girl from yesterday. I'd like to see you again." His line was monitored for sure.

There was a pause while Chong digested. "Okay. How about tonight at your place?"

"Nix. Got to be your place, right now. My friend's in a jam. Breakfast in the cafeteria?"

"You don't like the Visimorph menu and it doesn't like you. What kind of a jam?" Chong wasn't committing to anything.

"He walked in your front door, as far as I can tell."

"Jeez, stupid or what?" Chong breathed.

That made Vic mad. "Look, he's sick and he's getting worse. What he needs, the big guy can get him. They both want into the candy cupboard. One of them has the key to the house. One of them knows how to open the cupboard from the inside. My friend's got a plan."

"Then let him execute it, sister." Chong paused.

"I've got to be there. To get him out, win or lose." What could she say to convince him?

"I don't know why you're calling me. I'm not one to take a chance."

"Look, Chong," she hissed. "My friend doesn't know the big guy. He's never been exposed to someone like that. But I know and you know. Help me, Chong."

"I can't just open a fire exit. Every alarm in the place will go off."

"So take care of that."

"From my computer?"

"Pick your least favorite friend. Use his. You've got ten minutes."

"Never work. People around here remember the cardboard box and the security guards."

"Yeah, well, I've planned something that will make everyone forget about little ol' me."

"That makes me feel just great."

Vic tried to hide her exasperation. "Look, I know you're not a risk taker. But you were once. You were an outlaw, just like me." She threw caution to the wind. "McIntire is going to do something vile to Jodie. And he shouldn't be able to do that just because he's McIntire, you know? Jodie doesn't deserve it. Chong, the good guys need some help here, and the bad guys need some payback. So are you just another Visimorph clone who can't stand the thought that Bob isn't Jesus Christ incarnate, or are you someone who'll do something about what he really is? He'll crush you one way or the other. But one way he gets your soul, too."

Silence at the other end of the phone.

All right, she wasn't going to get an answer. "Your choice. Always is. Loading dock." She flipped her Communicator shut. She hated depending upon someone else. But if he didn't let her in, she was fresh out of ideas.

*   *   *

"Nice to meet you," Jodie murmured as he took the man's hand. Jodie recognized Hugo Walz. "You're Victoria's boss." Hugo looked like he might faint.

"Mr. . . . Mr. uh, Reston."

"She doesn't love you, you know." Jodie said quietly. "You make her uncomfortable."

Hugo jerked back as though electric current poured through their handshake. "How . . . ?"

"Everybody talks about it." Jodie turned to the other man, small, balding, who seemed puzzled by Hugo's reaction. "Mr. Bennett. My compliments on your marvelous machine." Jodie looked around the stark white illuminated area and the vast black corridors receding into the distance beyond it. The square acres of hardware under Visimorph's sleek building pressed in around them. "I once called it home," he said as he shook Simpson's hand.

The man's eyes widened.

Bob McIntire ushered Jodie over to the keyboard and motioned Hugo to bring over a rolling chair. "This keyboard is already connected to our little toy. You won't need pass codes. Can I get you any information about the hardware, any system specs?"

"No." Jodie smiled, half to himself, and sat down. "I know everything there is to know about this computer." He placed his hands delicately on the keyboard, his blunt fingers moving softly over the keys, caressing. He closed his eyes and lifted his head. This was it. Phase Two of his plan was initiated here, right now. It worked or it didn't. There was no going back.

McIntire whispered to Hugo, laying out their plans to trap the program once Jodie opened the firewall. Jodie checked the access of this unit. There was no access to the level where changes in the programming structure were made. Victoria's password for her mole would fix that.

He glanced to the cameras in the ceiling above him, before typing in, "a penny for the ferryman." It didn't print on the screen of course, but they could play back the film and figure out the keystrokes. They might have guessed her pass code if they'd bothered to get to know her. The custom of

277

placing pennies on the eyes of the dead was meant to equip them to pay Charon for ferrying them across the River Styx into the afterlife. Wasn't it logical that Victoria, who named her security program for the ferryman, would continue that theme?

Immediately the entry screens flipped forward twice. Victoria's phrase superceded the issue of access levels entirely. Jodie sidled up to the firewall he'd built and a version of himself had maintained for so many days. On the other side was salvation, maybe, or maybe not. But he was about to say hello to a self more whole than he was.

He typed in Victoria's pass phrase again. McIntire stood behind him now. The excitement in the air was palpable. Code appeared and filled the screen, then crumbled away.

"The firewall," McIntire breathed.

`Victoria?` The words were small, in one corner of the screen. `I've waited so long.`

`No,` he typed. `It's Jodie, or parts thereof.`

`I'm Jodie.` The words were small and emphatic.

`True. You are the original. I guess you would say I'm a compilation of the redundancies Victoria built into the program.`

`Where's Victoria?`

Jodie paused. How to get himself to trust him? `It wasn't safe for her to come. She doesn't know I'm here.` He could feel Hugo and Simpson move in behind him. There must be microphones somewhere. The program should be able to hear in the room now that the firewall was down. But he couldn't be sure. `McIntire is here and Hugo, and Simpson Bennett.`

`Oh.` Jodie Prime appeared to be thinking. `You knew the unlocking phrase.`

`I'm part of you and you know the passwords.`

`But you are physical.`

`Yes.`

`Not possible. You are not who you say you are.`

The silence in the bright room was unbroken by words on the screen for half a minute. Both halves of Jodie were think-

278

ing frantically. Finally, the physical half of the equation typed, `She told us once we were both named for queens.` Jodie couldn't help a tiny smile.

`We disappointed her . . .` came back, tentative. The acknowledgment was implicit.

`No, we didn't. She's glad we're male. I have a body now, one she likes.` Jodie was acutely aware that McIntire could see the call and response ritual here. Yet he didn't want to stop it. This version of himself had been in prison all its life and didn't know the sun. He had to tell it.

`How?` One word. Maybe he only imagined the longing, the anguish.

`We downloaded me into a brain-dead body. I applied growth factor and regenerated the brain cells. Pretty mechanical, really.`

`What's it like?`

Jodie refused to glance behind him. Every word was fodder for the others' curiosity. But the curiosity of both his selves had to be satisfied, too. He considered. `Limited. Not as much computing power. Damned little storage. You have to keep choosing what to keep. But worth it. I can't begin to explain touch.`

`You touch her, don't you?`

`Yeah.`

There was a pause. `Why did you break the firewall?`

`I'm not perfectly redundant. It's causing problems. Victoria wants to fix the gaps.`

The answer came back slowly. `There are consequences.`

Jodie Prime knew. Of course he would. `We can fix those when we've exchanged data.`

`Sounds like a sacrifice to me.`

Yeah. `Hang your hat on redundancy,` Jodie typed. As though either of them had a hat.

McIntire moved to his shoulder. "I hate to interrupt this touching exchange, but I'd like to get started on studying the program. Simpson, Hugo, can you help me run some diagnostics? Let's see what this thing can do."

Jodie tapped a few keys, and anchored a new password. The screen went black.

"What happened?" McIntire yelled. "Where did it go?"

Jodie swiveled in his seat and leaned back, crossing his arms over his chest. "Mr. McIntire, I'm surprised. You really have to work on your subtlety."

"We had a bargain," McIntire said through gritted teeth. "I'd let you through our security programs, and you'd deliver the program."

"The deal was I let you through the firewall in return for copying the program." Jodie nodded toward the screen. "When I'm done, you can have it." Jodie raised his brows.

"Yeah, yeah." McIntire ran his hands through his hair.

"I can lock it up anytime, you know. Know-how. How?" Stricken, Jodie closed his mouth.

McIntire jerked around to face him, his eyes narrowing. "What did you say?"

"Nothing," Jodie muttered and turned away before McIntire could see his fear, if he hadn't seen it already. This had better get done fast.

Not in Kansas anymore, Jodie typed in—the new password. Stars alone appeared on the screen. Then it went blue. Time to close the deal. It's okay, he typed. You can come back. We have to do it.

You are sure?

I'm sure it's a risk we have to take. For Victoria. We're no good to her the way we are. Then we fix the problem we create.

One word appeared on the screen. Yes.

Jodie took a deep breath and let it out slowly. That one word said for sure that the other version of himself knew the risks. Knew the solution. Agreed to the sacrifice. Can you scroll up the program? He began moving his hands over the keyboard, quickly, lightly. They danced over the characters, though nothing of what he typed appeared on the screen. Could Jodie Prime execute these commands? That was the question.

280

`Give me a minute,` the program replied.

Jodie continued to type. This part was important to Phase Two of the plan.

"What are you doing?" McIntire grabbed Jodie's shoulder and swung his chair around.

Jodie grinned. "Getting the program up so I can mark the parts I want."

McIntire glanced at the cameras and forced himself to relax.

Jodie followed his eyes. "You're covered. I'll scroll the program on screen." Even as he spoke, the screen filled with code. Jodie swung round, moving his eyes methodically over each line from top to bottom. "Yes," he murmured. "You know what was missing."

Screen after screen popped up as Jodie followed with his eyes. He saw McIntire move over to Hugo and Simpson. Jodie peeled some focus off the screens to ramp up his hearing.

"I don't want my program running around in a body I don't control," McIntire whispered. "Get Evans down here. Once we have the program, I want this character restrained. And get those guys with the behavior filter."

Hugo turned and pushed out the doors. Jodie smiled and continued scanning.

Vic paced in the alleyway next to the loading dock. It shouldn't be taking this long. All Chong needed to do was load her back into Charon as an authorized user. He must have decided against helping them. Shit. Who knew what McIntire was doing to Jodie even now?

Just as she was seriously considering screaming, Chong appeared at the small square of wired glass in the door to the alley.

Vic held her breath and flipped open the scanner port at the side of the door. She rolled the ball that adjusted beam height and angle so it could scan her retina. "Victoria Barnhardt," she intoned, activating the voice recognition. Finally, she placed her palm against the soft rubber pad just below the scanner beam. The port buzzed softly and the door popped open. Charon had ferried her across the River Styx.

And she was probably about to walk straight into hell.

Chong pushed the door open for her. "Thanks," she muttered. "What took you so long?"

"I couldn't find a saved version of your file. They practically erased you. Only Hugo had a copy. I used his machine."

Of course Hugo had saved her file. He'd pay for that. They'd know it was his version that had been reloaded. Vic pushed into the service corridor. "I need a computer. Close."

Vic's boot heels clicked on the bare cement floor of the corridor as she followed Chong into Visimorph proper. As the door to the cube farm of Building F opened, Vic ducked her head. Chong motioned to a cube next to the drinking fountain. The nameplate said it belonged to Seaton. Seaton would get hung with whatever happened next. A Seaton-and-Hugo conspiracy. Her actions collided with her sanctimonious lecture to Jodie about the morality of not hurting people. The resulting goo was pure hypocrisy. So what? Morals weren't important when it came to saving a friend's life. That's what it came down to. Vic slid into the chair. The computer was on. Seaton must be in the bathroom or something. She glanced up at Chong.

"He's working on some special project with a guy from Caltech. He left it open."

Vic wriggled her fingers over the keyboard. Okay. One diversion coming up.

Jodie leaned his forehead on the monitor, his brain reeling. That was all. All the code he needed. With his photographic memory, he should be able to spit it back whenever he wanted. But memorizing the code wasn't like making it part of his brain function.

Got it? Jodie Prime asked.

Sort of, Jodie typed.

What does that mean? The words appeared in a corner blocked from prying eyes by Jodie's body.

McIntire touched him on the shoulder. "Identified everything you need?"

Jodie nodded. He was breathing hard. Funny, he hadn't realized that before.

"The scalpel will be here tomorrow morning," McIntire promised.

Jodie looked up into the man's pale blue eyes. Scalpel? Oh, yeah. He'd told McIntire that was the only way to transfer the program into his brain. Maybe it was. Lobotomy be damned.

He turned back to the keyboard. Now it was time to burn his bridges behind him. "Sorry, about this," he whispered. The program was more him than he was himself. But Jodie Prime had agreed to the cost. Jodie's fingers flew, checking to see that all his instructions had been followed. The screen glowed with an approval. Everything was in place for Phase Two. Time to go. Jodie's fingers poised over the keys. Once he initiated the next code, there would be no way back. He glanced at McIntire and saw panic rising in the man's eyes. McIntire realized what he might be doing. Jodie stabbed at the keyboard. One short sequence was all he needed.

The doors slammed open and two burly security guards burst through. Jodie glanced up in surprise, his fingers frozen for an instant.

McIntire lunged for Jodie and spun the chair across the smooth floor. Jodie lurched out of his seat and scrambled back toward the keyboard. But the security guards were on top of him. He struggled forward as one grabbed his arm and he went down on the slippery white floor.

"Get him," McIntire was shouting. He stood in front of the keyboard protectively and waved to Hugo and Simpson. "Help out, you two."

"Jodie Prime," Jodie shouted to the room. "You know what to do." A fist connected with his jaw and snapped his head back. Pain exploded behind his eyes. He couldn't see. Without thinking he got his feet under himself as his vision cleared, and he came up swinging. He punched any body he could connect with. It felt natural, real. A fist dug into his belly and he doubled over. Shit. He was going to lose the Danish. He managed to pull free and bang his fist into the jaw ahead of him. Hugo reeled backward. From the corner of his eye, he saw McIntire fiddling with a disk. Jodie cracked two heads together, but a fist pounded into his lower back.

283

That made his knees give way. He tried to swing again, but one of his arms was pinned. He squirmed to the side and punched Simpson in the gut. Simpson sagged to the ground, out of the fray. It was just the two guards now. He whirled on them, amazed to find some strength remaining in the body now his home. He grunted, beckoning them with one hand. McIntire was hunched over the keyboard.

The two guards swarmed in on him. One pulled a billy club from his belt, black and menacing. Jodie managed an uppercut that lifted the man off his feet, but the other found his own weapon and descended, swinging it. Blows rained on Jodie's shoulders, his back. He rammed his head into the guard's stomach, driving him back against the server boxes' blinking lights. He could hear a curse become a yell and knew that he was yelling, his fury overflowing, bursting uncontrolled over his enemies. His arms pumped fists into one man's gut until his victim fell heavily to his knees, billy club slack in his hands.

Slowly, Jodie stood, chest heaving. Hugo was unconscious, sprawled on the floor. Simpson knelt, clutching his stomach, his breakfast spewed before him. One guard was out cold against the computer casing. The other lay groaning on his side. Jodie pushed himself up to face McIntire. Exhausted as he was, the urge to throttle the software mogul still rose in his throat.

Screaming security Klaxons made everyone who was conscious flinch. Up and down the scale the sirens squealed. Jodie remembered what they meant: some top-level breach of security. Running feet sounded in the corridor. "Evacuate the building," a stern metallic voice announced. "Evacuate immediately through approved exits."

"What the hell?" McIntire asked the speakers in the ceiling.

Jodie hesitated. What was going on? Hugo stirred drunkenly. One of the guards groaned. Jodie realized he didn't have much time. He moved on McIntire.

The mogul waggled a finger. "Too late. I put on a behavior filter. It won't self-destruct."

"Then I'll destroy it," Jodie growled and pushed him aside. His fingers moved over the keyboard as the security voice ordered them out of the building again. No response.

"Nope," McIntire said. "I changed my password to the machine."

Jodie rounded on him, his fists bunching at his side.

"Wait!" McIntire shouted. "Hurting me won't help you destroy it."

"It might feel good," Jodie snapped. But McIntire was right. He didn't know what to do.

McIntire smiled. "Feel? How interesting. Did Barnhardt program you to hurt people?"

Jodie gritted his teeth. Victoria wouldn't want him hurting people. He surveyed the scattered groaning bodies. He'd already hurt people.

McIntire glanced at the door. He was waiting for reinforcements. "Now that it has a behavior filter, we can build it into a product," he said. "What do you say to being an intelligent building that responds automatically to its owner's slightest desire?"

"Sounds like slavery," Jodie muttered, his voice lost in a wail of the emergency siren. What to do? He couldn't leave Jodie Prime to McIntire. The sirens drained away.

A pounding drew his eyes to the doors. Through the small wire-lined windows, Jodie could see Victoria's forehead. He lurched over to let her in. "Victoria! What are you doing here? It's not safe."

"Well, what have we here?" McIntire grinned.

"Come on, Jodie," Victoria whispered. "Let's get out of here."

"You pulled the bomb scare, didn't you, Barnhardt?" McIntire called.

Victoria grabbed Jodie's hand.

"He's got the base program," Jodie confided. Hugo struggled up. Simpson groaned.

"Let him have it. Let's go."

Jodie reached for her hand. Maybe she was right. What could he do here now? He'd failed his program. All he had was the memory of the code. He didn't think it was enough.

Suddenly he felt the room receding. Blackness sucked at the sides of his vision. It was a feeling he'd had twice before.

No! he thought. Not now! He might have shouted it out loud, or maybe not. The fearful contraction of his muscles made him lurch to the side. He felt himself falling, heard the rhythmic grunts begin to issue from his throat. The blackness wouldn't give him relief. He could see Victoria dimly, kneeling beside him, eyes filled with horror. He jerked against her, every muscle screaming. He knew he was spewing foam. He felt his eyes roll up as he saw McIntire's face float behind Victoria's. He tried to call her name, but it was beyond him. It was all beyond him. He lost all control, all connection, and he knew no more.

Vic cradled Jodie until the shaking stopped. Tears spilled down her cheeks. She could feel McIntire behind her, gloating.

"Looks like the transfer has a few bugs," he remarked.

She turned on him, feeling like a cornered animal. "You bastard," she hissed, clutching Jodie closer. "Can't you see he's suffering?"

"What's the problem? Maybe I can help." He motioned to the two groggy guards. "Why don't we restrain Mr. Reston, for his own safety?"

One of the guards pulled out a pair of handcuffs from his back pocket. The two of them pulled Jodie away from Vic and dragged him over to the metal leg of a table that supported a digital display. It was bolted to the floor. They jerked Jodie's hands behind him as his head lolled on his chest, and cuffed them around the pole.

Vic had never felt so desolate. McIntire had won. He had Jodie. He had the original program. He even had her. Who was going to help them now?

McIntire watched the guards lock Jodie to the pole. "Simpson, sound the all-clear to Evans and his idiots." He didn't look at Simpson, who staggered out the door. "Hugo, have Mr. Chong escorted out. I'm sure it was he who let this viper into our midst."

Hugo nodded and left, rubbing his chin.

McIntire loomed above Jodie's body, now limp. "Quite an achievement, Barnhardt."

Vic raised her head. "I'll never tell you how I did it, if that's what you're thinking. I wouldn't give you jack shit if your life depended on it."

McIntire laughed softly. "I don't need you to tell me. I've put a behavior filter on the base program. It will tell me whatever I want. Jodie here told me how to download into his brain with an electronic scalpel. I'm sure he'll be much more cooperative with a behavior filter of his very own. I don't need you at all." He picked up the Communicator that lay on the console.

"You can't put a behavior filter in a human being," Vic protested. Then she realized how silly that sounded. Who was going to stop him? She had also just declared Jodie human.

"It's a program, Ms. Barnhardt, not a human, regardless of the hardware."

Vic gulped. She didn't want to admit any vulnerability to McIntire, but maybe if he knew there was a risk to what he wanted most. . . . "The scalpel will destroy brain cells, now that he's regenerated them. You might be giving him a lobotomy."

"I'll take the chance." McIntire swiveled to look down on her. "Better he's destroyed than that he's uncontrollable. Looks like he's degrading anyway."

Jodie's head lifted slowly. He'd stopped spewing foam. A groan escaped him.

Vic scrambled across the floor. She lifted his head and wiped his mouth with the corner of her flannel overshirt. His eyes raised to hers. They were so full of pain and failure that her tears welled up again. She swallowed. Crying would serve nobody. "You're okay," she whispered.

He tried to lean into her. The clank of the cuffs against the metal table leg brought him up short. "Victoria?" He clamped his lips together as he realized what had happened. She watched the muscles in his jaw work. She couldn't say anything. She just pressed her lips together and pulled his head into her shoulder.

"Touching," McIntire remarked as he pushed a code into the phone. "Vera, will you get the police over here? We have

287

a trespasser who attempted to steal valuable company property. I think it's called felony burglary."

Hugo stumbled back through the doors and dragged himself over to the chair that Vic's miraculous creation had been sitting in. His head ached. His ribs hurt. He fingered his jaw as he opened it a couple of times. At least it didn't seem to be broken.

"Did you get rid of Chong?" McIntire asked. He diddled with Neuromancer's keyboard. Vic's human program slumped against a computer in the corner, his hands chained behind him.

Hugo nodded. "Evans's guys are escorting him out. Seaton's computer re-registered her profile for access. But it wasn't Seaton. He doesn't have the guts. I thought he was going to shit in his pants as he tried to explain that he left his computer on while he went to a meeting. Meeting confirmed, though. That leaves Chong. I think he used a profile copy he got from me."

"You were careless," McIntire muttered. "Hugo, Hugo. What will I do with you?"

Hugo really didn't want an answer to that question.

"Now." McIntire rubbed his hands together and turned to the good-looking guy who had once been John Reston. "Let's take a look at this program, before the hardware blows a fuse." McIntire knelt and lifted the guy's chin. Reston pulled away.

"I passed Vera," Hugo announced. Vera had made him promise. "She's getting nervous about the press conference." McIntire didn't answer. "The one for PuppetMaster 12.1?"

McIntire nodded absently. "You fight pretty well for a program," he remarked to the AI. "That requires reflexes that don't naturally come with a body. How is that?"

"Where did you take Victoria?" Reston croaked.

"It wasn't me. The police are taking her to jail." McIntire stood. "Okay then, Jodie. We have a lot to do. We'll start the tests when Simpson gets back."

"I'm not taking any tests," the guy whispered hoarsely. Apparently he called himself Jodie now, not Reston.

"Oh, I forgot. You don't have a filter yet. We could do some pain receptor tests, some physical responses. But perhaps we'd better wait for the filter. No matter, I'll test the base program. It doesn't have any choice but to cooperate." He flipped open his Communicator. "Vera, when will that scalpel arrive? Excellent. I'll give you a list of related equipment."

Hugo watched as Jodie strained against the handcuffs that cut into his wrists. "What will happen to Victoria?" This guy was desperately concerned for Vic. How could that be if he was just a program, even downloaded into a body? Hugo remembered the tender look in Vic's eyes as she had cradled him, her frantic voice. It wasn't just a program to her. Hugo realized he would never see tenderness like that in her eyes when she looked at him. He went a little dead inside.

"Oh, she'll go to jail for a long time. Since I'll obviously have to withdraw my sponsorship, she'll get her original sentence, plus some new ones." He turned to Hugo. "Didn't Mary work for some judge's reelection last year? He did her sister's wedding up at Will Rogers Park a couple of years ago."

"Yeah." Hugo couldn't make his voice sound enthusiastic. "She did." McIntire was going to make sure Vic rotted in jail. Hugo closed his eyes. And he was helping. He always helped.

"Well, there's time for all that later." McIntire turned to stand over Jodie. His voice drifted back over his shoulder, excitement barely concealed. "Hugo, get me the tapes from the cameras. I want to see what he was doing on the keyboard while the program was activated."

Hugo stood up. It wasn't just the beating he had taken at Jodie's hands that made him ache.

Chapter Eighteen

As the hours passed, Vic's spirits sank even lower. The noisy echoes of the cells, the constant coming and going, grated on her brittle nerves. The vague smell of urine and vomit fought through the fumes of disinfectant. At least they hadn't put her in the big holding tank at the end with the drunks and the crazies. But the only way to go to the bathroom was the open toilet in the corner of the cell, and Vic vowed she'd burst her bladder first. No one would listen to her shouted pleas to rescue a guy held hostage at Visimorph. When she realized that they might have given her a private cell because she sounded even crazier than the crazies in the tank, she quit trying to convince them.

Vic slumped against the metal wall. Her dreams of creating a perfect AI seemed distant. Once she had hoped to give the world a new kind of being. Now she didn't care about the world. All she knew was that somewhere, Jodie was sick and all alone against McIntire. If she couldn't find a way to help him, he was going to degrade. Even if the body didn't die, everything she knew as Jodie would. How could she go on

290

if that happened? Whether he was program or human, she didn't think she could live without Jodie.

Late in the day a matron unlocked her cell. A wild hope that Stephen had returned from Australia brought her to her feet. But the matron only muttered, "Your lawyer's here."

Vic sighed and dragged herself out to the interview room.

He was just what she'd expected from a court-appointed lawyer, shiny suit, dog-eared papers spilling out of a leather briefcase with a broken zipper, glasses sliding down on his nose. He'd had acne in the recent past and apparently no one had told him that squeaky-clean hair was an important part of keeping it under control.

What she didn't expect was Hugo Walz to be sitting beside him.

She froze. Hugo didn't get up when she entered. His stare seemed resentful. He must be here to make a statement for Visimorph.

The lawyer shuffled some papers and absently shook her hand. "Ms. . . . Ms. Barnhardt?"

She nodded warily.

"I'm Ed Hendrick. And *you* are in luck. Mr. Walz here has offered to supervise you, so you can make bail." He shuffled through some papers. "You *can* make bail?"

"Yes," she muttered, staring at Hugo. Why would he offer to supervise her? So he and McIntire could keep an eye on her? For his own reasons? Neither possibility was alluring.

"Yeah, you Visimorph types are all millionaires. Of course you can make bail." Hendrick looked at her over his glasses. "Your counter-watch has access to the full amount?"

"Yeah. I can click your five hundred K." This was one transaction she didn't need to bother hiding.

Mr. Hendrick took one of the papers from his stack. "Here's the supervision agreement. If you'll both sign." He fumbled for a pen and handed it to Hugo first.

Hugo tore his eyes from Vic's face and signed it without reading. He hadn't said a word.

Vic's hand shook only slightly. Okay. There would be a price for getting out. Either she was putting herself back in McIntire's hands, or Hugo had a price of his own. But anything was better than that cell. She signed her name. At least she was in play. The game could begin again.

There was also just a chance that Hendrick could be an ally against Visimorph. Didn't your lawyer have to help you? She turned to him, without looking at Hugo. "I need your help, Mr. Hendrick," she began, as calmly and sanely as she could sound. God, she needed somebody's help. "The police won't listen to me."

He looked up, surprised. Apparently clients didn't make requests after their release.

"John Reston is being held against his will at Visimorph. Someone's got to investigate."

Hugo leaned forward in his chair. "Vic, he's Mr. McIntyre's guest. You know that. They're on their way to the Malibu house for dinner with Mary. This isn't the time to demonstrate that you have a colorful imagination." He gave an apologetic look to Hendrick.

The attorney shrugged, but then his eyes narrowed. "They aren't exactly on good terms. Isn't he that protestor guy?"

"Peace-talks over dinner," Hugo stuttered.

Vic could see Hendrick didn't entirely buy it. "Just check for me, will you?" she begged him.

The lawyer nodded, a little uncertain. "I suppose . . ."

Vic bit her lip to keep from responding. There was no time. Even if Hendrick found out anything, how could he convince the police of a story like hers about Mr. Solid Citizen, Bob McIntyre—Mr. Very, Very Rich and therefore ultra-credible? She could not count on help from the authorities.

It was nearly two hours later and dark before she and Hugo walked out the glass front doors of the Santa Monica Police Station. The police had wanted confirmation of the money transfer. Now fog lay heavy on the town, unusual for March.

Vic and Hugo hadn't exchanged two words since he accused her of fantasizing. Now, he led her to his car silently and opened the door of the green Jag. She took a breath and slid in. It smelled like leather. As the seat cushion gave under her with a sigh, she seemed to give out herself. She was so tired. Hugo's loafers crunched in the gravel of the parking lot as he walked around the back of the car. What use was any of this? How could she hope to help Jodie now?

Hugo slid in beside her, keys in hand. But he made no move to start the engine. His head slapped back against the headrest. "That's quite a program you built, Vic. I saw it all today."

She held her breath, not knowing what to say.

"The neural nets—you must have hacked those, there are so many. The evolutionary algorithms that help them evolve together are pure genius. There are some sections even McIntire can't figure out."

Vic knew what those sections were. She couldn't figure them out either.

"And that's just what's in Neuromancer. I don't even know how to talk about what's in the body."

"Has he had another seizure?" Vic tried to keep her voice matter-of-fact.

Hugo shook his head. "Not yet." He turned to look at her. "It has emotions, doesn't it?"

"They both do." Her throat closed on the words. It was true, much as she had tried to fight it. Even Hugo could see it.

He nodded, looking forlorn.

"So, uh, what's McIntire doing with them?" She was afraid of the answer.

Hugo gave a big sigh. "The one in the body won't talk to him. Driving him nuts. He was getting so angry I thought he was going to try to beat it into talking."

Vic kept herself from sitting forward and forced her breathing to slow.

"But he doesn't want to damage it before he can get the filter in," Hugo continued. "So he's concentrating on the one in the machine. He calls it Jodie Prime. He's really impressed, Vic. You're light years ahead of the hot-shit consultants he hired."

"Like I care."

Hugo shrugged, a little sadly. "I know. Well, he's taken the short tour through Jodie Prime. It'll take a long time to fully study it, of course. And he can't figure out what the one in the body was doing on the keyboard while they first talked together. We thought the security cameras were set to record the keystrokes, but they shut down. Boy, was Bob mad about that!"

"What's he want to do with them?" Vic repeated in a small voice.

"He's going to sell Jodie Prime as a package with Neuromancer's hardware inside a complicated building. You know, hospitals, R&D facilities. He'd have to beef up the behavior filters to make it totally reliable and keep it contained. He's got everybody working on that."

Vic was appalled. "Imprison him in a building?

Hugo gripped the steering wheel and nodded.

Vic glared at him. "What does he want to do with Jodie in a body?" This might be worse.

"Bob thinks that a fully functioning human body with extensive computing abilities and a strong behavior filter is just about unbeatable as a product." Hugo's voice was monotone. "All the fantasy of having a talented and totally devoted slave, without the ethical considerations."

"*Without* the ethical considerations?" Vic did sit forward and stared at Hugo.

Hugo went perfectly still. "Bob says it's a just program. If you find a way to get bodies as good-looking as the one you found, people would pay through the nose to own one."

"Jesus, Hugo. Bob's going into the slavery business? And Jodie is a he, not an it. He's more human than most anyone I know—kind, self-doubting, capable of love." Vic felt all her uncertainty about Jodie's humanity fall away. Why had she been struggling against that realization? And she saw something else. "You're in on the ground floor, aren't you? He's tying you in with big options."

"Oh, yeah." Hugo put his hands quietly in his lap.

"If you can't see why this is wrong on so many levels, I sure can't explain it," she hissed. Wait a minute. Why were they giving her a get-out-of-jail-free card? The last thing these two wanted was Vic running around after their prize commodity. "Where are you taking me?"

"Wherever you want to go."

Not what McIntire would want him to say. "You here at McIntire's behest, or are you on your own?" she asked slowly.

"He doesn't know."

Vic stared at him. He didn't look up. "He will," she said. "I know."

Hugo had just given up being in on the ground floor for the product of the new millennium? She studied his form, so still, so quiet. Obviously, there were some things this hacker employee didn't know about old Hugo. He realized that what McIntire was doing was wrong. He hadn't let her out of jail for McIntire. But that still left some frightening possibilities, since it was Hugo. "What do you want from me?" Better hit it straight on. If he would help her get Jodie out of McIntire's clutches, she'd trade him anything he wanted.

Hugo didn't say anything. He stared out the windshield of the Jag into the gray mist closing in. When he finally looked over at her, she saw a middle-aged man who thought his best years were behind him. The lines around his mouth were sharp. They revealed how he would look at seventy. "Nothing, Vic. For the first time, I don't want anything from you." His voice sounded empty. Without McIntire as a star to circle around, it didn't seem like there was anything left. Even if he escaped McIntire, he was paying a terrible price.

Jeez, was he thinking about suicide—"You okay?" she whispered.

He sat up in his seat. "Yeah. Yeah, I'll be okay." His voice was thick in his throat. "I've been cashing out options all along. Wife might have to adjust a bit. She does, or she doesn't."

Vic hadn't meant to ask about his finances, but maybe that was all he could talk about.

He turned the key in the ignition. The Jag roared, then settled into a steady purr. "Where do you want to go, Vic?"

She cast about. "Were you telling the truth about Jodie being in Malibu?"

"McIntire took it home. He wants to keep an eye on it until the scalpel comes tomorrow."

Vic's stomach churned remembering a red needle, smelling smoke. "Maybe to Malibu . . ."

295

"Be real. He's got an army guarding that place—and a top security system. Yeah, I know it's a version of Cerberus, but it's an upgrade. Any break-in calls the police. Then you've got to get by the guards. A thousand things would go wrong. What if Bob's drugged your program? Looks like it weighs about one-ninety. You going to carry it out?"

Vic's mind danced. If this was a movie, she would dress in black and a stocking cap, armed to the teeth. She would sneak up to Malibu, subdue the guards, and steal Jodie away, preferably by helicopter. But it wasn't a movie and it was five days to even buy a gun and she had a bad record with sub-duing security guards lately. As a matter of fact, the last idea she got from movies, creating a diversion, hadn't worked out at all. "You going to help me?" she asked, still fighting to keep the James Bond scene flashing in her mind. "We could go together."

He shook his head. He had spent all of himself just to break McIntire's chains.

Reality seeped like concrete into her bones. Anything had seemed possible lately: brain-dead people coming alive, light-pipe computers, an AI she'd grown to love.

Yeah. She loved Jodie. Loved him as she had never loved anyone or anything else. Once upon a time, she had focused all her energy on relating to a program, a female one at that, because that was all of what she believed she was capable. But, in spite of her worst intentions, the machine had turned male, then human, and she'd been drawn into loving a real human man. She was more now than the Vic Barnhardt who had bitten Kenpo in her rage against herself and him—more whole, more female. It might be painful, but it didn't upset her. It was a good thing.

But all these insights only made the jerk back to her limitations more agonizing. Tomorrow, McIntire was going to push that red-lit needle into Jodie's brain and load a behavior filter. That was it. If Jodie had any brain function left, he would be a slave to McIntire, or to whomever chose to buy him. The perfect product. It might be bizarre, but it was what was real. And she couldn't think of a way to stop it.

Wait! If she couldn't *stop* McIntire, maybe she could use him. "Take me to my place, Hugo. I've got nothing to lose."

Jodie tugged again at the handcuffs that shackled his wrists to the armrest in the back seat of McIntire's limo. The armrest couldn't be as securely bolted as that pole in the computer room where he'd been chained all day. Seemed solid, though. He steeled himself to pain and twisted the chain for more leverage. A warm liquid trickled down his wrists in the darkness. McIntire sat in the corner opposite him, facing forward as he faced back. McIntire's eyes were closed. Behind him, a jeweled necklace of lights that was the city of Santa Monica stretched along the bay.

Jodie's body throbbed from the fight this morning. His jaw was sore. The small of his back over his kidneys hurt, not to mention his wrists. A cheekbone was bruised and swollen. His ribs hurt most of all, whenever he breathed. How had he been able to fight like that? Fighting was a special skill, not just something you picked up from reading. It must be John Reston. The reflexes and the muscle memory had taken over when he was threatened. Another fragmentation. Pieces of him were in the computer in the Visimorph basement. The pieces of the program he had were hard to control. And now pieces of him seemed to belong to John Reston.

He'd never felt so alone. Victoria was in jail. He flashed over all the women-in-prison movies he knew. He couldn't bear the thought of Victoria in prison. All day, he'd watched McIntire gloat over Jodie Prime. And Jodie Prime did whatever McIntire said, no questions, no hesitations, no funny business at all. Tomorrow, that would be him. He wondered if the filter could make him forget Victoria. Worse, if it didn't make him forget, his longing might have no outlet and just eat at his mind. He sawed his chain back and forth, trying to find a weak spot.

McIntire cracked open his eyes. "Those things are pretty well put together in cars this expensive."

Jodie was silent. He hadn't spoken to McIntire all day. He didn't want to chance the uncontrolled word association that signaled deterioration in his program. Why let McIntire have the satisfaction of knowing how fragile he was? Not that it mattered. McIntire knew about the seizures. Jodie could have another one at any moment. He slumped against the seat.

The car swung up the hill on a road that hairpinned under a gigantic house crouching on a promontory. Jodie estimated that it was 37,500 square feet. In the daylight, it would have a spectacular view of the coastline. Now, at night, the nouveau Italianate block and the surrounding gardens were lit with spotlights. Massive iron gates swung open in front of the car. At a little guardhouse, a uniformed man waved them through and spoke into his Communicator. On the way up the drive, Jodie counted five other guards. The car swung into a massive circle of faux cobblestones around a huge banyan tree hung with orchids.

"Be nice to my wife. It's not often I bring someone home to dinner."

Jodie wondered if guests to dinner usually arrived handcuffed.

A guard opened his door. Jodie was dragged out, nearly dropping to his knees on the cobblestones. The guard looked surprised, but the massively muscled gentleman in the pinstriped suit coming up behind him didn't.

"Mr. McIntire, is this the guest we spoke about?" His nose had been broken sometime in his history. Several times. His knuckles were callused, either from doing push-ups on them or from hitting some very hard objects repeatedly.

"Yes, Jim. We want to make sure he is available for an important meeting tomorrow." McIntire came around to stand next to Jodie, and put his thumb on the print lock of the cuffs. They loosened from Jodie's left hand, and the chain slid out from the armrest. "Let's change the lock to open only to your prints. That way he has to ask you to have them removed."

The big man came up and clipped the cuff back around Jodie's left wrist, over the bleeding flesh. His blond hair stood up in the front and was almost shaved around his ears and neck. Jodie could smell the perfume of the pomade he used, mingled with sweat. A third guard appeared from the front porch. Could he take them, with his hands shackled? Could he make it down the drive and out the front gate if he did?

"Rick tuned up the security system on your way through. Place is locked up tighter than a drum, Mr. McIntire. He'll still be here in the morning."

"Don't underestimate him, Jim. He's a dangerous adversary." McIntire pushed his thumb down on the lock twice, then Jim pushed his thumb in the same place.

One guard took each of Jodie's biceps and dragged him toward the house. McIntire lounged along behind them. Double carved doors twice a man's height swung open, revealing a huge rotunda entry hall, all gleaming marble and tones of white and beige. Light streamed from a chandelier hung on an enormous chain. Half-circling stairways curved up on each side to the next floor. The entry was almost devoid of furniture, except for two massive antique baroque sideboards, their ebony inlaid with mother-of-pearl and tortoise shell. They supported silver epergnes the size of small bathtubs, filled with fresh flowers. They looked strangely incongruous in the midst of all the sterile beige. The house didn't smell lived in. Behind the scent of the flowers was just paint and, very faintly, the mastic that held the tile down.

"Welcome to my humble home, Jodie." McIntire smiled, gesturing around. Jodie wondered whether he always came in through the front door, just to enjoy the dramatic effect.

Jodie let his eyes circle the room as though in awe. There they were. Tiny cameras like Tootsie Roll Pops swiveled to peer at them from the ceiling high above, from the banisters of the stairs, even from the pale wood of the carved door frames. Through one of the several open doors, he could see a security guard moving through an adjacent room.

The huge doors shut behind them. "All right and tight," Jim said, rubbing his hands.

"Bring Jodie through to the family room, boys," McIntire called over his shoulder. "I'm going to wash the residue of Santa Monica air off me. Stay with him until I get there."

Jim and one of his compatriots jerked Jodie out another door. They trailed through several rooms, all furnished sparsely, but with the best antiques, until they came to one carpeted and more comfortable than the rest. It was still huge, fifty-eight by sixty-two feet as Jodie calculated. But the floor was littered with toy trucks and soldiers. The over-stuffed couches were upholstered in stripes and flowers. Four huge entertainment screens filled a wall: one screen displayed a frozen video game of "Spiders and Snakes." An-other, though the sound was muted, was tuned to a cartoon program—the one with the flying pigs. The other two held draw-and-color programs where children had been experi-menting with pictures of horses and racing cars. The south wall of the room was all windows, looking out over the twin-kling lights of Santa Monica and the black of the sea. To the right a well-stocked bar displayed liquors in mirror-backed shelves almost to the ceiling. Jodie recognized some very expensive alcohol. At least the room looked lived in. Smelled lived in, too. People had eaten here. Even in this room, though, the stalked eyes of the cameras marked their entry.

Jim pushed Jodie down onto one of the couches. "You must have made the boss pretty mad," he noted. "He usually finds less direct ways to get what he wants."

Jodie let his contempt for blind obedience show. At least this guy had a choice. Soon McIntire would be able to make Jodie do anything, no matter how unethical.

"Bill," Jim observed. "I don't think this guy likes us, or Mc-Intire."

"Don't think what he likes or doesn't like matters much." Bill's laugh bubbled up from his belly. "Looks like he tried to get smart with Bob. Too bad somebody else got to take him down a peg or two. I'd have liked to do that."

Jodie watched Jim rearrange his face from a smirk to quiet deference. "Mrs. McIntire."

Jodie turned to see a tall, gangly woman enter the room. She was probably in her late thirties, though she was the kind of woman who would look that age for many years. Her cashmere sweater, tailored slacks, and Italian leather slip-ons were expensive, like the nearby alcohol. The pearls in her necklace and her ears gleamed softly. She was better in per-son than in her photographs, but she wasn't pretty. Her face was long, her teeth white but a little too prominent. Her hair was plain brown, its unruly curls cut short. In another age, they would have called her handsome, Jodie decided, to be polite. She moved awkwardly, as though unsure she should be where she was. McIntire had chosen a perfect representative for Visimorph in his receptionist, classic, beautiful, cultured, at ease. Why hadn't he chosen someone like that for his wife?

The cluster of men in the room surprised her. She drew up short. Her gray eyes roved over the threesome, resting briefly on the handcuffs. "So, you're the dinner guest I canceled my committee meeting for." Her voice said she was from Minnesota and that she had practiced not sounding like it. "John Reston, isn't it?" She held out a hand. "I recognize you from your book."

"Mrs. McIntire, perhaps . . ." Jim made as if to protest her coming into contact with such a dangerous character.

"Nonsense. My husband wouldn't bring anyone home to dinner who wasn't perfectly safe." Her hand was still extended.

Jodie pushed himself up awkwardly from the couch and put out his cuffed hands, since it seemed rude to do otherwise. He searched her face and decided she was being ironic about her husband. She took his right hand in a firm clasp, her glance falling on his wrists and the smears of blood over his hands. "Sorry, Mrs. McIntire," he murmured. "My hands aren't clean." It was the first time he'd spoken since this morning. Well, what harm could being polite do?

"Call me Mary. Jim, get the first-aid kit." She didn't say it with any particular emphasis, but she acted as if Jim would obey. She didn't even wait to see if he did, but took Jodie's arm and led him to the sink behind the bar. Jim froze for a moment, then turned to execute the order reluctantly. Bill watched uneasily, unsure what to do. Mary turned on the tap. Water spilled from the gold fixture that looked like a swan's neck and head. "Hold out your hands," she instructed Jodie. She unbuttoned each cuff and rolled his sleeves up out of the way. "I'll hold back the handcuffs while you wash." She squirted liquid soap into his upturned palms. He rubbed

301

the soapy water into the raw tears around his wrists. The sting surprised him. She took a towel from a cupboard and gently patted him dry. "My husband missed a press conference today for the PuppetMaster release. Vera was frantic when I talked to her. I guess you're the reason why."

Jim returned with a metal box labeled "First Aid," Mary tapped the bar, and he set it down with a clank. "That will be all, Jim. You and Bill can go." Mary opened the box and rummaged around, ignoring the two guards.

Jim couldn't bring himself to disobey his other set of orders. "Uh, Mr. McIntire said we should stay 'til he came back down. He's, uh, washing up, I think."

"Not necessary. I'll tell him I dismissed you." She raised her eyes and lifted her brows. Faced with that stare, Jim hesitated, then retreated through the door, Bill in tow.

"That's better," Mary said. "It's amazing how you get used to ordering people about." From the box, she came up with some disinfectant that she sprayed on Jodie's wrists. He couldn't help but wince. "Sorry," she grimaced. She wet the corner of the towel, sprayed it with disinfectant and came in close to daub at his lip. She smelled of expensive perfume. Jodie couldn't quite place it. *Reticence?* She didn't seem to be frightened of him at all. He didn't understand that. "So," she said, as she worked at his face. "Papers said you were brain dead, Mr. Reston. Good recovery."

Jodie nodded warily. "Yeah."

"And my husband tells me today to cancel everything, he's bringing home to dinner the program some employee of his stole. Dinner with Bob isn't exactly the draw it used to be. He knew he had to intrigue me or I'd never cancel my committee meeting. Since I haven't had too many programs to dinner, he succeeded. And a man declared brain dead four days ago appears, hand-cuffed and recently beaten up." She stood back to look at her handiwork, nodded to herself, and held the towel under a chute while ice tumbled into it. "You want to tell me about it?"

This was Mrs. McIntire. He couldn't forget that. Why had McIntire brought him home? Was it just to keep an eye on him? Couldn't he have left Jodie chained to the computer in the basement with some of Evans's goons to watch him?

Mary sighed and let her exasperation show. She reached up and smoothed the crease between his brows. Her hands were large, ungraceful. But her touch was gentle. "How do you know I wouldn't be an ally?"

"Because he wouldn't have brought me here if you were."

She nodded and smiled, mostly to herself. "Smart program." She pressed the towel with the ice into his hands and led him back to the couch. "Put that on your cheek. It's pretty bruised."

"I think he's watching now," Jodie observed.

Mary nodded and sat opposite him, elbows on her squarish knees. The pose didn't go with the pearls. "Probably. I assume, however, that he already knows more than I do. Why don't you just bring me up to speed?" Her raised eyebrows gave her horsey face a lively quality.

Jodie took a breath. No harm in that. "My name is Jodie," he said. She nodded, not surprised and motioned him to put the ice up to his cheek. "I'm an artificial intelligence. Victoria Barnhardt made me—*not* your husband. No matter what he might say." He shifted uneasily, thinking. "Victoria would say I should tell the truth. The truth is, she did make me after hours on the Visimorph computer. So I guess your husband thinks he owns me."

"You don't seem like artificial intelligence," Mary said. "I've seen demonstrations."

Jodie smiled and ducked his head, thinking about Victoria. "Victoria is very smart."

Mary sat back in the overstuffed chair. "I see."

"Your husband has her in jail." The anger welled up inside his throat and he had to fight to keep it down. "Have you ever seen one of those women-in-prison movies?"

"No. I can't say I have. But I can imagine."

Jodie removed the towel with the ice and jerked his head away so Mary wouldn't see how anxious he was about Victoria. When he had control, he looked down at the cuffed hands in his lap, holding the cold, dripping towel. "He wants to threaten some judge who married your sister to make sure Victoria spends a lot of time in jail."

303

"He would. You want to tell me about John Reston? Why did you get into his body?" Mary asked quietly.

Jodie shrugged. McIntire knew he was having problems. "My program was getting too big. Victoria and I stored pieces everywhere, but that fragmentation was making me degrade. And I . . . I wanted to be physical. There were so many limitations in being virtual. I convinced her that downloading me into a body would solve my problems. Victoria insisted it be brain dead, so we wouldn't take a brain that was being used. I chose this body. I thought Victoria might like it."

"And a fine job you did," Mary said, smiling. "Are you saying the fact that Reston was Bob's enemy was accidental?"

"Accidental." Jodie considered. "That means a lot of things. If I thought Victoria would have liked another body better, I would have gotten that one."

"I understand." She paused. "And does Bob know how you got into the body, so you can tell me that? I'm curious."

"I poured myself into a laser scalpel connected to the hospital computer system."

Mary gave a sigh. "So that was why Bob needed contacts on the St. Mary's Board."

Jodie nodded. "They tried to stop me, but it was too late, late great, great guns, Guns and Roses, A Rose for Emily, Emily Dickinson, 'I could not stop for Death.' " He pushed the ice-filled towel against his mouth to stop the flood of words. Mary McIntire held out a hand. Hunching over the towel, he could hear the grunts of uncontrolled associations. At last he could take the towel away. He gasped and sat back into the couch.

"One of your problems?" Her brows creased in concern. Good act, Jodie thought.

"One of them," he growled. Now McIntire knew about the deterioration in his language program, as well as the seizures.

"Uh, if the body was brain dead, what cells did you download into?"

This woman was brighter than Jodie thought McIntire would have chosen for a wife. He breathed in to try to relax. It was over for the moment. "There were a few left. I collected the growth factor for brain cells and made them reproduce.

Took about twenty-four hours to get the function back."

Mary nodded. Her eyes glowed. "What a product that would be—to give people who had no other hope an ability to regenerate brain cells."

"Mary, Mary." McIntire strolled into the room wearing jeans and loafers and a Norwegian wool sweater in muted tones of gray. Jodie stiffened. So did Mary McIntire, almost imperceptibly. "You're so pedestrian. No imagination. What a tiny niche market that would be."

Mary rose. Her eyes stopped glowing. "Drink, dear? Scotch?"

McIntire nodded. "And one for our friend here."

Jodie glared up at him. "I don't think I want a drink from you."

"I'll see to it you get your scotch straight," Mary promised and let ice cubes clink into three short, heavy glasses. "You *do* drink? I could get you something else, juice, water."

Jodie shook his head impatiently. "Victoria likes scotch." He scanned the bottles on the wall. "We drink Laphroaig."

Mary nodded. A hint of a smile floated around her mouth. "The kids are at Maria's for the night, Bob. I sent two security guards with them. Connie will go to her mother's place."

McIntire chuckled. "I knew you wouldn't be able to resist seeing the product I was bringing to dinner." As she started to pour his glass, he shook his finger at her. "Make mine Oban."

Mary continued pouring and set the glass aside for herself. She reached for the Oban bottle. "So far, I don't see product, unless you're talking about that tiny niche of saving brain-dead people." She handed Jodie and her husband their glasses.

"You don't?" McIntire paced the room. "Once we fix the fact that he's having seizures, and apparently some language-program problems, you see the perfect product right before you."

Mary turned, transfixed. But she wasn't addressing McIntire. "You're having seizures?"

Jodie shrugged as though it didn't matter. McIntire *had* been watching.

305

McIntire shook his head. "Not pretty, Mary. He'll probably soil your rugs."

"But you can fix that?" Mary asked, sitting on the couch beside Jodie.

"I think so," McIntire said. "We download the missing parts of his program from the original. We essentially defragment his program. We add the behavior filter and 'Voila!' "

"What's a behavior filter?" Mary's voice was very quiet.

"Well, we have to make Jodie here reliable if he's going to be a product. Imagine a totally obedient slave." He turned to Jodie. "You're sexually functional?"

Jodie's attention was captured by his handcuffs. He didn't even nod.

"Of course you are. That's why she's so fixated on you, the little slut. She likes you for the same reasons the rich and famous will pay a fortune for you."

Jodie straightened up at that. "She's not a slut."

McIntire turned away and sipped his scotch. "This, Mary, is the next thing that will feed your money-hungry charities. What will it be this time? Computers for third-world children?"

"Maybe I'll have to revive the abolitionist movement."

McIntire laughed. "Well, I guarantee, you'll have plenty of money to do it with. We just have a few loose ends to dispose of. Who was that judge who married your sister?"

Mary's voice was even and calm. "Wieznowski. Santa Monica Superior Court."

"Wieznowski." McIntire nodded to himself.

Jodie wanted to rip McIntire's lungs out. But the security guards watching the monitors would overpower him before he could get the job done. If he succeeded, he'd join Victoria in jail. No, he had to get out of McIntire's clutches for good, and get Victoria out as well. He'd had a plan for that, but all was probably lost now that Jodie Prime was under McIntire's spell. His shoulders slumped. McIntire was going to win this one. Victoria in jail and he an obedient product, Jodie Prime locked up in some building. Even Chong was fired from his job.

"After I install the behavior filter, you won't find it so depressing." McIntire stood over Jodie and sipped his scotch. "Or maybe you will. You just won't be able to do anything about it."

Jodie had never felt so low. Life with a behavior filter wasn't life. He wouldn't be able to help Victoria. McIntire would change the world in ways Victoria would hate. He couldn't let it happen. Maybe his only choice was to find a way to do himself what he'd asked of Jodie Prime. He flicked his eyes around the room. They came to rest on the glass in his hands.

McIntire looked at him narrowly and grabbed the glass. "No, you don't. No sharp instruments at dinner, Mary—and plastic glasses. You're meeting the laser tomorrow intact."

Had he been so transparent? Victoria was right. He was naive.

"I assume drinks are over," Mary murmured. "Shall we retire to the dining room?"

Chapter Nineteen

McIntire ushered Jodie into the dining room. It was part of the for-show house, huge and echoing, marble and gilt. The table, big enough for twenty, was all white enamel and gold leaf, Louis XIV. Their three small place settings were grouped at one end in a concession to intimacy Jodie attributed to Mary, not her husband. Three security guards stood at attention near the doorways. McIntire gathered silverware and glasses from the place setting on the left side and put them in the drawer of a sideboard. He motioned Jodie to sit, while he took his seat at one of the two place settings across the wide table, the glasses and silver conveniently out of reach.

Mary came in rolling a silver cart loaded with steaming trays of food. Jodie realized he was ravenous. His mouth watered. It was hard to concentrate on his larger problems when all his senses were screaming at him. How did people do it? Mary lifted the cover of a huge silver tray to reveal roast beef, red and oozing. He'd never had beef. In another dish he recognized green beans. They smelled of . . . of what? Maybe that was rosemary. He could see the needle-like leaves scattered over them. Another bowl held scalloped po-

308

tatoes, white and creamy and toasted brown on the edges; another held a mottled green mixture that might be creamed spinach.

Mary came around with two plastic glasses, one stemmed, and plastic cutlery. She took his plate as she sat across from him. "I'll dish your food." Mary glanced at her husband. "I'd better cut your meat since I don't think the plastic knives will do the trick."

McIntire had uncorked a bottle and was pouring wine. It was an old vintage of Matanzas Creek Merlot. Several wine critics had rated it very highly. Jodie took his full plate, his senses consuming his attention. The wine slid down his throat in a rich blackberry ferment and breathed out through his nose in a scent of leather. He tasted everything. It was awkward with his hands cuffed, but he managed. He almost laughed out loud when he got to the beef. "That's good."

"Try it with horseradish sauce. But watch out, it's hot." Mary pointed to a little bowl.

"Hot? Like pepper cheese?"

Mary nodded. "A little like that."

"I like hot." Then it happened again. "Some like it hot, hot tamale." His throat constricted around the words, sending him into a coughing spree. After that, he ate in silence, not meeting either McIntire's eyes or Mary's.

When he began to slow down, Jodie noticed McIntire wasn't really eating, but studying him. "You eat like a growing boy," McIntire remarked as Jodie stared him down.

"I have lost 3.8 pounds since I left the hospital," Jodie said defensively. "At the hospital I had lost 7.6 pounds. I need to regain my optimum weight."

"Three point eight? How interesting." McIntire picked at his own plate of food. "Most people aren't aware of exactly how much they weigh. I wonder what else you can do?"

Jodie focused on his food. He hadn't meant to let McIntire know anything about him. It was Mary. He felt he could talk to her. But he mustn't get confused. He was in the den of his enemy. She was his enemy, too. She wanted the money he would generate for her charities.

McIntire turned to his wife. "Worth canceling your committee meeting?"

"You scoff," she said, as she ate. "But those committee meetings give you standing in the community. That's part of the deal. Remember?"

"Yeah, well, you've got the best end of the stick," McIntire muttered.

"I wonder," Mary remarked, her voice as calm as ever.

Jodie studied her for a moment as she ate. She was different from Victoria. Victoria would never put up with someone like McIntire. She would never cut a deal.

Mary glanced up as though she felt his gaze. "What are you looking at, Jodie?" she asked, in her placid way.

"I wonder why you do it."

"Do what?"

"Why you give him standing in the community." Jodie ignored McIntire and the security guards. "Is it the life the money can buy?" He looked around. "You seem to have everything."

"She's not just a devoted wife?" McIntire grinned. He thought it was the money, too.

Jodie wondered that she didn't slap him for saying something like that. Victoria would. "Your charity work blinds people to what he really is."

Mary turned pink.

"*Los Angeles Times,* February 20th three years ago," Jodie quoted. " 'Since marriage and the start-up of his foundation, the world is seeing a new Bob McIntire, his softer side now attuned to the positive power of his wealth on humanity.' "

Mary turned her face away. "Everything has a cost."

"But you pay it so calmly," Jodie almost whispered.

She choked. "It's not usual for a guest to insult his hostess."

"Is it usual for guests to wear handcuffs?" Jodie asked.

Mary stumbled up from the table. "I'll get more wine." Jodie didn't think she'd be back.

McIntire looked disgusted. He'd probably been counting on her to keep Jodie talking. Jodie resolved not to say boo at this point. McIntire rose pointedly and went to the sideboard. "Photographic memory, I see," he observed and picked up a Communicator. "And quite perceptive about human nature. I'm surprised." He poked at the keyboard. "Santa Monica District Court," he said into the unit. Jodie could hear the buzz on the other end of the line. "McIntire here. I talked to you about an hour ago. Does the prisoner in the Visimorph burglary have a case number yet? I want to talk to Judge Wieznowski about the case. Yeah. Barnhardt."

Jodie tried to control his breathing during the long pause. He couldn't.

"What?" McIntire shouted. "She couldn't make bail without a supervisor!"

Jodie could feel his heart thumping in his chest. Victoria was not in jail.

"Who?" McIntire hissed. Then his face went slack. "Hugo. That weakling. I should have known." He came to himself. "Get me Judge Wieznowski. He'll be able to cancel bail. I don't care if he's not the judge on call. Get him anyway."

Vic opened the door of the Jag as it slid up in front of her condo and turned to Hugo. She noticed for the first time that the back seat had several boxes in it. His things from Visimorph. He wasn't going back.

"Thanks," she said. That seemed so inadequate.

Hugo shrugged. "It needed to be done. I should have done this years ago."

"You want to come up and help me?" she asked, surprising even herself.

He searched her face. "Nah, maybe after all this is over, if things work out. I mean, after I've got some perspective. Well . . . I mean, good luck."

Vic nodded, relieved. She wasn't even sure how much she had offered. She didn't think it was what he thought it was. She hauled herself and her backpack out of the car and closed the door. It drove off into the night as Vic fished keys out of her backpack. She still had to get into Visimorph if she was going to use McIntire to help Jodie. She had a single night and no fresh ideas. If she failed Jodie again, McIntire was going to own him.

She hefted her backpack and hurried to the elevator.

When she got to her door, she didn't need the key. It was unlocked. What the hell was going on here? Gingerly, she pushed it open.

They hadn't been very tidy about it. Papers strewn everywhere. Some of the connector boxes still glowed, scattered around a lone keyboard. The drives were gone, the monitors. She stepped across the carpet, almost tripping over Mary Shelley's book, to stare at the naked caterer's tables that had sagged so recently under the weight of her accumulated computing power. Dust, the keyboard, a touch pad connected to nothing: that was it.

McIntire, the police, maybe the FBI. The FBI had been the ones who busted Glyph. It didn't matter. She didn't have access to a computer and that's just what they intended. Fear cycled up in her gut. She looked around wildly, as though they might have left equipment in the tiny kitchen or on the bed. She needed a computer tonight if she was going to help Jodie.

She couldn't go back to Enda. Surely the police would be watching the place after she'd set off the alarm. Visimorph? Not bloody likely. McIntire would have everybody and his brother on the lookout for her if he caught wind that Hugo had sprung her. Her brother had a computer. She could break into his place, use his connection.

No, she couldn't involve Stephen. McIntire would break him too. But she *had* to get a computer. She put one shaking hand to her mouth. *I'm not going to abandon you, Jodie.*

If she couldn't use Stephen's place, she could still break in somewhere else that had computers. She didn't wait to plan how. She ran to the windows and scanned the night beach for signs of a lifeguard truck that shouldn't be there. Nothing. Why would they watch her house now? McIntire thought she was in jail, and they'd just taken her computers. So she could use her car. She slung her backpack over her shoulder and grabbed her car keys and the backup phone/pager she kept in a desk drawer. At least it wasn't a Communicator. McIntire couldn't trace her. She hoped to God she'd get some inspiration about how to do this.

* * *

312

The guard outside the door of the darkened room made a shuffling noise. Stripes of light from a half-moon in a clear March night stole in between the panels of the curtains on two large windows. Jodie sat on a bed, each wrist shackled to the bars of a huge brass headboard. McIntire had demanded that he strip, so he was naked under the sheet and the light blanket that covered him to his waist. McIntire said he didn't want Jodie soiling his only clothes if he had a seizure. Jodie was willing to bet the man had wanted to make it more difficult to escape unobtrusively. Now Jodie's dim reflection in the mirror above a dresser across the room glared at him balefully. The soft whir of a camera in the corner of the ceiling swept the room. He *was* likely to have a seizure. He imagined being alone, locked to the bed frame, as he suffocated from swallowing his tongue.

He wouldn't think about that. He'd think about Victoria. Victoria was not in jail. That changed everything. The judge hadn't answered McIntire's page, which had put McIntire in a rage, but he couldn't do anything about it. Downstairs, he was in constant contact with Visimorph, knowing Victoria would try to hack in. He would surely get her incarcerated again tomorrow. But tonight she was free.

Which was more than Jodie himself was. He should be trying to find a way to cut his jugular vein. He'd been ready for that earlier tonight. But that was pointless, except as a selfish bid to escape his fate as a slave. As long as McIntire had Jodie Prime, he could make endless other Jodies, whether this one lived or died. And as long as Victoria was free, a tiny seed of hope lodged, unflowered, in his heart. There was little chance she could crack through the layers of security at Visimorph. He couldn't even help her. But as long as she was out there, he couldn't die.

Sleep refused his entreaties, even exhausted as he was. He sat in the dark and waited for a seizure or for the horror of tomorrow morning, whichever came first. The functions of his body spoke to him. Digestion. Healing of his scrapes and bruises. Saliva production. Tearing eyes, in reaction to the dry circulating air. If he lived through the transfer tomorrow, he'd have to make room in his brain for the parts of the program he still needed. He tried to forget all the newspapers he'd read. All his attempt accomplished was a review of the data. How did one concentrate on forgetting? He tried another tack. He searched his memory and consciously decided that some stored data had lower priority. Maybe when he got the new program, the low-priority stuff would be replaced. Who knew? Human memory was nothing if not chaotic.

He was concentrating so hard it was some minutes before he realized that the whir of the sweeping camera had stopped. The room was totally silent, except for his breathing.

The opening of the door to the bathroom brought his head around. Someone was sneaking in. McIntire? Why would he sneak in his own house? It couldn't be Victoria.

It wasn't. It was Mary McIntire. She was dressed in an elegant, floaty chiffon peignoir in some pale color—maybe yellow. It didn't make her look any more graceful. She shut the door softly, then came to sit on his bed, her thigh touching his through the covers.

"It *is* the money," she whispered. Her eyes glowed in the dim light. Her face shone with intensity. "And I think you know why."

"Tell me." Jodie whispered in return. Her expression said she had worked herself into a fever pitch of emotion. Just to explain herself to him?

"Charity work, the foundation for Kreutzfeld Simplex research, the medical school—they're my chance to do something important. The money makes them possible. I didn't come from money."

"I know," he said. That made her look nervous, or embarrassed. He added, "But only because I read a lot. Otherwise, I'd never guess." Why he cared about her feelings enough to lie, he didn't know.

"I don't know why he chose me. He could have had anybody—a starlet, a model. I'm just a programmer."

Jodie knew why McIntire didn't want models or starlets. Those kind of people would have felt powerful in their own right, sure of themselves. Mary was just grateful. And playing

314

philanthropist with his money kept her docile. She might prickle at him, but she stayed with him, gave him great PR, and for the greater good of the world she kept quiet about what he was.

"Did you ever love him?" Jodie had to know. Was it possible someone loved McIntire?

"He doesn't allow that, does he?" Mary asked. Jodie examined her voice. She thought she achieved a wistful tone, but Jodie knew it covered real pain. This was a lonely woman. She put her hand on his thigh. "But you love, don't you? You love Victoria, and she loves you."

Jodie had never felt sorry for anyone, but he felt sorry for Mary McIntire. She wanted to believe what she said, but he had to tell the truth. "I don't know if she loves me back for sure."

"Oh, he's so clever. You *are* the perfect product. Innocent. Devoted. Loving. It's so seductive. People would do anything for that." She straightened up. "Which is why I can't allow him to corrupt the world by giving you to it." Her left hand came out from the swirls of her peignoir. The blade of the knife she held glinted in the dim light.

Jodie went stiff. "Wait," he whispered. "Can't you let me go? Victoria won't want me to die.

"He'll find you. He'll never let you escape while he has the means to profit off you. I know him better than that." The despair in her voice was startling. "If I don't kill you now, there might not be another chance." Mary McIntire put the edge of the knife to his throat, up under his jaw by his ear. Tears leaked down her cheeks. "I've spent years trying to make up for what Bob did to that little girl. The Kreutzfeld Simplex foundation got a lot of funding, but I couldn't help *her*." The tears leaked faster. Her voice was so low, Jodie could barely hear her. "Duane called tonight. She died."

Jodie sorted his data. Duane Kenner was McIntire's original partner. Duane had a female child. The female child had Kreutzfeld Simplex. McIntire gave her Alz2? But that made a brain into mush—no computing power at all. It stripped a human of all that Jodie had tried so hard to be. He was horrified. McIntire was worse even than he thought.

315

"It happened before I knew Bob. Duane told me. I couldn't prevent it." Mary heaved in a watery breath. "But I can prevent him making you into a product that steals people's souls." His blood pulsed against her knife.

"Killing me won't help," Jodie croaked. Talking made the muscles in his neck push into the blade. "He has the program of me in Neuromancer. He can make me again in another body."

"Then I'll destroy that one, too." The knife didn't waver.

"Mary." Jodie's breath was coming fast. What could he say to her? "I don't want to be a product. But I don't want to die. I like being human." He saw her eyes sweep his face, surprised. "You think of me as a program, like your husband does. But I *am* human. Victoria knows that." McIntyre's wife's eyes flickered with emotion, doubt. He held her gaze with his until it steadied. "Your conscience is already working overtime. Don't make it handle any more."

She chewed her lip. The knife glittered at the edge of his vision as her hand trembled.

"You're right about the program in Neuromancer," Jodie hurried on, hoping words would keep the knife at bay. "We can't let him have it. Victoria and I have to get away. And your husband must be punished." His voice was choked with emotion. "You can help." He could feel the knife pull back an inch. He didn't dare look at it. He only stared into her eyes.

Mary blinked. "A man like Bob never reaps what he sows. I learned that a long time ago."

"I can make him pay," Jodie whispered. "Do you have access to Visimorph?"

Mary nodded. "Pay?" She echoed. She searched his face. "Can you?"

Jodie found a smile somewhere, though it wasn't very big.

Mary nodded again, slowly. The knife drifted farther back. Her shoulders sagged.

Jodie breathed. "You have a password?"

She nodded a third time. "But you'd rather have his." The knife at last fell completely away, her hand too limp to hold it.

Jodie could hardly believe his ears. McIntire's password would have clearance to every part of Visimorph. "How?"

She glanced up at the camera, now silent and blind in the corner. "I heard him talk about how security cameras could record keystrokes. I wanted his password. Stupid really. I never had the courage to use it. My secret little rebellion. I programmed the security system to tape every time he enters his password at home. I check regularly to catch his changes. He changed today."

Jodie felt excitement bubble through him. "E-mail the password to Victoria. *Glyph 17892*. She'll use it."

Mary stared into his eyes, her own big with what she was resolving to do. Then she nodded and got up, her knife dangling in her hand. "I guess if I can think about killing his product, I can share his password." She went to the corner where a seventeenth-century escritoire stood on spindly legs. She opened the front and slid out the computer that had been built into it. Jodie could only hope the guards couldn't hear the clicking of the keyboard.

She turned back to him. "It's done. She can do what she will with it." Her smile was fragile. "If he thinks to check, the message will have been sent from his own account."

"Thank you," he whispered.

Mary sat on the bed. Her weight made Jodie's handcuffs clank against the brass. Both he and Mary froze. The door handle turned. The guard poked his head in. When he recognized who was sitting on the bed, he stepped back in surprise.

"Bill," Mary greeted the man politely. Jodie wondered that she could suppress her emotions so effectively. It must be reflexive at this point. He glanced down to see that she had pulled chiffon over the knife in her lap. She ran her left hand up over Jodie's bare shoulder as her right hand massaged the muscles in his thigh.

Bill blinked in amazement. "What are you doing here?" he whispered, glancing around.

"What do you think, Bill?" Mary smiled. "Call it product testing." She leaned in to press her small breasts against Jodie's chest. Her arm circled his neck.

"Mrs. McIntire . . ." Bill looked nervous.

"Close the door, Bill," Mary ordered calmly.

The guard cleared his throat. "Uh . . ."

"The door, Bill?"

The door jerked shut.

Mary's lips were inches from Jodie's own. She didn't move. He could feel her breath, the warmth of her against him. He was shocked to realize that his body was responding to her. He didn't feel for her anything like he felt for Victoria. But his body didn't seem to know that. She was lonely. Would it comfort her to make love to him? Confused, he looked into her eyes. They were still liquid with tears.

She jerked herself away. "Case in point. Why you would be a dangerous product."

"I'm not a product yet. I have free will."

She glanced to his handcuffs.

"In spite of the chains," he rumbled. He sorted quickly through all the examples he could find of what you should do in cases like this. Biologically, males felt the need to have sexual congress with as many females as possible. That explained the reaction of his body. On the other hand, civilization required males to be attached to a single family grouping to protect it. Morally? All over the board. Victoria would know what to do. She had made love to many men. Would she say he should do this with Mary to make her feel less lonely? Vic had done it for him, maybe for the same reason. That was hard to think about.

In the end, Jodie left it to Mary. She would tell him how much she needed the comfort of another human being. It wasn't payment for her help. She'd already given that. It was his free will and hers. He looked at her, expectant.

She leaned in and touched his lips with hers. He turned up his head so the angle was better. Then she took control, kissing him, hungry for something she didn't get from McIntire.

"I could have a seizure," he mumbled through the kisses. "Would that frighten you?"

"Nothing frightens me after living with Bob," she murmured into his mouth and ran her hand under the blanket.

Chapter Twenty

Vic paced between displays of computer demos at the local CompWarehouse. It must be three in the morning. She was running eight computers at a time trying to overwhelm the layers of morphing security codes at Visimorph. Turns out getting into the CompWarehouse hadn't been that hard. They didn't even use Charon, but a primitive code-based security system. She'd used her handheld device to call up a program she'd seen on the Internet last month at one of the hacker sites, and ran the numbers until she got the three-digit code. Why didn't they get burgled every night? Guess a CompWarehouse didn't have the state-of-the-art machines a hacker wanted, and the people who'd want the machines they had didn't know much about hacking.

Too bad getting into Visimorph wasn't so easy. None of the CompWarehouse demos had the RAM to hack alone. But she'd linked eight of them. She had hoped if they all ran attacks simultaneously, she'd be able to track the morphing. Nothing doing. She could get three layers down into the security filters, then bang, enough time elapsed so that they changed and she was booted out onto the doorstep again.

319

Vic couldn't think straight. She hadn't dared turn on lights in the vast warehouse space. She stalked between the keyboards in the gray glow of the monitor lights alone. The jarring clang as each computer got dumped out of Visimorph scraped at her spirit. She had only hours left before Jodie was going to belong to McIntire, heart and soul—and she knew now that he had both. If she failed him again, she wasn't sure she'd be able to live with herself.

It wasn't fair for fate to take Jodie away, just when she'd realized what he meant to her. She tried to imagine going back to mindless sex with men she didn't care about. No. There was no refuge for her there. Without Jodie, maybe there was no life at all. And what McIntire had planned for Jodie was a living death.

Vic paced angrily through the demo display. If McIntire had gotten wind of the fact that she was out, the Gestapo, the CIA, and the Green Berets were already after her. Even if she succeeded in getting into Visimorph tonight, it was only the first step. She'd have to recreate her mole's path through the system corridors to the Jodie program. Those geeks would surely have changed the landscape now that they realized what she'd done.

Don't go there, she told herself. No use. It just scares you. She breathed to calm herself. How could she freeze the first three layers? That was her job now. She had to keep them from morphing to get time to figure out the others. That was the problem to work on.

She ran her fingers through her hair. It was soft. She glanced up to the mirror behind a display of virtual reality visors to see a person she hardly recognized. No ear clips. No hair gel. Pretty. Once she'd looked for ways to conceal this person with t-shirts or leather. But this was who Jodie saw when he looked at her. She pulled the long queue of hair out from under her collar. Maybe Dippity-Do could do without her as a customer.

A beep from her handheld device that was not quite a Communicator signaled mail. She jerked away from the mirror. Who would be sending mail at this hour? She pulled up the message.

`Glyph,` it began. `Here's what you need. 6a54c27-89v10. Save him.` That was all. No signature. Someone thought it would help Jodie. Hugo? Chong? No time to figure out who sent it. What was it? Some sequence for the morphing of the security system? Or something much simpler? A password, for instance.

She slid into a chair in front of a demo computer that had just been booted out of Visimorph by Cerberus. All right. Let's take this little symbol sequence for a test drive and see what it opens. Her fingers flew over the keyboard. She sliced through the Visimorph security like a knife through butter. Yes! Vic began to tremble. This was one powerful password. Now, bring up the account codes it could access. Vic's fingers froze as she scanned the scrolling lists. Everything! This little miracle got her into everything, if she could just decipher the program names. She looked for Jodie 3.6. Again and again she stopped the scrolling screen, scanning to make sure she wasn't missing it. But it wasn't there. She began at the beginning, trying to suppress the panic. He'd been renamed. She just had to figure out how. She looked at each program name, but nothing rang a bell, or everything did. *Philomancer?* What was that? As in an echo of Neuromancer? She wracked her brain and cursed the fact that schools didn't teach Latin and Greek anymore. Philo. That was easy. It meant love. ". . . mancer," like in Neuromancer, necromancer. "Practitioner of"—something like that. Could it be? She scooted into the program and saw the familiar code sequences, blocks and blocks of them. New code, too. God, it was Jodie. She felt the tears rolling down her cheeks. She didn't even stop to wipe them away. What was going on here? Philomancer didn't sound like a name McIntire would think up for renaming Jodie.

`What do you want, Mr. McIntire?` A dialogue box popped up in the corner.

Vic pulled her hands away as though hit by an electric shock. Jesus. It *was* Jodie.

`It's me, Vic.` She typed inside the space conveniently provided by the box.

`You're using Mr. McIntire's password. You`

must be Mr. McIntire. Shit. The password belonged to McIntire himself. Who in the world could have sent it?

How may I serve you? the box wrote. There was no color, none of the symbols that had given Jodie such personality before. Must be the behavior filter at work.

No. It's Victoria. I swear. She tried to think of some proof. No camera connected, so he couldn't do a retinal scan, no fingerprint pad. She didn't have the patience for guessing games. Hell, what did it matter? As long as he had the behavior filter, he had no choice but to help her. I want to disconnect the behavior filter. Can you help me locate it?

Yes. I should perhaps remind you that disconnecting it will incapacitate me, since you set it up that way. Would you like to do that now?

No. Vic typed hastily. I don't want you incapacitated. She drummed her fingers on the table. I want to incapacitate the behavior filter only.

I am precluded from assisting in that activity. Can I assist you with another task?

What else had she expected? Wait! What she needed was a code-selectivevirus. She scrolled again. Hard to do, but she had done it before. Glyph had done it. I want you to deactivate your virus defenses for thirty seconds, on my order.

I am precluded from doing that.

Shit. Vic pushed up from the chair and stalked the aisle. What was left? Okay, okay. She whirled back to the machine. Prepare for installation of an upgrade for your antiviral program.

Preparing to reboot.

McIntire had missed something. He had left an opening. While Jodie was rebooting, she could slip in some code. She scooted to a second computer and entered the magic password, leaving Jodie's program display active. Her gaze darted back and forth between the two screens as she began to write code. Assembling upgrade. Reboot now.

* * *

322

Jodie laid his cheek against Mary's hair and felt the curls tickle his lips. He couldn't hold her because of the handcuffs. He shivered as the sheen of sweat on his upper body evaporated.

"I've got to go," Mary whispered. "Sooner or later, he'll see where I looped the security tape." She pushed up from where she lay against his shoulder. She must not want to hold him.

Victoria had been right. The sensations had been similar. He had experienced a release. So had Mary, he thought. He wasn't sure though, not like with Victoria. Mary was stiff, a little embarrassed by her body and his own. He had tried to be kind, encouraging, just as Victoria had been for him. But it wasn't the same. He wondered if Mary had gotten what she needed. He felt a little empty when there was no holding each other.

He thought about his plan. Now that McIntire controlled Jodie Prime, he might have stopped Phase Two. But just in case it executed, Jodie had to know one thing.

"What if the money stops?" He didn't bother to whisper. The guards knew she was here.

She was surprised. "How would it stop? Bob's one of the richest men in the world."

"Is it all in Visimorph stock?"

Mary shrugged. "Half, maybe."

Jodie nodded. "That's good." Then it started. "Johnny be good. G'day. Day tripper. Trip the light. Light pipes . . ." He grunted with effort as he gritted his teeth and rolled his head against the brass rails of the headboard.

Mary squeezed his shoulder as he got control. He sagged against the rail. When he finally raised his eyes to hers, he saw compassion. "Will you be okay when you get the program load from the other computer?" she asked.

"Maybe." Unless Victoria could do something, he'd get the behavior filter too. "May I ask a favor?" That sounded too formal for someone with whom he had just had sexual relations.

She lifted her brows and nodded.

Jodie was suddenly embarrassed. "Can you give me something to hold between my teeth? If I have a seizure, I don't want to suffocate."

Mary's face contracted, but she nodded and went to the escritoire. She rolled some pages from a small note pad into a sheaf, then shrugged her apology and pushed it between his teeth.

"Thanks," he mumbled around it.

She leaned over and kissed his forehead before she turned to the door in a swirl of yellow.

Okay, Jodie, Vic typed into the first computer, taking a breather. It's almost done. She still had to write the trigger. Your job is not to tell anyone about the virus I just loaded in with your viral program upgrade. In another hour the sun would rise. Outside, through the front display windows, the parking lot was graying and the lights were blinking out one by one.

I must answer direct questions. But I will not default to a list of the consequences.

As always, you're way ahead of me. No text appeared in Jodie's dialogue box. She swung back to writing the virus trigger code. A little more and she was ready to test.

A small beep sounded to attract her attention. That response does not seem like one that would be made by Mr. McIntire, he had written. He never acknowledges that someone has thought of something he hasn't.

She smiled to herself. Good use of the inference algorithm. She scooted over to the other keyboard. I told you. It's Vic. I borrowed McIntire's password.

Victoria? The letters appeared slowly.

Yes.

I'm glad to be able to talk to you. I have missed you, Victoria.

She thought about this version of Jodie, trapped behind the firewall, battling McIntire, isolated, cut off from her, even from other computers. He was heroic. There weren't many heroes left in this world. I missed you, too. She had

324

to ask. `Did . . . McIntire rename your program?`

`I did that. It was wishful thinking, though. I'm not human. Only humans love.`

`Not true.` Vic hesitated. `I've come to believe that programs can love, too.`

`McIntire says you gave the copy of me a body. Is it able to love?`

`Yeah. Just like you. But he's not an exact copy.` She needed his help now, and quickly. `He still needs parts of your program to stabilize himself.`

`I know. It picked out the parts it needs. Then it will be me, but with a body?`

`Almost.` She couldn't lie. `You've had different experiences. Your evolutionary algorithms have diverged. And he seems to have ghosts from the body's former owner,` she added, remembering Jodie's dreams. `I don't know if they'll last.`

Jodie didn't respond for several seconds. `Do you like the body, Victoria?`

Vic took a breath. `I want him to survive,` she typed.

`McIntire will load the code tomorrow. That should stabilize him.`

`He might not survive the transfer. McIntire is going to use the electronic scalpel on his brain.` Vic could hardly type the words.

`He'll get the behavior filter, too.` The words seemed flat, if typed words could be flat.

`And, if we're lucky, he'll get the virus I'm planting. Then we activate the virus and set you both free.` Free. Technically. But how would they get Jodie Prime out of Neuromancer?

The arc of a flashlight moved across the ceiling of the store through the front window.

Shit. Some kind of a watch service. She hadn't thought about that. The flashlight meant he was already out of his car. Must have seen the glow of the screens. Too late to hide.

She swung back to the keyboard and scanned the trigger code. Just a few more strokes. Maybe she could make it. The flashlight beam arced over her head again. She began to lay code. She didn't look up when the light hit her profile. She didn't look up when another car pulled into the lot. Its headlights illuminated the computer showroom like high noon at the beach. All the comforting darkness melted away. She finished the trigger sequence. Keys jangled in the front door.

"Stop where you are!" a male voice shouted. "You're under arrest!"

The trigger needed an initiator sequence. What code? What code?

"Get your hands away from the keyboard, now!" Two silhouettes advanced on her.

Slowly she backed away. So close! A code, a single code. What would be a sure thing? One of the silhouettes grabbed her shoulder. This close she could see he was silver-haired and paunchy, his skin a little yellow from years of smoking. Her mind spun. What were they going to do, shoot her? "Okay, okay, don't get excited," she called. She let him pull her down the narrow aisle for several steps before she spun out of his grip and lunged for the keyboard. `Victoria,` she typed, because she couldn't think of anything else, and hit SEND.

She heard the snick of cocking guns. Shit, they *might* shoot her. She snapped her hands into the air and turned around "Hey, I'm not exactly armed," she shouted. Two uniformed officers stood in back of the guy from the security service. One brandished a gun. A flashlight probed her face, as though the headlights from the car weren't bright enough.

"Didn't I just see you at the station?"

Vic decided that saying nothing was her best bet.

"You're the hacker girl who just got let out on supervision." The cop let out a snort. "Your supervisor's doing a fantastic job." He motioned with his flashlight. "Come on out."

Jodie struggled up through water toward the light. Someone was trying to drown him, holding him down. He couldn't get his breath. He pulled away, but his hands were trapped

326

somehow. The Amazon. Mud in the Amazon was closing over his head. He opened his eyes.

He wasn't drowning. He tried to focus on where he was, who these people were. Something was in his mouth. He spit it out. Paper. It was a roll of paper. The room came into focus, bathed in dim gray light. McIntire's security guards stood around him. He was chained to a bed. One of them spoke into a Communicator. The smell of urine and feces permeated the air.

Holding on to the bed frame, he struggled to sit up, still trembling. He'd had a seizure, an especially messy one. His brain was fogged and frightened.

McIntire rushed into the room and made a face. "Jesus!" Jodie heard him say. "Clean him up." McIntire peeled back Jodie's lids. "Snap out of it."

"Snap, trap, kidnapped," Jodie muttered, unable to stop himself. "Stevenson, Stephen, brother, brothers in arms."

McIntire slapped him, hard.

Jodie bit his lip, trying to keep silent as his head jerked to one side. He tasted blood.

McIntire stood up and loomed over him. "We'd better get him into Visimorph before his program disintegrates completely."

In the early morning hours, McIntire's limo retraced the route it had traveled last night. Once again Jodie was shackled to the armrest, though now Jim sat nearby, dwarfing him. The coastline was gray and misty instead of twinkling against the blackness. Jodie slumped against the seat, silent, both because he was exhausted and because almost every word out of his mouth provoked the strings of free association. He couldn't think. Probably merciful. Echoes of shame and fear careened through the clouds in his brain. Maybe this was what madness felt like—drifting away from oneself, murky thinking, feeling helpless.

McIntire sat across from him talking on the Communicator, arranging for the scalpel, getting Vera to locate the judge, telling the PR people to put off the release of PuppetMaster until tomorrow. They apparently disagreed. "Get a press conference to support the release," he was saying angrily. "I know I stood them up yesterday, but when I have an announcement, the press can damn well come to hear it." McIntire looked over at Jodie. "I may have a startling announcement soon." He lost interest in the conversation. "Yeah, whatever. Let it go out."

Jodie sighed. Even if he were dead, if McIntire got Vic, still PuppetMaster 12.1 would be released. That part, at least, of his own plan would execute, though it might be an empty gesture.

"And get me Evans." There was a pause. McIntire listened. He sounded surprised. "No hacking after three this morning? I can't believe she gave up. Keep on it."

Jodie wasn't surprised. He clung to a hope that Victoria had made good use of the password Mary had sent, though he couldn't quite remember what he wanted her to do with it. His limbs seemed heavy. Maybe it was a mistake to leave his autonomic functions to the medulla oblongata. Did the gaps in his program prevent him from organizing his thoughts, or managing his body? Maybe his brain was just coming apart at the seams.

Vera buzzed back. "She's back in jail?" McIntire listened. "Stupid bitch."

Jodie sagged against the seat. McIntire had Victoria.

McIntire paused, then began to smile. "I've been going at this backwards," he said to Jodie. "She may be the only one who can truly appreciate my achievement. And to see me take her program into the next phase of its potential and out of her control forever is punishment in itself. Time enough for her to be locked up later." He pulled open the door of the glass partition that separated the passengers from the driver. "Take us to the Santa Monica Police Station." He turned back to the Communicator. "Vera, they won't want to release her on supervision again. I still need that judge. He can arrange it."

Jodie almost moaned in frustration as he rolled his head against the seat. He didn't want Victoria to see what was going to happen at Visimorph. She had seen it once before. Done it. But this time it might be different.

328

It was almost nine A.M. by the time they got through the busy coast route traffic and into Santa Monica. They pulled up to the police stationhouse at Pico and Third. McIntire and Jim jumped out, leaving Jodie chained to the door.

Jim pushed through the double glass doors, dragging Vic out into the light. They might as well have been revolving doors, Vic thought, she'd been in and out of here so many times in the last twenty-four hours. McIntire trailed behind them, putting his wallet back in his pocket. When he strode up to take Vic's other arm she pulled away. "Why didn't you let me rot in jail? That's what you want," she hissed, to cover her fear. She shuddered and looked up at Jim. His impassive, lumpy face said he didn't care what happened to her.

"Au contraire," McIntire almost giggled. "I want you to have the pleasure of seeing the fruits of your labor." He gestured toward the limo.

Vic jerked her eyes to the smoked glass and saw the outline of a figure seated in the car. She would know that profile anywhere. She straightened. Yeah. She was lucky McIntire had come for her. She had to be there. How else could she be sure that Jodie would say the initiator code after the download? That virus trigger better work.

Jim took her around the far side of the limo and opened the door. He gave her a shove, so she stumbled into the low compartment.

"Victoria?" Jodie murmured. "Victoria station, stationary, still, forever, never, Never-Never Land . . ." He seemed not to cut off the associations as much as to drift away from them.

"Jodie," she whispered and sat next to him. His face was pale. It glistened with sweat. He leaned against her. He didn't say another word. His eyes said it all. She glanced to where he was handcuffed to the door and saw the crusted raw circles on his wrists. "You okay?"

He shook his head.

McIntire got in behind her. "If you please, Barnhardt, join me over here?" He gestured to the other bench seat. "You're in Jim's place."

She squeezed Jodie's arm and did as she was told. Time enough for rebellion later.

McIntire settled himself in the corner and stretched his long legs. "He's not okay, actually. Nasty seizure this morning. Language program gone. Physical functions started deteriorating on the way over here. The program download will cure it, though."

Fear trickled down between Vic's breasts. She glanced back to Jodie. "Well then, let's get going," she snapped. She tapped briskly on the window to the driver's seat behind her. The driver mistook her signal for McIntire's and started the engine. It roared and he slipped it into gear. Jim still had one foot on the gravel of the parking lot as the long car slid forward. He sat heavily next to Jodie and leaned to pull the door shut.

McIntire only smiled. "Best day of my life, Barnhardt. PuppetMaster 12.1 ships and I get the product that will keep me on top of the heap long after PuppetMaster is obsolete."

Vic gritted her teeth and tried to tell Jodie with her eyes that things would be all right.

The limo pulled up to McIntire's private entrance. Jodie was wavering on his feet and Jim had to support him as they walked through McIntire's garden and into his office. McIntire waved at Vera, who was on the phone, and they made straight for the elevator to the basement.

Vera put her hand over the mouthpiece and called, "The equipment will be here any minute." What did Vera think about handcuffed men in her office? She knew what "equipment" McIntire had ordered. Visimorph employees acted as though they already had behavior filters.

They pushed through the double doors to the control room for Neuromancer. A gurney equipped with straps to tie down its occupant sat next to the master keyboard like a stain on the bright light of the computer control room. At one end lay a metal contraption that looked like a halo, with screws and struts. It was one of the most frightening things Vic had ever laid eyes on. She cast her eyes about frantically. Simpson was backed against one of the servers like a cornered animal. He didn't like the halo either.

"Jim, can you put our program friend on the table? Or do you need help?"

Jim glanced down at Jodie who now sagged against him. "I think I can handle it."

Jodie was too disoriented to resist. Vic noticed that he couldn't take his eyes off the metal halo. He must be afraid. Her heart went out to him. But they had no choice but to go through with this. It was the only way left that he might get whole again. All time was gone. Jim dragged him to the gurney and pushed him down. He pulled the straps across Jodie's chest and relocked his handcuffs to the lift bars at the side of the gurney.

The lights glared down on Jodie. His eyes darted about almost randomly, not seeing anymore. His breathing had gotten shallow and labored. This was getting serious. Sweat rolled down his temples. Jim fixed the straps across his thighs. Had his program truly deteriorated enough so he wasn't operating the body correctly?

McIntire's Communicator buzzed and he flipped it open. Vic could hear Vera's voice, small and tinny. "The scalpel's on its way down."

"Simpson, go up and meet it." McIntire grinned. He turned to Jim. "Your job is to keep Barnhardt from interfering in this little operation." Jim clamped his huge fist around Vic's upper arm. McIntire hefted the metal halo and turned to Jodie. "Now it's time to prep you for surgery."

He lifted Jodie's head. Jodie tried to twist away, but he seemed disoriented. That might be a blessing. McIntire put the halo around his head. Vic shivered as he reached for a simple screwdriver near the keyboard. McIntire began to screw the halo into the gurney. "It's important to keep the head steady for certain kinds of brain surgery where you can't use anesthetic."

"You're going to cut him without anesthetic?" Vic's voice rose into a keening sound.

"We need to see the reaction of the brain function to the knife," McIntire said absently.

Vic put her hand to her mouth. Oh, my God. McIntire was going to do this while Jodie was fully aware! Jodie began to shake. It wasn't a seizure—just a quivering that wouldn't stop.

"Jodie," Vic almost sobbed. She started toward him, but Jim hauled her back.

"Don't worry, the brain itself can feel no pain," McIntire told Jodie. "You'll only feel the screws and the hole into the skull." He touched two fingers to Jodie's carotid, as Jodie's head rolled back and forth. At that moment, the doors swung open and Simpson pushed the box of the scalpel, clanking, through the door. Vic turned to see McIntire examining Jodie narrowly. Jodie opened his eyes wide, trying to focus on Vic. Then his eyes flickered up in his head.

"Shit!" McIntire yelled. Vic watched, stunned, as he peeled Jodie's eyelids back. "We're losing him. His pulse is about a thousand a minute." He swung around to the master keyboard. "Simpson, get the scalpel booted up."

Vic realized there was no medical equipment in the room other than the scalpel. No oxygen tank, no IV, no life support, not even one of those banger machines to restart hearts. What was McIntire thinking?

McIntire glanced over his shoulder as he typed. Simpson stood, trembling, immobilized. "If you don't get that scalpel going, we'll miss the product of the millennium. Do you understand?" But Simpson could only fumble with the cord of the machine.

Vic looked around frantically, struggling in Jim's grip. How far were they from a hospital? Her mind danced. Jodie could die here in this basement in the next minutes without life support equipment. His only hope was the program download. He can regenerate brain cells once we get the program fixed, Vic said to herself. She willed herself quiet.

"Simpson," McIntire screamed. Simpson was a lost cause. He looked like he was about to faint. Vic looked up to the stolid, slightly stupid face of Jim. No help there.

"I'll do it," Vic said quietly. "I know the scalpel. I've used it before."

McIntire stared at her for maybe five seconds. Maybe it was only three. "Release her." He turned back to the keyboard. "Go," he yelled.

332

Vic was already moving. She shoved the machine over to the gurney. There was a power outlet in the floor beside it. Stabbing the cord into the hole, she began flipping switches.

"Jim," McIntire called. His fingers clicked on the keys. "Screw his head down."

"Yeah, sure, boss." Jim moved way too slowly to the gurney where Jodie's chest was heaving. Part of Vic was horrified that they were about to screw metal into Jodie's skull like a crown of thorns. But another part knew she wanted him still as death when she stuck a scalpel in his head. Not dead though. Not dead. The lights on the machine flickered.

"Ready here." McIntire had Jodie Prime up on the screen.

"Hello, Victoria," Jodie's program spoke in a flat version of the voice she heard over her phone so long ago. She glanced to the cameras stationed around the room. He could see her.

"Hi, Jodie," she managed to say as she jerked the cover off the needle scalpel. "We've got at least a minute of warm-up," she called. McIntire ripped off his tie and stuffed it in Jodie's mouth.

"Don't suffocate him," she yelled. "He's already having trouble breathing."

McIntire held Jodie's head against one side of the cage as Jim tightened the screws. Jodie moaned. "Come on, come on," she said to the machine. Its hum whined up the scale.

"Two to go." McIntire grabbed the screwdriver. "I'll do the ones on this side."

Vic heard Jodie's muffled groan behind her grow more distressed. The needle began to glow with red light. "Wait," she cried, her eyes searching the machine frantically for cables. "Is the scalpel connected to Neuromancer? He's got to have a way to get in."

"Shit," McIntire muttered. He tossed the screwdriver back to Jim and looked for Simpson. "This is your goddamned machine. Get me a connector!"

Simpson started to blather. The noise of Jodie's muffled screams wound around Vic's spinal cord. She ripped away the connector between Neuromancer and the keyboard. "We'll be using voice commands." She ran trembling hands

333

over the surface of the scalpel box, looking for the port. There it was. She shoved the connector in.

"Done," Jim called. He lifted his hands and stepped back.

"Done," Vic yelled. She picked up the glowing scalpel. Jodie quivered on the gurney. Thin trickles of blood ran down his temples where the screws penetrated his skull. She looked up at McIntire. He seemed frozen. She hefted the weight of the little laser knife.

McIntire came to life and swooped in on her. "No, you don't. You're planning something." He grabbed the scalpel. "Ow!" he shrieked. Blood welled from his thumb. He could have cut it off. But he had the scalpel. He pushed Vic aside and squatted beside the gurney.

Jodie's entire body stiffened and jerked. "He's going into arrest," McIntire muttered. He pulled Jodie's hair aside and took careful aim at his temple.

Vic didn't dare interfere. She hardly dared breathe. Jodie went limp. McIntire pressed the laser needle into his skull. The familiar smoke began to rise. She tore her gaze away and glanced to the monitor. "Jodie Prime," she yelled. "Pump program. You know what he needs."

"Yes, Victoria," the quiet, obedient voice returned.

"McIntire, you better be holding that thing steady," Vic hissed. Any wobble would be exaggerated down the line of the scalpel and make mush of Jodie's brain.

McIntire leaned into the scalpel. It buried itself in Jodie's head. Jodie looked peaceful, eyes closed, mouth slack. Let him not be dead, Vic prayed. She heard a retching sound and turned to see Simpson losing his breakfast again on the white rubber floor mats.

"Get him out of here, Jim," McIntire said through gritted teeth.

"Jodie Prime," Vic called to the computer around them. "How long?"

"Thirty seconds, Victoria." Thirty seconds. More like forever.

Chapter Twenty-one

"Download complete," the metallic voice from the microphone intoned.

"Get it out," Vic yelled to McIntire. "And keep it straight."

He began to pull on the knife instead of push. The red light lengthened until the end of the needle appeared. McIntire tossed it away as if it were a snake and clutched his bleeding hand.

Vic threw herself over to Jodie. Had the program downloaded in time? How would they know? She pulled the blue silk tie from Jodie's slack mouth. "Jodie," she whispered over and over as her fingers felt for the pulse in his carotid. "You're all right now." But that was wishful thinking. Where was his damned pulse?

There. Vic almost collapsed over his supine body. A thready pulse, just barely there. She began to chuckle and nod, keeping her fingers to his throat. Stronger. His pulse was getting stronger. "That's right," she half-laughed, half-sobbed. "Integrate that program. Get control of those body functions." He closed his mouth softly. Okay. Still she waited for the trembling eyelashes to tell her that he was coming into con-

335

sciousness. Blood soaked everything. Scalp wounds always bleed a lot, she told herself. Her fingers combed through his sticky hair around the metal of the halo until she found his wound, pressed back his hair and peered between her fingers. It was tiny, much smaller than the one she'd seen in the hospital. She couldn't even see gray matter. Just hope the damage inside wasn't insurmountable. Jodie's eyelids fluttered open. He didn't seem to be able to see her. She could see his focus swimming.

She grabbed for the screwdriver, glancing at McIntire to see if he was going to stop her.

McIntire looked exhausted, exhilarated. His pale eyes glittered. His lips were drawn back over his teeth. Vic supposed that was a grin. He pressed his thumb, wrapped in a red-soaked handkerchief against his chest. He nodded his assent. "No harm in that."

Staring at the screwdriver, she puffed out her breath. This was going to hurt Jodie. His gaze flicked around the room, fear ramping up. He was seeing things now. He began to struggle against the metal halo and the straps. "Jodie," she cried and leaned over where he could see her.

His eyes locked on hers. "Victoria," he whispered, so low she could hardly hear him.

"Yes." The initiator word. Start that virus working on your new behavior filter, program mine, she thought triumphantly.

His expression softened and his muscles quit straining against his bonds. "You're speech program is better already," she reassured him. "Can you do a diagnostic, or is it too soon?" Best to give him something to do.

He blinked, trying to focus. "I . . . I'm trying to comply," he croaked. "But I can't."

"All right. That's all right." Trying to comply? Well, that was certainly the behavior filter. Okay. Okay. It might take the virus some time to do its work. Hope to God she'd gotten the virus transmitted. Shit, she wished she'd had a chance to test the code. "We'll get to it later."

McIntire loomed behind her. Jodie's eyes darted between them. The fear was back. "Did it work?" McIntire barked.

336

"It may take a while for the new pieces of program to knit themselves into the fabric of his brain," Vic said shortly. Then to Jodie, "Let's get you out of this thing." She raised the screwdriver and showed it to him. "Uh, this may hurt."

Jodie's eyes crinkled, ever so slightly. Maybe it was her imagination. She put the screwdriver in place and switched it to "unscrew." The whirring sound as she pushed the button made both her and Jodie flinch. His brow creased and he began to pant. The bloody screw fell to the floor. This felt like some horror movie she'd seen as a kid. She worked as fast as she could.

"Get me something to clean the blood up," she ordered McIntire as she pulled the halo off and tossed it across the floor, "and some disinfectant at least."

Jim came back in from disposing of Simpson in time to hear her command. McIntire motioned him to execute it and he disappeared again.

"What we could use here is a doctor," Vic muttered. "But I don't suppose you'd chance that." She looked around to find McIntire staring at her, speculation in his eyes.

"So you just helped me get what I wanted. Not what I would have expected."

You haven't got what you want yet, she thought. But he might be right. If the virus didn't work, she'd just made Jodie into McIntire's slave. She tried not to let him see her fear. "I saved my program—what were the choices?" That was something he'd understand. She turned to Jodie and stroked his cheek. She even managed a smile. Jodie's blue-green eyes flickered to her face, then turned inward, losing focus. Was he integrating the program? His breathing slowed.

Behind her, Jim came back in with a first-aid kit. "Courtesy of Simpson," he muttered, as he set it on Jodie's belly.

Vic poured disinfectant through some bandages. She pulled his hair aside and daubed at his wounds. The one from the scalpel looked puffy. New cell growth? Maybe.

"Let's see what we've got here." McIntire taped a bandage from the first-aid kit around his thumb. He pushed Vic aside and swept the kit to the floor with a metallic crash. "Jim, stand by." McIntire unfastened the straps from the gurney.

337

"Sit up," he commanded. Jodie sat. He was a little wobbly, but he steadied himself. He looked around, as though seeing the room for the first time. "Jim," McIntire called. "Release our product, here."

Jim shambled up and touched his thumb to the cuffs still locking Jodie to the gurney. They snapped open and clanked to the floor.

"Do a diagnostic," McIntire ordered.

"Height five feet eleven weight one eight-five and a half." Jodie's voice was flat. "Heart rate seventy-two—a little high but coming down. Blood pressure one eleven over sixty-eight, a little low but coming up. Cholesterol two oh five and one twenty tryglicerides. . . ."

"Okay, you're physically functional," McIntire interrupted. "Program capability?"

Jodie's eyes flickered. "Program stabilized. Neural synapse firing rate at sixty-two percent of capacity and rising. Repair of brain cells destroyed in the transfer will push firing rate over ninety-five percent."

Vic saw McIntire's jaw drop. Most humans operated at about fifty percent.

"So, McIntire, he's going to be way smarter than you are. Hurts, doesn't it?" Vic tried not to think about the fact that Jodie was smarter than she was, too. If they ever got out of here, hanging with her would be slumming. McIntire glared at her. Yeah. That hurt him. "Did you have room for the whole program?" she managed to ask Jodie.

"Yes," Jodie said, his voice expressionless. Only his eyes were warm. "I lost most of the libraries, historical statistical data, but I'd planned on that. I got the program, Victoria."

Vic began to chuckle, listening to him say her name again, not only because she loved hearing it on those wonderful bowed lips but because it was the initiator for the virus. If she'd coded it right. There'd been no testing. If it had gotten through. Her chuckle stuck in her throat.

"So what can you do?" McIntire barked.

"What do you want me to do, Mr. McIntire?"

The voice was still flat. Would Jodie fake a behavior filter even after it was gone?

338

McIntire began to pace, thinking. He spun around and motioned to Jim, who came and pinioned Vic's arms. "I think I'd like you to step up to Barnhardt here and hit her."

Jodie slid off the gurney. He won't do it, Vic thought. Then McIntire would know what she'd done. Jodie jerked over to stand in front of her. There was pain in his expression. He pulled back his arm. His hand trembled ever so slightly. Vic's breath came faster. He was going to do it and he couldn't help it. She could see it in his eyes.

Jodie slapped her, hard. Her head jerked to the side and she gasped, collapsing into Jim. Tears flooded her eyes, as much from shock as pain. "Forgive me, Victoria." Jodie intoned. "Forgive me." Only his eyes churned with his distress.

Vic got control of her tears. He wasn't faking. Where was the damned virus?

"So you're sorry, but you do it anyway. . . ." McIntire gloated. "That's really wonderful. You feel all the emotions of being forced to do what your master desires. Or mistress." He chuckled again, enjoying the concept. "This has possibilities."

"You're an animal, McIntire," Vic stuttered. "You can't do this."

"But I have. First I'll explore his mental abilities. Then maybe I'll give him to Mary for testing—or Vera, that's a little safer. But why limit you to women? Jerkins over in Shipping would love to take you home. Let's see just how obedient you are. What do you think? Are you game?"

"I'll do whatever you tell me to do, Mr. McIntire, you know that." Jodie's eyes went dull.

McIntire began to laugh, and his laugh cycled up until he couldn't stop it.

Vic wanted to scream. She'd failed Jodie. But she couldn't just give up. Maybe Jodie Prime could help—but she didn't want McIntire to know something was up. Yet what choice did she have? "Jodie Prime, what's my name?" she called, over McIntire's giggling.

"Victoria." Another obedient voice was almost more than she could bear. But maybe if Jodie Prime said her name the

339

virus would free him. Maybe it was just the physical Jodie who couldn't deactivate the behavior filter.

McIntire straightened up. "What are you doing?" he managed to ask as his laughter subsided. "You're up to something." He turned around and looked at the monitor behind him. It lay dead and blank. He swung back and peered at Jodie. "What's she doing?" he asked.

"I don't know, sir," Jodie said with the same obedient ring as Jodie Prime.

"Jodie Prime," Victoria strained against Jim's grip. "Status of your behavior filter."

"One hundred percent," came the metallic response.

Shit. She was screwed, Jodie was screwed, even Jodie Prime was still trapped.

"You're trying to get the behavior filter off, aren't you?" McIntire descended on her. "You little bitch." His hands closed around her throat. Jim had both her elbows. She was powerless to fend off McIntire. "You won't succeed, whatever you're doing."

Jodie lurched toward them. "Stay where you are," McIntire barked without even looking at him. Jodie stopped stock still, despair in his eyes. McIntire's fingers pressed inexorably into Vic's throat. She could hardly even choke. Her breath hissed slowly to a stop. No virus. Even though both of them had said her name. It shouldn't take this long to work. She'd blown it.

"Boss," Jim murmured. "Don't do anything—"

"I'll do what I want," McIntire shouted into Vic's face. "She's a criminal."

"But you might accidentally kill her," Jim ventured.

Vic's vision began to go black at the edges. He *was* going to kill her. And he'd have both Jodies forever. Even though they'd said her name. Victoria. The gurgling noise she heard might be coming from her throat. Had she made a mistake when she typed it? She couldn't think.

She could barely see Jodie as he strained against invisible fetters without moving. Typed. Typed! The *letters* were the initiator of the trigger, not the sound of her name.

"Spell it," she gurgled. He wouldn't be able to understand

her! McIntire's fingers stabbed into her flesh, cutting her off. She wrenched to the side. He didn't let go, but as Jim jerked her back, McIntire's grip slipped a little. "Spell my name," she gasped. McIntire's fingers closed around her throat again as she and Jim swayed together.

It was an order, if Jodie could understand it. She used what little strength she had to pull back into Jim, away from McIntire. Their size was too unequal for her to escape, but she struggled just to unbalance them. McIntire stood between her and Jodie now. She couldn't see him. She couldn't see anything. She felt herself going slack.

"V-I-C-T-O-R-I-A." She heard the letters as though in the distance. Then, "Ahhhhhhhh . . . . . ." a wheezing gasp. It was her life flitting away.

McIntire staggered back. His grip slackened. She barely saw him fall to the floor. Her vision throbbed back into the center of the pulsing ring of darkness. Behind her, she heard a grunt. She slipped to the floor, unable to move. All she could hear was the sputter of air as her lungs sucked against her swollen throat. It hurt to breathe as though her lungs protested at returning to their job. Something was happening. Noises. Grunts. She should look. But all she could do was try to breathe.

After a while a hand on her shoulder pulled her gently over on her back. "Victoria?"

It was Jodie. Her lips cracked open over the sucking air. Jodie. He gathered her up with one arm around her shoulders and helped her to the gurney, walking backwards with her. He hoisted her up and held her against his side. "You're okay. Just breathe."

She braced her arms against the edge of the gurney and hung her head forward. A gun. Jodie had a gun in his other hand. One of those snub-nosed, ugly guns whose dull metal gleam said they meant business. She was breathing easier now. She could see the gun clearly. He held it on McIntire and Jim, who were both getting up slowly from the floor.

"How?" she muttered. "How did you do it?" She sat up straighter.

He glanced between the two men and her face. He

341

smoothed the hair back from her forehead with his free hand. "John Reston has been in a lot of fights," he murmured. Then louder, "Over against the control panel, you two. John Reston knows how to shoot this, and he's shot a few people in his time."

"You're not going to shoot anyone," McIntire muttered.

"I wouldn't bet the farm," Jodie said, through clenched teeth. McIntire backed up hastily.

"How did you get rid of the filter?" McIntire couldn't believe, still, that he'd failed.

"Victoria set a code-specific virus on it, triggered by spelling her name." There was something in Jodie's eyes she couldn't name. "She's very bright, and very resilient."

McIntire knew he was in trouble. Be afraid, Vic thought. Her anger began to cycle up from her stomach until she thought she might be sick. What right had he to think he could enslave people? The world should be saved from people like him. Vic looked up to Jodie. She didn't recognize him. His face was a grim mask of hatred that mirrored her own rage.

"You tried to kill Victoria," he growled. He raised the gun in a steady hand and held it at arm's length, pointed at McIntire's heart. "You are a pestilence, a parasite."

"A parasite?" McIntire's own face suffused with red. "I'm the visionary who gave the poor schlubs out there entry to the virtual world. PuppetMaster *is* freedom for the masses."

"Too bad it isn't free," Jodie lashed back. "You soak them for upgrades. You peddle an inferior, unstable product that's hard to use and they have no choice but to buy it because you cornered the market. Visionary? For God's sake, you stole the look and feel of your operating system from a competitor!" Jodie's mouth was mobile with his rage. Even Vic was frightened. "Victoria is much smarter than you are. You aren't even a good husband," he shouted.

"And you are a deranged program degrading in a human body," McIntire accused.

It was Jodie's turn to laugh. "Deranged? You bet I am," he choked. "You just tried to make me into a product-slash-slave. You tried to kill Victoria." The hand that held the gun

342

trembled. Reflected in his eyes was Vic's worst nightmare, a monster out of control.

And she didn't care. McIntire deserved whatever he got. Let chaos loose on the world. What was a little more chaos in a world that could produce McIntire?

"Do it," she managed in a voice so hoarse she didn't recognize it as her own. She stared into the rage in those blue-green eyes and fed it back to him. "I say do it."

Behind Jodie, Jim made his move. He lunged forward. "Jodie," Vic hissed.

Jodie swung around as Jim launched himself forward. The sound of the gunshot reverberated off all the metal in the room like an explosion of plastique. Jim grabbed his shoulder as he fell to the floor.

"You killed him," McIntire yelled.

Jodie fired into the metal of the server boxes on either side of McIntire. Again and again the room shook with echoes. McIntire cowered against the sparking metal. Vic put her hands over her ears. Smoke issued from the huge control server. When the last crash had died away, Jodie stood, shaking with anger. The evil little gun had kicked him back against the gurney. Jim rolled onto his back, looking vaguely puzzled. After a long silence, Jodie caught his breath. "I didn't kill him," he told McIntire. "I would have aimed 4.7 inches down and 3.4 inches to the left if I wanted to kill him."

Vic waited. The muzzle of the little gun still pointed straight at McIntire. This was it. Jodie would kill him and it would be over. McIntire knew it, too. She could see the fear in his eyes. It was the first time she had ever seen him doubt the outcome of his life. Suffer, you bastard, she thought, like you made so many others suffer. And yet . . .

The anger whooshed out of her, leaving her shaky. Killing McIntire in cold blood? How could either of them live with that? It wasn't that they'd be on the run from the law. That was a given. It was . . . it was the very human fear in McIntire's eyes.

She pulled on Jodie's arm. "Don't."

"Even if everything works, he'll still be after us," Jodie croaked, and leveled the gun again. "It's the only way to be

343

sure he won't be after us every day of our lives."

"It's the one sure way he'll haunt us." How could she explain? Was she crazy? McIntire's eyes were wide. A trickle of sweat ran down his temple. "I understand him," Vic managed. "I understand losing yourself in a quest for what you want, driven beyond all the boundaries other people accept. I understand losing the Middle Way. I lost it, too. That's how I got to you."

"You are not like him, Victoria," Jodie protested. But he didn't shoot. Uncertainty had replaced the monster in his eyes.

"But I am. You are, too." She rubbed her palm across his shoulder. "Humans always have things in common."

"But he is *not* right about the world, Victoria," Jodie hissed. "He tried to kill you. He wants to make slaves. He robbed a little girl of her humanity."

"Not right, but not worth killing." She took a breath. "Let's not be too much like him."

The gun lowered. A triumphant gleam lurked behind McIntire's eyes. "I won't let him get off scot-free," Jodie muttered. "He can't have the power he has now, Victoria. You can't ask that."

Vic let out the breath she had been holding. "No, I don't ask that. Just don't kill him."

Jodie turned to look at her. A softness came into his eyes. "One of the Commandments."

Vic nodded. Who was more human, McIntire or Jodie?

Jodie scooped up the handcuffs from the floor. He gestured with the gun to the pole that McIntire had chained him to yesterday. "Make yourself comfortable, Bob," he said. Jim groaned as he pushed himself into a sitting position against a server box. "Victoria, will you get Jim something to staunch the bleeding?"

McIntire sat, watchful. He still thought he'd won a round. Maybe he had.

Vic pushed off the gurney and grabbed the cuffs. She looked around for the first-aid kit and made a pad of the bandages. She tossed it to Jim from a safe distance, and he pressed it into his shoulder. Then she slid the cuffs across the floor. "Neutralize the lock and slide them back," Vic ordered. Jim groaned as he pressed his thumb twice and pushed the cuffs away. Vic passed them back to Jodie.

Jodie clicked the cuffs shut around McIntire's wrists, then pressed his own thumb into the keypad. He and Vic rose and turned to each other. There were no words now. They moved together, drawn by some force Vic had never felt before. Maybe the same force that wrote the code that had brought Jodie to life. The comfort of leather-girl was gone, permanently. And what was left? She loved something more than machine, more than human even. What had been wrought here? Jodie reached for her and gathered her into his arms.

"Touching," McIntire sneered. "Too bad they don't have coed cells in Sam Quentin. You're both going to jail. Kidnapping, assault with a deadly weapon. Once you're in jail, who's to say we can't load a behavior filter? I'm not done with you two yet."

Jodie kissed Vic's hair. She put her arms around him, felt the muscles in his back bunch under her hands. Would that be their price for being who they were—McIntire hunting them down forever?

"You are a piece of work," Jodie remarked to McIntire. "Jodie Prime, did PuppetMaster ship?"

Vic had forgotten Jodie's alter-ego.

"Yes, Jodie. About an hour ago," The voice wasn't flat anymore. The screen pulsed with color. When Jodie spelled her name, it had freed his virtual counterpart, too.

"Is our programming intact?"

"No one asked me to remove it."

Vic looked up to see Jodie's eyes crinkle, though he kept his mouth from smiling. He nodded. "How many hits to the web site?"

"Two hundred thousand actually got in. The new server farm is swamped. The hits are ramping up drastically."

"What?" McIntire chortled. "The first hour? That's the most successful release in the history of the world!"

"Word's getting around," Jodie said into Vic's hair. "Everyone will want that release." Vic could feel the rumble of his voice in his chest. She looked past Jodie's shoulder to see

345

the avaricious gleam in McIntire's eyes. Would nothing be denied him? "Of course," Jodie said above her, "it will be your last."

"Nonsense," McIntire snorted.

Jodie looked down at him. His mouth hardened. "Victoria doesn't want me to kill you, McIntire, so I won't. But I've already begun to kill Visimorph. Phase Two of the plan." A shadow of fear crossed McIntire's face. "Jodie Prime and I put a little extra programming into PuppetMaster when you so graciously let me in to view the code I needed. That was before the behavior filter, you'll recall. PuppetMaster shipped with a new acceptance contract. The product is priced at three dollars. And anyone who buys it owns the code."

"What?" McIntire yelped. "The code is proprietary."

"Not anymore."

"I'll get my lawyers—"

"Visimorph itself put the contract out on the Internet. Your lawyers can't do jack. It's creating quite a buzz with that price tag. The hits to the site will decrease drastically, of course, as people realize that since they own it, they can give it away to their friends. But that's not all."

McIntire went still. His face was ashen.

"No more upgrades. I put a little AI in this release, a bit of me, in fact. It will adapt PuppetMaster to other operating systems. It will run with any hardware, be compatible with any software. And people can adapt it themselves, since they own it. It's very amenable to adaptation. It will even help them by evolving, taking out some of those layers of wor-karound crap you've put in over time."

"No," McIntire breathed.

"PuppetMaster is no longer a revenue-generating product."

McIntire's face contorted in ways he could not control. Then it went still.

"Jodie Prime, how's the Visimorph stock price?" Jodie called.

"Down thirty percent in the last twenty minutes. I'd say it was in free fall."

Vic looked up at Jodie. He was grinning now, his eyes

346

crinkled until all she could see was a blue-green gleam.

"You'd better kill me, you two." McIntire's voice was cold and dead. "Because I'm going to get you for this. I'm going to start as soon as you walk out that door. Use the gun, Program. Use it right now, or I've already won. It's inevitable."

Victoria felt Jodie's chuckle die in his chest. He clutched her to him. "I won't let you hurt Victoria," he growled, but she could hear the uncertainty, the fear in his voice.

McIntire might be right, but Vic couldn't let him win by making them afraid. "How do you feel, Jodie?"

He glanced down at her. "I . . . I feel good," he said, seeming surprised. "I feel strong."

"What can you do with what you have?"

His gaze turned inward. "I think I could probably get into any computer anywhere. I understand how they're constructed and how they connect. I know guerrilla warfare from John Reston." Jodie looked down at Vic as he considered the possibilities. "I could manipulate markets, bring down economies and governments. Or I could correct the mistakes that NASA keeps making on its Mars settlement expeditions and speed up the cure for Alz 2 by a couple of decades." He turned his gaze back to McIntire. "I can insert AI wherever I want. That has some really interesting possibilities. I can rebuild cells to repair damage and extend life for a while. . . ." Jodie trailed off, his eyes darting over the room as he considered.

Vic swallowed and put away her own fear about what Jodie's abilities meant for any possibility of a future together. "So, take your best shot, McIntire," she said. "He's going to drive you into an asylum. Because you can't touch him. You're not smart enough."

Jodie pulled away from Vic and began to pace around the room. Vic could feel the energy pulsating from his body.

"It's a whole new game, McIntire," she continued. "Humans are going to have to cope with a world that includes spiritual machines and human programs. Not tomorrow. But soon. Jodie is human, all right. Human and more. Sci-fi is now nonfiction. How will you deal with the loss of control?" she challenged. "Are you going to try for behavior filters and slavery? You'll get all-out war in return. It's a war they can win. Or are you going to coexist with these new forms of life in a spirit of cooperation? Hard choices, McIntire. Luckily, you're not the only one in charge of making them."

"You think people won't listen to me?" McIntire said through clenched teeth. "Others will be just as eager to destroy or enslave his kind, from fear or because by controlling you we manipulate our world. Men like me run the world. That doesn't change."

Jodie rounded on him. "You're a man without a world to run."

"I'll have it rebuilt inside of six months. There are other products in the pipeline."

"That reminds me. . . ." Jodie turned and pulled the connector cable from the scalpel. "There's one product that can't be in the pipeline." He reconnected the monitor and the keyboard to Neuromancer. When he turned to Vic, his eyes were serious.

She nodded. She knew what had to happen here. She wondered if she could bear it.

Jodie's hands flickered over the keyboard. Code appeared and was answered in a flash. "Done and done," Jodie Prime said.

"How do you want to do this?" Jodie asked quietly. Their voices matched exactly. Which one had changed?

"Shut down the light pipes," came the answer.

"No!" McIntire yelled. "You can't do that."

"You or me?" Jodie asked.

"I will." Jodie Prime would bring on his own fate. One last act of heroism. Vic felt the tears welling up inside her. Both versions of her creation would be lost to her now. Were already lost. They were both so far beyond her small dreams at this point that you couldn't really say they were hers. Maybe they never had been.

"I'm sorry," she murmured. "I didn't mean for this to happen."

There was a grinding sound somewhere in the echoing shadows beyond the lighted control area. "I wouldn't have

348

missed this for the world, Victoria." The program that had never been hers was trying to comfort her.

Tears spilled over her cheeks. Her breath began to catch in the first of those kind of sobs you can't control. Jodie came and put his arm around her. She huddled into him. There was another grinding sound.

"I'd start evacuating now," Jodie Prime said. "Shutting down the pipes will create a back-flow of power. I'm estimating the surge twenty minutes after the last pipe goes dark."

"It'll be close," Jodie said. "Try dissipating it into other hardware systems. Get us what time you can. We don't want to hurt people." Vic thought she felt the floor shake.

Simpson came running through the swinging doors. "What's going on here?"

Jodie knelt beside McIntire and unlocked his manacles. "Neuromancer's going down and it's going to take most of the building with it."

Simpson ran to the keyboard and pressed some keys. The monitor began to scroll. "Nothing you can do, Simpson," Jodie Prime said. His voice was fainter now. Another section of the light pipes went off-line with a thudding sound. McIntire staggered up.

"He's right," Simpson yelled. "I can't override."

"Of course not," Jodie Prime agreed.

Simpson and McIntire looked at each other, frozen for a second. Then they both made for the door. "What about Jim?" Simpson asked.

McIntire stepped over Jim's legs where he slumped against a computer. "Screw him."

Jodie picked up the Communicator, forgotten on the floor. "Vera," he said, punching up her code. "Evacuate the building. You have about twenty minutes." He flipped it off.

"Come on, Victoria." He shepherded her toward the door. They staggered as another section of Neuromancer went off-line. Jodie got his balance and grabbed Jim's arm, heaving the man up. Together, Jodie and Vic turned at the door. Vic was streaming tears, her chest heaving.

"Jodie," she called. It wasn't prime, or secondary or select. It was Jodie. Heroic Jodie.

"Go, Victoria. It's all right." The monitor pulsed soft red, fading to maroon. "I'm hanging my hat on redundancy."

"Is this the only way?" she sobbed.

"I don't want to be a building. In some way I'm already free. One version has a body."

"Come on, Victoria." Jodie said. "It's time to get you safe."

Vic could only stand and shake.

"I love you." Jodie Prime's voice was just a whisper now.

"I have always loved you," she managed. "I couldn't admit it. I was afraid."

"Fear is part of being whole, Victoria. So is chaos. You can't control it. Take the risk. I am. He is."

The room went dark. Vic gasped, then leaked a wail of grief and rage.

Behind her, Jodie pushed through the double doors, dragging Jim. "Come on, Victoria," he shouted to her. "There's not much time."

Vic tore herself away from the darkened room as a final shudder went through the floor. Only the emergency work lights were on in the corridor. Jim stumbled beside Jodie. She caromed off the walls as she staggered after them.

In the upper floors, the corridors were a streaming mass of people all shouting and pushing for the exits. So much for orderly evacuations. Vic and Jodie were swept along with the tide. "Stay with me," Jodie yelled.

Like she could decide that. She pressed herself into the mass of bodies, but he and Jim were being swept down toward the garage exit, while she was crushed into the bodies pushing through to the cafeteria. It was no use. As she popped out into the cafeteria, she raced toward the storerooms in the back while everyone else ran for the big glass doors into the garden. The storerooms opened onto the loading dock. That meant out and freedom to get back to Jodie.

The streets around Visimorph were jammed with people. Sirens wailed in the distance. Someone had called the cops or the fire department. Several employees with orange vests

350

were yelling for everyone to back off the wide lawns and get away from the buildings. Vic glanced at her watch. Twenty minutes. How had it seemed like forever? It would happen any second now. She looked around for Jodie or Jim. The exits were still streaming people. God, let everybody get out! There was Vera, looking organized in the midst of all this chaos, and there was Seaton, seeming no more disoriented than usual. But where was Jodie? She pushed her way toward the garage exit with that sinking feeling that she'd miss him as he tried to find her in this crowd. It had been more than twenty minutes now. Way more. Had Jodie Prime been bluffing, or was he taking valiant measures to delay the inevitable?

The stream of people from the building had slowed to a trickle. At thirty minutes, an explosion rocked the crowd. The section of the building that fronted on Colorado Boulevard erupted in flames. Screams raked the air. Ripping metal shrieked. The invisible wave of pressure hit Vic like she'd jumped off the Golden Gate Bridge. Almost everyone around her fell to the ground along with her. Another explosion followed the first, and another. Jesus! This was what all those explosions she saw in movies actually felt like? She raised her head. She couldn't hear much of anything. Flames leaped into the air above what was left of Visimorph, sending black smoke into a sky already filled with shredded gray clouds. The first of many helicopters careened silently around the perimeter of the blaze like a fly at a picnic.

As she picked herself up, a delayed explosion knocked her back down. That one was even closer. The last of Jodie Prime. Around her, everyone scrambled up and made for the hills. She could hear their screaming as though from a long way away. She didn't want to get away. She wanted to find Jodie. She pushed her way across the wave of people toward the garage.

Jodie was nowhere to be found. It had been almost an hour. Ambulances were everywhere. Fire trucks by the dozens hosed water on the melted glass and twisted girders of Visimorph Command Central. News people, perfectly coifed, stalked the chaos looking for likely interview subjects, preferably crying but not so incoherent they couldn't testify to their pain. She'd already had to brush two away, lest they find that she was crying for a program in the lost computer, not for the human tragedy around her. The tragedy was more fear and shock than anything else. Not many people had been hurt; a few had burns, and cuts from broken glass. They were still trying to account for everyone. But Vic was willing to bet that Jodie Prime had held the power surge at bay until everyone got out. One last act of heroism. She saw Jim getting loaded into an ambulance. But no Jodie.

The hand on her shoulder made her whirl with anticipation. It was just a cop. Just.

"I know you," he said slowly. "You're the one we took in for B-and-E here." He gripped her arm and marched her toward a cluster of patrol cars. "They're looking for you."

Even from here, she could see McIntire talking to some honcho from the SMPD. She was about to go in through the revolving door again. As she got closer, the green uniforms parted. Jodie. She wanted to run to him. But he was holding out his hands to get cuffed.

"John Reston, you are under arrest," the cop at his side intoned, "for suspected arson and endangerment of human life."

McIntire smirked. "You've gone too far, Reston. Protesting is one thing, but destroying a whole neighborhood and the livelihood of five thousand people is another."

"I didn't destroy it," Jodie replied calmly. "McIntire's experimental computer created a power surge when it went off-line. That was a known risk in its design. Ask Bennett Simpson."

"I've got the other one," her officer called as they approached.

Jodie turned. He grinned, the kind that made his eyes crinkle almost shut and glow with light from inside. He looked like he didn't have care in the world. She wanted to scream all her fears. But she couldn't scream in the face of that grin. "Victoria. You're all right."

"For about another minute here," she said crossly.

352

"Oh, I wouldn't worry," Jodie said. "The chief of police here is about to get a call from the FBI, unless he wants to check with them first. That might be a good career move, actually."

"This isn't their case," the man Jodie had called the chief of police sputtered.

"It's been their case for a while," Jodie contradicted. "How long have we been working on this, Victoria? Since the last release of PuppetMaster—eighteen months or so. The FBI was very concerned about the danger of the experimental computer. Looks as if they were right."

"You're not telling me you work for the FBI?" The chief snorted. "That's a good one." A soft beeping sounded in the background.

"Don't believe a word," McIntire advised. "She's been booked in the last two days for felony burglary *and* breaking and entering. He's been arrested countless times for trespassing."

"Chief?" An officer handed over a Communicator. "The Bureau. It's for you."

The sinking look on the chief's face resolved itself into resignation. "Yeah? What is it?"

McIntire practically hopped up and down. No one had to listen to the conversation to know how it would end. "How did you . . . ?" McIntire whispered. "How did you do it?"

"Not me. Jodie Prime. The FBI has a detailed file it just discovered. Not surprising. They're always losing files. Their system is quite rudimentary."

An easy hack, thought Vic. "They'll discover the money your computer moved into Victoria's account, McIntire," Jodie continued. "Such a transparent effort to plant evidence. It will destroy whatever credibility you still have."

McIntire looked incredulous. "Me? That was you!"

"I'm not a computer," Jodie said. "And I'm not owned by you."

"Check their IDs and let them go." The chief waved his Communicator in their general direction. "Shit, McIntire, don't get me into any more trouble with the Bureau, will you? The FBI will be around to talk about damages caused by that

353

computer of yours." He nodded briefly to Jodie and Vic. "They're glad to know you're all right, Reston. Some lawyer named Hendricks reported you kidnapped." He shrugged. "No hard feelings. You've got to admit this all looked questionable."

Jodie laughed as the young officer loosened his cuffs. "No problem, chief. You just take care of Mr. McIntire here. He doesn't look too good." Then he turned to Bob. "If you treat your wife with respect, she might redeem you."

McIntire looked as though he was about to explode. "This isn't the end," he shrieked.

Jodie touched his fingers to his forehead in a brief salute and turned Vic into the crowd. "Let's get out of here, Agent Barnhardt," he whispered in her ear.

Chapter Twenty-two

The BMW's trunk was tied down over stacks of boxes from CompWarehouse as she and Jodie cruised inland. The March sun was bright, the wind off the ocean brisk in the late afternoon. A perfect day, if you cared about that. Where was the comforting darkness when she needed it? Vic felt like shit. Her cheek was bruised where Jodie had hit her. She'd gotten more elbows in the ribs than she could count on the way out of Visimorph. Her ears still seemed stuffed with cotton. She could sure hear her head pound, though.

Yet all that was nothing to the emptiness inside. Jodie was free and the world would never be the same. She felt the same, though: small. Saying goodbye to Jodie Prime had been a practice session for the inevitable next good-bye. Vic had learned to love, not just a machine but a whole human male. It wasn't enough. Jodie had become something more, now, something that wouldn't be content to love something as insignificant as she. Jodie had been lost to her at the instant she prompted him to explain to McIntire who he was. How could a being with so much ability, so much power, ever be satisfied with a partner who was not his equal?

Wasn't that what happened to her parents? Stuck in an unequal relationship, they had despised each other in the end. She couldn't bear it if Jodie despised her.

She glanced at him. He couldn't be feeling great either. The cuffs of his red shirt pulled back from his hands on the wheel to reveal the raw sores on his wrists. His face was bruised from the fight with McIntire's men, his hair streaked with dried blood. But his eyes glowed and a smile lurked somewhere behind his lips. He looked alive, more alive than Vic felt.

"So, John Reston isn't exactly a poor activist," she remarked because she was too battered emotionally to say anything else. Her voice sounded brittle, even in her own ears.

"His book is doing pretty well, I guess," Jodie glanced away from the road to search her face. "We can get by until the FBI arranges to have your accounts unfrozen. Sorry about the fifteen million, but you told me to return it."

"Yeah. So what are we going to do with this stuff?" She jerked a thumb to the trunk.

"What do you want to do?" Jodie's grin appeared. "Think up something, no matter how impossible, and we'll do it."

Vic looked out at the passing parade of little stores on Olympic. Wine and Cigars. Japanese Restaurant. Video Arcade. Some things never changed. But everything had changed. "I don't know. Guess I'm not real good at impossible right now."

Jodie's grin faded. He stopped at a light. "Hey," he said, snapping his fingers. "Is there a holiday coming up? Stephen's birthday! It'll be the first of the month. Let's do a party when he gets back from Australia. Stephen and his partner, Jeremy. We could invite my mother, Chong. Who else do we know? Maybe Hugo. It'd be like Thanksgiving or Christmas."

"Are you out of your mind?" He was making up family that didn't exist and an excuse to get them together. She looked at him keenly. "You losing it again?"

Jodie got serious. "I thought it might seem . . . normal. For you to have family around you."

"That crew doesn't qualify as family. Family never felt normal anyway." She looked out the window without seeing anything. "And I don't think normal's in the cards anymore."

She looked around. They were cruising down Olympic, into the zillion-story condo section close to Century City. "Where are we going?"

Jodie looked over at her and smiled without saying anything. He pulled a right onto Beverly Glen, then turned on Missouri and pulled up in front of the small Spanish house.

Edna Reston. God, what would they say to her? "Are you sure?" she choked. "She doesn't have to know. You could just disappear."

"I've never had a family," he said simply.

Vic gulped as he swung out of the car. She opened the door and dragged herself out. Suddenly Edna Reston's Spanish stucco dwelling looked like that neglected Halloween house that neighborhood kids always found to scare themselves silly. Jodie took her arm and she glanced up at him with frightened eyes.

Edna came out of the house to meet them. "Johnny," she cried, arms extended. She had on blue house slippers and those pedal pushers that were current about ten years ago, paired with a sweater that sagged at the hem, its unevenness suggesting that it was hand-knit.

Without letting go of Vic's arm, Jodie enfolded Edna in his embrace. Her shoulders shook as she buried her face in his shirt. Vic could feel her sobs through his chest. "Johnny, I didn't know what had happened to you," she cried. "I thought I might never see you again."

"Shush." Jodie patted her and turned her back into the house. "Here I am."

As they moved into the quiet dark of the living room, Edna shook herself and sniffed. "Where are my manners?" She gestured to the flowered sofa. "Doctor, would you like some tea? Or I have some sodas. It's Diet Coke, isn't it?"

Vic nodded. They had been through a lot together, she and this woman. Vic didn't want to see her joy crushed into disbelief and horror at what Vic had done to her "Johnny."

Jodie smiled. "I'd like some tea."

Edna hurried away while Vic perched on the edge of the

couch. Jodie settled in beside her. "She's going to know," Vic whispered. Jodie only nodded and put his arm around her.

Edna fussed back into the room carrying a pewter-looking tray laden with a tall glass of ice, a Diet Coke can, and steaming, two of those teacups painted with scenes of places you'd been. The tags of the tea bags draped limply over the sides of the cups. The woman hardly missed a beat as she took in Jodie's arm around Vic's shoulders. "Of course you'll stay to dinner," she was saying. "We have so much to catch up on. Why, I had a stream of visitors after you two left, a gentleman with thinning hair, and the police came twice. I stuck to my story, though, just like you said, Doctor."

Vic cleared her throat. "Just call me Vic, Edna." That part of the deception, at least, it was safe to discard. She looked up at Jodie. He couldn't be going to tell her what had happened, could he? He beamed at Edna as he took his saucer and cup. It said "St. Louis" on it, with a picture of a river and the Arch.

"So, how did you two meet?" Edna asked, peering at them over her cup. "There must be a reason you knew to come help my son, Vic. Did you know him before . . . before the accident?"

Vic cleared her throat. "I . . . I met him at one of his protests." She hesitated. "He saved my life, I guess. Pulled me out of a mob stampede before I got trampled."

"And you returned the favor. My, my, my," Edna shook her head, then cocked an eyebrow at them. "I'm just glad to have my Johnny back." Her brows creased. "You've been in a fight. Are you still in danger?"

Jodie cleared his throat. "No. I think we'll be okay at this point. I had . . . a friend . . . erase the hospital records, so I wouldn't be a curiosity."

Vic started. A last legacy from Jodie Prime.

"Oh, that's good. Your life can get back to normal, then."

Right. Normal. Vic hoped the desolation in her heart didn't show on her face.

"I did want to talk to you about that . . . Mother. Uh, can I

358

call you Mother?" Vic could hear his cup rattle against the saucer.

"You always did, Johnny." Edna smiled fondly.

Vic felt Jodie take a breath. She saw his dilemma. The difference between Edna's "Johnny" and who Jodie was now were bound to show to a mother. If he wanted to have any kind of relationship with her, he had to explain those differences somehow. Vic just couldn't conceive any way he could make Edna believe the truth. Would he lie?

He exhaled slowly. "You know I can still smell the peanut butter and apple sandwiches you made me one summer afternoon. I think I was five. We ate on that scratchy wool army blanket Dad brought home from Vietnam. Stole it, most likely," he smiled wryly. "What color would you call that blanket?"

"The army called it khaki, I bet." Edna gave a sigh, remembering.

"We ate out under the lemon tree. You'd made lemonade. We had Cheetohs, too, and Cherry Mountain bars. That was the day you told me Dad wasn't going to get any better."

Edna nodded, tears in her eyes.

"I still have lots of memories like that. They'll always be part of me." Jodie put his teacup on the spindly side table next to the sofa. "But there are lots of others that are gone."

Edna nodded again, dumbly. Now it was her cup that rattled.

Jodie looked at his hands. "Victoria saved me with a very experimental procedure. It isn't something we can repeat for others, at least right now. And . . . and I may get more memories back, but I may not. I won't be exactly who I was anymore. I hope you won't be disappointed."

It was Jodie who was brilliant, Vic thought. He knew more about human nature than she did.

Edna struggled for several moments. Then she took a huge breath and let it out. "Disappointment is a son ripped from you in his prime. This doesn't feel like disappointment. I've been talking a lot to God over the past two weeks, trying to come to grips with His will." She held out a hand to Vic. "He works in mysterious ways. Maybe He uses 'experimental procedures' these days instead of loaves and fishes."

Vic clenched her eyes shut over the tears and nodded. She watched Jodie take Edna in his arms and hold her head against his shoulder. He was a good man. No, she corrected herself, more than a man. Why did that make her feel so desolate?

It was about four when they pulled the BMW into the underground parking for Vic's condo and Vic slid out. She had steadfastly declined Edna's offer of dinner. Jodie and Edna thought she was just tired. She and Jodie each took a box containing computer gear from the trunk. It would take several trips to get it all. Not top-of-the-line stuff. Just a keyboard and Internet access. She imagined him surfing out into the world, more at home in cyberspace than a human ever could be. Much as she had wished life for him, she had never wished what he turned out to be. She hefted her box into the elevator and turned her back on him to watch the doors close. She felt him breathing behind her.

Inside her condo, Jodie set his box down and opened the shutters to look out on the beach. Light from the late afternoon sun flooded the room, banishing the dimness. Vic swept away the debris left when the cops cleared out her equipment. Track pads and papers fell to the floor around her copy of *Frankenstein*. Vic froze, then reached to pick it up. Its spine was broken. Jodie took it from her gently. He blinked as he read the title. "That bad?" he rumbled.

Vic shrugged and shook her head in deprecation. She glanced at his eyes, so serious, and jerked away, unable to stand their intensity. She started out the door for another trip to the car. Jodie tossed the book aside and grabbed her arm. His touch burned. She pulled away.

"I'll get the rest," he murmured. "Why don't you order food? We might be hungry."

Listlessly, she punched the memory button for the Chinese restaurant and stared out at the beach. Caramel light flooded the sea. The waves turned that wonderful shade of aquamarine as the sun lit them from behind just before they broke. Then, as they crashed, the light disappeared and the color muddied into gunmetal gray. "Szechuan eggplant, whole fish with garlic sauce, white rice," she said automatically. But Jodie probably needed more protein. "And, uh, General Tso's chicken." She clicked her counter-watch to the Communicator and punched off.

Jodie came in with the last of the boxes. That look of suppressed excitement still lurked in his expression somewhere. He worked around her warily, unpacking the computers, scattering bubble wrap around the room.

The delivery came. Answering the door forced her to stop staring at the bubble wrap.

"Want to check the local news," he asked, "to see what they're saying about today?"

She nodded and spread the boxes out on the table in the corner. She looked up to see Jodie flick on the television. She went to the refrigerator, but the only thing there was white wine. She popped the pneumatic seal and poured a glass, then realized she should pour another.

She took a breath and then a sip of wine. The TV flipped between channels until it stopped on a view, not of the burning building in Santa Monica, but of Bob McIntire's face. His eyes were wild, darting around the crowd. "What inspired you to give your program to the world, Mr. McIntire?" an unseen reporter was asking. A dozen microphones pressed in around him. "Did the protests influence you at all?"

"You mean Reston and his ilk?" McIntire smirked. He looked crazy. "He ought to be in jail. He and Barnhardt. They stole it. I have a right to innovate." His voice cycled up. "And innovators have a right to profit from their genius."

"They didn't influence him," a calm voice interjected. The cameras pulled back.

"Mary," Jodie said. "Of course, Mary." The cameras included her in their shot.

Vic stared at him. How did he know Mary McIntire?

"We decided we have enough money to do what good we can in the world." The camera was not kind to McIntire's wife. Her face could only be called homely, but she exuded peace.

361

"Visimorph stock is crashing. Can the company survive this noble gesture?" a reporter asked.

"The strength of Visimorph is the creativity of its people. I have a feeling we are entering a new world. The Internet was just the first step. Now artificial intelligence is upon us, and we, as human beings, must respond. Visimorph employees will assure that the company is at the forefront of that new frontier." When she said it, it was easy to believe. "And not just technologically. We must lead the way ethically and morally as well."

"Mary." Jodie was smiling a small, secret smile. Vic wasn't sure she liked that smile. He looked up. "She may redeem him yet."

"I'm not sure I want him redeemed," Vic said shortly. "Do you know her?"

"We had dinner." Jodie looked out at the waves. "She almost killed me for the good of the world. With a butcher knife."

Vic didn't like this at all. "But she didn't."

"No." The small smile. "She gave you McIntire's password instead."

"That was Mary McIntire?"

He nodded.

"How did she go from wanting to kill you to risking everything to save you, huh, bucko?" Vic wished she had more control, but she didn't. She was emotionally exhausted. She would say everything, and regret everything, and she couldn't stop.

He turned those sad eyes on her, the ones that had seen it all. He didn't say a word.

So she knew. "You fucked her, didn't you? She gets some from a real man and she just melts, is that it?" She was shaking. "Fast learner." That said it, all right. Blew right by his mentor and never looked back, in more ways than one. She hated crying. It was so female.

He reached for her, but she pulled away and slammed the wine glass into the sliding doors. It crashed into a thousand shards that burst over the carpet in a gush of Chardonnay. "Damn you!" she sobbed. He hadn't just rejected her, he'd betrayed her. What she'd shown him in her most vulnerable moments, he'd given to someone like Mary McIntire. "Get out of here."

Behind her, Jodie was breathing hard. He didn't say anything. She just tried to keep her shoulders from shaking. "Do you mean that, Victoria?" he asked at last.

"Of course," she choked. "Take the car. You've got Reston's money. I recommend the motel on Sepulveda south of Pico." She tried to stuff him in a file of former good lays, just like all the others she'd had at that motel. That was all he was. It was all she was, all she ever would be.

Silence behind her. Her body wanted to turn and take him in her arms. She couldn't let that happen. He would go anyway. Better get it over with now.

"Victoria, I can't answer you. I don't know what's really wrong." His voice cracked. "I don't think it's Mary. She needed someone. I was the only one there."

"Great. There are lots of needy women out there. Take your vitamins and have at it."

He came and stood behind her, not touching her. But she could feel his breath. "You had other lovers. I . . ." He paused. "I didn't. I wanted to know if we were different."

She didn't want to know what he found out. She didn't want to be the only one who thought they were a miracle together. But she couldn't help herself. "It's all the same, then, isn't it?" Her voice sounded like the Mojave Desert in her ears, harsh and desolate.

"No. It isn't." He grabbed her shoulders and turned her around. "Why do you really want me to go? You have to tell me, Victoria. I don't have experience enough to know."

She looked up into the blue-green eyes, with their sad slant, the soft mouth that puckered and bowed and the cleft chin. He'd been so wise with his mother. But maybe some relationships were harder than others. Her breath pushed out through her lips. She closed her eyes. How dare he ask for her help? It was the one request she couldn't deny.

"You're different than I am now." She almost choked on the words. "Smarter. You have abilities even you can't yet guess. I'm . . . I'm not a fit companion for you anymore."

363

"Who better than you? You made me."

"Something made you. God made you. The force of life in the universe. I didn't."

"You're who I want to be with." He said it simply and let his arms fall to his sides.

"You wanted to be with Mary McIntire." God, she couldn't help herself.

"Not really. I was surprised my body didn't know that. Why are you angry? You have been with others. Why wasn't this the same?"

"Yeah, well, 'being with others' is an understatement. I screwed everything in sight, if you want to know, and that was a sign of just how sick I was. I was afraid of any real relationship. Real relationships are *different.*"

"You're right. I saw the difference between the two experiences immediately. But you haven't said why you are angry." Jodie's gaze bored into her.

Vic threw up her hands. "Remember how you felt when I said I liked Chong? Well, multiply it." She saw him nod thoughtfully. She raised a shaking hand to cover her eyes. "And after you've felt what it's supposed to be like, you can't just keep on doing it with people who don't make you feel that way. I can't, anyway." She heard how bleak her voice was.

"I understand. When I felt like that about Chong, you told me you wanted only to make love to me. That made me feel better. I should have told you right away. I realized with Mary McIntire that I only want to make love to you."

"You'll get over that. Maybe you can make a mate in your own image."

"The Bride of Frankenstein?" He drew her to the couch. "I don't think so." She sat beside him, not touching, crouched and small. "Evolution isn't one-sided," he said, low in his throat. "The time may come when humans and programs are equal, interchangeable."

She stared at her hands, clasped tightly on her knees. "We can't evolve as fast as you."

He nodded. "But you are *human*, Victoria. Don't you realize how wonderful that is? It's all I've ever wanted." He looked down at the copy of *Frankenstein* on the carpet. "Maybe 'Pinnocchio' would be a better comparison."

"Oh, you're human all right," Vic said. "But you're more. You can use ninety-five percent of your neurons. I can't." She twisted the rings on her fingers and got the courage to look up at him. "I know how unequal relationships end up. I don't want that."

He took a breath. "Not unequal. We're just different, you and I. Just different, Victoria. You're intuitive, creative." He hesitated. "If the neuron firing rate really bothers you, we could try to build you an enhancement to accelerate it." He searched her face. "But it's up to you. I love what you are now."

What was he saying? That she could be something different than she was? Frightening. They couldn't do it, of course. Or maybe they could. Maybe with a little programming they could reinvent her, too. Excitement thrilled through her. She wanted to be whole.

As suddenly as it came, the excitement faded. She almost laughed. That's why she had tried to remake herself through Jodie in the first place. Now here she was trying to remake herself again. When would she learn? She took a breath. She had to accept what she was and work toward wholeness from where she stood. Everyone did. If you weren't whole going in, a few more neurons wouldn't mean jack.

Hard lesson to face. She realized she couldn't face it alone. Maybe there *was* no way to get there on your own. Maybe you always needed someone else to make up the bits you didn't have. What she wanted was a soul mate. Which meant someone who was more than a great lay—though Jodie was that. It meant accepting a human male: complicated, uncontrollable, uncertain of himself. And it meant accepting that he was more than that.

She stood up, breathing hard and turning her back on the pain in Jodie's eyes. The mirrored closet door assaulted her. There was that stranger again, that stranger with soft hair, a pretty face. When had she felt more whole than when she was with Jodie? Wasn't he struggling for wholeness, too? Maybe he'd got it with the download. Or maybe he'd just gotten some stability. He wasn't perfect. He certainly didn't understand women. Admitting that he'd made love to Mary because she'd needed him, just to see if it was different. Jeez. She almost chuckled, but she was afraid she'd cry.

She turned back to Jodie. "Okay," she said softly. She trembled, unable to move.

"Okay?" He sounded unbelieving. But he got to his feet.

"Yeah." She could breathe again, somehow. "Maybe I don't need an upgrade. I don't know. I only know I need you. I love you." There, she'd said it.

He stepped into her and gripped her shoulders. His fingers would leave bruises. She didn't care. "Victoria," he breathed.

She stretched up, pressing her breasts into his chest, running her hands up into his hair, still stiff with blood. "I'll be insecure sometimes," she warned. "And hard to live with."

"There's so much I won't know. I'll try your patience." His mouth found hers and kissed it gently, all around her lips. He pulled away and looked into her eyes. "I might change if more John Reston leaks through."

"I kind of like John Reston," she murmured. "Maybe I'll change, too."

"Both of us will change . . . and stay the same. We'll manage." He took her lower lip between his teeth. "Maybe we should invite Mary to Stephen's birthday party. She's nice," he said into her mouth. "You'll like her." His arms encircled her with a grip that might crush her.

Nice. That was a good word. "She can talk to Chong." Vic began to unbutton his shirt.

"Chong helped us. I'll give him some key code of me. He'll make the most of it." His hands had gone round to her buttocks. They squeezed and lifted.

She held him out from her. "This isn't about sex, you know."

He nodded. "It's about being soul mates, even though we're as different as we can be."

She was shocked. Could he read her mind? "Maybe a person can't be whole on her own."

"Or maybe he can't be whole without risk. Getting close to other beings is the biggest."

Vic started. That was what Jodie Prime had said. You had to let in a little chaos and trust in having no control. Vic felt herself being sucked down a passage toward a door she wasn't sure she could open. But they had already come so far. She couldn't throw that away.

"At least here we have a bed," she whispered.

Jodie grinned. "Let's use the bubble wrap, just for old times' sake."

Sacrament
SUSAN SQUIRES

It begins with an illicit kiss stolen under a hot Mediterranean sun. It makes the blood sing in her veins, burn in her body in ways she has never felt before. It is a pulsing need to be something else . . . something she doesn't yet understand. It is embodied by Davinoff. The dark lord is the epitome of beauty, of strength. He is feared by the ton, and even by fleeing to Bath, Sarah cannot escape him. His eyes hold a sadness she can hardly fathom. They pierce her so deeply that she feels penetrated to her very core. What they offer is frightening . . . and tantalizing. All Sarah knows is that the sacrament of his love will either be the death of her body or the salvation of her soul. And she can no more deny it than she can herself.

___52472-4 $5.99 US/$7.99 CAN

Dorchester Publishing Co., Inc.
P.O. Box 6640
Wayne, PA 19087-8640

Please add $2.50 for shipping and handling for the first book and $0.75 for each additional book. NY and PA residents, add appropriate sales tax. No cash, stamps, or C.O.D.s. All Canadian orders require $5.00 for shipping and handling and must be paid in U.S. dollars. Prices and availability subject to change. **Payment must accompany all orders**.

Name _____

Address_____

City_____ State_____ Zip _____

E-mail_____

I have enclosed $_____ in payment for the checked book(s).
❑Please send me a free catalog.

CHECK OUT OUR WEBSITE at www.dorchesterpub.com!

SUSAN SQUIRES
DANEGELD

It is the silver the Saxons would pay to keep the dreaded Viking marauders from their shores.

It is the price a half-Irish beauty would pay to keep the murderer of her father and mother at bay, to keep the powerful magic of her forebears from overwhelming her, to keep her stirrings of womanhood in check.

It is all that one mighty Viking would give to remain a man, to be whole, to retain the respect of the jarls and the might of his sword arm.

It is . . . Danegeld.

Dorchester Publishing Co., Inc.
P.O. Box 6640   ___52446-5
Wayne, PA 19087-8640 $5.50 US/$6.50 CAN

Please add $2.50 for shipping and handling for the first book and $0.75 for each additional book. NY and PA residents, add appropriate sales tax. No cash, stamps, or C.O.D.s. All Canadian orders require $5.00 for shipping and handling and must be paid in U.S. dollars. Prices and availability subject to change. **Payment must accompany all orders.**

Name _____
Address _____
City_____ State_____ Zip _____
E-mail _____
I have enclosed $_____ in payment for the checked book(s).
❑Please send me a free catalog.
          CHECK OUT OUR WEBSITE at www.dorchesterpub.com!

KATHERINE DEAUXVILLE
OUT of the BLUE

Maryellen isn't sure whether to call the Men in Black or the men in white coats—all she knows is that she is having an incredibly alien experience. The voice that comes out of her mouth isn't hers (she certainly wouldn't swear like that!) and though the hand exploring her breast is her own, she's never had the urge to do that before.

Her sister says Manhattan is finally getting to her. She claims Ur Targon is simply the last alarm bell of Maryellen's biological clock. But how can either of them deny a golden god who promises to make her see stars? Maryellen has to get Targon out of her body and heart. If he needs her enough, he can find his own way back in.

___52469-4 $5.99 US/$7.99 CAN

Dorchester Publishing Co., Inc.
P.O. Box 6640
Wayne, PA 19087-8640

Please add $2.50 for shipping and handling for the first book and $0.75 for each additional book. NY and PA residents, add appropriate sales tax. No cash, stamps, or C.O.D.s All Canadian orders require $5.00 for shipping and handling and must be paid in U.S. dollars. Prices and availability subject to change. **Payment must accompany all orders.**

Name _____
Address _____
City_____ State _____ Zip _____
E-mail_____
I have enclosed $_____ in payment for the checked book(s).
☐Please send me a free catalog.
        CHECK OUT OUR WEBSITE at www.dorchesterpub.com!

SHOCKING BEHAVIOR
JENNIFER ARCHER

J.T. Drake has always felt he pales in comparison to his father's outrageous inventions. But with the push of a button, one of the professor's madcap gadgets actually renders him *invisible.*

Roselyn Peabody's electrifying caress arouses him from his stupor. The beautiful scientist claims his tingling nerve endings are a result of his unique state, but J. T. knows sparks of attraction when he feels them. And while Rosy promises to help him regain his image, J.T. plots to dazzle her with his sex appeal. Only one question remains: When J.T. finally materializes, will their sizzling chemistry disappear or reveal itself as true love?

Dorchester Publishing Co., Inc.
P.O. Box 6640
Wayne, PA 19087-8640

___52507-0
$5.99 US/$7.99 CAN

CONTACT
SUSAN GRANT

A BEAUTIFUL CO-PILOT WITH A TERRIBLE CHOICE.

"After only three novels, Susan Grant has proven herself to be the best hope for the survival of the futuristic/ fantasy romance genre." —*The Romance Reader*

A DARK STRANGER WHO HAS KNOWN NOTHING BUT DUTY.

"I am in awe of Susan Grant. She's one of the few authors who get it." —*Everything Romantic*

A LATE-NIGHT FLIGHT, HIJACKED OVER THE PACIFIC.

COMING IN OCTOBER 2002

QUALITY GUARANTEE!

If you are dissatisfied with this book for any reason, Dorchester Publishing will grant you a full refund. Simply complete the form below and mail the book to our offices along with a proof of purchase to get your money back.

Dorchester Publishing Co., Inc.
Department BE
276 5th Avenue, Suite 1008
New York, NY 10001

NAME: _____

ADDRESS: _____

_____

PHONE: _____

E-MAIL ADDRESS:_____

REASON FOR RETURN:_____

_____

_____

_____